W9-ATN-802

Acclaim for the novels of Kim Wozencraft

WANTED

"Wozencraft writes with nervy brilliance . . . the novel switches from procedural to prison story to escape novel . . . without losing momentum. A chiller."

—*Booklist*

"Gripping . . . a great story that is very hard to put down."
—*Star Phoenix* (CN)

"Wozencraft has a remarkable talent . . . her characters come alive on each page . . . the book will keep readers guessing to the end. *Wanted* is hard to put down."

—*Tulsa World*

"[A] powerful thriller."   —*YRB* (Yellow Rat Bastard)

"It's impossible not to remember the hit movie *Thelma and Louise* when reading *Wanted*."

—*Times Union* (Albany)

"For addicted crime-novel readers desperate for a fix, here's some methadone."

—*San Francisco Chronicle*

"Writes with equal authority and pathos about their opposing worlds . . . a deftly told jailbreak caper that provokes thought and goose bumps."

—*People*

More...

"[A] straightforward, satisfying thriller . . . *Wanted* boasts impressively authentic detail . . . Wozencraft's plainly spoken, richly populist style serves the material well, and the story moves faster than a speeding police car."

—*Entertainment Weekly*

"Wozencraft's knack for nonstop action will keep readers engaged from the very first page."

—*Publishers Weekly*

"[A] well-crafted surprise ending." —*Texas Monthly*

"Fast and literate suspense . . . gripping all the way."

—*Kirkus Reviews*

"This is writing so powerful it will blow you away. Kim Wozencraft's characters step right off the page as living, breathing people, in a slam-bang thriller that doesn't let up until the final page."

—Tess Gerritsen, author of *The Sinner*

"A perceptive character study of two troubled souls on the lam, *Wanted* is unpredictable and absorbing. Kim Wozencraft sure knows how to craft a crime novel."

—Perri O'Shaughnessy, author of *Presumption of Death*

"*Wanted* is a top-notch read from a first-rate author. Kim Wozencraft has what it takes to go all the way. She writes like an angel carrying a .45 Magnum, and *Wanted* is a twin turbo of a novel. It should come with seat belts. Kim Wozencraft is back, with a vengeance."

—Keith Ablow, author of *Murder Suicide*

"Thelma and Louise are a couple of schoolgirls next to the pair of heroines who tear through Kim Wozencraft's *Wanted*. A high-speed emotional thriller that grabs you from the start, it's also a white-hot indictment of what passes for justice in the United States—where crooked cops, malicious prosecutors, and a dystopian bureaucracy destroy more lives than all the drugs on the street. Gail and Diane's desperate bid to outrun the shock troops of a sociopathic society is at once terrifying, exhilarating, and inspirational. These are two powerful women refusing to bow down to the tin god of jurisprudence gone insane. You'll never stop rooting for them."

—Ian Spiegelman, author of *Everyone's Burning*

MORE PRAISE FOR KIM WOZENCRAFT AND HER NOVELS

"Harrowing authenticity . . . The writing is quite good, the dialogue pungent and true."

—*The New York Times Book Review* on *Rush*

"Written with the brisk, torchy compulsion of a thriller . . . Her lean, athletic prose is matched by the lucid speed and economy of the narrative."

—*Washington Post Book World* on *Rush*

"Powerful." —*People Magazine* on *Rush*

"Gripping . . . *Rush*'s power comes from its vivid writing and its raw, compelling story."

—*New York Magazine* on *Rush*

"Spellbinding . . . addictive—tense and dramatic, full of incredibly real characters, a steamy Texas landscape . . . truly compulsive reading."

—*Cosmopolitan* on *Rush*

"With an unquestionably authoritative narrative voice, Kim Wozencraft commands readers into its harrowing story."

—*Publishers Weekly* on *Rush*

"In this brave first novel, Wozencraft has dared to expose an ugly and seldom seen side of our 'drug war.' *Rush* is a tough, scary, and heartbreaking book."

—*Baltimore Sun* on *Rush*

"A gripping narrative . . . swiftly paced, thrillingly exact . . . focused and involved."

—*Los Angeles Times Book Review* on
Notes from the Country Club

"Explosive in its portrayal of domestic violence . . . A novelist of amazing—sometimes frightening—depth and perception."

—*Richmond Times-Dispatch* on
Notes from the Country Club

"Wozencraft's depictions of the raw edges of victimization . . . are vivid and wrenching."

—*Miami Herald* on *Notes from the Country Club*

"A richly written, deeply felt work."
    —*New York Newsday* on *Notes from the Country Club*

"Compelling, poignant . . . Sharp imagery and a sure-footed sense of place."
    —*Publishers Weekly* on *Notes from the Country Club*

"Wozencraft's characters are potent and unforgettable."
    —*Booklist* on *The Catch*

"Pertinent things to say about the seductive qualities of a life lived outside the law."
    —*The New York Times Book Review* on *The Catch*

"Powerful . . . A carefully crafted, character-driven tale that . . . finds bitter irony in the dark furies that drive those who want to do good."
    —*Kirkus Reviews* on *The Catch*

"A thriller, with a love triangle at its core . . . a struggle worth exploring."
    —*The Los Angeles Times* on *The Catch*

Also by Kim Wozencraft

The Catch

Notes from the Country Club

Rush

WANTED

Kim Wozencraft

St. Martin's Paperbacks

NOTE: If you purchased this book without a cover you should be aware that this book is stolen property. It was reported as "unsold and destroyed" to the publisher, and neither the author nor the publisher has received any payment for this "stripped book."

"Talking at the Texaco" written by James McMurtry © 1989 Short Trip Music (BMI) / Administered by BUG. All Rights Reserved. Used by permission.

"The Ballad of the Crimson Kings" written by Ray Wylie Hubbard © 1996 Mt. Karma Music. All rights reserved. Used by permission.

WANTED

Copyright © 2004 by Code 3 Communications, Inc.

All rights reserved. No part of this book may be used or reproduced in any manner whatsoever without written permission except in the case of brief quotations embodied in critical articles or reviews. For information address St. Martin's Press, 175 Fifth Avenue, New York, NY 10010.

Library of Congress Catalog Card Number: 2004048385

ISBN: 0-312-93914-0
EAN: 9780312-93914-4

Printed in the United States of America

St. Martin's Press hardcover edition / September 2004
St. Martin's Paperbacks edition / February 2006

St. Martin's Paperbacks are published by St. Martin's Press, 175 Fifth Avenue, New York, NY 10010.

10 9 8 7 6 5 4 3 2 1

For my sisters

ACKNOWLEDGMENTS

My heartfelt thanks to my first-rate agent, Betsy Lerner, and my wonderful editor at St. Martin's, Jennifer Enderlin. Your guidance and encouragement made all the difference. Thanks to Donald J. Davidson for his close reading and excellent copyediting, to Bill Schaap for being in my corner, and to Blair Breard and Annie Nocenti for reading and commenting on early manuscripts. My love and appreciation go out to my mother, Terry Wozencraft, and to my family, the Stratton crew: Richard, Maxx, Dash, and Sasha.

ONE

There were times the deep night shift seemed as if it would go on forever. Driving the quiet, deserted roads near the outskirts of town for nearly three hours now, Diane hadn't been able to shake off the fatigue dogging her after a scant three hours sleep. All day long she'd been in court, trying to doze in what was supposed to be a chair, but was in fact an instrument of torture approved by the purchasing department. Called in on her off-duty hours, she'd spent the entire day waiting to testify against a hot-shot internet whiz dressed like a rapper, an asshole from the moment she'd approached his gleaming black Porsche after watching him bust a red light and miss a cyclist by inches.

She had slipped out without a word when the judge excused her, was home in bed and trying hard to get to sleep before six. Back at the station by 10:30 P.M., sitting in the briefing room in her navy blue uniform downing a second cup of coffee, she was fighting her eyelids as the sergeant reminded everyone that somewhere out there on the streets there was bound to be some psychopath with a .45 under his front seat, just itching to get pulled over so he could vent his frustration on the police. Gravity was winning; her eyelids eased down. She shook her head and took a gulp from her mug, got a mouthful of grounds. Chewed them up and swallowed. That ought to help. The sergeant droned on . . . be careful out there. . . . She'd been hearing this sort of thing for almost three years now, since Officer Renfro had recruited her from the campus of the University of Texas at Bolton at not quite twenty-one.

"Wellman," the sergeant said sharply. "You with us here?" Diane's eyes jerked open to the low rumble of laughter from the men in the room. She straightened in her chair.

"Sir," she said, nodding yes. Her back ached from trying to sleep in that courtroom chair all day. Forget about the psychopaths, she'd thought drowsily, it's the damn-fool citizens who really take the toll on the cops.

Now, as she cruised past a lone 7-Eleven, a fast-food outpost on the development frontier at the edge of town, fluorescent light spilled out past signs advertising SuperMegaGulp Slurpees and onto the deserted blacktop of the parking lot. During the day, construction workers congregated at lunch to fill their bellies with microwaved chili dogs and smoke Marlboros. Diane thought about pulling in, but couldn't bear the thought of another cup of coffee when she hadn't even hit the halfway mark in her shift.

"Two A.M. and all's well," she muttered, making a left that would lead her out toward the edge of her district, where there were still a few farms around. It was silly, maybe, to risk getting caught out of her assigned area, but she wouldn't go very far out of her sector, not like the time she'd got busted halfway across town after having a quickie with Renfro. That had been stupid, the first and last time it had happened.

And anyway, Lake Bolton was close, the night was slow beyond belief, and it wouldn't be ten minutes before she'd be back where she was supposed to be. If she happened to get a call, her response time wouldn't indicate that she'd been out of her district. It was harmless.

When she eased onto the narrow rock road that wound around the lake, she killed her headlights and took it slow. She loved the way the moonlight reflected off the crushed white caliche, lighting up the roadway like it was the surface of the moon itself, and broke into little curlicues of light on the water when a sunny or a turtle broke the surface. Diane could smell the heat coming off the green, springtime grass, even this long after sunset.

And then she saw movement. Or thought she saw movement. And then knew she saw movement. Someone darted across the road, twenty feet up or so, right over by the narrow lane that led back to where the kids liked to go and make out, smoke a little grass, drink some beer. Usually by this hour the last of them were gone, leaving crushed, empty aluminum cans littering the sparse grass and dusty ground beneath the umbrellas of oak trees. Maybe there were a few die-hards back there, still partying.

She hit her headlights and caught the figure just as it ducked into the brush, even while a voice in her head insistently reminded her she was out of her district. Ignore whatever it is and get the hell back where you belong. But she'd gotten a look, things weren't right, this was no teenager. She registered the information automatically: white male, midthirties, medium build, maybe six feet. Brown hair. Beard. Blue jeans, dark blue T-shirt. She hadn't seen his shoes. She was good at this, she knew. Her instructors at the academy had been more than impressed with her observation skills and memory. And though she'd taken a thorough trashing from her otherwise all male class when they were practicing building searches and she said in class that intuition could play a role, that was exactly what she was feeling right now: intuition. And it wasn't good.

She eased down the lane, looking for movement, for lights, for anything. As she wheeled through a curve in the sandy road, her headlights bathed a low oak tree just a few feet off the lane.

Beneath it, a body.

She was out of the car, gun drawn, scanning the area, radio in hand calling for backup, fast. Talking low, quiet, urgent. Shit. It was a body. Seriously dead. Shit. She wasn't supposed to be here.

A teenager. He was propped up against the oak tree, as though taking some afternoon shade. His mouth was sealed shut with duct tape. His hands were folded in his lap. He was wearing sunglasses. Blood covered his chest and seeped out through the gashes in his chest, soaking into the thin cotton fabric of his T-shirt.

Diane heard static, realized the dispatcher was calling her, requesting that Diane confirm her location as the north end of Lake Bolton. Shit. She blurted into her radio, "Yes, okay, I'm out of my district."

"Two-forty," the dispatcher replied. "Repeat, please. You're breaking up."

"Just get me some damn backup here fast and an ambulance and Crime Scene, okay? Jesus. The north end of Lake Bolton. I'll turn on my lights. Notify the S.O."

The dispatcher's voice crackled in the night, there was a brief flurry of voices as she ordered units to respond to the call, and then there was silence. And then there was the snap-crack of someone stepping on a very dry twig, over by her squad car. Adrenaline burned clean into her fingertips. Diane turned, her gun held close, aimed skyward, and saw the man slip toward the driver seat of her squad. Damnation. She crouched, ran, and ducked behind a tree. She hung her radio in her belt and pulled her Kel-Lite from its loop. Peeked around the trunk. Stuck her flashlight out around the other side of the trunk and pressed the button. The beam cut a cylindrical swath, caught a face. A glimpse of pale skin in the glare of light as a man turned. It was him, the one on the road, and she could see anger glinting from eyes mostly covered with shaggy hair.

"Freeze!" Diane's voice commanded obedience. The man turned quickly, ducked into the driver's seat of her squad car and slammed the door.

"I said freeze!" Diane raged, moving toward her car, crouched, aiming at the windshield. "Stop!" And then was instantly blinded by the glare of her headlights. She threw an arm up to shield her eyes and dived behind a tree, sprawled there, her gun still held on the car.

The squad's rear wheels spun, spewing sand and dust into a cloud around the car, then hit hard dirt and dug. The car backed out, the driver alternately gunning the engine and slamming on the brakes as he careened backward down the winding lane, veering abruptly, a moving target. Diane tried to hold her aim on the driver's side and cranked off six rounds. Emptied the cylinder and grabbed a speed loader from her belt. By the time she got fresh ammo in, all she could see were brake lights as the car, her car, completed a three-point turn, lurched into drive, and fishtailed into the night, slinging caliche behind it.

She stared after it. And then she screamed out, "Your ass is grass, motherfucker!"

And stood there feeling stupid. More than stupid. Stupidly inadequate. Totally fucked.

Fuck. Fuck. Fuck. She stomped the ground futilely, trying to pound her anger at herself into the dirt. Her ears were numb and ringing from the gunshot blasts. Her lungs filled with dust churned up by the car. Her car. Shit. The jerkoff stole her fucking squad. Things could not get more fucked up than they were right now. His ass was grass, that was all. She heard the sound of her engine fade into the night.

"Dipshit," she muttered. "Asshole." She didn't know if she was talking about him or herself.

She looked around, following the beam of her flashlight as it swept the area. She walked back over to the gruesome sight under the oak tree. Seventeen maybe. Maybe not even that.

She shone the light past the dead boy. She walked down the road, toward the picnic table, sweeping the lane and the woods that edged up against it with the beam of her flashlight. The usual litter. The light flashed off the gleaming silver aluminum of a Silver Bullet—the teenagers in town were fond of Coors— off by itself in the bushes. Diane stepped off the road, began picking her way through the brush to retrieve it. She pulled a pen from her pocket so she could lift the can by its opening without putting any prints on it.

It was then she practically stumbled onto the second body.

And the third.

She felt something leave her. She did not know what it was, what to call it, the thing that evaporated from the area right around her heart. Not innocence, certainly, but something like that. Some kind of hope or belief in human possibility. Or maybe it was just fear, doing this to her.

They were girls. Teens, too, bound hand and foot with duct tape. It was strapped over their mouths, as well. They were all cut up. Multiple stab wounds. Their pants were missing. Thighs already going blue with bruises.

Diane stood staring, listening to her heart pound in the silence, horrified at the sight of the dead kids, really feeling for the first time what it was to be near a lifeless human body. Mutilated. Her stomach was an empty balloon, her lungs pressured like she was deep underwater. She couldn't swallow. Couldn't talk. She stood in the shadows, watching the trees light red, white, and blue as a Visibar whirred atop the first of the Sheriff's Office squads to arrive. They'd come Code 2, lights only, running silent, hoping not to chase anyone off.

She stepped back out onto the lane, walked back toward the oak tree.

The sheriff himself, Gib Lowe, stepped out of the car, a junior deputy in tow. Diane motioned them over, and Gib Lowe, a man who at forty-something had enough nervous tics for the entire Sheriff's Office, stood there patting at the strawberry blond curliness that stuck out above his ears but was in scarce supply on the rest of his scalp and scratched at his belly, which hung over his belt just a little.

"Dead, huh?" Lowe looked at Diane as though he'd just said something profound.

She nodded.

"What the hell are you doing out here"—he looked at her name tag—"Officer Wellman?"

"Workin' deep nights."

"That don't explain what you're doing out here. Far as I know, your jurisdiction ends at the city limits. This here's my territory. Sheriff's Office territory."

"I just cruised over to take a look at the lake," Diane said. "For a minute. Trying to cool off, wake up a little."

"Where the hell's your car? They got you on foot patrol or something?" The deputy had a smirk on his face.

"I saw someone," Diane said. "Out on the main road. I followed him in here." Nothing to do but look the sheriff in the eye. "He stole my squad."

"What?" Lowe looked at her, maybe even actually saw her.

"He stole my car."

The sheriff stood looking at Diane silently. He didn't laugh. He didn't even smile or sneer. He just looked at her. And then he pulled out his radio and pressed the transmit button.

"All units, be on the lookout for a city PD vehicle, stolen just a few minutes ago, being driven by a . . ." The sheriff paused and looked at Diane.

"White male," she said quietly, and gave the rest of the description. The sheriff repeated it into the radio, broadcasting Diane's embarrassment for all in the Sheriff's Office to hear. Diane could picture it: every deputy on duty and all those back at headquarters, everybody smiling and snickering and shaking their heads. What kind of fuckup would go and let somebody steal their patrol vehicle? Sheriff Lowe snapped his radio back onto his belt.

"Don't you worry, darlin'," he said, "we'll find the nasty old man stole your squad." Diane wanted to slug him. Instead, she pretended to ignore his remark. He put his flashlight back on the young man's body. Folded his arms across his belly and stood staring.

"Damn." Lowe chewed on his thin lips a long minute. "That's Minister Logan's son, idn' it?"

The junior deputy shrugged. "All's I know is he's deader'n a doornail." He didn't move, stood there and kept on staring at the dead kid.

"Looks like he's been stabbed about two dozen times," Lowe said. "Damn." The junior deputy shook his head and spat. Lowe turned to Diane.

"This fellow you saw," he said, "the one stole your car. You think he did this?"

"I do," Diane said. "And there's more," Diane said quietly. Lowe's head jerked up.

"More what?"

"Bodies," Diane said. "Over there. Two females. Roughly the same age."

"My Lord and my God," the sheriff said, almost like he was praying. He nodded at Diane. "Lead the way."

A train of about six S.O. cars wheeled off Lakeside Road onto the narrow drive leading back to the park and came to a halt at the crime scene. A couple of ambulances showed up, and with all the lights going on the tops of all those cars, the trees seemed to swirl around the scene, limbs joined, dancing, spinning, circling, and the lights brilliant red, white, and blue. Diane stood in the middle of it, the blood of three teens seeping into the earth, the ambulance attendants yanking gurneys out the backs of their wagons, the deputies striding purposefully around, destroying footprints and any other evidence that might have been had, all the officiousness, and the swirling and swirling of red, white, and blue, and she wanted to suggest that the sheriff back everybody off until Crime Scene could gather what they needed, but she was acutely aware that she was in some pretty deep shit. Not in much of a position to suggest to the man how he should do his job. Even if he was a moron.

And then, right on cue, here came Channel 7 News. Diane bet it was none other than Brett Dallas, that asshole reporter who'd been on the PD's case any number of times. He had some kind of vendetta against the cops, was one of those people who recoiled at the sight of a uniform. Always looking for an angle, that guy. He'd even asked her out for a date once or twice, but she knew what he was after, and it damn sure wasn't her.

She faded back into the shadows as Brett approached, just in time to see Gib Lowe kneel next to the body sitting at the base of the oak tree. Lowe rested an elbow on his thigh, rested his forehead in the palm of his hand. His intensity sent Diane into a free fall that started in horror and went on to some strange place where she almost needed to laugh. Please, somebody crack a joke so I won't look like a beast, snickering at death. And Gib Lowe's self-consciousness as he knelt next to the bodies almost did the trick. Still as a statue, he looked like a kind of Bible Belt take on Rodin's *Thinker.*

"I swear," Lowe said as he stood up. He shot a quick glance around the crime scene, made sure the media was paying attention, looked again at the dead youth. "I swear by God, son, I'll find who did this to you and bring them to justice."

By then the photographer from the Bolton *Morning Tele-*

graph was on the scene and able to capture the moment for the front page of the Saturday morning paper. Thankfully, nobody but Diane noticed when Renfro slipped up and tapped her on the shoulder. She followed him back down to Lakeside Drive, where he'd parked.

As they drove back toward the station, she hung her head out the window, taking deep breaths of air, trying to clear the scent of death from her nostrils. Renfro offered her an Altoid. She took the whole tin from him, stuck a couple of mints in her mouth, and pocketed the rest. Renfro just drove, not saying anything until Dispatch called him back to the station so the shift sergeant could give Diane the proper ration of shit for being, as he put it, "the fuckup of the month. Maybe even the year." She stood in front of his desk, knowing that what he was saying was true, that there were no excuses, nodding at the appropriate moments. He fell silent, waiting for her to say something. All she could do was shrug. He was right. She'd blown it big-time. He softened then and said, "Look, I know you were running on almost no sleep. We've all been out of our district at one time or another. But you pulled a hell of a time and place to get caught at it."

"Maybe I should have just left. Gone back to my district and let somebody from the S.O. find the bodies. That what you're saying?"

He looked at her seriously. "Could you have?"

"If I could have, we wouldn't be here right now. I saw the killer, Sergeant."

"Good enough." He nodded at the door. "Go get some sleep."

But she had to stay at the station, describing the suspect to a technician who entered the information into a computer to generate a sketch of the suspect. And after that she had to wait until the sheriff's deputy came and took her written statement about what had happened. It was the same one who'd arrived with the sheriff, first on the scene but for Diane. From the minute he walked in the door, he acted like he didn't believe her.

TWO

Eighteen years, and Gail Rubin has not seen a sunrise. She has not seen the moon. At some point in her life she had known what it was to lie in a soft, comfortable bed and feel a cool evening breeze flow through the window and over her body at the end of a hot summer day. But she could not summon the memory, buried as it was under years of lying sleepless on a thin, lumpy mattress spread over a steel slab, night after night, hearing keys clank against the guard's thigh as he walked down the corridor at midnight. Then again at three A.M. And again at six o'clock. When she reached out, her hand touched a cold cinder block wall.

But tomorrow. It was finally almost here. Tomorrow was her parole hearing. She couldn't think about it. She couldn't not think about it. She had seen them four years ago. Usually prisoners tried every two years, but Gail held out. She hadn't even gone that first time until she had a solid ten years inside, and still the examiners had looked at her all the way through the hearing as though she were perhaps slightly insane. Maybe they were right. Maybe ten years inside had caused her to lose her mind, and everyone knew it but she. The years. The days. The hours. The minutes. How many minutes had she spent behind bars? How many seconds? Tomorrow.

She heard Johnson marching down the hall in his erratic almost double time, with a stutter step thrown in every few yards. Corrections Officer Johnson, angry as a chain saw, sad as a humpback moon. Hup, two, three, four. Right on time as usual, stepping off from the control room exactly at midnight. Count time, ladies. She heard children singing in her head: *We're all in our places with bright, shiny faces. Oh, this is the way to start a new day.* From preschool? Forty-odd years ago, when it took every bit of Gail's four-year-old willpower to keep her head down on her little wooden desk for an entire half hour. Even then she hated confinement, and sometimes she could feel her hands going numb from the pressure of her head on her arms as she struggled to maintain the required position.

Johnson's voice shot through the cell bars almost in his wake as he moved briskly down the corridor, occasionally tapping a cell bar with his pen. "Lights out, Rubin." He moved fast, and was all business. Lock the locks. Hang the keys on his belt. No smiles. No slack. No chance of mercy if he caught you in the wrong, even on a minor infraction. If he saw you smiling, he'd come over to find out why and make sure you weren't by the time he walked away. Some of the hacks were friendly enough, or at least civil. Johnson was civil enough most of the time, but he took it upon himself to make sure that prisoners didn't forget what total scum they were. His eyes told you that.

Gail slipped a marker in her book, closed it, and put it on the small desk as she rose to hit the light switch. She heard the woman in the cell next door, Rhonda the Rodent, splashing water. A little late-night primping, and Johnson on duty tonight.

"Rhonda." Gail pressed her face gently against the bars, speaking quietly.

The splashing stopped. "What?"

Gail stood there, wondering what she'd been about to say to Rhonda. The thought had evaporated. Probably for good reason, Gail thought. Probably I was going to say something to let Rhonda know that I know what's going on. But who the fuck cares what's going on?

"Never mind," Gail said. "I found some."

"Some what?"

"Toilet paper," Gail said. "I thought I was out."

"Wouldn't have mattered," the Rodent said. "I only got the roll I'm using."

Gail knew it was a lie. The Rodent was a legendary hoarder. Rhonda had a lot going for her in the Department of Tits and Ass, but she had a face like a weasel and the demeanor to match. God. This place. This awful, smelly, noisy, soul-killing, stupid, messed-up place.

Before Gail went to the board the first time, she'd waited what felt like three eons. She could have gone earlier, but her attorney said it was unwise. Mel Schapp would sit across from her in the cramped, barren attorney visiting room and watch her tears fall, wiping a few from his own cheeks before folding her hands in his. "If you go to them before they think you've fully recognized the seriousness of what you did—and paid a serious price for it—they're going to slam you. You'll wind up staying here twice as long as if you wait. Listen to me," he would say in a pained voice, "I know you're a good person. What got you here were naïveté and a misguided political sensibility. And yes, you can say you're a political prisoner. Some people would go for that. But not a judge, not a parole board. They're not even capable of hearing it. There are no political prisoners in the United States. Bring it up? You'll convince them that they're right to keep you in prison. They'll think you still believe violence is a legitimate means of effecting political change."

She didn't believe it, if she ever had. They'd gotten her with weapons and explosives in the basement of a rented home. She and Tom Firestone both, only a few weeks after they were engaged. Tom was the true believer, and his fervor was contagious. Not that she was trying to lay responsibility off on him, but Gail had never and would never intentionally harm another person, no matter how much good it might do for society as a whole. For her, terrorism was not an option. Property crimes with a message, that had been her limit. She felt sometimes, in those days, like a failure for not being able to cross that line. She wondered if she would even be involved if it weren't for Tom. She didn't know if she was being chicken on the merits or if she'd been drawn into something way over her head while searching for love. About the only thing she did know, in her own heart, was that violence was wrong. Always. Unless you were defending yourself against an attack. It was not a sentiment she had ever dared to put forth at the meetings. But there were many like her in the organization that called itself Free Now. It was a large and eclectic group of people, likeminded in their desire to stop what they saw as criminal activity by the United States government, but full of dissension when it came to how best to do it. It was only a hard-core few, at the center of things, who felt human life was a legitimate sacrifice. They were the ones who'd robbed a bank in Philadelphia. They were the ones who'd shot two guards and a teller when things didn't go as planned. And they were the ones who got away with around two million dollars which somehow never made it to the organization's coffers.

The rattling of Johnson's keys in the lock to Rhonda's door brought Gail back to the confines of the cell. She turned away from the wall and covered her exposed ear with an ancient feather pillow long ago turned to lead. Even through the pillow, Gail could hear. Johnson had a great voice, a sexy voice, deep and inviting. It came through the walls.

She began humming softly, nothing she recognized as a song, just random notes to fill her ears beneath the pillow. Johnson was either too stupid to see what Rhonda was up to or he was being willfully ignorant. Not that Gail had any sympathy for hacks, but she knew that Johnson was going to face the modern equivalent of a lynch party when the Rodent decided to cry rape.

There were those like the Rodent who would fuck a guard in exchange for special treatment. And there were those who chose to take lovers. Truly it was concupiscence. Gail smiled to herself but couldn't take the smell of dead feathers anymore. She removed the pillow from her head. Just tune it out. She herself had been courted over the years, and briefly had a relationship with another prisoner that broke up after she found herself unable to tolerate the partnership in the fishbowl of prison. Everybody knew everybody. Any confidence would be out on the tiers in a matter of hours. She had become, after a few years of secretive, occasional, and completely purposeless masturbation, celibate. She was most comfortable if she consciously harnessed her libido and steered the energy in other directions. She read, studied, wrote, went into her head and explored. She had, in her fifth year of incarceration, developed a literacy program to teach prisoners how to read. Her instruction had been so successful that her program had been adopted by the entire federal prison system. Back when they had programs. Now it was strictly about warehousing.

A radio blared from somewhere down the tier, echoing loudly, a young black kid from the sounds of it, half-singing, half-rapping in front of a mix of rock and funk . . . *just another brother in lockdown* . . .

"Turn that shit down!" someone shouted.

"Suck my dick!" a squeaky female voice shouted back, but the volume went down.

Gail sighed, pulled her scratchy green wool army blanket up and smoothed it against herself, pinned it to her sides with her arms. She was long and slender under the blanket. She tried to imagine what she would look like with a baby in her belly. The huge swollenness of it. She had been pregnant once, for less than ninety days, before having to terminate. She still hated the word. Right after college in Oklahoma, where she'd gone to study Native American cultures and to piss off her parents. They wanted Yale, or Columbia, or Brown, and Gail could have gone to any of them, but she was so tired by then, sick of the whole upper-middle-class-Eastern-liberal-we-are-the-world-but-send-your-kids-to-private-school scene. She felt contempt for her perfect spacious bedroom in her parents' perfect spacious, gracious house with the perfect Connecticut lawn and the swimming pool ever blue in the backyard and Juan, who came to make sure the lawn and garden behaved themselves, and Sunday brunches next to the pool and just the whole goddamn calm suburban mess. Come graduation day from Doris Canne Girls Prep, Gail was outta there.

She wondered now, if she'd stayed closer to home, done the Ivy League thing her parents wanted, which, they assured her, was only because they wanted her to be happy, she wondered if she might right now be sitting in her kitchen waiting for her children to come home from school. She saw how the women looked when they came back from the visiting room after having seen their kids. The strangest mix of happiness and despair showed in their eyes. Some of them were full of stories from home and eager to talk about their kids' accomplishments, some saddened into a cold and lonely silence as soon as they returned from the visit.

She stared up at the bottom of the bunk above her. Gail had watched as the war on drugs brought more and more women into the system. Young ones, too. Mules mostly. Fools for love, mostly. And most of them were just plain fucked. Like the Rodent. Busted for holding three grams of cocaine when she was nineteen. Three measly grams. And then again, when she was twenty-six, for a half ounce. This last time they got her with an ounce, but linked her very loosely to a conspiracy involving multiple kilos. Didn't bother the prosecutor that she wasn't really part of any plan, she was only dating one of the conspirators, or maybe just trading sex for coke. Three strikes, she was out. No matter that the sum total of the drugs they got her with wouldn't fill the shirt pocket of a Colombian general's uniform. Rhonda the Rodent got mandatory life with no parole. Even the judge had no say in the matter. Why not fuck the guards, when you came right down to it. Fuck them and they'll give you cocaine or pot, give you good food, look the other way when you're having a little glass of hooch late on a Saturday night, kicking back with the girls. Gail understood why Rhonda did the things she did. Unless some miracle legislation came along, or some president who had a set of balls to go with his wandering penis, Rhonda was going to die here. Here or in some other cell somewhere in the vast gulag of the exponentially expanding U.S. penal system.

Gail sat up, tossed off the blanket. Shit. It was overwhelming sometimes. Living next door to such a case. She had to get out of here. Had to. But tomorrow. At least Mel thought so, and that was something. He never had before. Gail had tried to keep her shame and anger and self-doubt in check that first time, and she would try even harder tomorrow. But she couldn't really be blamed if her take on the matter was tainted. Eighteen years is a long time to live in a concrete eight-by-ten room with three cinder block walls and a fourth made of steel bars. Hell of a lot longer than a half hour is to a little girl in kindergarten sitting perfectly still with her head down on her desk, pretending to sleep.

Gail turned onto her belly, pulled the blanket up over her shoulders, positioning it carefully so the scratchy wool wouldn't touch her face or neck. She was in a T-shirt and boxer shorts. Prison-issue stuff. When she had first arrived, prisoners were allowed to have boxes of clothing from home sent in twice a year. No more. Street clothes were outlawed. They wore leftovers, hand-me-downs from the army and air force. Gail had been around long enough to cop one of those puffy green silk bomber jackets with the orange lining inside that were so coveted in winter. They kept you warmer than the peacoats. And she had a bag made of the same material, big and blocky, but with a large looping handle she could hang over her shoulder, kind of like a satchel. It went with her everywhere but to work and workouts. In it she carried her journal, notes for her case, articles she sent to magazines. She'd even published a few, in the *Nation, Texas Monthly,* and a couple in *Prison Life* magazine. But she'd backed off from doing a whole lot of that lately. It made the authorities nervous, and she didn't want any unnecessary animosity coming toward her so close to her parole hearing.

Things quieted down, finally, but for the Snorer down the hall. That was the hardest noise to fall asleep against. Painfully, incredibly loud. Poor girl. It sounded as though she were barely getting any oxygen at all. Gail focused inside her head, pictured a warm white light there, right in the center of her brain. Made herself relax. Felt the tension draining out of her neck and shoulders, felt her weight sinking onto the pitiful excuse for a mattress. Tomorrow, she would rise early, do some stretches, dress carefully. Go to chow. Return to her cell to await her appointment. When called, she would be composed and earnest and ready to communicate her heartfelt regret for the mistakes she had made in her youth, and she would defend herself carefully and without attitude. She would convince the examiners.

They would recommend parole.

She could not consider the alternative.

She drifted toward sleep telling herself this: It's time. You're ready. You deserve a second chance. But she could not let go of the word *maybe*. Maybe, just maybe, deep down inside, there was a part of her that wasn't sure she deserved a second shot at anything. Maybe her crime had been too heinous. What if she hadn't been caught and the guns and explosives had been used? What if people had been killed by them? Maybe she could stay in prison for the rest of her life and still never feel that it was sufficient punishment for the stupidity she had exhibited back in her twenties. That was what really haunted her: the possibility that what she had done to get herself locked in prison for all these years was simply a matter of stupidity. Yes, she had loved Tom. Yes, she had thought they would marry and have children. Or maybe not marry and have children. But they would make a family, one way or the other. She wondered if it had been desperation, a feeling that if things with Tom didn't work out, then they would never work out with anyone. For a long time after the fiasco in Oklahoma, when the boyfriend who swore he would love her forever split town the day after learning she was pregnant, she'd been certain she'd never have a family. But Tom was her soulmate, she was sure of it. He knew the way things really worked, he saw the preposterousness of the system, how it crushed people and doomed them to wage slavery. He refused to be part of the gimme-gimme-gimme culture of Amerika, Inc. He hated war. He wanted to help bring about something better. A better world, he said, for their children. For all the children. It would take drastic measures, but he was committed. And he needed Gail. Wanted Gail. Loved Gail. His passion was contagious.

Tom was on the streets now. Had been for two years.

She hadn't heard from him.

She explained to herself that he couldn't contact her. He was on parole. He couldn't write. Couldn't take calls from her. Any contact with a prisoner or ex-convict on his part would be construed as association, and he could be in violation, have his parole revoked and be sent back inside. She had to understand that.

But she didn't. There were ways. There were people who could carry messages. He could write to her under a pseudonym. He could have a friend write. Anything. Anything would have helped. She didn't expect him to declare true and undying love for her. Just something to let her know he was thinking about her, since he was out and she was still in. Just to let her know that it hadn't all been some kind of ruse.

That way if she had done the crime for love, and not because she believed it was the right thing to do, she could at least think that it had, truly and actually, been the real thing.

She tried, but couldn't picture him. His face was a blur, surrounded by curly black hair. He was in blue jeans and a denim work shirt. But she could not see his features. Could not remember his smile or his eyes. Maybe that made it easier to lay things off on him, if that's what she was doing. She didn't know anymore. She didn't know if she had ever really believed in what they were doing. And didn't know if that was because she despised violence, no matter the terms in which it was couched, or if she considered herself a coward for not being able to get out there and toss Molotov cocktails with the best of them. And what was all this anyway? What did it matter at all except that tomorrow morning she had to convince three parole examiners that she deserved to be let out? She deserved to be free. Why couldn't she embrace that? Maybe the time inside had taken away her ability to believe in anything. Perhaps all these years living in the criminal element had enabled her to attain a perfect state of anomie: wholesomely alienated and without purpose. If that was so, then tomorrow was just another day in paradise, and it did not matter what the examiners decided. She lay in her bunk, perfectly still. If she moved, she would shatter into a million particles of dust. Her soul would transmogrify from the ethereal to the material, and it, too, would perish.

She had talked about culpability several times with the rabbi who came to visit the prison and lead services every other week. He had counseled her not to be so hard on herself. Chaplain Fuentes, whom she had worked for many times over the years, had told her the same thing. "Forgive yourself," she said. "I know you, and you are not a criminal. You are not a bad person." Gail had worked at it, and at times had achieved it. Other times she thought about those guns, those cold hard rifles and the frightening boxes with the forbidding labels on them, all stacked down in the basement like cartons of home-made pasta sauce or something, just out there on metal shelving, waiting for the police to come and find them, and she was chilled with fear. She knew the chaplain was right: she was not a bad person. So how could she have done that? The thoughts whirled in slow circles in her head, moving ever more slowly until, at last, her eyes fell shut and her consciousness floated out through the bars into the ether of dreams and freedom.

THREE

Diane picked up the mike and gave dispatch a 10-4. Too hot, the early spring evening, and the people of Bolton were taking it out on each other. The call was her sixth of the shift, and that was far from over. At least she was off deep nights. So far, since she came on at three, smack-dab in the middle of a real scorcher of an afternoon, there'd been a barking dog, a stolen bicycle, a shoplifter, a bit of teenage vandalism—some kids had wrapped a two-story house in toilet paper—and something else she'd already forgotten about but had dutifully recorded in her log in the backseat of the squad. And now this: a domestic disturbance.

She pulled to the curb several houses down from the address of the call. Walked briskly toward the house, a single-story ranch, midblock, with similar homes dotting the length of the street. She approached cautiously, looking for anything that might be out of place. No sign of trouble. She'd barely got her finger off the doorbell when a woman in cutoffs and a Ricky Martin T-shirt opened the door and led her through the living room toward a shouting match in the kitchen. She rounded the corner just in time to see a couple of curtain climbers grab pork chops from a platter on the kitchen table and hurl them at the wall, shouting "Dinner sucks! This food sucks! We want McDonald's!" When they saw Diane, they clammed up, and then their jaws dropped open like they'd never seen a woman in uniform before.

Dad sat watching them, a slight smile on his lips.

"He started it," the wife said. "Threw the entire bowl of whipped potatoes and another one of gravy smack against the new wallpaper that I spent all last weekend hanging myself."

"You ought to've just hung yourself," Dad said. Diane glared at him, and then past him at the wallpaper, which had grapes and cherries, a purple and red color combination that looked to her like something you might buy at the Our Savior Thrift Shop in Overton, Texas, where she had grown up. On calls like this, she hated her job.

Again at the husband. "What an awful thing to say." He looked at Diane, the smirk still on his lips. She'd never known her own father, but if he was anything like this, just thank God she hadn't. She stood looking at the wall where clumps of whipped potatoes were splatted and gravy was dribbling down. This was such bullshit. They didn't need the cops here. They needed a damn kindergarten teacher. This was just plain stupid. It was so stupid she had a hard time not laughing out loud. Stupid people in a stupid house living stupid lives. They just didn't get it. She looked at the pork chops on the floor, thinking how her mother had never once made pork chops when she was growing up, thinking how she could only remember once or twice her mother making some Shake 'N Bake chicken, and burning it each time, and how she'd always just kind of fended for herself in the kitchen. She could scramble an egg by the time she was six. Her older brother Kevin brought home shoplifted groceries and put them in the fridge or in the cabinets, or sometimes, when their mother was so drunk he couldn't stand the sight of her, he just left the bags on the counter and went back out, shaking his head and cursing quietly. Diane would put the stuff away and then go back outside into the swelter of a steamy hot, pine-scented East Texas summer and look for a bit of shade.

The salad was still on the table. None of them had touched it. Iceberg lettuce and, from the looks of them, the tomatoes had been picked stone green and wrapped in cellophane so they could half rot, half ripen. Diane's eyes followed the gravy down the wall. The baby had crawled over and was eating potatoes off the floor. Diane looked to the wife, with her tear-stained cheeks and frizzled hair, and then to the husband, with his dirty T-shirt and his jaw jutted out against any kind of authority that dared show up as a female, and on to the kids, who were staring at her badge and gun so hard they couldn't even see there was a human being under all that uniform and gear.

Her backup arrived—it was Renfro—jangling smartly through the front door, holding his flashlight like a club. She waved an okay to him. Will Renfro relaxed, walked up, and shifted his weight to his gun leg, rested his arm on the butt of his revolver, still holstered. It was a cop form of gangster lean, but with Will doing it, it wasn't at all threatening. He just wanted somewhere to rest his arm.

"Should we go now?" Diane asked. She turned to the wife. "Y'all gonna make it to dessert here without tearing the place down? Or do we drag this asshole off to jail for a night?" It was her turn to smirk at dear old dad. Diane knew it would come down to a fight if she tried to take him in, but she wasn't afraid to get physical. He could see it, and didn't look so tough now. Renfro looked down at his spit-shined black tie shoes to hide his own smile.

"We'll be fine," the wife said. "Thank you, Officer. I'm sorry for your trouble."

"No problem," said Diane, thinking that as soon as she and Renfro were out of there, the wife would be apologizing to the whole damn family. No doubt about it, Diane had just met a woman who said I'm sorry at least a dozen times every day. You could get through life easy that way, long as you could deal with the bad taste the words, when used just to get by, left on your tongue. Before turning to leave, Diane picked up a fork and stabbed it into the salad bowl, stuffed a wad of greens into her mouth. She chewed. The family stared; their eyes got even bigger. She swallowed, and smiled at the wife.

"Delicious," she said. She turned back to the kids. "Never forget," she said. "Do not forsake your leafy greens."

Outside, on the smooth suburban street with a decent-size

oak centered in each manicured lawn on either side of it, Diane leaned against the door of her squad and made a note on her clipboard.

Renfro leaned up next to her, looking over her shoulder as she scribbled notes on her report. She felt his shoulder next to hers, not touching, but close enough that she could sense his strength. It wasn't pushy, though, it was something like gentle, the kind of strength she could just sense would always be used to a good end. It was a nice feeling, one Diane couldn't help but respond to. You couldn't ask for a better backup than Renfro.

"Civilians," Renfro said, shaking his head, looking at her with a sideways smile. "That fella in there must've got his Ph.D. from the University of Stupid."

Diane kept writing. "Glad you showed up," she said. "It looked like he was gonna get rambunctious there for a minute."

"He ought to know better than to take you on."

"Right." She slipped her pen under the clamp on the clipboard and looked up at him. He had really cute ears. You couldn't say that about a lot of guys, but you could about Renfro. Not that she ever had.

"I was just about to check out on a Long 5 when they called me to back you up," he said. "Join me for dinner break?"

Diane tossed the clipboard into her squad. Renfro had a new haircut, his sandy brown locks cropped closer than she'd ever seen. She liked it. It brought out his eyes, blue tinted toward turquoise, keen, street smart. He was, as she'd overheard Katie Ryan say in the women's locker room one morning, a fine physical specimen. True enough, but that was as far as any relationship went for Officer Ryan, and Diane herself preferred a man with a brain. That meant for slim pickings in the PD, but right from the start she'd recognized that Renfro made the cut. And was nice on top of it. It was too much. She still wasn't sure she trusted it, this thing they had between them, and part of her kept what she hoped was a safe distance.

"We keep showing up at restaurants together, people are gonna start talkin'." She slipped into her squad, rolled down the window, and cranked the engine.

"Fine with me," Renfro drawled. "Why don't you meet me

at Harbingers." He rapped a knuckle against the roof of the squad. "I hear they got a special on pork chops this evening."

At dinner, Renfro set his walkie, volume just audible, upright on the gold-specked white Formica tabletop right next to the metal contraption that held slightly greasy glass salt and pepper shakers on either side of two neat stacks of packets. Real sugar was wrapped white, next to the pink-packaged artificial stuff that confused humans into thinking they were losing weight, but mostly just gave cancer to rats. Renfro was one of those wiry types who could eat like next Sunday was the Rapture and not put on an ounce. Diane, not wiry but trim and athletic, sported a healthy appetite herself, and was unafraid of chicken-fried steak, or chicken-fried anything for that matter. If there was cream gravy on it, she would eat it.

"Perfectly good food all over the floor." Renfro stuffed a flaky chunk of biscuit into his mouth. "What gets into people?"

"Marital bliss," Diane said, looking at him significantly.

"My folks are still married. Still love each other. It happens."

"The odds suck."

"You gonna go through life all alone, never have kids, never give the family thing a chance? What're you scared of?"

"Not you, that's for sure." She had the feeling the smile on her face looked like just what it was: naked self-defense.

He gave her a look, willing to make it all a joke, all just in fun, nothing to get upset about.

She lowered her voice to a whisper and leaned across toward him like they were conspiring on a diamond heist. "So? You heard anything?" It had been nearly six months since she'd found the bodies out by the lake, and the DA and sheriff had wasted no time arresting a lowlife speed freak named Rick Churchpin for the offense. They'd taken him to trial in record time, produced a dental forensics expert who testified that bite marks found on the victims matched dental imprints taken from Churchpin's teeth. They brought out a couple of young Mexicans who told the jury that they had repaired Churchpin's Chevy Nova and returned it to him the afternoon of the murders. Tire tracks at the scene matched those on the Nova. And, most damningly, Sheriff Lowe himself took the stand

and swore on the Bible that while Churchpin was incarcerated in the county jail awaiting trial, he had confessed to the crimes. It so happened that the deputy on duty went home sick that night and the sheriff came in to relieve him because he happened to be working late in his office. He'd brought Churchpin out of his cell and had the defendant mopping the cell block when Churchpin was suddenly overcome with the need to confess. Sheriff Lowe, who knelt with young Churchpin there on the concrete jailhouse floor in the small hours of a Saturday morning, had listened in horror as Churchpin, tears streaming down his face, detailed what happened the night of the killings. He hadn't been willing to sign anything; he only wanted to unburden his soul to Sheriff Lowe. And the sheriff hadn't wanted to risk interrupting things to get a video camera running because he knew for sure that it would frighten Churchpin into silence. When the defense raised issues of hearsay, the judge said that in light of the sheriff's position as a peace officer in the state of Texas, he would allow the testimony. Read: The case had shocked and inflamed the good citizens of Bolton. Elections were looming in the fall. The DA needed closure, and needed it fast. Later in the trial, perhaps thinking in terms of reversible error, the judge instructed the jury to disregard the sheriff's testimony. But the damage to Churchpin was done. The jury promptly dispatched him to death row. Diane had been outraged. Churchpin's father was black, his mother Mexican, and the man she'd seen that night was as white as they come. So far, her efforts to point out this discrepancy to the DA had been met with disdain and a trip to Chief Thompson's office, where she was encouraged to forget about the whole thing. Hadn't he forgotten about the stolen squad car, which had never been recovered? She didn't know how to reply. The thing that pissed her off most about the theft, after her emotions had settled and the embarrassment abated somewhat, was that she'd lost her autographed copy of *The Big White Lie,* an exposé of the drug war that she'd been carrying in her briefcase in case she got the chance to read on her dinner breaks. At least the chief hadn't found out she was carrying a book on duty. That was against regulations.

Renfro slipped down in the booth and stretched his legs out under the table, and then shifted forward abruptly.

"I have it from a very reliable source that the high sheriff of Breard County has taken up residence in that big old cell on the top floor of the county jail. Had it carpeted. Moved right in and made hisself at home. Like it's his goddamn penthouse apartment or something."

"Very funny." Diane took a long sip of iced tea. "Come on. I'm serious. You know what I mean."

"No, for real," Renfro said. "I hear ol' Sheriff Lowe is partying hearty."

"And you believe that horseshit?"

"Hell, I heard he already had his way with two prisoners right there in his penthouse. One girl Narcotics busted on coke, another just some sorry-ass hooker from the south side. About half skanky I bet. Don't see how he could even look twice at a slice like that."

"Water seeks its own level," Diane replied too quickly. When she was in high school, she used to worry that she'd turn out like her mother, even though she was the farthest thing from it. She took a mouthful of french fries, grabbed her napkin and wiped ketchup from her lips. The waitress hadn't blinked when Diane had ordered French fries and whipped potatoes to go with her chicken-fried steak. She knew Diane could rarely decide between the two, and usually ordered both. Diane felt Renfro's ankle rubbing up against her calf, felt that little electric-charge shiver sensation that shot right up and made her quiver, quickened her heart like a robbery-in-progress call, and made her want to lean across the table and kiss him. She glanced around the café. Nobody had noticed, but she pulled her leg away and shot him a not-here look. He sat up straight and dug back into his pork chop, his eyes never leaving hers.

"Don't get all moony-eyed," Diane said quietly. "We have an image to uphold here."

Renfro looked around the café, too, and back to her.

"Nobody gives a hoot," he said.

"I do," Diane said. "I don't wanna get called on the carpet cause you can't wait till we get off."

"Get off?" He smiled and eased up, passed her the ketchup. "I'm sorry," he said. "I just can't be near you without jumping up at attention."

"Well, at ease, or parade rest, or whatever." Diane put some whipped potatoes in her mouth but all she could think about was kissing Renfro. He was the best kisser she'd ever encountered, not to say that she was any expert. Sometimes she thought maybe it had something to do with the possibility that he loved her. He sure acted like it. It scared her. Last thing she wanted in the world was some kind of serious relationship where everybody could get all tearful and messed up and wind up hating each other. Forget about that.

"Touchy tonight, aren't we," Renfro said.

"Maybe."

"But not touchy-feely?" He gave her that look of his.

She wasn't going for it.

"Damn, girl. What's the major malfunction?"

"Lowe's a criminal!" Heads turned. Diane lowered her voice. "You know it as sure as we're sitting here."

"Maybe I do, but I know better than to try to make some big deal out of it. I just thank God I turned in my deputy badge and got the hell out of there before that fool took over. I feel sorry for the deputies in this county. Being city police is a lot better deal, you ask me."

He'd asked her once when was the first time she ever thought about becoming a cop, but she didn't tell him it was when she came home from seventh grade one day and her mother had just turned a trick in the bedroom and Diane almost bumped into the john on her way in the front door. They'd stared at each other for an insufferably long moment, shame turning Diane's cheeks the color of the oleanders outside next to the porch. And as embarrassed and horrified as she was, that was just how cool and big-dog-unconcerned the john was. He looked at her like she was dirt, and she watched him swagger out to his Toyota pickup, one of those pip-squeak pickups that couldn't even call itself a real truck. She glared after the truck as it disappeared down the street: Look at me again, asshole. She would get his respect, someday, if she even wanted it by then. She would get respect from everybody in Overton. Except maybe her mother. Her mother didn't know how to respect anything, even her own self.

"Renfro," she said now, "Sheriff Gib Lowe is no fool. He's fucking evil."

"Aw, come on, Diane." Renfro winked. "An' here he's got everybody thinkin' he's doin' the Lord's work."

"Like putting Rick Churchpin on death row? That's a fine piece of investigating, thank you, Jesus."

"Churchpin was nothing but a bottom-feeder. Don't tell me you're feeling sorry for him."

"I'm not feeling sorry for anyone. But he didn't do those murders."

"I'm not so sure."

"Did they even call me to testify? I was there, for God's sake. The killer was white, Rick Churchpin isn't. Doesn't even remotely resemble the guy I saw. I can't believe that fuckin' Al Swerdney has the balls to even call himself a district attorney. I go to him with what I saw and he tells me the case is secure without my testimony. He doesn't want to do anything that might confuse the jury. Fuckin' slimebucket."

"Hey," Renfro's voice was low and soothing. "We've been over this. Calm down, girl. It's not worth getting all worked up over. I'm sure Churchpin's attorneys will appeal. Maybe you'll get your say then."

"Yeah. Get called by the defense? Fuck up the case for the prosecution. I'll be a damn laughingstock. And there goes any chance of promotion whatsoever. I'm tellin' you, I'm ready to quit this job. It's all just horse crap. Might as well be a lawyer."

"That'd just be horse doody with better pay and not as much risk. Come on, you love the streets. You know it."

Diane sighed.

"I just wish somebody would rob a bank or a supermarket or something. I've had enough bullshit calls to last till next Easter."

"Diane."

She took a deep breath and sighed it out slowly.

"You know," he said, "if you were serious about law school, you know I'd like, if you wanted to, if you went here to the university, I'd like . . ."

"You'd like?"

"You could stay with me. At my place. You know, since you'd be payin' tuition and all that." He was looking at her so earnestly, she thought she might melt.

"That's so sweet, Renfro." She took another breath. "The truth is, I don't know what I'm doing. I haven't made any decisions. I'm just pissed off about what's going on around here. It's not right."

"Maybe you didn't see the killer. Maybe that guy was just out there doing something else—I mean God-knows-what at that hour, probably something wrong—but maybe he wasn't involved and he just freaked out and took your squad. Isn't that possible?"

"Listen up. You tell me, honest to God, that you believe Gib Lowe's case against Churchpin. Tell me for real." She sat waiting for his reply.

"He was a cadet once," Renfro said quietly.

"Churchpin?"

Renfro nodded. "Back in high school. Rode with Detective Efird several times when he was in the program, back when Efird was a patrol sergeant."

"What on earth happened to him?"

"Crystal meth," Renfro said. "Speed happened to him. Efird tried everything, but Churchpin took it upon himself to dive down deep. Talk about a waste. He used to be a pretty good kid."

"See what I mean? And now he's on death row! It's fuckin' outrageous. It's the sheriff who ought to be there. How in the name of God does he get away with it? I mean, really."

"Who's gonna call him on it?" Renfro shook his head in exasperation. "You? Me? Hell, him an' the DA are in tight together and busier than a couple of hens pecking on a fire ant mound."

"Tell me something I don't already know."

"How about this: I'd like to take you out to the backseat of my official City of Bolton 2003 blue-and-white Chevrolet patrol vehicle and rip your uniform off and fuck you till you say uncle."

Diane felt her cheeks go red in spite of herself. Damn him.

"Just you try it. You'll be the one yelling uncle."

He smiled at her. She smiled back, but shook her head no. No way.

He chomped down on what was left of his pork chop—the bone—held it between his teeth and growled at her real low.

She tried not to laugh, but couldn't help it, then saw a couple staring at them across the blue linoleum tiles and sobered herself up right quick. Sort of.

"Renfro," she said, almost snickering, but not intentionally, "you're gonna get both of us into deep doo-doo if you don't straighten up." He did so, assuming an almost military bearing as he finished off his fried okra, handling his utensils with precision and grace.

"Officer Wellman," he said officiously, "allow me to get the check." He picked up the small rectangle of green recycled paper, torn jagged from the waitress's book, smoothed four dollars onto the table, placed the ketchup bottle on top of the tip, and sauntered to the cashier's stand. The cashier reached for the check. Renfro reached for his wallet, or made a gesture as if he were about to. The cashier looked at him, gave ever the slightest nod no, and slapped the check onto the metal spike next to the register, facedown. On the house.

They walked out into the heat. Diane felt it coming off the blacktop parking lot, up through the soles of her boots. She was sweating before she reached her squad car, and happy to pull off her hat and get inside where there was air-conditioning. Renfro walked over and tapped on her window. She grabbed the handle and rolled it down.

Renfro eyed her with unabashed desire. It went right into her, pulling her toward those lips of his.

"Damn it, Renfro, what am I supposed to do?" She sat back in the seat.

His hand brushed across hers as he turned away, smiling. And then, over his shoulder, "Officer needs assistance. Follow me." He got into his car and gunned out of the parking lot. Headed south on Main.

She went north.

For about two blocks. And then she couldn't say no; she pulled a smooth U-turn and sped to catch up to him.

The city of Bolton was growing so fast that entire neighborhoods were springing up practically overnight. What once were fields of cotton or wheat, or pastures for cattle, were being cordoned off, sliced into neat sections, paved, prepped, and plumbed, and receiving houses that could be assembled in a matter of weeks and still achieve the label Custom Home. The buyers chose the brick, the façade, the roofing color, the wallpaper, the carpet, and the wood paneling from large loose-leaf notebooks which held samples. Six weeks later, there sat the house. Small tank trucks pulled up out front, and men in white uniforms emerged to spray a thick green coating of sticky stuff wherever dirt had persevered in the midst of all that pavement. Three days later, weed-free lawn was sprouting. Swimming pools, cool blue ovals or rectangles or kidney bean shapes, appeared in backyards. Privacy fences went up.

It was the strangest thing. Diane would take her two days off, currently Tuesday and Wednesday, and by the time she came back to work there would be three new streets to memorize, and already people were moving in. Far be it from her to judge, but it seemed that if anyone truly deserved the death penalty, it should be the planners and architects who designed the suburbs.

She followed Renfro, and they drove past the finished neighborhoods where not a single kid was outside playing on the beautiful green lawns sustained by copious watering. It was either too hellishly hot or all the kids were plugged into TVs and computers—who knew?—but they drove past those homes and through the sections where only the skeletons of houses stood naked against the dusky blue sky. The concrete was clean enough to eat off. Diane remembered how, when she was a kid, she and her friends would go barefoot down the pavement, using their toes to pop the translucent bubbles in the ribbons of tar that separated the concrete segments of Stadium Street. Sometimes the other kids got in trouble with their moms for getting tar all over their toes, but Diane's mom never gave her any problems over it. Or anything, for that matter.

She followed Renfro at what she hoped was a discreet distance, though once they were out there in the boonies, there wasn't really any such thing as discreet.

The destination was a nameless cul-de-sac laid down in what used to be a horse pasture, way out on the edge of town. Soon it would be a neighborhood, complete with gas grills and patios and azaleas under the windows. Or maybe wax leaf ligustrum: something spiky, to keep teenage burglars from crawling in the windows and making off with the Playstation and the Compaq. Renfro parked and got out, leaned against his car, waiting as Diane pulled in behind him. He gave her a big smile and was yanking at his Sam Browne even before he got to her car. She got out and stood watching as he opened the back door to her squad and pushed her briefcase to the floorboard, then came around the open door and grabbed her, pulled her to him, and laid into her with one of his kisses.

Hot damn. Somehow they got into the backseat, and him on top, but they hadn't quite got their gunbelts all unfastened, and it was a mishmash of thumbs and fingers and buckles and Renfro knocked a couple of bullets out of the little leather loops that held spare ammo on his belt, and got frustrated even while he was kissing his way down Diane's chest, and then suddenly all the guns and leather and ammo and radios and belts and zippers and cuffs between them were out of the way and he was inside and pumping hard and kissing her lips and making beautiful humming grunts and Diane was loving it, moving with him and feeling it building and they could just as well have been naked on a deserted tropical island as in the backseat of a squad car at dusk in East Texas.

Then they heard the radio spit static, but it was too late, neither one of them could stop. Diane felt her insides blossoming like a gorgeous pink flower and the feeling went clean down into her toes and Renfro was God's gift to woman and somewhere over there behind it all she thought she heard the dispatcher's voice over the radio. And then she was sure of it. Holy shit. It was. It really was.

"Two-forty." Pause. "Two-forty come in." Pause. "Two-forty we have a possible Signal 27 at 48 Brookshire Road." Static spat out of the radio. "Two-forty?"

She gasped and pushed Renfro off her, and he rolled into the tiny space between the seat back of the front seat and the edge of the backseat, so squashed he stuck there, lodged, not even making it to the floorboard, and Diane yanked herself free and ducked around the open door and threw herself bodily into the driver's seat, grabbing the radio as she landed.

Then, into the mike, trying not to sound breathless, "Two-forty, ten-four, 48 Brookshire, I'm en route Code 3." She tossed the mike to the floor and started the car and jumped out to tug Renfro free of the backseat. He almost knocked her over when she finally pried him loose; he caught himself and steadied them both and yanked his pants back up, buckling and cinching, checking to see that his gun hadn't got knocked out of its holster. Diane pulled things back on fast as she could.

"Damn," Renfro said.

"Damn straight," Diane replied. She leaped into the driver's seat and threw the car in gear. Renfro grabbed the door frame, leaned in to kiss her.

"Gotta go," Diane said.

"You're a first-rate copulator," Renfro said, smiling large.

"Out of my fuckin' district, too." Diane peeled out, and heard Renfro shout after her, but with the engine noise she couldn't make out what he said.

She turned off the lights and siren three blocks from the location of the call and parked two houses down so she could approach on foot, quietly and cautiously. It occurred to her as she neared the plain frame house, in need of a new coat of white, that she hadn't heard Dispatch order a backup, though she was sure they had. She had just been too flipped out to hear or remember it happening.

The front door was locked. She pulled her gun and eased cautiously around the side of the dark house, scanning for movement. There was nothing. She found the back door ajar, pushed it open slowly, pulled her Kel-Lite from her belt. The kitchen. Small, clean, tidy. Nothing amiss. Stood listening. Somewhere in the neighborhood, a dog was barking. The house was silent. Down the hall, following the cone of her flashlight. Stepping lightly and quietly as she could, calm, tuned in, trying to sense whether anyone was there.

The body was in the back bedroom.

It stunned her, the scent filling the room. A woman, her lifeless body still warm, blood still oozing from her wounds. There was so much of it. That was what Diane smelled. Blood. The weirdness of death, the primeval fear of a lifeless body, pressed her back. She had to force herself to stay. It was as though, if she got too close, the dead body might try to suck out her own life energy, take it from her, inhale it, and rise up from where it lay, leaving her the one dead on the ground. She felt ancient, in a time when humans were still walking wobbly on two feet, not yet sure they were meant to be upright, still able to see gods and monsters. She stood motionless in the doorway, the ghost of the murdered woman on the bed peering over her shoulder.

She could hear sirens blasting their amplified electronic noise through the thick summer air, drawing closer in the night. Soon there would be red and blue lights strobing through the small window that faced the street, just above a small wooden desk that looked to have been ransacked. The desk was the kind you would find in an unfinished furniture store, this one painted yellow and stenciled with small lavender flowers around the top edge. Diane stepped over, watching every footstep, careful to disturb nothing. On the desk, a flimsy shoebox, its top tossed to the floor. Inside it were letters, opened, presumably read, and replaced in their envelopes. More letters were strewn over the desktop, obviously gone through in a hurry. She didn't touch, but could see a return address on one. Rick Churchpin, #00986-345, Ellis Unit One, Huntsville, Texas. Diane knew the address: death row. One of the open letters on the desk began: Dear Mom. In one corner of the desk, a neat stack of what looked like household bills. On top was a phone bill, addressed to Juanita Churchpin.

She looked again at the body, in its blood-soaked white blouse and pressed blue jeans. Blood sank into the bedspread beneath it, staining like spilled wine. What was the saturation point? When would it start pooling? The woman's lips were pulled back in what must have been a grimace of horror, but death had softened the expression, until she seemed merely confused, indecisive about something.

Rick Churchpin's mother. Jesus Mary and Joseph. Churchpin's mother, stabbed, just like the teens at the lake.

She pulled her radio from its holster on her belt, keyed the mike.

She summoned CID and Crime Scene, went out to her car, and pulled a roll of bright yellow crime-scene tape from the trunk, began securing the area. Neighbors were starting to gather. Diane got out her notepad and began preliminary interviews, ignoring hostility in the eyes of some of the teenagers and young toughs in jeans and T-shirts, some with bandannas tied tight around their heads, who gathered curbside across the street. Rick Churchpin's crowd: speed-freak scooter nasties who went with heavy metal and Budweiser to campfires out past the city limits on Friday and Saturday nights. He had been an oddity among the mostly white faces. Connected by methamphetamine.

The men arrived, Detective Efird from Criminal Investigation, and Lewis, the Crime Scene officer, a wannabe necrophile whose skin looked like he bathed in formaldehyde, having an almost chartreuse tint to it year round. A wacko if ever Diane had met one, and she had met way more than one since joining the PD. Efird, less than a month back from an extended vacation, looked like he'd spent it in a tanning booth. Rumor around the PD was that it wasn't a vacation so much as it was a recuperation. Efird motioned her inside the house with a nod of his head. He looked like he'd crawled out of bed, stuffed himself into one of his several brown suits, and forgotten to comb his spiky brown hair before he left the house. It looked shorter than Diane remembered it, too. But he had managed to shave, as he always did, no matter what odd hour he was called to a crime scene. She'd never seen even a hint of a five-o'clock shadow on Efird's face. Probably because of that cute little cleft on his chin that he no doubt liked to show off. He was holding an almost full bottle of Dr Pepper. Diane stood next to him in the narrow, dark hallway outside the bedroom while Lewis went in with his camera and fingerprint kit.

"ID'd her yet?" Efird tore open a skinny package of peanuts with his teeth, tucked the little strip of plastic into a suit pocket and painstakingly poured the peanuts into the Dr Pepper.

"It's looking like she's Rick Churchpin's mother. Name's Juanita."

Efird put a thumb over the bottle top and gently swirled the peanuts around in the Dr Pepper. "How dog-ass weird is that, almost a year after her shitbag son lands on the Row?"

"Very weird. Or else it makes perfect sense, you ask me." Diane folded her arms across her chest and waited for more from Efird. He stood looking at the room, taking it in.

"There's a bunch of letters from him on the desk in there. Looks like somebody went through them."

"Don't much look like there's anything worth stealing in this dump. You on split shift?" Efird looked down the hall toward the living room. He took a swig of soda and crunched some peanuts.

"Evenings. Off at eleven." Diane stared after Efird's gaze. The place was small, and definitely in the poor part of town, but Churchpin's mother had obviously kept a nice home for herself.

"Me, too. Bunch of us're goin' drinkin' down at the Chase after work. Wanna come?"

"Can't." Diane turned her attention back to the bedroom.

"I thought you wanted to be a detective," Efird said.

"Yeah," Diane said. "Be a detective. Not date a detective."

"Oh," Efird said, smiling, "I forgot. You're spoken for."

"Whatever gave you that idea?"

"Rumors fly in the halls of the PD." He was smiling at her. "Hey," he added, "don't be so touchy. Renfro's a nice guy."

"True," Diane said. "But I am most definitely not spoken for."

"That mean you'll join us?"

"I doubt it."

Efird motioned her out to the hallway. She followed him to the living room. They stared around the room. Efird seemed preoccupied. Diane wondered if he was seeing things, clues, that she was missing.

"You knew him," she ventured.

"Churchpin? Yeah. Years ago. Sorry little motherfucker."

"I heard he just took a sudden wrong turn."

"That he did," Efird said sadly.

"Did you know her?" A nod toward the bedroom.

"Not really. Met her once when she was dropping him off at the station. He was a cadet, you know. Rode with me a few times."

"I heard."

Efird seemed surprised. "You did? From who?"

"Rumors fly in the halls of the PD."

"Yeah." He smiled and shook his head. "He could've been a good cop. Got lost after high school."

"I talked to the neighbors," Diane ventured.

"Let me guess. Nobody saw nothing."

"One guy, lives across the street, said he saw a small black car cruising the neighborhood a few days ago, just about dusk."

"Oh, that's helpful. My mother drives a small black car. So do thousands of other folks. No make, no license?"

Diane shook her head no. "He said he wasn't paying much attention. Just out on his porch having a smoke and happened to notice it made a few passes."

"Did he say what he was smoking?"

"Nobody else had anything to say," Diane added.

"All right, then." Efird stood. "You'll stick around till Lewis finishes up? Make sure a copy of your report lands on my desk first thing?"

Diane nodded. "You're leaving?"

"You talked to everyone?"

"The neighbor to the right isn't home."

"I'll stick my card in his door on the way out. Not much

else I can do here at the moment. You change your mind, we'll be over there at the bar about eleven-thirty or so. You know where it is, the Chase?"

Diane nodded, and Efird downed the last of his Dr Pepper.

"Looks like you've got it pretty well under control here." He gave Diane a vague salute. Efird was tall, and his shoulders filled the door frame as he headed out the front door.

Diane walked down the hall and waited, watching through the bedroom door as Lewis did his thing, moving around the body with reverence, dusting the windows, the door, the dresser drawer pulls. He painstakingly gathered the letters and put each in its own plastic evidence bag. She thought for a moment she should call the captain on duty, see if he'd like to send a different detective out, but that would only bring trouble. It seemed like Efird should have stuck around, but at the same time she was flattered that he'd left things in her hands. Or maybe he'd done this kind of thing enough times that he was tired of hanging around until the doors were shut and taped off, knowing that there really wasn't anything else to be done at the moment. There were no leads. A small black car. He was right. Where would you start.

He'd seemed so sad there for a moment. It surprised Diane. A lot of folks in the department thought that Efird was a waste, a lost cause. Ever since his girlfriend had locked herself in his bathroom one night last December and blown her head off with his .357 revolver, Efird had been on a slow but steady mission, attempting to drink himself into oblivion. A lot of guys would already have succumbed, but Efird's capacity for alcohol and his ability to work while hungover in extremis were fast making a departmental legend of him. Still, he seemed salvageable. Diane had sometimes wanted to say something to him, wanted to try to help him, but didn't know how to approach the subject. The memories of her mother's relationship with alcohol prevented any kind of hopefulness on that subject.

Lewis was just finishing up when Diane heard footsteps entering the living room and moved quickly to intercept whoever it was. She made it as far as the end of the hall when Sheriff Gib Lowe rounded the corner and brushed past her with a brusque, "'Scuse me there, darlin'." She wheeled around and went after him.

"Sheriff? Hold up, Sheriff Lowe. We got Crime Scene in there."

Lowe turned, recognized Diane, and broke into a big smile.

"That yours?" he asked. "Out front? They find the one got stole or did they break down and give you a new one?" He was speaking extra loud, as though making an announcement to a crowded room without the aid of a microphone. The house filled with the deep-chested laughter of the sheriff and Lewis. Diane felt about three inches tall, but didn't let on.

"Sheriff," she said, "this is not a county case. Thanks all the same."

"Not like that last one, eh, darlin'? You'd best go have a chat with the district attorney about this, because I just got off the phone with him a few minutes ago and he has personally instructed me to investigate this case." He had that look on his face, a look that came all the way from caveman days to right this very minute and said to Diane: Go home and play house, little girl.

The ambulance attendants had stopped gossiping and were looking down the hall at them. Lewis stood at the bedroom door, staring openly at them, fingerprint brush in one hand, poised as though he were about to dab paint onto a canvas.

"Sheriff," Diane said, "could I have a word with you out back?"

"I'm kinda busy here, sweetheart. Move along now," the sheriff said, turning away from her.

"Sheriff Lowe," Diane interrupted, moving between him and the doorway, "you can't just come in here and—"

"I am following the district attorney's instructions. Now I'll thank you to let me get about my business."

"This isn't right!" Diane felt her face go hot. She knew she was losing it. He wanted her to act like a pathetic little girl and she was.

"Look, Officer Wellman, I don't have time for this bullshit. I've got another homicide on my hands here." He tried to step past her.

"It's not your case." She stayed in front of him. He stopped, surprised.

"Let's understand something here. The victim is Juanita Churchpin, no? The DA wants me handling this. Odds are it's related to the Lake Bolton murders—which you may recall I handled quite effectively. The Sheriff's Office officially took over this investigation as of right about ten minutes ago, so you can go back on out there on the streets, where you're needed, I'm quite sure. Unless you'd care to go on in the kitchen and rustle us up a pot of coffee." He started to push past her, but Diane reached out and took his shoulder. He spun abruptly, knocking her arm loose.

"You got your car keys with you? I'd hate to see you lose another squad. Those things are expensive, you know?"

"Sheriff," she said. "This is my case. I intend to follow through. You're not stealing my case."

"Far as I know, you are not a detective." Sheriff Lowe leaned in close enough for her to see the blood vessels in the whites of his eyes. "Just you listen to me, Hotshot." His words came out whispered, full of spite. "I been policing since you was in diapers. I know more about a crime scene than you do about changing a goddamn tampon, and you're absolutely fucking right, you're not lettin' me steal your case because it's my case."

"Why," Diane spat, "so you can put another innocent man in jail?" She thought he might explode right then and there. His face went red and bulgy; his fists were balled up and ready to strike her if she said one more word. She stepped back. First rule of self-defense: Create distance from the attacker. She sent him a message with her eyes. Come on ahead, asshole. I'm ready.

He slowed his breathing, Diane watched his chest as he regained control. He stepped to her, leaned in close again.

"Get the hell out of here." He stalked past her and into the bedroom.

It took every bit of self-control she had to make herself turn and walk away from it. Okay. All right. Bide your time. She made sure Gib Lowe could hear as she pulled her radio from her belt and checked clear of the scene, advising Dispatch that the Sheriff's Office would be handling the case as per instructions from the DA's office.

She walked across the sunburnt grass of the front yard toward the sidewalk, thinking how Gib Lowe bragged that when it came to solving crimes, he had been blessed with something akin to ESP. But it wasn't witchy, it was God-given, this ability he had to discern through vibrations at the crime scene just exactly what had happened and how it had happened. Once armed with this knowledge, Gib Lowe had the wherewithal as a first-rate investigator to determine who had done whatever it was that had been done against the law, and then make the facts of the case fit his version of the crime. He was a master.

That was fine. That was all just dandy. Let him go on ahead and think he was handling this case. Just like he thought he was home free with Rick Churchpin.

Diane climbed back into her squad, her face still burning with anger, ignoring stares from the clumps of people who'd gathered to watch the action, some of them standing on their porches in bathrobes or pajamas, figuring the emergency nature of the situation allowed them to come out however they were. All those people who knew nothing, had seen nothing, had heard nothing. Diane tried usually not to fall into the cop trap of thinking the public at large was simply a huge gathering of assholes, but whenever she saw them all standing around staring at some minor or major tragedy like that, with those looks of something between fear and consternation and thankfulness (the there-but-for-the-grace-of-God look), she had a hard time not seeing them as a herd of cattle. And anybody who'd ever been within shouting distance of a cow would have to know that a cow was dumb as a fence post.

She drove out of there, away from Sheriff Gib Lowe and his distorted self-image, away from the bloodied body of Juanita Churchpin, away from all the dumb-ass neighbors who would doubtless get tired of watching and return to their easy chairs and TVs in twenty minutes or so. A few blocks away, she pulled to the curb and took out her tape recorder to dictate the details of the murder scene to be transcribed and typed onto a report by the women in the records division. She made sure to note that the DA had instructed the sheriff to take charge of the investigation, and that any follow-up would have to be co-ordinated with Sheriff Lowe. Maybe the Chief would raise hell, but she doubted it. The Chief liked things quiet. He wasn't fond of squabbles between agencies.

She cruised the domestic streets, driving slowly, with the windows down, feeling the heat of the evening and knowing that there'd be no relief from it, even in the dark middle of the morning, the three A.M. time when the only people on the streets were burglars lurking in the shadows, drunks trying to find a way to whatever miserable place they called home, and teenagers who'd crawled out their bedroom windows sometime after midnight seeking the freedom of a summer night: beer and cigarettes, maybe even a little whang-dang-doodle.

Maybe when Efird heard, he'd pitch a fit and get the case back. If he even wanted it. He didn't seem to want much of anything since last December. The word had come in early, traveling fast, sweeping down the fluorescently lit hallways of the PD and into the briefing room like Mr. Clean, swirling white-tornado style from mouth to ear to mouth, leaving a low murmur in its wake. Efird's girlfriend. .357. Bathroom door locked, he begged her to come out. Kaboom. Brains and bits of skull bone all over the mirror.

It didn't surprise Diane that he'd got so messed up over the thing. She tried to think how she would react if Renfro pulled a stunt like that, not that he ever in a million light-years would even think of it. Renfro was fundamentally happy, and it was one of the things that attracted her to him most. But if he ever did . . . whether she respected Efird or not, she felt bad for him over that, over what he must have gone through. Most of the PD had turned out and seen him standing tall at the funeral. He'd done the macho Texan thing. Stood like a statue. Not a tear shed. Just took the dead girl's mama in his arms and calmly rocked her while she wept, shaking, on the verge of col-lapse. It was the man's place to be strong in these situations, and that seemed to Diane like an awful burden to bear. Maybe part of why so many of them seemed to be a mess.

It was nearly ten-forty before she realized ten-thirty had come and gone. She had to gun it to get back to the station in time to check out and leave her squad car to some lucky duck working deep nights.

She hung the car keys on the motor pool pegboard and stormed toward the locker room. Ran headlong into Renfro.

"Whoa," he said, grabbing her arms. "Where you rushing off to?"

"Home," she said curtly.

He moved in close, spoke barely above a whisper, still holding on to her. She shrugged loose from his grip.

"You okay?"

"Fine," she said. "I'm just tired and need to go home."

"I'll call you."

"Please don't," she said. "I need some sleep."

He stepped back, shrugged. "Fine, then. Whatever. You call me." He moved past her into the men's locker room, not looking back.

Her legs felt heavy as she stepped into her civvies. It was true. She was tired. Wrung out from the crime scene, the crime itself, angry at herself for being so impulsive that evening with Renfro. She could've got busted again, out of her district, and the simple fact was she shouldn't be fucking around on duty. It meant more to her than that, this job, even though lately she had more and more been thinking she had to get out. What she needed to do was meet people who weren't cops, circulate in the larger world. Hah. Like that would ever happen. Not as long as she was a cop it wouldn't. And as much as she was doubting herself in the career department, when she walked into something like she had tonight, it brought out something in her that made her feel, if not needed, at least necessary. She wanted nothing more than to find the person who'd killed Juanita Churchpin and put the cuffs on him. That would be sweet. So very, very sweet.

She said her good-nights as she walked through the brightly lit halls of the PD, opened the door to the heat, and made her way across the blacktop to her ride, a deep green Jeep Wrangler, gleaming like new because she took the trouble to keep it that way. She cranked the engine and gunned out of the parking lot, jabbing the button on the CD player. She thought about going to the Chase, but decided better of it. She'd already had one big-time fuckup today. She could join Efird and his pals another night, when she wasn't so ragged out. Tonight she would go home. Get some rest.

The music came up loud, and all she could think was just screw Gib Lowe. Screw him and the jackass he rode in on. Maybe the high sheriff could officially throw her off the case, but nobody was gonna tell her what to do with her off-duty hours.

FOUR

Gail opened her eyes to morning and the brief illusion of freedom, quickly crushed by full consciousness in the instant of realizing where she was.

But today.

Today.

The corridors went on forever. Dark green linoleum floor, spit-shined with a buffer in the small hours of morning. There were plaster white walls, painted white and white again and white the year after that, white on white on white. White broken by doors, gray metal doors with heavy-duty locks and changeable nameplates. Case managers. Psychiatric associates. Storage rooms. Conference rooms. Staff lounge. Door after door, and Gail followed the hack and tried not to hear the keys banging against the blue polyester of his uniform pants. *Clank clank clank,* heavy brass keys, *clank clink clink.* The hacks had a way of walking: I'm in charge; don't fuck with me. Gail followed, growing colder as they approached the conference room. Already she was shivering, and she wasn't even there yet. She should have brought a sweater, but she wanted to show them the degree of compliance: She had on nothing, not even a watch, that wasn't prison issue. Khaki pants and top. White T-shirt underneath. Work boots. Even her socks, prison issue.

She was complying with the rules. Her dark curls were pulled back in a ponytail at the base of her skull, held only with a rubber band. She wore no makeup. Her green eyes were clear and alert; she tried to make them friendly.

Door after door after door, and then a door with a plain wooden bench outside it. The hack motioned. Gail sat. The hack turned and walked back down the corridor. *Clink clank clink.* The sound faded.

Gail thumbed the manila folder in her hand. Heard a sigh from somewhere far away and then realized it was her own.

The door opened; a prisoner emerged and walked away briskly. Gail glanced over at the door and then went right back to her file, words flooding through her, phrases. Bits and pieces of thoughts from the last eighteen years pinging off the walls of her skull: bits of apology, bits of anger, bits of despair. Her molar was hurting again. The one the prison dentist kept telling her was just fine. Another prison dentist, the one before this one, had done a root canal and filled it back in '93. It had never been right. None of the dental work had ever been right. The door opened again. Gail remained motionless, afraid to look over. The man in the doorway, the examiner, was staring at the file in his hand.

"Ms. Rubin." He looked at Gail straightforwardly, with no trace of malice. "Chuck Rocco. Come in. Please."

She stood and followed him into the room. Closed the door behind her.

The room was clinically spare. Rectangular. Windows at the far end, curtained in green. A file cabinet. A brown wood-grain Formica-topped table in the center of the room. Three chairs on one side, steel frames scantily upholstered in drab orange Naugahyde, in which sat the parole examiners. One identical chair on the opposite side of the table, in which, Mr. Rocco was motioning, she should sit.

She pulled herself away from the door, walked toward the seat. God, it was cold in here. She sat. Wondered if they could see her heart trying to burst out through her sternum. Gail offered a polite smile to them, carefully placed her file on the table in front of her. They had stacks of files. They had a hundred more files than she did. She wasn't even sure why she'd brought a file. Something to hold on to while she waited, she guessed.

She recognized all of them from her previous visit. Next to Mr. Rocco sat Mr. White, the head honcho, basically unchanged in four years, still pale-skinned and red-nosed with a bad haircut but jovial eyes. The woman next to him smiled at her.

"Lorraine Gray," she said. "How are you today, Ms. Rubin?"

Gail heard herself saying *Time flies when you're having fun,* and almost gasped before she realized it was only in her head. She nodded politely to Ms. Lorraine Gray and wondered what kind of changes the parole examiners had been through in the last four years, how time had been to them, and how quickly or slowly it had gone. They remembered her, obviously. Or maybe they'd only checked her file and gleaned enough to seem that they remembered her.

Mr. Rocco clicked on a tape recorder.

"Gail Roselynn Rubin," Mr. White began, "DOB 03/16/60. Prisoner ID 09046–086? We are present today at the Federal Correctional Institution at Sundown, New York, for a hearing on your request for parole in the case of the *United States v. Gail Roselynn . . .*"

She was losing him, unable to follow his words. She could see his mouth moving and knew generally what he was talking about, but it was like a fog had descended between them and was soaking up the sounds. She couldn't hear him. Or maybe it was in her own ears. It was pressure in her head, swelling until she couldn't process the sounds. His mouth moved on, forming words, and occasionally he glanced up from his paperwork to catch her eyes. He didn't seem angry or unfriendly. He was just reading something. She tried to breathe more slowly, she swallowed a couple of times, and breathed, and breathed. There. It was abating.

". . . most impressive," Mr. White was saying. "We were encouraged to learn that you have completely renounced violence as a means of political change."

"Yes," Gail ventured. "Absolutely. Some years ago, in fact. I don't, I just—"

"We know," said Ms. Gray. Gail looked at her and nodded, afraid to do anything else for fear she would somehow insult this woman whose Morticia Addams hair was draped stringily over plaid-covered shoulders. This woman, and these two men in their Sears off-the-rack suits and government haircuts had the power to set her free. It was incredible, truly.

Gail stopped herself before she got lost in a free-fall speculation on the absurdity of the situation. She folded her hands in her lap. She looked from one to the other. They were human. She was human. We are all human here. Let's try to connect. Let's try to see eye to eye.

Mr. Rocco leaned toward her. "The literacy program you set up has been extremely beneficial to thousands of prisoners throughout the federal system. Do you enjoy it?"

Trick question. If she enjoyed it, he might think she should just by God stay here and enjoy it for a few more years, because prisoners weren't supposed to enjoy anything. Gail answered: "We meet Tuesday and Thursday evenings and Saturday mornings."

"Think it would fall apart if you're released?" Mr. White again. Gail tried a smile. She was afraid to think she'd heard what she knew she'd just heard. It was a hint. It was a clue.

"I'm sure I could find someone to take over my role."

Mr. Rocco gave a look at Mr. White. Gail couldn't read it, but he wasn't happy, that was apparent.

"Ms. Rubin," Mr. Rocco said, "not that we want to give you the wrong idea. We are in total sympathy with you. We've read the reports, read the letters of recommendation, the one from Senator Stratton was very impressive, and we know that you have made the change from self-styled revolutionary to model citizen. We believe, as do your case manager and fully one hundred percent of the prison staff here, that you are completely rehabilitated, and that you have accomplished that rehabilitation through your own efforts in addition to what the prison offered. And we believe that you pose no risk to society if we release you. These are the criteria that we must look at before making a recommendation to the Parole Board to release any prisoner. You've passed with flying colors."

"We fully support your request for parole." Ms. Gray again. Gail was having trouble staying in her chair. But something was up, they hadn't finished yet, and they hadn't said the magic words.

Mr. White pulled a sheaf of papers from her file.

"I should just read this to you, and then you'll understand the situation."

Gail tensed, tried to cover it. What was this? What situation didn't she understand? She'd been locked up long enough. She wasn't a criminal. She'd done her time.

"Gentlemen," Mr. White began, "I write to you today out of a deep sense of duty to try to avert a grave miscarriage of justice in the case of Gail R. Rubin, whose petition for parole I understand you are to hear in the near future. I feel there are some things you should know before you meet with Rubin and consider her request to be released from prison. As you may know, I was the lead prosecutor in the government's case against the numerous defendants in the infamous Bank of Philadelphia robbery of 1984 . . ."

Gail felt her body go leaden, sink against the seat beneath her. Alvin G. Langherd. Assistant U.S. attorney. Bastard. She felt her face burning, wondered how red it was. But none of them were looking at her. Mr. Rocco's eyes were on the ceiling. Ms. Gray's on her painted fingernails. Mr. White was bent over his letter, reading like an earnest third-grader.

". . . in which two bank guards and one teller were brutally murdered by marauding terrorists from the group Free Now, who made off with over two million dollars that bloody afternoon. You may also know that the government, after initially bringing indictments against Rubin and her codefendant in the bank case, subsequently declined to prosecute them on the charges. I want to make clear to you that the lack of prosecution was not in any way an indication that we felt unsure of our ability to obtain a conviction against Rubin in the case. It was simply that Rubin and her codefendant Tom Firestone had recently received sentences of seventy-two years on another case, this one for possession of explosives and weapons, the very case in which you are to consider Rubin's petition for parole. We were satisfied that seventy-two years was sufficient punishment and that additional prosecution on the bank robbery case would be a waste of taxpayer resources. It did not occur to us at the time that Rubin would possibly even entertain any hope of parole, much less petition for it."

"Let's look at the facts."

Gail stared at her hands in her lap, listened to Mr. White read Alvin Langherd's facts. She heard: We believe unquestioningly that Gail Rubin was involved in the planning and execution of the Bank of Philadelphia robbery. Rubin was a known associate of blah blah blah blah blah . . . Those weren't facts, those were suppositions. If he had any goddamn facts, why hadn't he taken her to court? She'd had nothing to do with that bank robbery and he knew it, and he knew she could prove it before a judge and jury, and that was why he'd refused to take her to trial, not out of any sense of fiduciary responsibility to the dead-ass lumpen taxpayers of America, Inc. Shit! Gail wondered if it was showing, if the rage building inside her was lighting up her eyes, making them glow green or some weirdness like that, because she had no idea how she was going to avoid losing it in the immediate future. She felt fingernails digging into the palms of her hands, realized they were her own. She kept looking down, did not raise her eyes to theirs. She might explode if she had to see them.

She had tried to force his hand, the U.S. attorney's, petitioning the court to be tried on the case, but he had filed a nolle prosequi, refusing to prosecute, and the judge had accepted it. Just like that. Real simple. We don't bring charges. You get no chance to prove your innocence. No chance to face your accusers. No day in court for you, sweetheart. Now, off to prison, where you belong.

She realized the room had fallen silent. Looked up. Mr. White had set the letter down on the table between them. Ms. Gray and Mr. Rocco were watching her. Well, thank God she wasn't crying. That would have been the worst. She would not shed a tear in front of these . . . these cretins.

"It's not that we aren't sympathetic to your situation," Ms. Gray said. Gail stared at her. Mr. Rocco had already said that.

Everyone remembered. Mr. White took a deep breath and placed his two thick hands carefully on the letter, smoothing it against the table.

"Short and sweet," he said. "The U.S. attorney wants another twelve years before we parole you. You heard his arguments. You may have paid for the possession case, but the Bank of Philadelphia robbery involved three deaths and the loss of two million dollars. That debt's a long way from being paid."

"But I didn't do it!" Gail stood up, leaned toward them. "I didn't do it! I wasn't tried, I wasn't convicted, and even if I'd been tried, I would have been acquitted! This isn't fair."

"I don't think you can say whether you'd have been found guilty or not. In any case, this is what the prosecutor wants."

What the prosecutor wants. She should have had Mel here with her. But they'd agreed it would make for a more cordial hearing if he stayed away. She knew what to say. Yeah. Only it hadn't mattered what she had to say. A decision had been reached before she ever sat down across from them.

Gail hovered at the edge of the table. She could not feel the floor beneath her. The walls moved. She saw them inching toward her. The three examiners sat staring at her with expressions of such bland ignorance that she wanted to slap them. She wanted to do something, anything, to jolt them out of their chairs and their complacence. She wanted to destroy everything: the table, the chairs, the stupid worthless files, the walls, the door, the entire damnable prison. Take it apart brick by brick, with her bare hands. Could she do that in twelve years?

She sat down, sinking into the dark place inside herself where she went for refuge from her very existence. She was no more. This place was not real. None of this was happening. There was no hell. There was no heaven. She was but a collection of particles that had fallen into one another's orbit randomly; she was only a series of chemical reactions that meant nothing more than the possibility of further chemical reactions. Life was something that happened to other people. Out there in the real world.

They stared at her, uncomprehending. Mr. Rocco picked

up the prosecutor's letter and tapped it against the table, straightening the pages and returning them to his file, and then returning the file to the stack of files next to him. All that hard work, categorizing and organizing and summing up human malfeasance, human possibility. All three examiners stood staring at Gail, lips tight, and then she was being led out the door.

She walked down the corridor, her knees weak from the effort of carrying her body forward. She walked. Fuck it all. She had eighteen years under her belt. They couldn't do this. They couldn't.

Twelve more. Twelve. When she went before them again, she would be fifty-six years old. Fifty-six. The numbers hammered at her. Eighteen in. Twelve to do. Free at fifty-six.

Fuck this.

Somehow she made it to her cell. The door was closed. She grabbed at the bars and pulled hard. Nothing. She pulled again. She thought she might be laughing, but then she felt the water on her cheeks and realized she was crying.

Locked out. She was locked out of her cell.

FIVE

The Chase was a carpeted dive in a suburban strip mall, everything all adobe and Southwestern-looking, the sign outside done in brown backlighted plastic, pleasing enough to the consumer of Dunkin' Donuts (to the left) or Taco Bell (to the right). Dark and air-conditioned, ashtrays at the standing tables you walked past to get to a place where you could sit down and drink. TVs at either end of a long, veneered bar. The stainless steel frozen margarita machine hummed gently under the blue neon glow of a Lone Star Beer sign hanging above it. Almost midnight, but the place was busy still. Ray Wylie Hubbard's "Ballad of the Crimson Kings" flowed from strategically placed speakers: . . . *some who can rise above blind faith, Others who just can't seem to pray, Then there are those condemned by the gods to write, They sparkle and fade away.* . . .

Diane stood at the entrance, wondering if she should've gone home after her shift the way she had last night. But she didn't want Efird to think she was scared of him, or scared of partying. It was important that he know she could hold her own, whatever the situation. On duty or off.

She spotted him at the same moment he saw her and stood to wave her toward his table. She recognized Rusk and Carter, both first-year detectives, hunched over their pastel green margaritas, listening intently as Katie Ryan, one of seven female patrol officers in the department, finished telling them something and downed a shot of something brown without so much as a grimace. Katie could handle just about anything, and liked to, word was. Diane was having second thoughts about being there. Get a Katie rep and you could forget about being taken seriously as a cop by anyone in the department. Katie was nothing but a cop groupie in uniform. And then there was some guy Diane didn't recognize, his long, light-brown hair pulled back in a ponytail. Sharp features, but not overly so, and wearing designer duds. Gold on his right ring finger, nothing on his left. Some kind of high-dollar watch on his wrist. Cell phone on the table next to his drink, which looked to be a margarita straight up, probably sickeningly sweet, from a mix, in a joint like this. Diane tried a casual nod in Efird's direction and walked toward the table, thinking she probably shouldn't have come here after all.

"Damn, girl," Efird said as she reached the table, "I thought sure you'd show up last night."

"I told you I wasn't coming," Diane said. "I stayed at the scene awhile."

"I waited here for you till they kicked my ass out, just hoping against hope."

"I'm sure," Diane said. "And anyway, doesn't matter what night it is, everybody knows to find you here, Eef." It felt a little odd, calling him that, like they were old friends or something. He didn't seem to notice.

"Gospel truth: they flung me out the front door." Efird laughed and flagged the waitress, pulled out the chair next to him. "Set your bones down, take a load off."

Diane sat, felt her pistol dig into the small of her back. She was in a tank top with a cotton blouse hanging unbuttoned and loose over it to hide the weapon tucked into the back waistband of her jeans. She reached around and shifted the gun to the right.

"You know everybody," Efird said. Diane nodded hellos around the table, until she got to the ponytail. He stood, reached to shake hands.

"Jimmy Ray Smith," he said. "A real pleasure." He looked

at her square on, and his hand was warm and strong, but gentle. Diane smiled at him, hid her surprise. She'd heard of Jimmy Ray. Just about everyone in law enforcement in Breard County, maybe even the state of Texas, had. Undercover agent with the Narcotics Service in the Texas Department of Public Safety. Started out as a pretty good trooper in the Highway Patrol, then got transferred to dope. Now, word was, he was a total cokehead, total pothead, even willing to snort crystal meth if that was all that was around, and his superiors supposedly knew, but he made cases, he made lots of cases, and that was all they cared about up there in suit-and-tie land. Give us numbers and your life is your own. He was stationed in Austin, but every so often drove up to visit with Efird. Ordinarily a state cop wouldn't condescend to be seen with the locals, but Jimmy and Efird had grown up together, gone to high school together, Jimmy Ray played wide receiver to Efird's quarterbacking on the football team. They were pals. But this guy didn't look at all messed up. And he came off as a gentleman. Maybe even a little sophisticated.

Efird turned to the waitress. " 'Nother round," he said. He looked at Diane. "Name your poison."

Diane looked at Jimmy Ray's drink, and he immediately said to the waitress, "Margarita, straight up, no salt, have him pour it with Patron, if you would."

Efird looked from Jimmy Ray to Diane and leaned back in his chair, resting his arm casually across the back of Diane's.

"Get that mess over on Brookshire cleaned up?" He took a long slow sip of his Lone Star, eyeing her over the top of his glass.

"I taped my report and sent it to steno soon as I got back to the office," Diane said. "You didn't get it?"

Efird lowered his beer and raised his eyebrows. "No."

"Sheriff Lowe showed up." Diane felt her face go warm, almost like she was embarrassed. "Said the DA ordered him to take over the case."

"What!" Efird's face flushed red, his green eyes flashed anger. "That ain't nothing but just a whole goddamn truckload of horseshit." He downed a shot of Turkey and slapped the shot glass hard against the table, like an Old West gunslinger about to step outside into the dusty street and draw, shoot some poor fool dead. "It's my case and like hell that sleazy-ass bastard is gonna steal it from me."

Efird leaned toward Jimmy Ray, confidentially, filled him in on the details, such as they were. When Jimmy Ray heard the name Rick Churchpin, he rocked back in his chair. "I've heard of him. Just about one sorry-ass motherfucker," he said. He flashed a smile at Diane. "Ever had any dealings with him?"

Diane shook her head no, not wanting to admit the circumstances under which she had run into Churchpin: He'd blown past her when she was working radar one evening out on the Loop. She'd been halfway asleep when the alarm sounded on the radar gun and the red digital numbers locked in the screen: 87 m.p.h. The speed limit was 45.

She'd thought for a moment he was going to run, and she knew if he did, he might well get away, considering the dog of a vehicle she'd drawn from the motor pool that afternoon. To her surprise, he didn't run; he pulled over and took his ticket and was reasonably polite. But if you wanted to maintain any kind of respect, you didn't talk about working radar to detectives and narcotics officers. You played it like you were only interested in matters of life and death, even though cars were definitely that. But traffic tickets not only were not sexy, they were humiliating, made you feel like a member of a shakedown crew: enforced fund-raising for the city.

"I couldn't believe it when that asshole showed up," she said to Efird. "Walked in like he owned the place and just smooth took over."

"Yeah, well, the motherfucker steps on my toes, he'll be taking over as the chief sanitation engineer of Breard County he doesn't watch out." Efird downed a big gulp of beer and stood up, grabbing Diane by the hand. "Hell with him. Let's dance."

He surprised her, took her hand and led her to the jukebox, fed in a couple of singles, and punched some buttons. She wasn't sure she wanted to dance with Efird, but it seemed harmless enough. It wasn't like he was coming on to her or anything. He was just wanting to get out on the dance floor.

The low-down voice of Steve Earle filled the room with an ache that couldn't be cured—*standin' there with them ol' transcendental blues*—and Efird was pulling her onto the tiny parquet dance floor.

"You don't mind, do you?" he said. "Just a dance?" He was sincere, making sure he wasn't pushing any boundaries. She shook her head no, and he wrapped himself close, but not too close, kind of loose and comfortable. He wanted her to enter the music with him, which seemed to her so much like the way her first real real boyfriend, in ninth grade, had been, so sweet and kind and just fine. Efird was gentle in a way she never would have guessed, in the way he held her close and danced, and took her out of herself and into a place of softness. She realized he was one of those guys who surprised you, once you finally saw them and let them into your life. Not the captain of the football team or editor of the school paper, not the class president or the Most Likely to Succeed or the class clown or the serious juvenile delinquent or drop-dead good-looking. Just a guy, a regular guy, a nice, decent, ordinary guy with a genuine smile. Efird could dance, and Diane went where he led, and they swirled on the dance floor, Diane losing herself in the song and Efird's capable arms.

She pulled herself closer, tuned into the music, let herself sway with the rhythms. Efird was strong and smooth, and he smelled ever so slightly of cologne, something kind of smoky and spicy.

"What are you wearing?" He responded by pulling her closer, whispering, "Michael for Men. But don't start thinking that makes me a faggot. It just smells good, don't you think?" She nodded, and he pulled her in again, in a kind of hug, still moving with the music. "Why," he whispered, smiling. "Turn you on?"

"You wish." Diane laughed, or maybe giggled was more like it, and he gave her a smile that took all the macho out of the words and made them just fun.

"You dance good," Efird said. "Ought to come out more often."

Diane nodded and kept following his lead.

"Or maybe you're too busy with Will Renfro."

"I'm just not much of a partier," Diane said quietly, letting the reference slide.

"Y'all gonna get married?"

"What?" She almost pulled loose from his arms. "No way. Definitely not part of my plan."

"What is your plan? Don't you want children?"

"Not that I'm aware of."

"What about your little old biological clock?"

"I forgot to set the alarm." She pulled back a little, eyed him. "Could we just dance out here? Would that be all right?"

"Hell, yeah." He pulled her back in and pulled a swirly kind of move that she had to struggle to keep step with, and no sooner was through that than he stepped back and twirled her under his arm, never missing a beat.

Marriage. Children. For her? Children for her? She thought about the woman in the Ricky Martin T-shirt with the whipped potatoes all over her wall and the linoleum lizard crawling under the table and eating leftovers off the floor. And the husband. Now there was a real catch. Fuck marriage. And no thank you, she didn't need babies to be fulfilled as a woman. She needed a detective shield, and maybe a law degree. She looked at the cute little cleft in Efird's chin and wondered if marriage had been on his mind that night his girlfriend killed herself. Maybe that was part of his devastation.

"So what're you gonna do about the Churchpin murder? Let Lowe have it?"

"Yeah," Efird said, "I'll let him have it all right. A right hook sounds about good." Diane chuckled, and when he moved his hand to press her head against his shoulder, she didn't resist. She noticed a button missing from his shirt. Found it endearing. Efird, the lunatic detective, the hardworking, hard-drinking hell-raiser who was always kind to women and children. He was a throwback of sorts, but kind of cute, in a disheveled, confused sort of way. She couldn't imagine what his apartment looked like, except that it would most likely have a chaos rating of at least 9.6. "He say anything about me while he was there? Any mention of Linda?"

"No." Diane said. "Why do you ask?"

"Because he's a motherfucker," Efird said. "A sorry-ass, no-good, lyin' sack a shit, and I know he's got no good use for me and tells anybody who'll listen. That's why."

Efird had actually said the name, maybe the first time since her death: Linda.

"Spanish for pretty." Diane wanted to ask a thousand questions, wanted the details of exactly what had happened that night. As though she could figure it all out, know what it was that drove the woman to put a gun to her head and pull the trigger. Rare, that. Women almost never went for the head. If they did use a gun, it was to the heart. She waited, dancing with Efird.

"Yeah," Efird said sadly. "Pretty. She was that." He pulled Diane in close again. "You know," whispering in her ear, "before she was with me . . ." He let the sentence trail off somewhere, tucked Diane in closer.

"Yeah?" She stepped with him, to the music, her boots right next to his as they moved in a tight circle on the dance floor.

"She used to be Rick Churchpin's old lady. Back when he was a cadet, when he used to come out and ride with me now and then. That's how I met her."

Diane stayed in close, hearing the music now more than feeling it, trying to get her head wrapped around the idea of Efird cruising the streets in uniform with Rick Churchpin riding shotgun, Rick no doubt taking in every word Efird uttered as the gospel of police work. And then winding up with Churchpin's girlfriend? She was trying to stay in step to Steve Earle, but here came James McMurtry in her head—*hey, what you up to, I already know, I heard the boys talkin' at the Texaco, it's a small town*—and she tripped on the toe of Efird's boot, but he caught her and smoothed things out like they'd never missed a step. She wondered how much more she didn't know about this place, and this man's history in it. She knew he'd grown up here and quarterbacked the football team to a state championship, the older folks still talked about that like it'd happened last season. But four years of college in a town like this didn't teach you diddly-squat about the local comings and goings. And even though she wasn't from that far away, it might as well have been another country she'd grown up in: she was still a foreigner.

"After he went and got his sorry self hooked into firing up the crystal meth?"

Efird pulled Diane back to him. He was feeling talkative now, holding her close and wanting to get closer. Wanting to open up a little. "Turned into a fuckin' loser but fast. Beat the shit out of her twice. I felt obligated to help her get away from all that." He was almost hugging her now, as if he were hanging on to her to keep her from running. "One thing led to another."

"She needed you," Diane said softly. Efird was hurting; she could hear it in his voice, and she could feel it in the way he was holding her.

"Never would've thought it," he said. "But I loved her. Didn't realize it."

Diane didn't know what to say. "It wasn't right," she tried. "What she did."

"Sometimes I'm a damn fool," he said, and then he went quiet and held Diane close for the rest of the song, just wanting to dance, it seemed. Just wanting to dance and not think about anything but the lonely song wailing out of the jukebox.

When it ended, Efird turned her loose, but held on to her hand for just a moment, let it slip slowly from his, reluctant to let go. He wanted her to be with him, she could tell. He wanted her but didn't want to admit it with words. That way he couldn't be denied with words. It wouldn't have to be for certain. She had a feeling that maybe Efird was a little more complicated than he let on, and a little more emotional than he would ever dare to admit.

He followed her back to the table, held her chair. She sat down and took a sip of margarita. Jimmy Ray was watching.

"Delicious," she said to him.

"Not like that stuff out of the machine." Efird eased his chair over closer to hers.

"Eef," Jimmy said. He gave Diane a significant look, like was she getting into Efird, and was his buddy gonna get laid tonight. She ignored it—but the answer is no—slipped down in her chair just a bit and looked over at the jukebox. He knocked a knuckle against the table.

"Hey, I gotta go pick something up. Old friend of mine. Y'all want to ride over there with me?"

"This ain't no deal, is it?" Efird eyed Jimmy Ray closely.

"Nah," Jimmy Ray scoffed. "I got to pick up a heater this dude's been holding for me. Strictly off-duty." He eyed Diane for a moment, openly sussing her out. "Model 18," said. "Glock." His look said he was letting her in on things, trusting her.

"Holy shit," Efird said. "Full auto?"

Jimmy nodded. "Bosses find out they'll have a full-on shit fit."

"What the hell you gonna do with that?" Efird asked.

"What the hell you think I'm gonna do with it? What'd you do back when you were undercover down there in Nacogdoches? Get down and dirty, impress people, buy shitloads of dope, that's what. Sorry-ass, motherfucking dope dealers see a Glock, they know you mean business."

"Hey, watch your mouth, son." Efird shot Jimmy a look.

Diane saw a look in Efird's eyes, a warning to Jimmy Ray.

"Easy, man." Jimmy Ray was staring back. "I thought—"

"Well, that's the problem right there," Efird said, smiling now. "You thought." He raised a hand, signaling the waitress. "Y'all ready for another?"

Diane pushed back from the table. "I'm good," she said. "I'm going to the little girl's room."

"Wait a minute," Jimmy Ray stood. "Y'all coming with me or not?"

"I've got to get home soon," Diane said. "I'm burnt."

Efird smiled at Jimmy Ray. "I'm with her," he said, turning to catch Diane's look and add quickly, to Diane, "Not like that. I just mean I'm tired and going home, too."

He was testing the waters, that was certain. Diane headed toward the back of the bar, half wanting to go with Jimmy Ray and meet his connection, not that she'd ever be interested in owning a fully automatic weapon. Still, she was intrigued. But this stuff about Efird having worked undercover. There hadn't been a hint of it, and usually there were at least rumors about stuff like that. This was news. She'd thought, like the rest of the department, that when he'd disappeared for six weeks back in springtime, he'd been on a long and much-needed hiatus from the job. Holed up in Arizona somewhere, trying to recover from Linda's suicide. Instead he'd been undercover, buying dope in Nacogdoches. And there was supposedly plenty of it down there. Lots of crack. Lots of crank. She wondered how often that kind of assignment happened. She wouldn't mind doing something like that. It would be one giant step toward a detective's shield, that was for sure, and would probably come in real handy if she ever got around to lawyering. She'd have to take her time, but when the time was right, she was going to ask Efird about it, try to get signed up. Anything to get out of patrol.

When she got back to the table, Jimmy Ray was gone and so was everyone else. But Efird. There were two fresh margaritas on the table in front of him. Straight up. No salt.

There was light out there somewhere. She could see it through her eyelids, which felt so heavy and sticky that it would take a monumental effort simply to open them. She couldn't, wasn't up to it. But she knew there was daylight out there somewhere.

Later. She would find it later. She slipped back into darkness. Behind her eyes, a massive headache was gathering, threatening thunder and lightning. Holy God, what was this? She fought, struggled to keep conscious, even if she couldn't open her eyes. She was not at home. She reached to feel whatever it was she was lying on, a couch she thought, the fabric rough beneath her fingers, like jute or hemp or burlap, she couldn't tell. She was someplace she hadn't been before. There was movement in the room, and the smell of coffee and the scent of—oh, God, no—Efird's cologne, and fear helped her open her eyes. The daylight spilling in the window shot through her pinholed pupils and exploded against her retinas; there were fireworks in her eyeballs. She cringed and winced and forced her eyelids open again. Not much better, but she managed to keep them open this time.

He was standing in front of a Mr. Coffee in a pair of boxers, pouring himself a cup. He raised the mug to her, offering. She nodded yes. Yes, please please please. She tried to pull herself up to a sitting position, but her body was not ready to respond to any commands. She lay there, semi-helpless. This was not a hangover. This was more than a hangover. Surrender. She should just surrender to the situation and eventually she'd be able to get up. She managed to look down at herself. Oh, God. She was wearing her tank top and her panties, that was it. And Efird was in his underwear. Oh, God. Her jeans were on the floor next to her, the butt stained with tire black. The aroma of petroleum wafted up from them. Just ask. Ask and get it over with. Then you can hate yourself in earnest.

"Efird," she said.

"How do you take it?"

"You'll have to tell me. I don't remember."

He chuckled. "Your coffee. Cream? Sugar?"

"Both. Lots of both. Make it beige." Her head felt like it might roll off her shoulders onto the floor and melt.

"What the fuck happened to me?"

"That I don't know."

"Are we in your apartment?"

He brought her coffee and helped her sit up. She was shaky, her insides wiggly. He pressed a hand to her forehead.

"Maybe you have the flu. Or something."

"What was in those margaritas?"

"Nothing special that I know of. We had two each. Hell, girl, can't you hold your liquor?"

"Whatever this is, it is not from tequila." She looked around again, still trying to focus. "Are we in your apartment?"

"Where else would we be?"

"It's so neat."

"Maybe I'm a neat guy."

She was focusing now.

"Maybe I'm hallucinating."

The place was spotless. Done in a western motif, if you could call what Efird had going on a motif at all. The furniture, including the couch Diane was now sitting on, as opposed to sprawling helplessly on, was wood and jute. There was a

Mexican rug on the hardwood floor and a matching blanket hanging on the wall. A small fireplace, and on the modest mantle above it a couple of large candles. And a bookshelf. With actual books on it. She never would have taken Efird for a reader. Hardcovers, even. She wished she could focus on the titles. She closed her eyes, tried again. Not happening. A *chile ristra* hung above the bar that separated the living room from the tiny kitchen. But what struck Diane most was the degree of order in the place. Things were put away. Things were where they belonged. She glanced down the hall to the bathroom, and Efird saw her looking.

"It wasn't here," he said. "I moved after it happened." Diane nodded, sorry he'd caught her wondering.

"What happened?"

"She locked herself in the bathroom and blew her goddamn brains out." Like he was talking about having had a flat tire on the way to work.

"I meant last night," Diane said. "To me."

"I don't know what happened. You just smooth passed out. I carried you outside, thinking maybe fresh air would help, but, girl, you were out. I almost took you to the hospital."

"I mean, what happened here? With you and me."

He looked shocked. And maybe a little hurt.

"What the hell do you take me for?" he said. "I mean, not that you aren't, you know, and not that I wasn't, you know, but . . . I'm not like that. I could never. I just wouldn't, that's all." He sat down next to her. "Besides, I knew you'd probably shoot my ass if I did." He smiled and sipped his coffee. His hair was all spiked out everywhere.

She thought of Renfro. Not good. If he heard about this . . .

"I feel like I've been drugged," she stammered.

"If I didn't know better, I'd say you had," Efird said. "It was like some kind of damn knockout drops or something. One minute you were there, and next minute? Lights out, Lulu. I thought to myself, damn, if only I could get her to talk to me, I might learn all her secrets." He laughed.

Diane smiled weakly.

"You all right?" Efird's voice came to her through fog. She managed a nod.

"I'm gonna take you home," he said. "We'll get your car later."

She managed to pull on her clothes and follow him to the parking lot. He helped her into his pickup. From somewhere far away she heard the engine start.

Her shades were on the dresser next to the bed in her apartment. Okay. So she could get them when they got there. Block out this godforsaken daylight. She'd thought it was morning, drinking coffee in Efird's apartment. She'd thought it had to be early morning, but now it was looking like most of the afternoon had gotten away and they were in the three P.M. heat of the day.

"Blueberry Ridge, that right?"

"How'd you know?" How'd he know where she lived?

"Hell, girl, everybody's seen Renfro's car parked over there. It's no secret."

Right. And what was she getting all paranoid about? Cops knew where other cops lived. They kept an eye out for each other. Everybody had their buddies on the department. You knew each other's cars, you knew each other's houses.

"Blueberry Ridge," she said. She wanted to open her eyes. "Over around back. West side. Number 212. Blueberry Ridge." Not that there was a blueberry to be found anywhere closer than the Piggly Wiggly grocery store twelve traffic signals down Loop 12, which circled around the city.

"Diane?" Efird's voice was sharp now. She felt his hand grip her shoulder, firmly. She forced her eyes open and looked over at him. He was there, a little blurry around the edges, but she could make him out.

"You all right?"

"Yeah." She closed her eyes again. "I just need to get home, get some rest." For a moment, she wondered if she were hungry, if blueberries would taste good right now. There wouldn't be any among whatever meager pickings might be available in her mostly empty refrigerator. The only thing she knew for sure was in there was salsa, and probably the tortilla chips in the pantry were stale anyway. But if she could just get inside, get some relief from all this relentless daylight. God, her head. She tried shading her eyes with her hands, but her arms fatigued almost immediately.

She felt the vehicle stop moving and heard Efird get out and close his door. Then he was around at her side of the truck and helping her out. She opened her eyes, shading them with her hands, watching the ground as Efird helped her up a flight of concrete and wooden stairs done in the style ubiquitous to the ubiquitous modern apartment complexes in Bolton.

She managed to get her key in the door and made her way inside.

"I'll be fine," she said. "Just let me get some sleep."

He stood outside the door, eyeing her carefully. "You sure?"

She nodded, using the doorknob for support but not wanting him to see.

"Call me. If you need anything."

She nodded again. "What time is it?"

"Almost four."

"Shit."

"Get some rest, you'll be all right."

"It's fucking shift change. I go on deep nights again tonight. I got to be in the briefing room at ten-thirty."

"Oh. Shit. Call in sick."

"I might have to."

"You want me to call you? Wake you up?"

"Yeah. Call me at nine. I'll see how I'm feeling."

"All right then." He looked at her again, bent down to get a good look in her eyes. She looked back, trying to pass inspection, knowing that a trip to the emergency room would only be an exercise in bureaucracy and would not look good on her personnel record. Even in her addled state of mind she knew that much.

"I'm okay," she said. "I just want to know who did this to me. And why. And how."

Efird stood back. "That's what I'm going to try and find out. I'll call you at nine." She locked the door behind her. Her lips were numb. Her fingers felt swollen. She walked to the kitchen and opened the refrigerator, stood in front of it letting the cool air flow onto her. There was a pizza in there. A couple of burritos. A container of cream gravy she'd brought home from Harbingers last time she was on deep nights, thinking to have it with biscuits next day, but then next day when she opened the fridge, there hadn't been any of those crack-open doughboy rolls of biscuits in there. She'd have to remember. Or maybe she could actually make a grocery list. Some people did that. Made lists. Lived organized lives.

She thought about Tylenol, and then remembered reading somewhere about how it was linked to liver failure when used to ease the pains of too much alcohol. But she hadn't had too much alcohol. At least she didn't think she had. At any rate she wasn't going to risk it. She closed the refrigerator door. Moving slowly now, easy does it.

Just bed. Sleep. Darkness. Please.

Her bedroom was an oasis of semidarkness, the sunlight blocked by foil taped to the windows. She set the thermostat at sixty-six and heard the central air unit kick on outside the window. Kicked off her clothes and crawled in between cool cotton sheets. She pulled her comforter up to her chin, tucked her arms under her pillow, and lay there. Her head was still pounding, but not so painfully now. More like a throb.

She stared at the phone on the nightstand. Whatever this was, she would sleep it off. Efird would call and she would go to work.

The light on the message machine was blinking. Probably Renfro. She didn't know what she would tell him. What she would not tell him. If someone had dropped something in her drink, well, she guessed that wouldn't be any weirder than that mom who hired a couple of dimwits to try to knock off her daughter's main competition in the local high school cheerleading tryouts. Not that she thought anyone had tried to kill her. They'd just wanted to fuck her up. And who knew? It could have been Efird. It could have been Jimmy Ray. Could have been anyone at the table. The place to start, as always, was with why. It comforted her, in an odd way, that she knew it hadn't been that asshole sheriff. And here he was the only enemy she really knew she had.

She stared at the light on the machine.

Blink. Blink. Blink. Blink.

She closed her eyes. She would see Renfro tonight, at briefing. She'd probably tell him everything, whether she went in there intending to or not.

SIX

The cell door slammed open and Gail lurched upright, wrenched from the midst of a dream, not sure where she was until she focused on the opening in the bars where Johnson stood just behind a young woman, motioning her into Gail's cell.

"What's—" Gail started sleepily, but Johnson silenced her with an upraised hand and a frown.

"We'll figure it out later," he said. "I got no place else to put her."

"What about right there?" Gail said, thumbing at the wall toward the Rodent's cell. She glared at Johnson.

"Meet your new best friend," Johnson said tightly. He slammed the cell shut and marched back down the hall.

Gail sighed, lay back down. The woman stood in front of the cell door, staring at the upper bunk like she believed she could bore holes through the steel with her eyes. She looked to be barely into her twenties, and still had handcuff bites on her wrists. She tossed her bedroll up onto the bunk, climbed up, folded it out, and threw herself down on it.

Gail stared at the bunk above her.

"Damn them," the woman said. A drawl gentled the words just a bit but couldn't do anything to soften the anger behind them.

Gail lay waiting. Wondering what this one's story would be, and what fleeting relationship it might bear to actual truth.

"I've been on that goddamned bus for thirteen goddamned days," the woman said. "It doesn't take thirteen motherfucking days to get from Beaumont, Texas, to Wherever-the-fuck-this-is, New York. This is New York, isn't it?"

"Sundown," Gail said.

"Sundown," the woman said. "What fresh bullshit is this?"

Gail smiled to herself. The woman had the drawl all right. Definitely from Texas, or somewhere close to it. There was quiet; Gail heard her new cellie trying to slow down her breathing. She didn't know what had made her think she would have a cell to herself for more than a day or two anyway. That's how it was. The place was packed to overflowing.

Quiet. And then the woman rustled around, trying to get comfortable.

"Diesel therapy," Gail said.

"Huh?"

"It's what they call it. Keeping you on the road for days and days, taking all the time in the world. Somebody's bright idea of how to make sure you'll comply with the rules when you get here."

"Fuckin' perverts," the woman said.

Gail couldn't remember how many cellmates she'd had, but she knew she wasn't up to a midnight chat with this one. They came and they went. She stayed.

From somewhere far down the cellblock she heard laughter. Not the happy kind. She rolled over to face her wall, hoping the young woman in the bunk above would get it that teatime was over.

In the silence, the laughter flared down the tier again briefly and then died out. The cellie cleared her throat and Gail waited, but, nothing. She closed her eyes. Waited for sleep. Minutes passed. She hated it when she became aware of minutes. Of seconds. Of time.

"By the way," the woman said, "I'm Diane."

Gail didn't reply.

Diane lay in the bunk, first on her belly, and then curled on her side. The mattress was compressed to the point where she felt like she was on nothing more than a few layers of paper towel spread out over the steel bunk. The pillow smelled like moldy feathers, which was no doubt exactly what it was filled with. At least she was prone, and off that puke-stinking bus. She wondered what the woman sleeping on the lower bunk was in for. Wondered what her name was. She wondered if the woman would knock her off as having been a cop. She would have to be careful. Watch her language, watch her attitude, watch her walk. Watch every little detail, every waking moment. Talk about undercover. She flashed on Efird, on Jimmy Ray. On how they might do in this situation. If anyone asked why she was here, she would stick with what her paperwork said: possession with intent to distribute cocaine.

She looked around in the gloom. Cinder block walls painted light green. Concrete floor, a drain in the middle. You could hose the place down. Just like the holding cells at the PD. How many prisoners had she delivered there? Drunks and drug addicts, burglars and thieves, rapists, bar brawlers, wife beaters. She'd sat in the booking room, typed out the paperwork, handed the prisoner over to the jailer, and gone back out on the streets. Now, this time, she was on the receiving end. Her brother's words, that afternoon in the backyard when she'd poked gentle fun at him for reading Edgar Cayce: Karma is meeting yourself. Only it wasn't right. This was not where she was supposed to meet herself. This had all been arranged by a third party who had nothing to do with justice, poetic or otherwise, much less any kind of self-evolution.

He was the reason she was sitting here right now in this cage of concrete and steel, surrounded by other cages full of convicted criminals. She was as sure of that as she was that she'd been handcuffed by a dufus DEA agent who didn't know his ass from a hole in the ground but who was following-the-goddamned-orders-sir-yes-sir.

At least he hadn't shot her, or she him.

She was asleep when it happened. Not two hours after Efird

had left her. It had taken her awhile to relax to the point where
sleep might come, and when it did, she'd drifted in uneasily, a
woozy, slippery descent into unconsciousness.

The whoosh-slam sound of her door as it came off the
hinges brought her out of bed and upright onto her feet in one
motion. She grabbed her gun and hit the living room in position to throw down and crank off rounds until the chamber
was empty, wanting to, and then she was staring at two men in
blue and one of them was screaming, "DEA! Freeze! DEA!
Drop the weapon get down on the floor spread your hands!"
and so many other commands so fast that she'd done nothing
but slowly—v-e-r-y-s-l-o-w-l-y—lowered her nine-mil and
bent to place it gently on the floor.

They stood staring at her, weapons aimed, motionless, as
she moved deliberately to the couch and quietly took up a cotton blanket that had suns and moons and planets patterned in
it. And wrapped it around her naked body. And sat down.

"I am a police officer," she said. "My ID is in the back
room."

"We know," one of them said. "We have a warrant to search
your premises."

Diane sat down on the couch as a third agent entered, stepping over the splintered door, crept over, and gingerly picked
up her weapon.

"I want to see it," she said. The agent looked at her. "The
warrant," she said. "I want to see it."

It had been perfunctory. A confidential informant, his relia-
bility sworn to by one of the agents executing the warrant, had
declared to the agent that he had within the past twenty-four
hours been inside the residence of Diane Wellman at apartment number 212 of the Blueberry Ridge Apartments located
at blah blah blah in the County of Breard in the State of Texas
and had seen with his very own eyes a substantial quantity of a
white powdered substance which he personally knew to be cocaine. Signed by Judge Winston L. Smith, County Magistrate.

Diane handed the warrant back to the agent.

"This is bullshit. This is a fuckin' scam and you know it."

The agents stared at her. Waiting to see what she was going

to do. If she was going to get rowdy and have to be subdued. That was when she realized that they didn't. They didn't know it was bullshit. They thought they had the real thing: a dirty cop.

It hadn't taken long. There were only three of them. One stood guarding her while the other two looked about, handling things with great care, as though they were shopping for a special gift in an antique shop.

Soon enough, one of them worked his way through the kitchen and to the refrigerator.

"Holy shit," he whispered reverently. He reached into the freezer and came out holding a Ziploc baggie, the quart size, packed full of chunky white rocks.

" 'Sup?" The one guarding Diane turned to take a look. Diane sat staring at it. She was fucked.

"Come see," said the one at the freezer. "Looks like cocaine base to me." He dangled the baggie. "Looks like ten years to life."

Diane felt something twist inside her, some part of her center attempt to curl into a spiral, and then it went liquid and evaporated, almost at the same time. She couldn't move.

She sat, wrapped in the blanket with the planets and the stars and moon on it. Renfro had called her a hippie when he saw it. She sat.

Totally, completely, unequivocally, downright, absolutely, utterly, officially, and plenarily: Fucked.

She was yanked back to her cage by the sound of a chain saw false-starting from somewhere down the cellblock. It could not possibly be human, that sound. But it was. Down the tier, someone was snoring. A woman was snoring. And it was the loudest snore Diane had ever heard in her life, jagged as shattered ice.

This was real. She was here, in a cell, in a federal prison, and this was real.

It couldn't be.

But it was. And one man was behind it.

She wondered where the high sheriff of Breard County was right now, what kind of crap was floating around in the gray matter of Gibson Ezra Lowe, one of a select few assholes in the Great State of Texas who would truly benefit from a high colonic of the brain.

The numbness that had hit her after her parole hearing didn't abate. Gail walked in a dream world, a real-life, eyes-wide-open nightmare reality. Twelve more years. She couldn't do it. That was all. She wouldn't do it. Her new cellmate watched her from a distance, and that was just fine. They'd barely spoken after that first night. The closest they got was every afternoon at four, when they had to be on their feet at the cell bars for the standing count. Gail had usually been able to make, if not friends, at least decent acquaintances, of her cellmates. This time she didn't care. There were fleeting moments when she felt bad for Diane, but not bad enough to invite her to eat at her table during chow, or bad enough to help her out with the stacks of legal paperwork Diane was accumulating in her attempt to overturn her case. The papers piled up on the small table in the corner of the cell. Gail watched Diane struggle through them, trying to decipher the legalese. Maybe she would have helped if Diane had asked. Gail wasn't sure.

What was it she felt? Mostly she felt nothing. She simply didn't give a shit anymore. About anyone or anything. She was preparing.

Days came and went. Nights came and went. The sameness was humiliating. Gail did time. Monday through Friday, she left Diane sitting in the cell and went out the back gate with the landscape crew. Soon enough, Diane would be processed and assigned a job. The staff didn't care about moving particularly quickly or efficiently. Everybody, prisoner and guard alike, had all the time in the world. The more of it you wasted, the less it seemed to drag: a kind of inversion-perversion theory of relativity. For some, mostly the guards, wasting time came naturally. For others it was a learned skill. A few of the prisoners had elevated it to an art.

For most of her time inside, Gail had tried to function as though she were in the world at large, and, for that, landscape was a plum assignment. She gardened, something she might well have done in her leisure time had she actually been a citizen in the free world.

Today, she dug in the dirt, rooted out slugs, crushed them between rocks. She'd never enjoyed that part of it before; it was simply something that had to be done to protect the plants. Now she ground the slimy little things between the rocks and imagined them to be fingers on the hands of the Honorable Alvin Langherd, prosecutor extraordinaire, the fingers that had gripped the yak-back into which he'd dictated the letter that his secretary had input into some government fucking computer before sending it to print, which had caused the fucking government printer in Alvin Langherd's secretary's office to spit out the ink on the pages of the letter that contained the words that scared the esteemed members of the parole commission into denying Gail.

Her freedom.

But she didn't let up on her work. She mashed the slugs and grimaced at the sick irony: Work will set you free. Now was not the time to draw attention to herself by changing her behavior. Just go on as before, saddened, but not devastated. Devastation would make the hacks watch her more carefully. She had to show them that she was truly reformed, that she had truly accepted the System and Its Whims.

And she wanted the perks of landscape. The landscape crew had a pretty good scam going. Once every couple of weeks, one of the prisoners on the crew, a pot smuggler named Hillary, would drive her tractor out, way out to the perimeter of the hundred-and-twenty-acre prison compound, mowing the grass, until she got to a huge maple that had been standing in the same spot for probably more than two hundred years. Near its base would be a garbage bag, which Hillary would snag and tuck up close to her seat on the tractor. She'd pass the bag off to Lisa, the prisoner assigned to caretake the warden's place, an old stone house with several outbuildings and many, many rosebushes. The roses had names like Penelope, Cornelia, and Felicia. Gail's favorite was the Ballerina rose, which didn't really look so much like a rose, with its wide, flat white petals, just tinged pink at the edges. Whenever Lisa had stash,

Gail would stop by and admire the roses before following Lisa to the garden shed to get her share. Little by little, throughout the workweek, the women of landscape would smuggle the swag in through the back gate at the end of the day. The hacks there usually did only a cursory pat-down, but there was always the risk that you'd get pulled out of line and strip-searched.

They managed to import paper money, vodka, pot, makeup, beautiful stationery, hotel sewing kits (complete with miniature scissors that didn't work great but were better than nothing), little miniature penlights that did just fine for reading beneath the blanket at night after lights out, scented candles, incense, herbal shampoos, creams and lotions, and vitamins. The kind of stuff you couldn't get at the prison commissary.

The sun blazed, felt good on her back. What she wouldn't give to be out here early enough to see the sun rise. Just once. A sunrise. If she had to do time, best to do it outdoors. Maybe she should lay off carrying stuff through the gate. Blow things out here and she'd be stuck inside somewhere. Like the kitchen. Or the laundry. She liked doing her volunteer work in the library in the evenings, but she didn't know what she'd do if she couldn't get outside regularly. She turned on the garden hose, waited until the water went ice cold, and drank long from it. She rinsed her head down, soaking her hair.

Great green gobs of greasy grimy gopher guts, mutilated monkey meat, pretty little ponies' feet. . . . Diane heard the words in her head, some singsong remnant from elementary school, as she lifted a huge stainless steel pan of unidentifiable white glop onto the steam table . . . *great green gobs of greasy grimy gopher guts and me without a—*

"Wellman!" She turned to see a middle-aged man in white, with his name embroidered in red over the left-hand shirt pocket: Carl. He had on an apron that once was white. Carl had a face like a pug, and to add to it he had a large wad of chewing tobacco stuffed in behind his lower lip. He looked her over suspiciously.

"You ever work in the food service industry? On the outside?"

Diane shook her head no.

"Wash your hands," he said. "That's pretty much all you need to know. Everything else I'll tell you."

She nodded, fearless in the face of stupidity. A prisoner walked by carrying a vat of red Kool-Aid, only it wasn't real Kool-Aid. It was some kind of generic version. But it was what they got to drink every day. Already Diane knew that. Red Kool-Aid one day. Green Kool-Aid the next. And then red again, and then back to green. Every once in a while orange.

"When you finish up loading that steam table, you can go on back to the dish room. That's where you'll be during lunch."

Diane did something between nodding yes and ignoring him and went back to the kitchen proper to get another pan of food for the table.

Her first day of work. Until now she'd been stuck in her cell, digging through paperwork, trying to find a way to prove she'd been set up. It could easily be that most of that fifty-five grams comprised cut and there was only enough dope in it to make it illegal (which actually meant any amount of dope, even a trace). Whatever, the minuscule portion they'd tested came back better than eighty percent pure. Not even her dumbass lawyer believed her. Not that it mattered. It was a case of take the best deal you can get or you're going to jail for life with no parole. They offered twenty. The lawyer said take it, and Diane knew he was right. Take it and fight it later. A life sentence with no chance of parole was the death penalty in slow motion.

She was just thankful to have Renfro on the outside, sending in whatever he could dig up to help her with her case. He was risking his job, sending in papers under the name of a dead lawyer, marking the envelopes *Legal mail.* That meant the cops in the prison mail room couldn't go through it; envelopes were delivered to her still sealed. Though Diane wanted desperately to call him, she wouldn't risk it. There was random monitoring of the collect calls placed by prisoners; she was sure the chief back in Bolton would be first to know if she happened to get caught talking to Renfro on the phone. And any-

way, there was always a long line for the telephone. Usually the
wait was close to half an hour. Still it was difficult not to call
and ask him where the transcripts for the Churchpin trial were.
Probably on some court reporter's desk, awaiting transcription.

She lugged a large rectangular pan of string beans toward
the steam table, tempted to drop it and watch the beans explode upward, greenish-brown and soggy, and land scattered
across the red tile floor. What could Carl do, fire her? Put her
to work in the sewage plant? That would be all right. At least
she was used to working with shit.

She was soaked with sweat and hot water and nauseated from
scraping out bus tubs full of half-eaten food that had no right
to be called food in the first place when Carl came into the
dish room.

"Wellman!"

She turned. He held out a yellow slip of paper.

"Your case manager wants to see you. Go now."

Diane took off her yellow rubber gloves and green rubber
apron and took the slip from Carl and walked out of the dish
room.

Her case manager, Mr. Yeager, could have been Carl's
younger brother, except that he obviously lifted weights and
cared about his appearance. He motioned her to sit in the chair
opposite his very organized desk.

"You were a cop?"

Diane felt what was left of her stomach tighten into a knot-
ted little ball.

"Yes," she said quietly.

"Oh, don't worry," he said. "Nobody'll find out from me."

Right. Not even ninety days inside and the rumors were
starting. Wouldn't it be just hilarious if it was the staff in this
place that wound up getting her killed.

"Look," she said, speaking with caution, careful to control
her anger, "I know you've probably heard this more times than
you can remember, but I'm not guilty of the charges. I was
framed, okay? But I just want to do my time and do what I can

to fight the case and make things right. I don't need anybody knowing my business."

"What happened to you on the outside doesn't concern me." His heavy brows were pulled together in concentration. "Just you do your time and don't try to get over on me and we'll get along just fine."

"Not a problem," Diane said.

"Have you recognized anybody in here? Anybody recognized you? Anybody make you for a cop?"

"No."

"You're sure?"

"I'm sure. Why?"

"If there's any doubt, you know, about your safety or whatnot, we can put you in segregation, where we know you'll be safe."

"What does that involve?" Segregation sounded halfway decent. At least she wouldn't have to share a cell with that bitch, Gail.

"It doesn't involve anything," he said. He gave her a tight, almost embarrassed smile. "In some circles it's called the hole."

"Oh." She could picture it.

"It's our no-frills option."

"I think I'm okay where I am."

"You let me know if you have any concerns, any concerns whatsoever, for your safety."

"I will."

His chair creaked as he leaned back in it.

"Okay then." Another tight smile. "You can go back to work."

Diane stood up and turned to open the door.

"Wellman?"

"Yeah?"

"You know, if you were to decide to cooperate, maybe let us in on where you got all that dope, we could probably do something about your sentence."

She opened the door.

"Tell you what," she said. "As soon as I figure out where it came from, you'll be the first to know."

She closed the door softly behind her.

• • •

Gail filed into the landscape barn behind the others: Hillary, from across the tier, two women from one of the other units. Three others from still a third. Norton, the landscape boss, was leaning up against the counter next to the coffee urn. Gail didn't like the way he was looking at them. Norton smiled at them, looked right at Hillary, then spat out a big hunk of chewing tobacco into the empty Folgers can he used for that purpose. He put it on the counter and walked toward the ladder that led up to the storage area above the locker room. Gail felt a shiver of dread pass through her. They had major stash up there. No drugs that she knew of, or alcohol. That stuff was all in the garden shed at the warden's place. But there was plenty of other stuff: makeup, stationery, all that, and food. They kept the booty from their garden raids up there; it was the coolest spot in the garage and things didn't spoil so quickly.

Gail felt it in her gut, that feeling that she didn't even need to get because things were already over. They were busted.

Norton gave the crew another smile and began climbing the wooden ladder built onto the wall of the changing room. He started to whistle. "Whistle While You Work." He disappeared over the edge of the storage area.

Hillary moved over near Gail.

"We're fucked," she whispered.

A watermelon arced out of the storage area, almost hitting the ceiling of the garage before it plunged down and cracked with a huge, wet, seed-spitting splat on the pavement of the garage floor.

Norton leaned over the safety railing of the storage area, his eyes tiny black pits of anger in the raw red blister that was his face.

"Assholes!" he roared. "It's just like you. Worthless thieving, good-for-nothing jerks! Fucking thieves!"

The women stared up at him.

He pulled the machete from his belt and went to work on the vegetables, flailing away, hacking to pieces watermelons and corn and tossing fistfuls of green beans down at the women. They stood staring.

Whack! Whack! Whack! The machete blade sliced madly, slamming against the wood. Gail scanned the garage. Her eyes fixed on the counter next to Norton's office, beneath the wall where the machetes hung. It was still there, in the area off limits to prisoners: a chunk of steel, a bent and broken piece of mower blade. She had been eyeing it since her parole hearing. And this might be her last chance to get it. She had to have that blade.

She nudged Hillary and gave her a look, eased away from the others, and edged toward the blade, listening to Norton rant. Then she was there, reaching for it, and then she had it, cold hard steel in her hand. She slipped the blade in her pants, snug between her legs.

Norton's head appeared over the railing. Gail froze, standing in the middle of the off-limits zone. Hillary quickly bent and scooped up a handful of green beans and hurled them at Norton.

"Hey!" she yelled. "Who said any of that shit is even ours? We don't even go up there unless you tell us!"

Norton slammed his machete into the wood railing and left it there, vibrating, as he climbed awkwardly down the ladder, trying to move too fast. Gail slipped back over and stood behind the others, her heart slamming against her ribs.

Norton got right up in Hillary's face.

"I don't know who the fuck you think you are," he panted, "but you'd better get the hell out of here now. Before I charge you with assaulting a federal officer."

"With green beans?" Hillary laughed.

"Get lost," Norton sputtered. He stepped back, waved an arm to include the crew. "All of you," he sputtered, out of breath. "Get the hell out of here."

Hillary led the women out of the garage, toward the back gate. As they approached the concrete archway and the three hacks who manned it, Gail felt her head go light. Her ears were ringing. How could she ever have thought to get by with this.

She felt like she was carrying a suitcase between her legs. Like one wrong step and the blade would slip down her pants leg and clatter to the blacktop beneath her. That would be some serious shit. Weapons charges. A moment ago it seemed like she had nothing to lose. Now she realized she had everything to lose.

But it was too late. There was no place to go but to the back of the line at the gate, to await her turn to be frisked.

She fell in line, her heart still pounding. Damn it. You fool. Whoa. Hold on. Just relax. Relax and let it show on your face. Everything's just like it is every other godforsaken day you walk through this gate. Nothing's different. Nothing's changed. You're bored. You're tired. You're sick of being searched every time you come in and go out, because you're not doing anything wrong. She felt it then, her attitude coming back to her, that place of confidence and quiet she had found a million times over to deal with the daily indignities.

She watched the hands of the hack pat down Hillary. Hillary, who had just taken a big risk for Gail. But Hillary liked risk. Admitted it freely. She might be the one to ask, when it came time to find someone to go. When Gail went over the fence and back to the free world. She wondered what Hillary was holding. Whatever it was, the hack missed it. He sent Hillary through the gate. The next prisoner stepped up, was patted down, and sent through. Gail's turn.

The hack looked at her closely. Something was making him take too long. He stared and stared. Gail looked back, then tried to muster up some impatience. He bent over with a grunt, started patting at Gail's ankles carefully. Too carefully. Shit. He was taking his time, moving very slowly. He expected to find something. She glanced down, saw him looking up at her, and then the sound of footsteps, running, approaching, brought him suddenly upright. Gail turned to see Norton, machete in hand, as he puffed to a halt at the gate, face still red, greased hair askew, and glared at the prisoners.

"And you know what?!" Norton bellowed, "You're all fired! You'll go work at the goddamn sewer plant if I have my way. Now get the hell out of here!"

The gate hack looked at Norton and signaled the women to go on through. He walked over to Norton, put an arm around his shoulder. Gail didn't wait to see what happened. As she walked down the wide blacktop lane leading to the main compound, she tried to keep her stride normal. She walked and walked. The trail from the back gate to the prison compound was about a hundred and fifty yards. Today the trip was taking a hundred and fifty years.

"You're all fired," Hillary mimicked, "for possession of lima beans."

Hillary patted Gail on the back, letting her know she should relax a little, act like everything was all right. Gail laughed with the women around her, made her mouth move and smile, shook her head in agreement, but all she wanted was to get back inside.

Safe in her cell, she stretched out on her bunk. Diane was already there, at the table in the corner, reading papers.

Gail dug in her locker, and used a tiny scissors from her contraband sewing kit to snip an opening in the seam of her mattress. It wasn't easy. Her finger and thumb were raw before she had a sufficient slit in the heavy ticking.

Diane sat reading her papers, pretending nothing was going on, doing her best to ignore Gail's activity. When Gail stood up and turned her back to Diane, reaching into her pants for the blade, Diane spoke up.

"I'd take a walk if I could," she said. "But I can't, so you just go ahead and do what you have to do. I'm blind here. I'm not seeing nothing."

Definitely the right thing to say, not that Gail had much choice but to go ahead and do what she had to do. Still, she was impressed. She lay back down and slipped the mower blade inside the mattress and tucked the sheet back in place. She would restitch the seam later, after evening chow, when Diane could take a walk, and when her own hands weren't shaking like she had the DTs.

And then the next time Diane was at work and Gail was in the cell alone, she'd find a different place to stash the blade. Not that she was planning to hide it for very long.

• • •

She had to watch where she was going unless she was looking for an ankle injury. The track, a quarter-mile oval that circled the Big Yard, was dirt, pocked and pitted, but Gail ran almost every evening and had it pretty much down. Knew where the major pitfalls were. And this evening she definitely needed a run. And after, she would find Hillary and try to get a pulse on whether Hillary was ready to get the fuck out of this place. The problem was that Hillary was a short-timer, relatively. She had thirty-eight months to go. A failed escape would mean five years added to her sentence. Gail wasn't at all sure that even an avowed risk-taker like Hillary would want to deal with that kind of penalty.

She breathed to her footfalls, four in, four out. Nice and easy, in stride. She wouldn't push herself hard until the final quarter mile. As she passed the softball backstop, a dilapidated chain-link affair with two sets of small wooden bleachers angled behind it, a woman warming up to hit stopped swinging her bat to watch Gail jog past. Gail ignored it, kept her eyes on the track ahead, even when she heard, "Nice body." She didn't want or need any complications, especially now.

She listened to her footfalls on the hard dirt surface. The rhythm, the pattern. She tried to decide whether the sound they made was quiet or loud or somewhere in between. Right now, it was barely audible above the noise: the shouts and laughter, the *thunk* of a basketball, the *ping* of a softball off an aluminum bat, the smattering of applause at a nice hit. Park sounds. Humans at play. She glanced at her feet, striking the track. She knew how to run. It had kept her sane, or close to it, inside this place. She had to be able to run, and did so religiously, except when they closed the yard. Like the time a couple of years ago when they'd resurfaced the track, using loads of dirt from behind the medical unit, filling all the holes and making the track level and smooth. Gail enjoyed a couple of days where she could sprint that final two-twenty without concern for potholes. And then the authorities discovered that the dirt they'd used was full of illegally buried medical waste, including much-cherished syringes. Used, to be sure, but it was nothing a little bleach wouldn't take care of. Contraband heaven for the junkies, but the runners hadn't been happy when the hacks shut down the Big Yard for the second time in a month, this time to scrape up and schlep out the needle-laden, contaminated dirt.

Her routine now was to do a mile on Sundays, one and a half on Mondays, and add another half mile each day of the week until on Friday she was at three and a half miles. Saturdays she rested. The yard, and the track, were crowded with amateurs that day. Saturday evenings she had a regular card game with five other women, including Lisa, Hillary, and the Rodent. There'd been some tension since the Rodent began fucking Johnson, but the women decided among themselves to overlook the Rodent's total lack of judgment while she was at the card table. Everywhere else, she was on her own. When the weather was nice, they played at one of the several wooden picnic tables scattered about the infield of the yard, where they could watch the beginnings of some pretty spectacular sunsets. But when the sun hit the horizon, the hacks shouted out, "Yard's closed, ladies, let's go! Back to your units! Yard's closed! Yard's closed!" You could always tell the ones who enjoyed terminating even this little bit of freedom and pleasure for the prisoners. It was a kind of glee that carried in their voices as they swaggered and shouted, radios clutched in their fists.

Gail wondered about the mentality of these creatures, the guards, the keepers, about just how loyal an army they were. If the warden issued an order one fine sunny afternoon that the prisoners were to be lined up before the handball wall and executed by rifle, how many of these civil servants would participate in the slaughter? And afterward go home to their families or their boyfriends or their girlfriends or their lonely rentals with dust on the coffee tables and pop open cool ones and kick back in front of the tube. Bitch of a day, it was.

She ran. She had entered the prison having never been much of an exerciser. She was slender, able to eat without counting calories. In fact, her problem had sometimes, over the years, been a matter of getting enough calories to keep her weight up. There were the times she got really thin. Really very thin. And it wasn't true. You could be too thin. You could get skeletal without even trying, provided your mental condition was sufficiently scrambled. Gail had done it only once in her life, gone into some kind of funk where she was afraid to eat. Oklahoma. The guitar player. The baby that wasn't. Their future as a family lost to his fear of whatever. When she'd got back from Dallas and the clinic, she lived for two months on water and saltines. When she could bear to eat them. She wanted to die and was trying to starve herself, only she called it taking off excess fat. She watched herself go from a ten to an eight to a six to a four. Months later, after her friend Oshi coaxed her into coming back to herself, she took a little black skirt from her closet and held it aloft. It looked about the size of a handkerchief. She and Oshi had laughed about it. What else could you do? There had been only that episode, and though prison food could easily have sent her off on another tangent, she had managed to maintain her appetite. Sort of.

The sun was hanging low now, just above the triple bands of concertina wire that topped the chain-link around the Big Yard. It wouldn't be long before the hacks closed things down for the night. The few streaks of cloud hanging out in the distant sky were pink and orange underneath, while their backs had gone blue gray. Gail did not want to go back to the cell. It was a lovely evening.

She was on her last lap of a mile and a half, into it, imagining herself outside the fence, running through the woods, when she heard footfalls behind her. Someone staying right with her, on her heels. She sped up. They sped up. She slowed down. They slowed down. She shifted her weight, turned to look.

Diane.

"You tailing me?" Gail turned back and picked up the pace. Diane pulled up next to her, easily keeping stride.

"No," Diane said. "I'm leaving your ass in the dust." And with that she sprinted past Gail, her wavy brown hair flying free as she ran with abandon, with the ease and grace of a born athlete. Gail hit the start of the final curve on the track and broke into her own sprint; she could still do a respectable two-twenty, but it didn't come easy these days. She ran and panted and watched Diane breeze across the finish line, which was where the track went past the steps that led into the huge red brick building with its maze of corridors that was Sundown.

Diane was standing near the entrance, her arms draped loosely over her head, catching her breath. Gail approached, trying not to gasp too audibly. She had a stitch beneath her lower ribs, a sharp, stabbing pain. Nothing serious, just exertion. It would pass. And if she had her say, it would pass unnoticed by anyone but her.

They were silent, with neither of them knowing how to continue the conversation. They'd been living in the same cell for what seemed to Diane like years, but that brief exchange on the track was as much a conversation as they'd had.

"You can run," Gail said.

"Grew up chasing cows." Diane was relieved at the change of subject.

"How old are you?"

"Does it matter?"

Gail looked at her, waiting.

"Twenty-four. How old are you?"

"Does it matter?"

"You said it does."

"I didn't say anything."

Diane shrugged, turned, and took the steps by twos, yanking open the doors at the top and disappearing into the building without a backward glance. Gail bent over, rested her hands on her knees, breathed deep and slow, gulped air and more air. She stayed that way until the stitch faded from under her ribs, and then stood up to survey the yard. For the forty-seven thousandth time, it seemed. The sun was hanging low now, below the concertina wire that coiled along the chainlink, laid in between the V of barbed wire that ran the length of the fence.

Twenty-four. Another kid. In for drugs no doubt. Diane could be her daughter. And, man, could she run! Gail wondered if she could do distance, or was only good at the sprints.

• • •

"Count time!" Morning broke to the sound of Lard Ass, a huge black woman whose name said it all, yodeling through the corridors.

Diane watched as Gail got up silently and stood at the cell door, and then she dragged herself from her bunk, stretching and yawning, to take her place next to Gail. As Lard Ass passed, Gail stared after her and shook her head, smiling.

"The eighth wonder of the world," Gail mused. "The Federal Ass."

Diane snickered.

"Achieved," Gail continued, "only through years of sitting on it and collecting ye old government paycheck, putting in as much time—with as little effort—as possible."

After Lard Ass passed, Diane climbed back up on her bunk and sat leaning against the wall, waiting for the count to clear and the cell doors to open, feeling what seemed to be too much relief that Gail had spoken to her in friendly tones. But nonetheless feeling it, and suspicious at the same time as to why Gail would suddenly decide to be, if not friendly, at least civil.

No sooner had Lard Ass shuffled her way through the count, huffed back to her chair in the control room, and opened the cell doors than Lisa, one of the prisoners from across the tier, shot into the cell. She glanced at Diane nervously, then turned to Gail and plunged ahead breathlessly.

"I need some pee," she whispered frantically.

"What?" Gail looked at her, amused and concerned at once.

"I heard I'm on the pee list. For today. They'll pop me for sure if I give them my own. Got the chronic in my system. Smoked a joint yesterday." She held out a paper cup and raised her eyebrows pleadingly. "Please?"

Gail stood looking at the cup. She shrugged and took the cup and moved to the stainless steel loo at the back of the cell. Diane returned to her bunk and picked up a magazine; Lisa stood looking down the tier, attempting to give Gail some privacy.

A moment later, Gail held the cup out to Lisa.

"That's it?" Lisa stared at the cup. There wasn't even an inch of urine in it.

"I peed when I got up," Gail said. "Is there anyone else?"

"Not anyone I trust." Lisa looked like she might cry.

Diane slipped down from her bunk. "I can do it." Gail and Lisa turned to look at her.

"Would you?" Lisa pleaded.

Gail said nothing, but her look told Diane to go ahead.

Diane took the cup and retreated to the toilet. This was even worse than being at the gynecologist, where God knew there was enough pressure to produce enough urine for the tests. A pee test, she thought. I hope I pass.

She did, and when she handed the cup, amply full, to Lisa, she felt an odd sense of pride. And a sense of being just slightly demented at the same time.

"Thank you thank you thank you." Lisa turned to go but stopped herself. "You're sure it's—"

"It might as well be Eve's own," Diane said. "But how are you gonna . . . with them standing there watching and all?"

Lisa pulled a surgical glove from the pocket of her khakis and dangled it before her.

"Fill with needed pee," she said. "Tie knot at wrist. Place in body cavity. Plus, have a safety pin with you when you go into the pee room." Lisa popped back across the corridor to her cell.

"Good luck," Gail called after her. She turned to Diane. "That was stand-up," she said, nodding approval. "See you later."

And that was it. Diane was dismissed, left yet again to fend for herself. Gail would sit with her circle of established friends at breakfast, laughing and telling jokes or listening with sympathy to someone's latest woes, and Diane would find one of the tables where the leftovers sat. Some days she preferred working in the kitchen to having a day off. She was out of the dish room now, promoted to working the steam tables, slopping large spoons of alleged food onto segmented Styrofoam plates. At least when she was working she didn't have to deal with concern over what table she would wind up at in the chow hall.

SEVEN

Gail heard a jangle of keys and looked down the corridor to see Johnson standing there, leaning in the doorway like a gangsta. He could swagger without moving a muscle.

"What you got left?" he called.

"Just this section to mop, and then I still have to buff it," Gail answered.

"Get busy. I don't need you taking all night with this shit."

"Yassah, Mistah Johnson, suh," Gail called out. He dismissed her with a disdainful wave of one hand and sauntered back down the hall.

Norton hadn't managed to get any of them assigned to the sewage plant, though Gail was sure he'd tried. Hillary was assigned to the infirmary. She came home every evening convinced that she'd been infected with whatever virus was eating its way through the population, but never so much as ran a fever. Lisa had drawn library duty.

They'd gotten Gail, though, or thought they had. Her new job was to mop A Hall. Even though it was supposed to be a dog of a job, and was definitely a far cry from landscape, floor duty wasn't half bad, at least not to Gail's way of thinking. The hacks were down in the control room, telling bad jokes and war stories, the prisoners were in their cells, except those who, like Gail, had night jobs to do. There weren't very many of them. It was only janitorial stuff. She had the entire corridor, empty, to herself. Room. Space. Regular walls, no bars. The illusion of freedom.

She was lucky the lieutenant had assigned her to mop over in the administrative section, where she didn't have to deal with concrete floors. But she did have to deal with a very long corridor, which meant, first, going the length of it with an industrial dust mop, then filling a huge yellow mop bucket with hot water and antibacterial soap, attaching the wringer, wheeling the thing down to the end of the hall and making her way back, mopping, back and forth, back and forth. Then she had to buff it.

She watched Johnson disappear through the doorway and went back to mopping. Somebody had spit gum on the floor and she'd missed it with the dust mop, and now it was soaked with antibacterial mop water and she should pick it up. Back to the mop closet for some scratchy brown paper towel. She scraped the gum up and looked around for someplace to put it, flashing on her years in the graduate program at New York University, headed for a Ph.D., and the times on her morning walks to class when she'd see people walking their dogs and picking up dog poop with baggies or newspaper they carried for just that purpose, how they all shared a certain look, standing there holding a lump of shit. It seemed insane to her then to have dogs in the city, but she'd missed her old family pet, a shaggy white mongrel she had adopted from the pound in seventh grade and named Colette, after the writer. Colette had made it until the year Gail bailed out of the Institute for Law and Society, living at home with Gail's parents in Connecticut, always there at the front bay window on Friday evenings, waiting to see if Gail was coming home for the weekend. Those were the days of Abscam, the Russian invasion of Afghanistan, and the assassination of John Lennon, leaving Gail and her parents no end of subjects for argument. Her father had been apoplectic the time she had to call him, just after the start of the fall semester, to come bail her out at the 1st Precinct. He didn't seem to care that she'd been one of more than two hundred thousand demonstrators who gathered in lower Manhattan for an antinuke rally. She didn't dare tell him, on the long, mostly silent drive back to Woodbridge, that she'd met someone in the fingerprint line. No sense setting him against Tom Firestone before they even met. And who knew, maybe this guy was like Andre, the guitarist in Oklahoma. I'll love you forever. What? You're pregnant? See ya. Anyway, all he'd done was write her phone number on the palm of his hand and tell her he'd call. It remained to be seen. She apologized to her father for dragging him all the way to the city, and for the two hundred bucks it cost to get her out, but stood firm that it was worth it to stop some maniacs from blowing up the planet.

Her father, two months short of fifty-five and having already had a heart attack, ran one hand through thick silver hair. "No one is going to blow up the planet," he said. "Too many people have too much invested in this place to let it go up in flames." He'd driven silently for a while, and then offered a short, quick smile. "To be honest," he said, "I'm proud of you for standing up for what you believe." He reached over and squeezed her hand, and elation flushed through her. She wished in that moment she could be closer to him, but it seemed to her that her parents were a different species and true communication was out of the question. Maybe it was all those years of disapproving glances and tight lips when Gail dressed the wrong way, or wore her hair the wrong way, or didn't join the right clubs at school and didn't hang with the right crowd. "My daughter the radical," her father would say at dinner when Gail launched into a speech. "My daughter the Communist. What's wrong with the way things are? We're lucky here, to be living in this place in these times. You don't know how fortunate you are."

She would usually wind up in her room, listening to Joni Mitchell, or Dylan's "Blood on the Tracks," reading Zinn's *A People's History of the United States,* or Ginsberg or Plath or Sexton, with Colette curled up on the pale blue carpet next to the pale blue dust ruffle on Gail's bed. She had long ago given up arguing with her mother about room décor, and had taken her noxious posters of Che Guevara and John Lennon off to school with her. After all, she was only around on weekends these days. And after Colette died, she wasn't even around that often on weekends.

She rolled the bucket full of dirty water to the closet and struggled to lift it to the sink and dump it. She washed out the mop and hung it on its hook on the wall. She dragged the buffer out. It was a huge chrome contraption, impossibly heavy until you plugged in its long, dirty orange cord and pressed the thumb button on the handle, at which point, unless you were ready, it would career down the hallway, whipping you about like laundry hung out to dry on a windy day. Gail had discovered this some sixteen years ago, the first time she'd been punished with janitorial duties. The infraction had been possession of tuna fish, back in the days when she still ate things that had eyes. She bought three cans of the stuff, for a buck and a half, paid in quarters, which was the only money prisoners were allowed to have on their person. And no more than ten dollars' worth. Someone working in the kitchen had smuggled the stuff out and made a killing on the black market. Gail was the only prisoner busted. She assumed it was a test. If it was, she passed it. When the lieutenant had braced her about where she got the contraband, she'd stood firm.

She took a square of green wool blanket and spread it on the floor, maneuvered the buffer's steel wool pad on top of it, gripped the handlebars firmly and pressed the button. She moved down the hall slowly, taking the buffer from one side to the other, back and forth, back and forth, listening to the mechanical whir, watching as the linoleum took on a fresh shine. It took some strength to control the buffer, and Gail used it as a chance for an upper body workout. From that perspective, she didn't mind the task, and if she didn't mind doing it, it was no longer an effective punishment. She'd beat them again. And if Johnson wanted her to hurry up, she would damn well take her time.

She was about halfway down the hall, working distractedly now, plotting her parole strategy. She would need more letters. She would have to ask Mel to call out his heavy hitters. She'd need politicians, as many as he could come up with, to put some heat on the appeals board in Atlanta.

Who was she kidding? She'd already used all her ammunition for the hearing. There was no one else to speak on her behalf. She was fucked. She pushed the buffer angrily, swinging it wide from one side of the hall to the other, banging it against the walls now, letting the buffer bounce itself from one side to the other, and then—a thud as it hit against the door to the records room.

And the door popped open. Just a crack. It didn't swing wide and invite her in. It was a matter of carelessness. Someone hadn't pulled the door shut. Was it possible? Easily. These people didn't give a shit, most of them. The women who worked in records would rather be home doing their nails and watching soaps than filing paperwork in a government cabinet. They looked for any excuse to have a long lunch and come back half sloshed. It was always someone's birthday. Gail looked left. Looked right. No one. Not a soul.

She let go the buffer switch, and it spun to a halt. Checked the hallway again.

She pushed open the door and slipped inside, left it open enough that light from the hallway spilled into the room. She went straight to the Rs, and quickly enough found her file. Eighteen years and they had summed her up in less than two inches of paperwork. Or maybe they purged these things every so often. Her hands were shaking as she leafed through the pages. She was sure her heartbeat could be heard halfway down the corridor. Her presentence report: recommending that she serve 240 months for a crime that usually carried a sentence of 60 months. The BP-9s she'd filed over the years, accusing the Bureau of Prisons of failure to offer adequate medical care, adequate dental care, adequate educational opportunities, decent food. Her complaints were not numerous, but they'd been answered with terse bureaucratese. And nothing had changed. There wasn't much else in there. Reports from her case manager. All praising her attitude, her willingness to help others, her sincere efforts at her own rehabilitation. Shit. She shoved the folder back into the drawer and turned to get the hell out of there. She heard a noise in one corner of the room and froze, practically sick with fear. But how could anyone, why

would anyone be hiding there in the dark. She stood, afraid to
breathe. And then she saw it.

A mouse.

Creeping brazenly across the floor, eyeing Gail, then scurry-
ing quickly, staying close to the cabinets as it headed for the
open doorway. Gail thought she might pass out from the
adrenaline cocktail her body had just served her. She leaned
against a cabinet until she felt her balance return. She edged
along the cabinets toward the door.

And then a file drawer caught her eye: W.

She found the file quickly enough. Wellman, Diane, DOB
5/23/77, white female, yeah, yeah, yeah, come on, come on.
Cocaine possession. So it was true, young Diane was in for
dope. Holy shit. Gail blinked, looked again. At the time of the
offense, defendant was employed by the Bolton, Texas, Police
Department, holding the rank of patrol officer. She was well
respected by her fellow officers, many of whom expressed astonishment at her arrest on drug charges . . .

Shit. A cop. Not just a cop. A dirty cop. They'd sent a cop in
on her. She stabbed the folder back into the cabinet and slipped
out into the fluorescent brightness of the hallway. Eased the
door shut. The mouse was gone, made its escape. She turned on
the buffer. Back and forth. She couldn't think about it, it was
too much. Back and forth. Her heart still pounding, she worked
blindly, the floor glowed green, shining supernaturally, and
from somewhere she heard Gilda Radner and Dan Aykroyd arguing, It's a floor wax. No. It's a dessert topping. Floor wax!
Dessert topping! *Saturday Night Live!* She and her girlfriends,
seniors at Dorris Canne Girls Prep, the floating party that
moved from house to house each weekend, depending on
whose parents had gone into the city for a show and dinner.
Smoke a little pot, get the munchies, goat cheese was the latest,
and they'd listen to the Talking Heads or Patti Smith, laugh
about *Saturday Night Fever,* and wasn't *The Women's Room* beyond depressing, and every so often, a little cocaine around,
just to kick the party into high gear. Gail moved the buffer back
and forth, back and forth, and now these motherfuckers sent a
cop in on me. A fucking cop! In my house. In my cell.

What for? It made no sense. Why put a cop in with her? It couldn't be what Johnson said, that she had the only empty bunk in the joint. That was true enough, except for the Rodent, but that couldn't be the reason.

When Gail got back to the cell, Diane was on her bunk, face in her pillow, sobbing. It happened to everyone, sooner or later. Every new arrival, when they'd been in for a few months—or sometimes only a few weeks—and were beginning to realize that their lawyer wasn't going to pull off some stunt to get them out—immediate release!—when the enormity of prison, of doing time, hit them, they did the crash-and-burn thing. Some got suicidal. Some got hysterical. Most, like Diane, wept. Some for hours, some for days, some until they got transferred for a stay in the psych unit.

Gail moved carefully, as though she were afraid a wrong step would break something. She went to the sink and prepared for bed. She couldn't believe there was a cop lying on the bunk in her cell, crying like a teenager who'd caught her boyfriend with another girl. She got a glimpse of herself in the small mirror hanging by a wire above the brushed stainless steel sink that was about the size of the one in a commercial jetliner toilet. She saw her fear. Okay. Okay. Chill. Just cool on out here. Relax. She is what she is, and right now she's a prisoner. They got her for cocaine, that was in the report. DEA no less. Maybe she was a cop once, but she isn't anymore. She got caught holding, and now she's on the other side of the line. Maybe it was just like Johnson said. There was no place else to put her. Gail looked again in the mirror. There. That was better. Then she saw the tiny lines around her eyes. She saw her age. How long? What would she look like if she had to do another twelve? Most likely her hair would be the silver color of her father's the last time she saw him, in the visiting room so many years ago. She wondered if her eyes would be hardened by then. She thought she'd kept them soft, considering her circumstances. She didn't have a hard look about her. She was still capable of being open, gentle. She worked to stay that way. But in twelve years? By then, they would have stolen most of her adult life from her.

She took her toothbrush from the tin can on the sink edge. Heard Diane calming, sitting up and pulling her blanket about her. She put toothpaste on her toothbrush.

"I talked to my lawyer today," Diane said, her nose stuffed from crying. "This evening."

Gail kept brushing.

"They denied my Rule 37."

"Never heard of it."

"Motion to Reduce Sentence?"

"Thirty-five. Rule 35."

"Whatever. They denied it. I'm gonna have to do the whole twenty." Her sigh sounded like it might have come from Sisyphus.

And she would, too, Gail knew. The feds had abolished parole in 1987. If you got convicted after that, there was no parole board to deal with. You weren't eligible for parole. It was only because Gail was sentenced before the law passed that she had a shot. Most of the hacks and judges hated the new law. It made their jobs harder. It made for prisoners who had nothing to lose.

She rinsed her toothbrush and returned it to its can. Turned and leaned against the sink, staring up at Diane. The girl's face was swollen from crying. She was really hurting. So fucking what.

Gail thought about the cops who'd taken her and Tom in. FBI. They'd splintered the front door with a battering ram. Flooded the place with feds. Thrown both of them on the floor and left them there for six hours while they took apart the house. Methodical. They kept looking even after they found the stash in the basement. AR-15s. Shotguns. And the explosives. They filed possession of controlled substance charges for the half ounce of pot Tom had in the nightstand. Gail remembered herself on the floor that night. That person. That idealistic, fanatical, hungry-to-change-the-world young woman. My God. What had she been doing? What had she been thinking? There were times, late at night in her unforgiving bunk, that she considered herself to be the one meting out the harshest punishment she could ever receive. There were times she thought she could never forgive herself for what she'd done. Or been about to do, anyway. Sometimes she was actually glad she'd been caught. Hadn't been able to plant the explosives at the phone company. That had been the plan. Knock out communication in D.C. Watch the scramble. The plan was to make sure no one got hurt. Strictly a property crime, but one that said Up Yours to Uncle Sam. Other times she thought she would have come to her senses on her own, would have stopped herself when it came down to actually breaking and entering. She liked to think she would have realized that she didn't believe in what she was doing, that she would have been able to step back and separate what she felt for Tom from what she felt for the organization. Maybe. The word was full of promise. Maybe she would not have gone through with it. Maybe she would not have hurt her parents so. Maybe she would have found someone a little less fanatically idealistic to bring some stability and tenderness into her life.

"What are you staring at?" Diane's voice brought her back.

"You." Gail leaned toward Diane. "Tell me something. Why are you here?"

Diane wiped her face with her blanket and looked at Gail.

"I told you. I got framed. Someone planted a shitload of cocaine on me."

"Who?"

"DEA found it. Could be the agents put it there themselves, could be somebody else did and called them. Probably that. The agents seemed straight up."

"Some advice?" Gail watched Diane carefully. "Never trust a cop."

"Duh." Diane shrugged, neither a yes nor a no.

"Who would frame you? And why?"

"I have my ideas."

"Who'd you piss off? And why'd they send you all the way up here? Why didn't they put you down in Fort Worth, or over in Alderson? There are prisons a lot closer to Texas than this one. There are plenty of prisons in Texas. How come here?"

"God, what is this? You're like a fucking prosecutor or something, cross-examining me." Diane put her head down in her hands for a long moment. "I don't know why they put me here. I guess somebody wanted me way the hell out of Texas."

Gail waited. Nothing.

"Are you a rat? You snitch on somebody?"

Diane jumped down from the bunk, landing face-to-face with Gail.

"No! Shit no! What is wrong with you?! Somebody say I was a rat?"

Gail stood her ground, eyed Diane closely. This was important.

Diane raised herself up, straightened. She wasn't much taller than Gail, but her demeanor said that she wasn't afraid if things went physical. Gail moved in closer, until she could see the tiny flecks of gold in Diane's green but bloodshot eyes. This girl had seen some things.

They stood like that, eye to eye. They heard someone laughing from a cell far down the hallway. When Gail spoke, it was quietly, her tone sincerely questioning, inviting an honest answer.

"Why'd they frame you? What'd you do?"

Diane stepped back. She looked at Gail. Looked at the floor. Looked like she might start crying again. She stood staring at the wall behind Gail, seeing something from her past.

"Honesty is the best policy," Gail said, gently prodding.

Diane stuck her hand out, palm up, looked at the ceiling. "Oh, wow, it's raining platitudes."

"That's not a platitude."

"Whatever."

"Are you gonna tell me?"

Diane gazed right at Gail then, eyeing her openly, sizing her up. She was afraid to utter the words. She knew she shouldn't. But there was something, this woman seemed like a decent person, not some asshole criminal. She seemed trustworthy. Though Diane had never worked undercover, she imagined this was what it felt like to have your cover blown. Fuck it.

"I was a cop," she said finally.

"Whoa." Gail rocked back. The girl was telling the truth. A dangerous truth. Gail sat on her bunk. Diane edged over, questioned Gail with her eyes. Gail motioned her to have a seat. It wasn't like there were many options.

"Yeah." Diane pulled her legs up to sit cross-legged, folded her arms across her chest.

Gail slid back on her bunk until she could sit against the wall.

"A fuckin' cop. I can't believe it."

"It's not so weird."

"Yes, it is. Think about it. It's weird as hell."

"It's like anything else. You go into it all starry-eyed, and then you find out how it really is."

"Jaded."

"I guess."

"I can't see you as a cop."

"You don't have to," Diane cracked a smile, her lips still quivery from the crying jag. Shrugged. "I'm sure as hell not one now."

"How'd you . . ."

"I don't know. Just kind of fell into it. Got recruited at college."

"Was it yours?"

"What?"

"The dope."

"Absofuckinglutely not." Diane shook her head no, emphatically. "No way, no how. Never touched the stuff. Never."

"You must be pissed."

"I had a run-in with the sheriff. And the DA. I was gonna, you know, expose them."

"Maybe you should've just got out of there."

"They've got this guy on death row. I know he's not guilty. But they put him there. Framed him just as sure as they framed me. I can't let that happen."

"It looks like it's already happened."

"I mean the guy's a total asshole, and everybody in town knew it, but no way did he do this crime. Sometimes juries are unbelievably stupid."

"Tell me about it."

"I mean it makes me fuckin' insane. And I call the sheriff

on it, tell him I know what he's done, and next thing you know, my ass is in jail."

"Where on earth were you living?"

"Breard County, Texas, hon. The wild, wild west is alive and thriving."

"This is a joke, right? I mean, you're making this stuff up, right?" Gail stared at her, and Diane laughed, the kind of laugh that could easily disintegrate into hysterical tears.

"It's the absolute stone-cold gospel truth," Diane said. "And when I start freaking and feeling sorry for myself, I think about that sorry-ass Rick Churchpin sitting down there in Huntsville waiting for the executioner, and I feel lucky as hell." She got very quiet suddenly, sat looking at Gail seriously. "That's why I have to get out of here."

"What, you think you're going to ride into town when they've got him strapped to the gurney and save the day? That's not usually how things go in real life. Life is fundamentally messy and unfair."

"Like you're telling me something."

"If you want out of here, you'd better want out of here for a legitimate reason. Not because you want to be some kind of hero."

"Look, I'm not after saving anyone's ass but my own, okay? But don't sit there and tell me how to reason. What I do is my business. And what they did to me was major-league fucked up, and I aim to undo it."

"Why didn't you go to the media? They'd've eaten this stuff up."

"They tend to listen to the powers that be, not to some girl cop with three years under her belt. They'd've gone straight to the DA, the sheriff. I didn't particularly feel like getting killed."

"You were a cop. Who's gonna kill you?"

"Ah, the sheriff maybe? I mean I've heard he's shot three people dead. Off-duty."

"And you know that for a fact?"

"No. What I know for a fact is that he framed me. Or had it

done. That's what I know for a fact." Her anger energized her, not pleasantly. She stood up and started pacing.

"Diane," Gail said finally, "keep that up and you'll make both of us crazy. Sit down."

Diane perched on the edge of Gail's bunk and whispered.

"I've got to get out of here. I have to. I'll go nuts. I'll kill myself."

"Just please don't do it in the cell, okay?"

"I'm serious."

"So am I."

"Gail—"

"No. Don't even talk about it." God, this woman was hard-headed. "They say the walls have ears in this place. Get it?" She looked at Diane significantly. "Now tomorrow evening, if the weather's good, I'll take you to my weekly card game. You like to play cards?"

Diane threw herself down, pounded the mattress ferociously. Cards? Like she was gonna spend the next twenty years playing cards? She glared at Gail.

"You'll learn," Gail said. "Listen to me. I'll help you file your 2255—"

"Whatever the hell that is."

"Last resort. Habeas corpus. Not that it's gonna do much good. But maybe there's something."

"I don't need help with paperwork. I need to get out of here."

Gail sat up then, stabbed a finger at Diane.

"You need to listen. You need to do as I tell you. Stop obsessing, and pay attention to what I'm saying. Get a routine going. It's important. It's how you keep your head together."

"What, you think you're my mother or something?"

"I'm nobody's mother," Gail said angrily, and hated the empty sound the words made. "But I've got eighteen years behind me in this joint, and you've got all of about, what? Has it been three months yet? Got ninety days in? You'd do well to take my advice."

Diane stood and grabbed her pillow off her bunk, lay back on Gail's bunk, and put the pillow over her face. Then she lifted it off and lay staring at the bottom of the empty upper bunk above her. Someone had scratched into the metal: Soyez tranquille.

"You do that?"

Gail glanced at the lettering. "No."

"Know what it means?"

"French. Remain calm. Be cool."

"You did it, didn't you."

"I just said I didn't. You think I'm a liar?"

Diane looked again at the words. "Do me a big favor," she said. "You know that scene in that movie where Jack Nicholson goes into the loony bin and winds up being smothered by that big Indian after the shrinks cut out a chunk of his brain? Just take this pillow and fucking smother me. Right now. I promise I won't file charges."

Gail sat back against the wall. She heard the first jagged sounds of the Snorer rasping down the corridor. It sounded like a chain saw, she swore, a very big chain saw. Deep. Astonishing. It would be yet another miserable, worthless night in this miserable, worthless place.

"What did you do?"

"Who, me?" Gail laughed to herself, at herself.

"Come on. I copped out to you. So to speak. Fess up. You got a hell of a long sentence. Must've been serious."

"It was."

Eighteen years. The realization that had been lurking in the back of her mind, feeling like the beginnings of a massive headache, revealed itself. Another twelve years. Six short of what she'd already done here. The simple fact was, she couldn't do it. She was not capable. There would be no point to her life if she had to spend another twelve years in this place. There was no point to it now, except the hope that she would get out and know freedom. And she knew, though she loathed to admit it, that her appeal would be denied. She'd been considering it anyway. Leaving. Going. Running. If she made two columns, one labeled Finish Your Sentence and the other labeled Escape, there was nothing to put beneath the first one except Certain Death. That was it. If she stayed here, she would

die. Either by her own hand or out of the hugeness of a despair
that would soon consume her. If she escaped, there was danger, yes. Danger of getting killed. Danger of getting caught.
But there was also the chance that she would get away. She was
strong, had worked up to forty-seven pushups in a minute. She
could run fast and run forever. And once she got underground,
they would never find her. Her mother was dead. Her father
was dead. She had no sisters or brothers, no husband or children. Her closest friend was Mel, her attorney. And he would
help her, she knew. When it got right down to it, she truly had
nothing to lose but misery. And the hell-raiser sharing her cell
seemed game for anything. She reminded Gail of herself, some
twenty years ago. Naïve. Idealistic. Fiercely determined that
Good should prevail in the world. And wasn't it odd, that an
ex-cop would come waltzing into her life, just in time to help
her get the hell out of here. Gail trusted her instincts about
these things. And if it was a setup, fuck it.

She caught herself wishing that the hearing had come out
differently and got angry at herself for being pathetic. Gee. I
wish I wish I wish. She could spend the next twelve years doing
that. Sitting in a prison cell and wishing. Wishing what, that a
bunch of paper pushers had a shown a little common sense and
compassion? Good luck. No. She would not wish. She would
not wish, and she would not let them continue to punish her.
She had done enough time. She had given them her childbear-
ing years. No more.

She would act. She had only been planning it for the past
three years or so. It was her pastime, in those small hours of
the night when she found herself awake in her bunk, trying to
remember what the moon looked like. And she knew now that
Hillary wasn't the right one. Hillary was a prankster, but she'd
never go over the fence. The one who would go over the
fence, and help her get over the fence, was right here in the
cell with her.

"Diane." Her voice was low.

"Yeah?"

Gail leaned in close to whisper. "Are you serious?" She

waved an arm in a circle, to indicate all that they'd been talking about. To indicate escape.

Diane propped herself on one elbow, saw Gail's green eyes, intense in the glow of the hall light seeping in through the cell bars. She had reached her. She had gotten through.

"Tell me what you did. I don't ride with just anybody."

"Possession of firearms and explosives."

"Holy shit. What were you—"

"Planning? To blow up the phone company in Washington, D.C."

"For real?"

"A political act. A statement."

"When was this?"

"You were a sprout."

"I thought all that stuff was over in the sixties."

"It's been going on since the Revolution, my dear. You've heard of the American Revolution?"

"Once or twice."

"Yeah. Well, it's all a process, you know."

Diane didn't allow herself to think what would happen if they got caught. It wasn't part of the picture. What she knew was that she would rather die than spend twenty years in this hellhole for a crime she didn't do. And what else she knew was that she was by God gonna get her butt back to Texas and make sure that Mr. District Attorney and Mr. High Sheriff of Breard County were brought to justice. If the feds wouldn't do it, she'd damn well do it herself.

"Diane?" Gail reached around behind her, pulled open the stitching on her mattress. Took out the piece of lawn mower blade.

Diane looked at it, at Gail, at the blade again. "Hell, yes, I'm serious." She nodded. Slowly. Emphatically. A tiny smile. A raised eyebrow. Partners.

Gail smiled, and it was the first time Diane had seen a real smile on her face. Unreserved. It was hard to tell what the smile meant, as it looked like it took considerable effort. There was something painful about it.

"Good," Gail said. Her eyes were confident. "I hear they're going to let us have a barbecue in the Big Yard for the holiday. Burgers and dogs."

"What holiday?" Diane looked utterly confused.

"Independence Day," Gail said. She leaned in close again to whisper. "Ours."

EIGHT

Johnson had a kitchen apron on over his uniform and a big smile on his face as he stood near the entrance to the yard, a spatula in one hand and a barbecue fork in the other. He wouldn't let any of the other hacks cook. And prisoners were not allowed to hold the grill tools.

"Every year," Gail said. "Same old thing. Hacks cooking wieners and acting like they're doing us a great big favor."

"Beats the chow hall." Diane was happy to be out in fresh air. And psyched.

"Depends who's cooking." Gail, too, felt a steady buzz in her system, a thrill born of fear that she tried to breathe out of herself, nice and easy. Just another day in lockdown.

They strolled out, carrying their blankets and plastic spray bottles of water. They had quart bottles of Poland Spring to drink, which Gail had purchased at the commissary the previous Thursday, her regular shopping day. They were dressed in prison chic: cut-off fatigues, white T-shirts, short-sleeved khaki button-downs left open over the Ts. Steel-toed work boots, black. Gail's T-shirt was out, hanging loose over her waist. Under the shirt was wrapped a length of rope she'd found in the associate warden's garage and smuggled inside. She had her softball mitt, almost worn out after all the years of playing, and, wrapped in her blanket, the almost L-shaped piece of mower blade that had been hidden in her mattress. She had managed to squirrel away some masking tape when she'd been on paint detail some time ago, and with it had fashioned a handle on the blade by wrapping the longer part of it with a strip of old T-shirt and then the masking tape. It didn't exactly make a shank, but if she got caught with it, she would surely be charged with possession of a weapon.

Diane stood next to Gail, surveying the Big Yard, framed on two sides by the building, a three-story red brick. No way up that. The other two sides were framed by chain-link and concertina wire, wire that looked vicious, like it might cut your eyes if you stared at it too long. Juxtaposed against the cruelty of the wire was a magnificent oak tree, the only one inside the fence, that had somehow managed to flourish in the withering environment of the prison yard. It was close to the point where the chain-link intersected the corner of the building; it had been pruned through the years so that the lowest of its branches were a solid fifteen feet off the ground. Diane, looking at the place through calculating eyes for the first time, was taken aback by the size of the yard and the height of the fence. And beyond, acres of meadows rolled toward thick woodland that quickly headed uphill. It looked like it got steep fast.

Gail looked at Diane as Diane checked out the yard, the situation. The girl had a cool about her that said fuck with me at your own risk. Gail admired the attitude. Wondered if she'd had that, way back when.

The Rodent had already claimed their table, a faded brown one-piece picnic table near the middle of the yard, and was shuffling cards. Gail led Diane over, made introductions. Lisa and Hillary would join them later.

"Let's move the table just a little," Gail said. The Rodent looked at her sharply, but stood up and took one end of the table.

The women lifted the table and Gail led the way ten feet to the left, making sure the table was centered over a three-foot-wide manhole cover that, oddly enough, was almost smack in the middle of the yard. Gail had made discreet inquiries over the years, had learned that the cover was above the exterior controls for the prison's water system. She had managed, one sunny afternoon, to get a peek down through the rather large keyhole, using her contraband penlight to see the huge rusted pipes with their shutoff lever. There wasn't much room in there.

They played cards until a team of muscle-head hacks known as Nick and Nack hit the yard carrying large boxes of what turned out to be, not hot dogs and hamburgers, but steaks. The news was passed so rapidly that Gail could literally watch the word spread across the yard in a wave, as she did from her place at the table. Not just steak. Corn on the cob. Potato salad. The hacks, a skeleton crew for the holiday, looked as happy as the prisoners about the unexpected feast. Johnson threw himself into his job, singing and dancing as he tossed the first of the rib eyes onto the grill. Already the line was forming.

"Let's go," Hillary said. "As soon as word hits the units, all the layabouts will be headed out here. And you know these suckers won't have enough to go around." She placed her cards facedown on the table and weighted them with a water bottle. The others followed. They grabbed paper plates and plastic forks and knives and fell into line.

"How're we supposed to cut steak with this stuff?" Diane examined the flimsy plastic cutlery.

"I thought you Texans just gnawed it off the bone." Lisa's smile took the bite out of her words.

"Very funny." Diane stuck the cutlery in the pocket of her fatigues and affected a look of extreme boredom.

"I haven't used a real knife and fork since I was twenty-something," Gail said. "I'm not sure I remember what it feels like."

"That and a few other things," Lisa chided. Gail started to come back, but saw how intently Hillary was watching the conversation. Before Hillary arrived, before Gail decided to withdraw into herself, Gail and Lisa had been together for a time.

They made it to the front of the line before the steaks ran out. Gail took one, though she knew she wouldn't eat it. She gave it to the Rodent, as a little extra encouragement to keep her mouth shut. The corn was delicious and buttery. Even the potato salad was nicely done. At one point Gail leaned over to Diane and whispered, "This is really good. Maybe we should stay." Diane snickered, shaking her head no. It was the nervous laughter of someone who was about to risk her life: barely a laugh, almost a cry of anguish.

Midway through the meal, the Rodent raised her bottle of water in a toast.

"To Independence Day," she said. She turned to Gail. "Long may you run." The women tapped plastic bottles, took healthy swigs of water. Giggled at the absurdity of their situation.

And then, before she could believe it, Gail saw the sun taking a nosedive toward the horizon. It seemed to be happening surreally fast, even faster than on the regular days, when all she wanted was a few more minutes outdoors.

"Okay," Gail said. "This is it. Speak now or forever hold your peace." She looked from one woman to the other: the Rodent, Lisa, Hillary, Diane. Each gave her a silent nod. Gail looked around the yard. Two hacks, one strolling around the perimeter, at the edge of the track. Another engaged in watching the softball game in progress. She squeezed the women's hands and slipped beneath the picnic table.

It was as if time stopped, time speeded up, time went quantum on her, registering as a quiet roar in her ears, and she watched her hands pull the mower blade from her pocket and slip it into the keyhole of the heavy, rusted manhole cover. She pulled. She had thought it would be heavy, wondered if she'd even be able to lift it, had even hoped sometimes to be foiled by its weight and forced to return to her cell defeated, but her strength was fear-driven; the cover lifted easily.

"Okay," she said quietly, and looked up through the cracks between the boards of the tabletop, realized that the women were frozen in place. "Play cards!" she hissed. "Shit." They went into action. "Diane! Come on!"

And here came Diane, easing beneath the table and down into the hole in one fluid motion. Gail slipped in next to her. The women folded themselves practically into thirds to get their heads beneath ground level, and then they reached up and pulled the manhole cover into place.

Darkness, but for the keyhole, lit gray with the coming of dusk. The smell of damp earth and rust, and soon enough the smell of fear in their sweat. The pipes were cool and damp against their legs, the sounds of the Big Yard distant and unreal.

Diane nudged Gail.

"It's tighter than a bull's ass in here."

"Do me a favor," Gail whispered. "Don't talk. Nothing. Okay? We blow this, it's an automatic five years added to my sentence."

"Mine, too, I guess then."

"Yeah. No talking."

"This must be what it's like to be a mushroom."

"No talking."

Gail heard a sigh, heard Diane settling in against the rough concrete wall of the whatever it was they were in. She focused on her breathing, trying to slow it, on her heartbeat, too. She'd be surprised if it couldn't be heard all the way over on the softball diamond. It was hard to slow down. The fear was there and real. But as big as the fear, maybe bigger than the fear, was the excitement of knowing that soon, for the first time in eighteen years, she would be back in the free world.

Then she heard it, the hack calling out, yard's closed, back to your units, yard's closed. And Diane whispered, "Yeah, suckers, back to your units." Gail thunked her with her middle finger on the thigh and felt Diane wince at the pain.

"No talking."

"All right already. Jesus."

Someone, probably Lisa, tapped a goodbye on the manhole cover and there were the sounds of their card-playing accomplices standing up and shuffling toward the prison. Gail pulled the length of rope from her waistband, kneaded it as if it were a string of prayer beads. Please, God.

Disjunctive bits of grumbling stuttered in through the keyhole as prisoners headed across the yard to their units, angry once again at the sunset. And then static. From a radio. Gail and Diane froze. The hack was close by. Gail tried to get a look through the keyhole.

He had one foot propped on the bench of the picnic table, an arm leaned on his thigh. That was all she could see. But she knew he was looking around the yard, checking for anything amiss. She thought she might just pee her pants, right there. And then she felt Diane's hand taking hers in the dark and squeezing reassuringly. They stayed like that, hand in hand, sweating like they'd just sprinted a four hundred meter dash, until they heard the hack stand, his voice into the radio, "Yard's clear," and the fading of his footfalls on the soft grass carpet of the infield.

From far away came the sounds of the big heavy steel door being pulled shut and the locking mechanism inside clanking into place. Diane sat staring at the keyhole, waiting for blackness.

"How long now?" she whispered.

"I don't know how in hell you ever made it as a cop, since you apparently lack the ability to follow the simplest of directions," Gail said.

"Shut up!" Diane whispered. "Why can't I talk now? There's nobody even in the yard. You're like a fucking librarian or something." She paused. "Oh, that's right. You are a librarian. But now it's were a librarian. And we are not in the library. So shut up and answer my question."

Gail took a moment, ready to jump back at Diane, but realizing before she did that the girl was right. They could talk. Or whisper, anyway.

"Twenty minutes or so. As soon as it's really dark."

They sat in silence in the dank little hole and waited. That was the difference, Gail thought. I know how to wait. I know how to let time pass. This little hothead has the patience of a two-year-old.

Diane could barely maintain herself. She'd never been in a situation that would bring out claustrophobia. But this was torture. She flexed against the concrete, felt it hard and solid against her back. She needed to move. She couldn't move. She pushed again. Nothing. Get a grip. She reminded herself of her purpose: Get the hell out of prison. Get back to Texas and clear her name. Regain her job and her friends on the force. Regain her relationship with Will Renfro.

Talk about someone being stunned. He'd visited only once, while she was in local custody, and stayed only long enough to tell her he believed in her and there was no way she'd wind up in prison. But the chief had told him to steer clear, stay out of the way for his own sake and hers, so that's what he'd do. "Renfro," she'd asked, "what's it like to always be so freakin' level-headed?"

"I'll help you, girl," he'd replied. "I'm just not sure yet how best to do it."

If he'd tried, it hadn't done any good.

"You had a trial?" she whispered to Gail.

"Of course."

"Well, it's not like you had to. You could have just pled out."

"If I was guilty."

"Weren't you?"

"On the first case, yeah. Why?"

"They processed my ass through the system so fast it's like I still don't quite know how I got here."

"You plead guilty?"

"Not in this life."

"Jury trial? Or did you go before a judge?"

"Jury. Bunch of stupid-as-dirt citizens. Foreman didn't know his ass from a hole in the ground. I mean stupid."

"Maybe just misguided."

"Hard not to be when you're watching three DEA agents testify that they found a shitload of cocaine in the defendant's freezer. Those guys, those agents, I mean, could they really be that dumb, or were they in on it? That's what I can't figure."

"When it comes to drug cases, you don't need a motive. The drugs are the motive."

"When did you get your law degree?"

"When I got to prison, babe. Best law school in the country." She watched the gray light in the keyhole, waiting for darkness. It was close. Ever so close.

Diane half sighed, half smirked.

"But tuition's a killer," Gail added.

Diane curled up just a little, as much as it was possible. Her knees were against her chin already, her arms tucked close at her sides. But at least she was moving, even if it was only a slight contraction of her already contorted body. She relaxed, then tightened up again, let it go that way, like she was a fetus at the end of term, being squeezed to the rhythm of birth.

And then unexpectedly, she felt a sharp nudge from Gail.

"Ready?" They'd gone over and over it last night.

"Since before I even got here, darlin'."

They eased the manhole cover back, crawled out, careful to stay in the shadows, under the cover of the picnic table. Large vapor lights at the fence corners illuminated the perimeter of the yard, lighting it up like night tennis courts. It was brighter than Gail anticipated. She signaled Diane to help her replace the manhole cover.

"Okay. Let's go." A deep breath, and then they crawled out from beneath the table and ducked across the yard, headed for the oak tree. Gail readied the rope as she ran, and as soon as they were there she tossed it up, aiming to loop it over the lowest branch on this side of the fence.

It missed.

"Shit," Diane said. "Give it to me."

Gail ignored her. Tried again. Again.

"Dammit!" Diane grabbed the rope from Gail. She tossed the rope over the branch and pulled it through the loop, making a noose around the branch. She yanked it taut and handed it to Gail.

"After you."

Gail wrapped the rope around her right hand and began scaling the tree, walking up the trunk and using the rope to pull herself up. Diane got beneath and pushed. Gail struggled, reached, missed the branch, and fell, dangling by her right hand from the rope.

"Shit, Gail, come on!" Diane got up under her, spun her around, and helped her get her footing again. Pushed again.

No good. When Gail swung her arm out to grab the branch, she fell short and again fell. This time her hand came loose from the rope and she hit the ground heavily. She lay there, staring up at the tree, her thoughts swirling too furiously to be captured, except one: You're out of your mind.

Diane grabbed the rope and moved as far away from the tree as she could. Wrapped the rope around her hand, gripped it firmly and ran toward the tree. She jumped as high as she could, and grabbing the rope up high, literally ran up the side of the trunk and then jumped out from it, looping one leg over the branch and then grabbing it with her arm. She pulled herself up, then pushed herself against the trunk and tossed the rope back to Gail, who was still lying on the ground.

"Come on!" Diane hissed. "Get your ass up and move!" No sooner had Gail started to move than Diane raised a hand. "No! Wait!"

From her perch in the tree, Diane saw movement. She pulled the rope back up, tucked it in close. It was way across the field, in the employee parking lot, which was lit up like a football stadium. A hack, going to his car. She pressed herself against the branch, trying to become one with the oak tree. Watched as the hack got to his car, turned, and scanned the lot. It seemed to her he looked right at her. Why wasn't he getting into his car? Please, God, send him on his way. She waited, waited . . .

"What is it?" Gail was still on the ground, on her back, motionless.

Diane put a finger to her lips to signal silence. She watched as the hack finally turned and opened his car door. She heard the sound of his car's ignition, breathed a beautiful sigh, watched the car pull out of the parking lot and its taillights disappear down the long, winding drive that led out to the county road.

She snaked the rope back down and watched as Gail grabbed it.

"Just use your feet on the trunk and climb the rope. I'll grab you."

"That's what I was doing," Gail grunted, straining to get up the rope. Diane watched her, saw that she wasn't going to make it. But she had to. That's all. Diane shifted her weight back against the trunk of the tree, clamped her knees against

the branch, grabbed hold of the branch with her left arm and
swung down as far as she could. As Gail struggled up the rope,
Diane stretched down and latched onto Gail's wrist and pulled
with all her might, felt every cell straining to pull Gail up.

Whether it was sheer strength or the combined will of the
women, Gail made it into the tree, legs and arms all scraped
up. Diane could feel a burning on her thighs but wouldn't take
time to look.

"Okay," she said. "This way." She edged around the trunk
and out onto a branch that overhung the fence. The razor wire
gleamed beneath, a shark with its mouth wide open, ready to
consume them. It would take a serious jump to clear it. Gail
stood, gripping the branch above to keep the branch beneath
her feet from giving way under her weight. She focused on a
rock on the ground.

"If a little girl climbs a tree," Diane whispered, "it doesn't
necessarily mean she wants to be a little boy. Sometimes it just
means she wants to climb a tree." Gail turned, stared at Diane.
She couldn't believe what she was hearing. Diane was using the
words as a mantra, clinging to the tree trunk, waiting to step
onto the branch as soon as Gail jumped. She saw Gail staring at
her. She stared back. "Break a leg," she finally whispered.

In a single move, Gail stood, let go of the branch above her,
crouched, and leaped. She saw the razor wire beneath her,
threw her arms forward, plummeted toward the ground. The
shock of the landing almost knocked her out. She rolled in the
dirt, wound up sprawled on her back. She opened her eyes to
see Diane sailing toward her, flailing her arms and legs as
though she were running in midair. Diane landed on all fours
and rolled gracefully in a kind of sideways somersault that ab-
sorbed the impact of the fall and leapt to her feet. She reached
for Gail, pulled her up.

"Haul ass, man!" She tugged at Gail, pulling her along.
They ran, Diane breathing hard but strong, Gail gasping, gulping air.

Gail fell in behind Diane, tried to match her stride, focused
on her breathing. She felt her heart stammering in her chest.

Don't let the fear get you. Calm now. Just run. You know how to run. Just run. Breathe. Run. Breathe.

She heard their footsteps pounding across the earth, down the gentle slope of meadow toward the woods. A hundred yards now, two hundred yards from the looming red-brick prison. It was coming together. She ran, efficiently, using the pull of gravity on the downhill to lengthen her stride, but careful not to lose control.

Diane glanced over her shoulder and saw Gail right behind her, and behind Gail, in the distance now, the huge and menacing building, the yellow pink glow of the lights on the razor wire.

"Yeah!" Diane said, "Fuck all y'all."

"Just run," Gail said. "Shut up and run." She felt something warm on her leg, but who cared. Who cared, it didn't matter, she was running. Running. Away from the misery. The loneliness. The absurdity. Away from death, toward death, running. Something warm on her leg, just above the top of her boot. Blood dripping, she knew. Let it run.

They made the woods. Starting uphill now. Pushing their way through thick brambles, vegetation green and snaky, thick, solid trees, skinny youngster trees, Gail moved to the front, led the way in the darkness, walking now, struggling uphill, feeling as much as seeing. Five minutes or so in, and blind in the darkness. Gail took out her penlight. Its tiny beam seemed like a floodlight, cutting through the woods. She picked her way along, found a stick to use as a kind of dull machete, knocking out thinner branches. Mostly she tried not to. The less trail they left, the better.

She stopped when she felt her sock getting wet. Shone the light on her leg. It was not good. The gash was almost three inches long, and deep. Diane bent to look, breathing hard.

"I hope you brought your sewing kit." The words came out in gasps.

Gail nodded, her own chest heaving as she gulped air. Diane ripped a piece of her T-shirt, and tied it carefully around Gail's leg.

"That'll hold for a while," she said. "Now, which way?"

"Up. Until we hit an old logging road or a quarry road. That'll lead us somewhere."

"How do you know we'll hit one?"

"We have to, sooner or later. They're all over the place in these hills."

"How do you know?"

"I read. I worked in the library, remember?"

Gail shined her light ahead, began picking her way through the woods. She was sweating, tired already, but calming now, retrieving her sense of purpose after the insane sprint away from the prison. She glanced at her watch. They had almost an hour before the ten o'clock count.

Almost an hour before all hell would break loose in Sundown, when men with guns and dogs would come looking for them.

Sweat ran down Gail's forehead into her eyes, salt stinging, bringing tears. But she had her wind now. Breathing deep, hard, but steady and controlled. She slowed to a trot, forced by the underbrush, grabbed a sleeve of her T and wiped her face. Move. Keep moving. Her ankle was hurting now, or maybe it had been all along but she'd been too caught up to notice. She slowed to a walk, Diane at her side, keeping pace, the two of them following the tiny penlight beam through the woods. And then a deer-traveled path, barely a path, but discernable. Fewer brambles, only an occasional black-cap bush or young maple sprouting from beneath the surface. Last autumn's leaves had turned to soil; the trail was spongy beneath Gail's feet. She wiped her eyes again. The sleeve of her T-shirt was soaked. The entire shirt was.

Diane stopped suddenly; Gail followed suit. They listened, dreading to hear hounds, but there was nothing.

Then, water, singing quietly in the darkness, maybe fifty feet away. They left the trail, headed into the woods toward the music burbling gently in the night. Mother Earth's circulatory system.

They approached the stream; Gail sat and unlaced her shoe, took off her blood-soaked sock and immersed her leg in the water. She focused on slowing down her breathing. She let the icy water of the stream run across the wound, sat with her eyes closed and enjoyed the cessation of pain. She was there and could feel it; this was real. She would not wake up tomorrow morning in her cell. Diane stood next to her, one hand on Gail's shoulder, protective.

Diane knew if she stood still long enough and stared at one spot, shapes would begin to emerge in the darkness. There was moonlight now, visible in places through the treetops. In different circumstances, this place would have seemed magical to her. She felt Gail's breathing slow beneath her fingertips, felt the muscles in Gail's shoulder, which had been wound tight as steel cable only moments before, begin to soften. She knelt to examine Gail's cut. Not good. Diane had worked her share of car wrecks and domestic disputes: she knew when stitches were needed. She stood again, continued to stare into the woods.

There were lots of trees.

She helped Gail to her feet, tore off more of her T-shirt and rebandaged the cut. Tighter this time, to stem the blood flow. It wasn't as if Gail had lost a lot of blood, but the flow was significant, and steady, and would have to be stopped soon.

They stayed close to the stream, treading carefully in the dark, until they hit a shallow section. They took off their boots and entered. Waded midstream, thankful for the chance to move at a slower pace. They stayed in there for close to a mile, Diane reckoned, before it started getting deep again. She led Gail to the opposite bank. They laced on their boots, listening for sounds above the flowing of water, continued along streamside. Gail's feet were numb from the cold water; it felt, if not great, at least better than the swollen heat and pain from the laceration.

She bumped into Diane, who'd come to a dead and sudden stop in front of her.

"Wha—"

Diane raised a hand, ordering silence. Gail froze, held her breath, listened. And then she heard it. Still far off in the distance, but unmistakable.

The hounds.

They didn't bark. They didn't growl. The sound they emitted was a gagging croupy cough, from deep in the lungs, from a place stupidly primitive, and tamed to lick the hand of its master.

"Come on," Diane whispered. Gail pulled up her sodden sock and retied her boot. Diane took her by the hand and tugged her forward, breaking into a trot. Gail followed, hoping that the numbness in her ankle would last until they got God only knew where. Wherever it was they were going.

Back to prison. Tack five years onto the sentence for escape. No.

The fear brought energy. Gail kicked into gear.

They jogged, they ran, they struggled through brush and darkness. Diane felt oddly calm, remembering how she'd kicked butt on the annual obstacle course run at the PD, never finishing farther down than fifth, pissing off all the beer-bellied male officers whose idea of exercise was to lift a can of Pabst to their lips while they watched the NFL on TV.

Gail stayed right behind Diane, matching her footsteps, matching her pace. Just keep up. Diane picked her way, focused on the little patch of ground illuminated before her by the penlight. She felt like she was driving with one headlight through heavy fog at night, going too fast to really see what lay ahead.

She almost bumped into it. Felt it before she saw it. She came to a halt and shined the light upward, around her at shoulder level. She flashed on that night at the lake. The bodies. The memory brought nothing physical; her adrenaline levels were already maxed out, her heart pounding with exertion, her breathing hard but steady. And then she was able to focus. The light hit the raw, rusted cedar wall of a cabin.

A hunter's cabin. Dark. Hopefully unoccupied.

Diane flicked off the light and edged toward the cabin, feeling her way quietly. Moonlight seeped through the treetops, casting its gray-white shades in pools on the forest floor, flickering when the trees caught a breeze.

She stood for a long moment at the cabin door, listening. Gail wondered if Diane could hear her heart pounding. She thought her eardrums might burst from pressure.

A board creaked as Gail stepped onto the small porch in front of the place. Diane glared at her in the moonlight. Gail froze. She held her breath as Diane tried the front door.

It opened easily enough, but when Diane pushed the door inward it let out a loud whining creak perfectly suited to a horror film. Diane pushed the door forcefully, silencing it, twisted on the penlight and quickly scanned the room. A couple of musty bunks, a small table, a woodstove, a pantry, and some pegs with clothing hanging from them. It didn't smell like anyone had been around recently.

Gail stepped in carefully, her eyes wide, trying to see in the gloom.

"Not even locked," she whispered.

"Nah," Diane said, speaking normally, though it sounded quite loud to Gail. "Locks don't keep thieves out. They just keep honest people honest."

"Except us."

"I don't know about you, but I consider myself to be honest."

"We're breaking and entering, aren't we?"

"Two desperate convicts." Diane said. "In honest need of assistance before those fucking dogs get any closer. Let's move. What's here? Water? A few Band-Aids? Think a couple of hunters would begrudge us that?" Diane went for the cabinet, shined the light in, pushed things around. Metal cans scraping on wood.

"Anyway, the door was open. Looks like beer or prune juice. Name your poison."

"In a minute," Gail said.

"Gail. We don't have a minute."

Gail ignored her and sat down on a bunk, took off her shoe and the even bloodier sock. Diane put down the liquids and approached. Put the light on it.

"Ouch," she said.

"Ouch is right." Gail tried a smile, but her strain was evident.

Diane hurried back to the pantry, came out with a roll of duct tape and a rusted steak knife. She handed the penlight to Gail and began hacking at the duct tape. Took yet another strip from her T-shirt, which was by now cut off midbelly.

Fashioning thin strips from the duct tape, she made butterfly bandages, using bits of T-shirt to cover the center part of each bandage and prevent the tape from contacting the wound. She worked fast, one ear tuned to the outdoors, listening for the hounds.

Gail listened, too, but didn't hear anything. Hadn't for almost ten minutes now.

"Maybe they're lost," she said.

"Maybe they're right outside the door." Diane finished bandaging and saw that the bleeding was slowing; she took the penlight from Gail and returned to the pantry.

She came out with a black spray bottle and a package of what looked like elastic straps with dirty white pads attached to them.

"Oh, yeah," she said. She put the stuff on the table and eyed the clothes hanging on the wall. Gail sat, waiting. Diane turned around slowly, shining the light and eyeing the room carefully, really taking it in for the first time. She aimed the light high in one corner of the room, then darted it across to the other, and along the floor, and back up the wall.

"Gail, look!" she said suddenly.

Gail stared at the spot of light on the blank cedar wall.

"What?" she asked. "What is it?"

The light darted back across and landed on Gail's face.

"Tinkerbell!" Diane laughed and crawled under one of the bunks, banged around on the floor, came back out. Slipped under the other one.

"Here we go!" she said. "I knew they'd have a stash. Nine out of ten homes have a stash."

"What now?" Gail was ready for another prank. She heard wood scraping against wood, and then Diane emerged from under the bunk, pulled herself upright.

She was holding a revolver. A snub-nosed black revolver. And a box of bullets, it looked like.

"Colt," Diane said, admiring.

Gail stared, shook her head no.

"Three-fifty-seven," Diane added. "This'll sure as heck do in a pinch."

"Do what?" Gail asked angrily. "Kill someone?"

"Don't forget," Diane said, winking, "I'm a trained professional."

There was a hint of sarcasm in her tone that made Gail uneasy. Diane didn't take herself seriously enough. For the first time Gail could picture Diane in a uniform, a cop's uniform, with a gun and a radio and handcuffs and all the other crap cops had to carry on their belts. She could picture Diane standing around the station listening to bad cop jokes and war stories. Maybe even telling them.

"Leave it," Gail said.

Diane let the gun drop to her side.

"You're out of your mind," she said. "We've got armed men with dogs after our asses, and they want to take us back to prison, and you're telling me to leave it?"

"What are you gonna do, shoot them?"

Diane cracked open the cylinder and began stuffing bullets into it.

"I'm not sure what I'm gonna do," she said fiercely. "I'm only sure what I'm not gonna do, and that is I'm not gonna let them drag my butt back to jail. It's simple as rain."

They stayed staring at each other, each acutely aware that the dogs were back on track, baying again, that awful hoarse raspiness echoing through the woods. In the distance, but moving in the right direction.

Diane stuffed the gun into her waistband, just in the small of her back, and grabbed a denim jacket from a peg on the wall, slipped it on to cover the gun. She dumped bullets from the box, emptying them into the jacket pockets. She grabbed the elastic straps from the table and fastened them to her shoes, the once-white pads facing away from the soles. She tossed a couple of straps to Gail.

"Put these on," she said.

Gail moved slowly, as though distrustful of Diane's motives. Diane took the black spray bottle from the table and squirted liquid onto the pads on her feet.

"Give me your feet," she said. Gail lifted her feet and Diane sprayed the pads on the soles of her shoes.

"Good God," Gail said, "It smells like a rotten cabbage wearing cheap men's cologne. What is that stuff?"

"Coon urine," Diane said. "Masking scent. Hunters use it. Maybe it'll throw the dogs off." She shone the light on the bottle, turned it over, eyed the back label.

"For hunting use only," she read. "Danger! Do not apply to your body or clothing, you may be attacked." She stuck the bottle in her pants pocket and stood there.

"Diane?" Gail's voice was calm again.

Diane took a deep breath. "Let's go. Let's get out of here while this piss is still wet."

Gail grabbed a camo jacket from a wall peg on the way out, closed the door carefully behind her, and joined Diane near the stream.

"Moon goes same as the sun, right?" Diane was staring at the half-moon through the opening in the tree canopy above the stream.

"If you were the cops and chasing us," Gail said, "which way would you expect us to go?"

"Toward New York City, of course," Diane said. "But then again I might think that you would be thinking that I would be expecting you to head that way, so you'd head the other way just to throw me off, and in that case I'd think you were going north. What'd you have in mind?"

"The city, of course. But we'll take the long way. Let's head north."

"Okay," Diane said. "So which way is north?"

"The moon's still rising, so that's east."

"Okay. So which way is north?"

"Don't you know?"

"As a matter of fact I do," Diane said. "And I can read maps and remember landmarks and do all that kind of shit. I want to know if you know which way is north."

"It hardly matters as long as one of us knows."

"What if we get split up? Or have to split up for some reason?"

"Diane," Gail said, exasperation overcoming exhaustion, "at the moment I'm not capable of thinking that far into the future."

Gail broke into a trot along the stream bank, headed upstream, to the north.

But soon Diane trotted past her, taking the lead and picking up the pace. They ran. Again. And some more. And kept running. Gail tried to think about the stream, the calm of water running close by through the woods. She matched her breathing to her footfalls, as she had all those many years running around the prison track. It was a mental thing now. It had to come from her mind; she had to will her body to keep going when it wanted nothing more than to lie down. Stop. Be still.

They ran. Diane chased the tiny light on the ground in front of her, checked over her shoulder every so often to make sure Gail was okay.

But by the time the moon topped its arc, even will wasn't strong enough; the desire to escape wasn't strong enough; Gail's lungs succumbed and she stopped, bent over, gasping, hands on knees. Diane stopped and turned, took Gail by the arm, and led her over to the stream bank. She was breathing too hard to talk, but signaled Gail to stay where she was. Diane trotted about twenty yards or so from the stream, slipped the masking scent pads from her work boots, and ran in a large circle around a group of white birch trees that glowed ghostlike in the night. She made the loop three times, splitting away every so often and then backtracking, and then, stopping right where she had started, she pulled the bottle of scent from her jacket pocket and refreshed the pads, slipped them back onto her boots and trotted in a wide arc back around to the stream.

By the time she got back, Gail had recovered enough that she was no longer gasping. Still breathing hard, but not like before. Sweat poured down her face. She kept bending to wipe at it with the camo jacket, tied around her waist by the sleeves.

"Give me your straps," Diane said, holding up the bottle of masking scent. Gail handed them over. "Go on across the stream." Gail waded quickly across, hopping from rock to rock to avoid getting her shoes too wet. Diane sprayed the ground where they'd been standing and then leapt onto a rock in the stream, following Gail's path.

On the other side, Diane sprayed the pads again and handed Gail hers, then bent to strap on her own.

And then, from silence, from nowhere: the hounds. Close now, suddenly and irrefutably close, and getting closer. Diane looked up at Gail, nodded toward the woods, and they ran.

All out again, running for their lives, crashing through underbrush that nipped at their arms and legs as they pushed it aside, they trampled it underfoot; it grabbed at their boots, and Diane went down hard and the penlight went flying.

"Motherfucker!" she spat, pulling herself onto all fours, shaking her head to clear it. She crawled over to the light, picked it up, and pulled herself upright. Gail stood watching, panting too hard to be able to talk. She was weak with fear and strong with survival at once; all those seconds within minutes within hours within days within weeks within months within years within almost two godforsaken decades of her life, all that time, that no-beginning, no-end eternity of prison's miserable minutiae, the day-after-day drowning in a hellish bureaucratic maze of rules and regulations and regimentation and what the fuck did the moon look like these days, anyway? When you had a chance to stop and really look at it.

She looked up, and there it was, and then she was running again, chasing Diane, but she could see the moon, the glorious reflection of sunlight, the silence of it, the smile on its face, as if it knew a delicious secret that Gail could only guess at.

She ran, and from somewhere came a surge of strength; her breath came easier now, and she was light on her feet again, because she had to be.

How much later? A few seconds, an hour, an eon? Diane stopped, bent over, panting. Gail rested her hands on her thighs and tried to catch her breath. Diane took a deep breath and held it, trying to listen. Gail did likewise. It was good. They'd made time on the hounds; the baying was farther in the distance now, and it sounded like the dogs were off track, heading off at some weird angle into another part of the woods.

Diane smiled at Gail and nodded, took off running again.

Gail wished she had sneakers on instead of work boots. They were getting heavy.

She ran. She felt as though her lungs would explode soon if she didn't let them rest. She ran.

NINE

A bed of pine needles at the edge of a woods. Below, unlit highway: blacktop two lanes wide, a double yellow stripe down the middle warning drivers not to pass other vehicles. Farmland and woodlands on either side.

They sat, resting. Breathing quietly. An occasional car whizzed by, headlights glazing the blacktop gray. Diane didn't give them a second look, but to Gail the vehicles seemed small and rounded. It felt good to sit, breath normally, though the insides of her lungs felt dry, like a sponge left unused for days. She could feel the lactic acid building in her muscles. She'd be lucky if she could move tomorrow.

Diane lay back on the ground, resting her head on her arms.

"We got to move, you know."

"A few more minutes."

"How's the cut?"

"Bearable. I guess." Gail felt it throbbing, but numbed. Like someone had shot a dose of lidocaine in there. She couldn't believe she was sitting in the free world, and that the sprint away from the prison and the nightlong run for freedom had worked. So far. She was giddy with escape, but not optimistic. Diane seemed to be taking it all in as though a prison break was something you did every Thursday at five-thirty, like an aerobics class. Gail felt she would have to watch Diane, not let her confidence turn into something dangerous. The girl was on a mission, anger and zeal her worst enemies. But Diane had been there, no doubt about that. There'd been nothing to stop her from leaving Gail far behind once they were outside the walls, but she'd stuck true.

And it would come in handy to have an ex-cop around until things got way cooler. Until Gail Elizabeth Rubin and Sarah Diane Wellman were just names on paperwork somewhere in a file at the U.S. Marshals Service. Or maybe it was it all computerized now. Diane knew the ropes that could well be hangman's nooses to Gail.

"How long do you think they'll chase us?"

Diane sat up, stared out across the road.

"How long'd they chase you last time?"

"I don't know how long they were on to us. But they chased till they caught me," Gail said. "There had to be a rat. They knew exactly where we were and what we were holding."

"Ever find out who it was?"

Gail shook her head no. "I personally didn't try to. Some others did, but no one ever came up with anything."

Diane nodded, eyeing Gail.

"I'm sure the boys back at Sundown will be plenty pissed that a couple of females got over on them."

Gail tried to summon Tom Firestone's face to her memory. It wouldn't come. She could see his muscular build, she could see his shaggy brown hair and the beard he often wore, but his facial features were a blur. She wondered where he'd gone when they released him, what it had felt like for him as he walked out the front gate at Lewisburg, if he'd thought about the fact that she was still locked up even though they'd been convicted of the exact same crime.

"We get some hot dog on our case looking to make a name, he'll stay with it until he catches us." Diane looked like she wanted to hit something. "Or confirms we're dead," she added.

"You mean someone like you?" Gail sighed.

"I was never a hotshot," Diane said. "Some people even thought of me as a fuckup. But I didn't consider myself that either. Not really." She sighed. "At least those dogs are off our ass," she said. "That's a big improvement." The dogs had been left running in circles, she presumed, around that clump of birch trees she'd marked. Thank the Lord she'd made herself go hunting when her brother asked her along that time or two. She'd felt all jittery the first time she'd taken the shotgun Kevin offered and blasted away at a flock of ducks taken flight, and she felt stunned and surprised and not a little bit awful when one actually fell out of the sky and thunked dead to the ground. But they took it home and ate it so that made it seem not so bad. In fact, after she thought about it for a while, she'd decided it was a lot more legitimate than strolling up to the re-frigerated case at the Tom Thumb Grocery and choosing something wrapped in plastic and Styrofoam and pumped full of color. She'd liked the gamey taste, though Kevin had showed her how he soaked the duck overnight in milk to take some of that wild flavor out. Then wrapped it in bacon to soften the meat. "Bite into a duck and it'll snap right back at you, tough as a rubber band," he'd said. That time and one other were the only times she'd hunted. When Renfro tried to get her to go with him, she told him she'd rather hose down the drunk tank than shoot another animal. He'd picked her up and thrown her on the bed and called her a sissy, but by the time she was done with him, he floated out the front door of her air-conditioned, fully carpeted apartment on wobbly legs.

He had come back over next night and made venison stew before heading out to work the deep night shift.

"Come on," Diane said to Gail. "I'm just sittin' here mak-ing myself hungry. Or hungrier." She groaned as she pulled herself up.

Gail struggled to her feet. They stood there looking at the highway.

"I'm not hungry," Diane said. "I'm starving. Know any-thing about foraging?"

"I know how to spell it."

"I heard if you were really in a switch for food, you could eat acorns."

Gail stared at her. "It's not like we're stranded in the middle of the Sahara. Take a look." She pointed down the embankment to the roadway. "I can tell you from right here that we are within a couple of miles of a McDonald's. Where there's trash, there are humans."

"Dunkin' Donuts, too, from the looks of it. And a Sonic Drive-In. I didn't know they had Sonics in New York. God, could I go for a chili dog right now."

"For breakfast?"

"Hell, yes. I'm so hungry I can't think." Diane started off and Gail fell in next to her. "They say the stomach and the brain are intimately connected, you know."

"I wonder what it's done to my brain that my stomach has been deprived of anything even approximating real food for eighteen years now."

"I'll tell you this. One Sonic chili dog would cure all your ills."

"I don't eat anything that has eyes."

"Since when do hot dogs have eyes?"

They walked what they thought was north, but after the mad run to get away from the hounds, and with the moon down and the sun not yet showing any kind of glow in any particular direction, they couldn't be sure. The woods lasted a good half hour before turning into a large field of corn that stretched almost to the road. It must have been planted early, to be so tall this soon in the season. They stood for a moment at its edge, feeling the vulnerability that would accompany being out in the open.

"It's a big old world out there, isn't it?" Diane turned to Gail, only half kidding. Finally they moved from the protective cover of the woods, skirting the field, slipping in between the rows whenever a car passed. They were halfway along the edge of it when they had to duck in for a long line of cars, each riding the bumper of the one in front, one after the other. It was dark and green among the stalks, and the narrow rows still held the cool of evening.

Gail grabbed an ear of corn and snapped it from the stalk, sat down, peeled back the husk and bit in. Diane watched, and then ripped an ear off a stalk and began yanking back the husk. She bit in fiercely, and the crisp sweetness surprised her. It was almost like eating fruit, it was so sweet.

"I've never had it without butter and salt," she said. "And now, I'm just realizing, seriously overboiled."

"One of the perks of working landscape," Gail said, "you learn how to eat just about anything raw."

"I thought you learned that just from being in jail, let alone landscape."

Gail smiled, watched Diane's face shimmer from the strobe of headlights cutting rapid-fire between the leaves of the corn rows. She turned to look down at the cars zipping past. "God," she said, "I'd forgotten how fast things move out here. Forgot what it's like to be in a hurry."

"Speaking of which."

"Yeah."

Diane reached for another ear of corn and Gail saw the flash of the pistol in Diane's waistband.

"Diane."

Diane turned, eyebrows raised. She looked like a teenager almost, and the expression on her face was full of innocent curiosity.

"The gun. We should get rid of it."

Diane peeled her corn. Shook her head no. "There are things I'll trust you on, and there are things you got to trust me on. This one's my call." She snugged the gun into her waistband, punctuating her sentence.

"Look, it's like I said, I was never one of those hot dog cops who can't wait to get into some shit. I probably wouldn't even have stayed one, even if all this craziness hadn't come up. But right now, with the situation we're in, we need it. Or at least I need it. I'm trained. I'm careful. And I'm not looking to hurt anyone. Okay?"

Gail grabbed another ear of corn. "It only took me the first eight years of my sentence to figure out that any kind of killing is bad."

"Who the hell's talking about killing? I got no desire whatsoever to kill anyone. But, for God's sake, if we wind up with somebody close on our ass, it's a very effective aid to making them go away fast. Especially if they're busting caps at us. Which is a possibility. Or hadn't you considered that? You think those cops with those dogs wouldn't've shot us all to pieces if they got half a chance? This is for real, Gail. You of all people should know that."

"Live by the sword, die by the sword." It was a pathetically inadequate argument, but the only one she could come up with, because she knew that in terms of realpolitik, Diane was exactly right.

"I'm not living by it. I'm using it—strictly for self-defense—until I don't need it anymore. Let's go."

Gail followed, but she wasn't ready to give in. "It's like, if you don't have the tool, you'll find another way to get the job done," she said. "If you don't have the gun, you'll find another way out of whatever situation it is you're imagining you'll need it in."

"I'm not imagining anything. We're wanted, girlfriend. We are prison escapees. We are the enemy of the law. And what we need is the ability to keep the heat off our asses. It's just that simple."

"How do you know? We've obviously lost them already. Maybe we'll successfully disappear and live out our lives and—"

"Wait!" Diane stopped, put a shushing finger to her lips. "I hear something." She stood, listening intently, for a long moment. She let her hand drop to her side and let out a long sigh. "Sorry," she said, "it was only Prince Charming. Probably on his way to see Cinderella." She turned and resumed the pace, that of a brisk hike. "What floors me," she added, "is how in the fuck you can have even one iota of optimism left after all that time in that place."

"If I didn't, I wouldn't have survived it," Gail said. "That's what keeps you going. That or hatred and the desire for revenge, which I found I could not live with."

"Anyway, you can't lump it all into one ball." Diane turned, slowed her pace until Gail was at her side again. "Killing. What about the difference between just plain murder and, say, a mercy killing. Like one time I had to shoot a horse that had gone through some lady's windshield, just this time of morning. Poor thing's guts were strewn all over, his head landed draped over the steering wheel, but he was still alive and let me tell you he was suffering. The lady was already en route to the hospital, and this one traffic cop was standing there just staring at the wreckage, waving traffic by. I shot that horse soon as I saw what was going on. And I'm sure he was thankful. Relieved him of his misery. I just hope he appreciated the shit-load of paperwork I had to do for discharging my firearm. Probably why the traffic cop waited and let me do the honors."

"That was a horse. What if the lady driving had been suffering? You wouldn't have offed her, would you?"

"Of course not. All she had was some broken teeth, and I'd get charged with murder. But it might be, that if I knew she was a goner and she was suffering slow torture on the way out . . ."

Gail looked at Diane, shocked, and then saw the sly smile and realized Diane was kidding.

"Very funny."

"No, it's true, I agree with you: Thou shalt not kill. But what are you supposed to do? Sit there and let somebody do you in and not raise a fist to them? Maybe if you're Gandhi. But I'm not. Somebody jumps hot at me, I'm coming right back at them. I'd even thought about working homicide someday."

"Why on earth anybody wants to chase psychopaths and poke around dead bodies is beyond me entirely."

"Somebody's got to. Anyway, I think it's interesting as all get-out. And I guess I feel like, you know, justice should be done."

"Ah, justice. What a concept. Were you one of those cops who thought God was on their side?"

"Hardly. The creeps who framed me claimed God for their side." Diane smiled or grimaced or did something in between, Gail couldn't tell which.

"DA even preaches every fourth Sunday at the First Baptist Church. Heard him myself once or twice. Not that I'm a churchgoer, but I'd heard about him and was curious. Hellfire and brimstone, and quite the delivery. Good preacher, but one hell of a hypocrite."

Gail walked silently; Diane's sudden vehemence had unnerved her. She was numb from lack of sleep. They would have to find somewhere to crash, and soon.

And then, here came the sun. She watched it crest the ridge in the distance and was overcome with a feeling she could not exactly name, melting away her fear and filling her with something she hadn't felt in forever. Something like joy, maybe. It had been such a long time since anything so positive had suffused her being. Joy. She was not in a gray concrete cage somewhere, wishing she could sleep through another day. Joy. Just at walking along in the countryside, at being, at breathing, at blinking her eyes and looking again at the stunning beauty of the sunrise.

They'd passed only a couple of houses, rural poor, and now were nearing a ramshackle car radiator repair shop. Diane glanced at Gail and fell into a trot, leading Gail around behind the place, her eyes scanning the area. Not a soul. She eased up to the back door, moving quietly and with brisk authority. Gail stood staring as Diane rattled the back doorknob, then pressed against the wood of the door, as though testing its density.

"Locked." Diane took a step back, looked around quickly and kicked hard, planting her boot just next to the knob. The lock splintered loose, the door popped open, slammed against an interior wall, and swung back. Diane rushed in. Gail found herself staring at the doorway, not believing what she'd just seen.

"Get in here!" Diane hissed loudly. Gail did.

Diane was at the front display case, had it opened and was pulling out a couple of T-shirts and a canvas carryall. She checked the register. Empty.

"Are you out of your mind?" Gail stood, her arms hanging at her sides, her ankle throbbing again.

"People are gonna be going to work soon, it's now or never. Just chalk it up to necessity and move on." Diane was all business, looking around the place for anything else that might be useful. Gail only nodded, figuring it best to choose her battles. Diane tossed her a shirt.

"Time for a change of clothes," she said. She pulled the

denim jacket from her waist, and then the gun. She wrapped the gun in the jacket and stuffed it into the canvas bag. She pulled on her new blue T-shirt, stood waiting while Gail slipped into a red one. On the front emblazoned in bright yellow lettering: Bob's Radiator Shop—The Best Place to Take a Leak.

Gail rolled up the camo jacket, and Diane held out the canvas bag.

"One sec," Diane said, and disappeared into the bathroom. She came out with a first aid kit, the white plastic smudged with greasy black fingerprints. "Let's get a real bandage on that thing."

They sat on the floor and Gail watched as Diane removed the duct tape from Gail's ankle.

"It's looking okay," Diane said. "It's looking not half bad." She smeared some antibiotic ointment on it, and then wrapped it expertly in gauze and sealed it with bandage tape. Then she pulled off her socks and held them out to Gail. "Sorry about the sweat," she said. "But you can't keep wearing this." She held up Gail's bloodied sock, looked around the room. "Give me your other one." Gail removed her sock and gave it to Diane, who wadded up the bloodied one and stuffed it inside the clean one before stuffing it in the canvas bag with their tattered T-shirts. Gail sat looking at Diane's socks.

"I can't take these. You need them."

"I'm not hurt," Diane said. "You need 'em worse. Put them on, and let's get the hell out of here before some sorry-ass decides to come fix a radiator." Gail pulled on the socks and replaced her boots. Diane struggled into hers, wet leather against feet that were swollen from running since she could remember. She ignored the pain as she laced on the boots. Fuck it. Right now they needed a ride, and they needed it soon, before the news of a couple of escaped female convicts at large made it to the radios and TVs and Internet.

She led the way back out to the highway, and they walked quickly down the road, putting a couple of miles between them and Bob's Radiator before they stopped and crossed the road to the southbound side. Gail heard traffic approaching and stuck out her thumb. A van shot past, something about plumbing painted on the side.

Gail heard a car approaching and stuck out her thumb again. It hurtled past, its air wake blasting at them.

Diane walked over.

"Maybe I should try."

"You ever hitched?"

"Nope."

"What makes you think you'll be good at it?"

Diane rolled her eyes and shook her head. "Like it takes some special skill to stand on the side of the road and stick your thumb out? Call me Little Jack Horner and stand aside."

Gail understood then and stepped back, walked over to the signpost, pretending to be engrossed by the black-and-white state highway 209 sign. Of course Diane would have more luck. She was young. She was good-looking. And she had a reckless air about her that was as apt to invite trouble as it was to invite fun. Gail could almost see herself in Diane, herself carefree—or was it careless—all those years ago. She'd hitched all over the Southwest during her sophomore year at the University of Oklahoma. Even ventured to take a poetry writing workshop with Professor Matlin, whose favorite subject turned out to be the rage of the southern woman. Something about having to stand up on that pedestal and be treated with such politesse, or at least politeness, and all the while not being considered a full and complete human being with things like rights and freedom and a fully functioning brain, seemed to put the belles into a very bad mood. Couldn't even inherit Daddy's property, silly girls.

What was she talking about? She'd never been carefree. She was the serious sort, spent the semester trying to imagine herself a southern girl and writing some pretty awful poetry from that persona. Though the art of the line break and the nuance of language eluded her—she thought her poems pathetic, sometimes even bathetic—she had the anger part down. So much was going down: Reagan hit the White House and sprang the Iranian hostages minutes after taking the oath of office, Big Oil was back in the saddle, El Salvador tripped from the tongues of newscasters, AIDS sprang up, Bob Marley died (or was killed, who knew?). Gail had been up on things, she'd been onto America's malfeasance, she'd been ready to change the world.

The sound of a very large vehicle coming to a very sudden stop, its brakes howling like a trumpet mating with a tuba, yanked Gail from her reverie, and she looked up to see a large dump truck pulling toward the side of the road. You call, we haul! was painted on the green cab door in bright yellow. Diane was enthusiastically giving the driver two thumbs up, practically jumping up and down. She glanced over her shoulder at Gail and signaled her to come on.

The truck came to a stop, and the passenger-side door swung open.

"Where you headed?"

Diane didn't hesitate. "Where *you* headed?"

"NYC."

"That's exactly where we're headed." She flashed a smile at the driver. He nodded his okay.

"It'll be tight, girls, but I think we can manage." The driver looked to Gail like he'd got stuck in 1968. Long scraggly hair, beard, headband. T-shirt and Levi's. She remembered being in middle school and seeing the hippies hanging out in Town Park, with their Army-Navy bell-bottoms and beads and leather thong braided into headbands and necklaces and bracelets. Peace symbols and tie-dye everywhere. And her mother's half-frightened, half-intrigued looks as they drove past the park and the hippies smiled at the big powder-blue Cadillac cruising by. He had that same kind of stoner smile the hippies used to have and friendly eyes. Gail looked up at the cramped cab, stepped back and let Diane go first. Diane climbed up into the passenger seat, and Gail squeezed in after her. The seat wasn't made for two; it wasn't even made for a large one. Diane wound up perched half on Gail's lap as Gail locked the passenger door and pressed herself against it to give them each as much room as possible.

"Name's Mike," the driver said. "Gonna make it there?"

"Sure," Diane said. "We've been in tight spots before." Gail pinched her in the side. "You ever see a contortionist?" Diane continued as though she'd felt nothing. "They aren't around much anymore, but I saw one once at a circus that came through town back when I was a kid."

Mike looked to be listening with one ear, focused on his side-view mirror as he took the big truck through its gears and eased back out onto 209.

"There was this guy had himself all folded up into a glass case not much bigger than the aquarium I kept my Chinese fighters in. His legs all warped up around his shoulders, his arms and head tucked up under him. Incredible."

Mike shook his head. "Don't think I ever saw one of those. I'm not big on the circus anyway. I feel sorry for the elephants."

"I know what you mean," Diane said. "Myself, I'm an animal lover."

"You're not from around here," Mike said. He smiled. "You got the South in your mouth, girl."

"Louisiana," Diane said. "But not lately." Gail was impressed with how easily the lie rolled off Diane's tongue.

"That don't sound like a Louisiana accent to me. I've traveled. Used to haul rice out of Texas. That's where I'd say you're from."

"You ever been to Louisiana?" Anger, or maybe it was nerves, seemed to be creeping into Diane's voice. A minute earlier Gail had thought Diane was going to wind up being asked to dinner by Mike, and now it was turning sour fast.

"No," Mike said, "but I know it's a different accent than Texas."

"Never been to Monroe, Louisiana?"

"I told you already, no." Now he seemed to be getting miffed.

"Well, ask anybody you like," Diane said vehemently. "It can be mighty hard to tell one from the other. I'm just sure you're thinking about southern Louisiana, about New Orleans territory." There was something threatening in Diane's demeanor. Gail couldn't place it at first, didn't realize where she'd seen it before. And then Johnson popped to mind, with his swagger and piercing eyes, and she realized that it was that attitude that cops have in dangerous situations, where they give off an aura of absolute authority, where they know—and they expect you to know—that whatever the situation, they're going to come out on top. Before she'd got to prison, Gail had believed it had something to do with carrying a gun, but Johnson had it even though the guards didn't carry weapons.

Why Diane was suddenly getting all nervous now, after what they'd been through in the last nineteen or so hours—if you counted that steak dinner in the Big Yard—was a mystery to Gail. But whatever it was, she had to break the mood.

She reached out and turned on the radio. The high beautiful nasal twang of Jimmy Dale Gilmore filled the cab. Mike shifted in his seat, kicked back to concentrate on driving instead of on the testy little thing sitting so close to him. Diane turned up the volume and joined in, her voice rising with the song.

". . . although she shared his love of duty . . ."

"You like him?" Diane asked Mike. Mike nodded, kept driving, Diane turned to Gail. "I guess you never heard of him?"

"I prefer R&B," Gail said, "or rap. You know, the kind of rap where the black male artiste spends the whole song grabbing his crotch and spouting off about mowing people down with automatic weapons and getting rich as fast as you can so you can get lots of bitches and slap them around, yo. That's my kind of music."

Mike chuckled, shook his head. "Yeah," he said, happy to be in on a joke. "Me, too. Where you girls headed?"

"The city," Gail said.

"You two work at Bob's? Where's Bob's?" He leaned over to read Diane's shirt.

Gail didn't know where Bob's was, didn't know what podunk town they'd been at the edge of when Diane kicked in the door to the place. She felt Mike looking at her but pretended she hadn't heard him over the music.

"Just back down the road a ways," Diane said. "Place is a dump, ask me. But we don't work there. That's where we had to leave my car, and I collect T-shirts. I should've known better than to ever buy a Gremlin."

"Gremlin?" Mike guffawed. "Hell, it must have almost a million miles on it by now."

"Damn near," Diane said. "Though I'm sure the sleaze-butt dealer I bought it from diddled with the odometer. Anyway, I thought it would get me and Linda here up to the Catskills and back. We been camping. Man this is beautiful country. But I'm sure ready for a shower."

"I didn't want to say anything," Mike said, winking at her.

"I guess we'll have to take the bus back up whenever Bob gets around to fixin' the thing. It didn't sound like it was anything going to happen immediately."

"What about your gear?"

"Gear?"

"Your camping stuff."

"He said he'd keep an eye on it. Don't get me wrong. I trust the guy. I just don't think he's in a hurry to work on my car."

"Hell, a Gremlin, who would be?" He smiled at Diane and she smiled back and things were okay again.

"Wanna let me try this thing?"

"What thing? This truck?"

"Yeah. I'll betcha I can drive it."

Mike laughed and shook his head. "I don't doubt it for one minute. But there's liability issues, you know?"

"You don't have any water, do you?" she said, nodding her acceptance and settling again in the seat, trying to get comfortable.

"Back behind you, behind the seat there. There's a six-pack of Poland Spring. Help yourselves." Diane reached around and got a couple of bottles and gave one to Gail. She tried not to gulp it straight down, but it was difficult not to.

"I'm just plain parched," she said.

"Well, if you drink all the water," Mike said, "I got plenty of beer." He winked again, and Diane smiled sweetly, though she was thinking that if she met this guy in a bar, she wouldn't even ask him for directions.

Gail stared out the window, watching trees and fields roll by. You had to hand it to her, Diane was cool. And she was a good liar, seemingly totally at home with the ability to deceive. She saw Mike glancing over at Diane, reevaluating, perhaps trying to come up with a new angle of attack. Obviously he was interested in her. But he seemed unsure of how to proceed.

Diane folded her arms across her chest and closed her eyes, leaned her head back as much as she could in her cramped position.

The *Intrepid*, with its fighter planes on deck and tourists swarming about. The tugboat-looking red and green and white craft of the Circle Line, resting on the waters of the Hudson. And that blank space in the sky where the towers of the World Trade Center once stood. That day had been one of the few times, maybe the only time in the course of her eighteen years inside, when Gail was actually relieved to be in prison. It seemed like one of the safest places in the country to be, and probably was. What enemy of the state was going to attack the people who'd already been adjudged to be enemies of society?

Traffic was slow on the West Side Highway. Gail drank it all in, the sights, the smells; it had been eons. Every cell in her body was alive to it; it was almost as if she were breathing through her skin. Man. She was outside, she was on the outside, she was free. The city was hot and smelly, and she was taking in lungfuls of exhaust, and people were everywhere, people who had no idea how lucky they were to be walking the streets without some hack yelling at them to do this or do that, nobody there to command lights out or summon them to the captain's office.

Mike drove intently, looking for something, it seemed to Gail. She knew this road, and knew he shouldn't be on it—commercial traffic forbidden—but he'd said he felt lucky and curved around onto the exit when it was too late for protest from Diane or Gail. And so far his luck had held. But Gail wasn't sure he wanted his luck to hold. She wondered if he were trying to get pulled over. She wondered if he knew. He made a turn onto Twenty-sixth-Street and gave Diane and Gail a weak smile: home free.

Diane smiled right back at him and then Gail got a seriously bad feeling.

They were approaching Tenth Avenue when Diane pulled

the gun out of her bag and stuck it against Mike's ribs. She was cooler than cool, she was ready to use the weapon, and everybody there knew it.

"Park there," she said. Mike took a second look, but that was all he needed to know she wasn't open to discussion. He eased the truck to the curb in front of a warehouse and rested his hands in his lap.

"Do what you need to," he fairly whispered. "I don't want trouble."

"I'm real sorry," Diane said. Sincere. "You do like I say, and everything'll be swell." Inside she was scared out of her mind because she knew that if he tested her, she'd either have to shoot him or give up, and she knew he didn't deserve any of this trouble, but, goddamn, they had to get away. They just had to make it out of there, that was all, and if it meant she had to shoot the motherfucker, she would, only she would try really hard not to kill him but just to wound him enough to make him back off and let them go.

"I knew who you were already," he said. "I heard it on the radio."

"And you picked us up anyway."

"No. I picked you up before I figured it out. And then it was too late, wasn't it?"

Diane nodded. "There's no reason for anyone to get hurt here."

Mike held out his wrists as Diane strapped them together with what was left of the roll of duct tape.

"We appreciate the ride anyway," Diane said. "It was good of you." She strapped his ankles together and laid him out across the front seat, positioning him so the gearshift didn't dig into his back.

"We could keep going," he said. "I could drive you."

Diane looked out to where Gail was standing on the curb, glancing up and down the street, worrying.

"He wants to come with us," she said.

Gail stared up at Diane and jerked her head sharply to the left, like, let's go now.

"I'm really sorry about this," Diane said to Mike, and laid a strip of tape across his mouth. That was the first time he looked pissed, and she was feeling so guilty she didn't look twice at him before jumping down out of the cab and hustling east on Twenty-sixth, trotting after Gail, who was so angry she couldn't even speak.

"Where are we going?" Diane finally asked.

"To a pay phone," Gail answered. "If you promise not to shoot it."

"I wouldn't have shot him," Diane said.

"Coulda fooled me."

"Well, that's just the thing. You got to be believable or it won't work, and you'll wind up having to pull the damn trigger. It's gotta be real."

"Oh, it was way past real. I thought you were gonna kill him."

"Gail! I would not have shot him."

"You're a fucking maniac."

"Well, hey, sweetheart, we can just part ways here if that's what you're into. I mean, give me a fucking break. This isn't a goddamn fourth-grade field trip."

Gail marched in silence, Diane at her side. They headed south on Seventh Avenue, nobody taking a second look at two women in matching Bob's T-shirts and steel-toed boots. Gail sucked in the smells, the heat rising off the concrete, the aromas from the street vendors: hot dogs and sugar-soaked nuts and pretzels, it was intoxicating even in spite of the fear.

"How's your cut?" Diane finally asked.

"Hurts like hell, but there's no need to make conversation."

"I'm not. Do we need to stop?"

"For what?"

"Medical attention?" Her voice was rising. "There's a walk-in place right over across the street."

"Let's just get there."

"Where is there?"

"Close. Chill."

"No problem," Diane said. "You wanna be like that? Be like that. If I care. I don't even really fucking know you."

"Ain't that the truth." Gail ducked into a phone booth and deposited a quarter. Thank God, she'd brought the last of her coin money with her. Thank God, the prison only let you have quarters. Thank God, she didn't have to go inside a store and ask for change, or panhandle on the street. Thank God, Mike hadn't gotten shot.

Mel answered on the first ring.

"Where to?" was all Gail said.

"212–555–4776. In ten." Mel hung up.

She exited and nodded for Diane to follow. They headed east on Twenty-third, not uttering so much as a word, walking past bargain shops, restaurants, and apartment buildings.

"Food," Diane said.

"You got money?"

"Nope."

"All I have is enough to make a couple more phone calls. But we'll be there soon enough."

When Gail thought ten minutes had passed, she ducked into another phone booth. Diane looked after her, questioning, and then remembered the bloody socks in her bag and discreetly tossed them into a trash container near the phone booth, slam-dunking them so they went in deep.

Gail dialed the number. Mel again, this time at a pay phone.

"Me," Gail said.

"Seventy-eight Gramercy Park East," he said. "Cohen. Three-B." Again, he hung up.

The doorman raised his nose at them, but rang up and directed them to the elevator. As they rose slowly toward the third floor, Diane fingered the mahogany trim inside. "Kinda high-dollar for a bunch of Communists, isn't it?"

"Lawyer," Gail said. "He's my lawyer."

"Yeah, but isn't he a Communist lawyer? Aren't you a revolutionary? Shouldn't he be living in, I don't know, some kind of working-class place or something?"

"He works. And no, I'm not a revolutionary. But to answer your questions, this isn't his place."

"Whose is it?"

"We're functioning on a need-to-know basis right now, okay?"

Diane nodded like she understood, but Gail could tell she was hurt.

Then, as they exited the elevator, Diane stopped. "You don't even know, do you?"

"Now you're getting it."

At the door to 3B, Mel Schaap hurried them inside, closed the door, and then grabbed Gail in a bear hug, rocking back and forth in obvious delight, his face showing love and appreciation and gratitude, his smile sublime.

"God," he said. "I can't believe it."

Diane watched, half surprised that Mel wasn't in a suit. He had on khakis and a light blue button-down shirt, the sleeves rolled to three-quarters length. She couldn't imagine what it must feel like to have that kind of love coming at you. Mel broke off the embrace with Gail, and his eyes fell on Diane. There was a flash of something distrustful, but quickly covered. Diane said nothing. She'd never been on this side of the law. Go with your gut, she reminded herself. In situations like this, first impressions are everything.

"Come in," he said. "Come in. You two look perfectly awful. Like you just blew out of prison or something."

He showed them to the parlor, as there actually was still a parlor in the apartment. Gail took a seat next to Diane, on a couch. A soft, comfortable place to sit. It was heavenly. Some kind of heavy cotton upholstery. Pale green, almost the color of an olive. There was a fan in the middle of the ceiling, turning slowly, taking its time, making a gentle breeze in the room. The windows were open, and Gail heard cars passing outside, bits of conversation floating up from the sidewalks as people strolled down the street on a summer evening. The ceilings were high, the apartment a prewar.

"Can I get you something?" Mel asked. "A glass of wine perhaps?"

"A shower," Gail said. "A shower would be sublime."

"I'd like some food," Diane said.

He looked at Gail. "Follow me."

Once in the bathroom, with the door locked—by her choice—and the feel of cool, clean tile against her bare feet,

Gail let the tears come. She was hungry, too, but food could wait. The thing she wanted most in the world right now was to be alone. She let the tears fall silently. Not that she was sad or confused or frightened, though she was all of those things, but the tears were of relief. Relief at the first real experience of privacy and comfort in eighteen years. Nobody down the hall screaming, no fear that a hack would show up and order her to the captain's office, no worry that someone was going to try to brace her when she went to chow. Privacy. Her own little space in a crowded world, even if it was a borrowed space. She sat on the toilet and carefully peeled off the bandage. Diane had done a good job, but the wound was still open. Congealed blood filled the space between the torn edges of her skin. Probably she should keep it dry, but forget about that, she was going to take a shower.

The warmth of the water flowing over her skin was nothing short of bliss. She took some shampoo and lathered her hair, took some soap and lathered her body. She couldn't believe how civilized it felt, to be cleansing herself alone instead of in a gang shower with six other women. The little things; that was it about prison, it was all the little things you lost that made it so hellish. The soap smelled of lavender. In prison the hardcore disinfectant disguised as soap smelled something like Lysol. She stood and let the water run over her, rinsing slowly, luxuriously. She was safe here, though it was temporary. She knew it. Mel was a rock.

But in the back of her mind was a waterfall of thought, small, inconspicuous, but there, slipping along just inside her skull, quietly, over and over: What am I going to do now? What next, what next, what next?

Out in the parlor, Diane was unnerved at being in the hands of the enemy. She thought back to her swearing-in ceremony, when she'd stood with the other recruits and raised her right hand and swore to protect and defend, among all the local interests listed in the oath, the Constitution of the United States of America. Aside from having memorized that part at the beginning, We the People of the United States, in Order to form a more perfect Union, establish Justice, insure domestic

Tranquility, et cetera, et cetera for some junior high school class, and of course studying the various amendments that had some bearing on street-level law enforcement, the search and seizure one and the speedy trial one, Diane hadn't actually been exposed to a great deal of the Constitution. But she did not doubt that she was in some way failing to defend it by hooking up with Gail's crew—a network of radicals. And then again, she no longer had any legal obligation to do so. They had kicked her off the force, they had used, or rather abused, the law to put her in jail, they were as much her enemy now as they were Gail's. Even though Gail didn't seem to think of them as the enemy anymore. It was like she'd been going through a phase as a teenager and had grown out of it. All she seemed to want to do was blend in: find a place to live and get a job and become part of a community. Diane couldn't imagine. The idea of shopping for groceries was enough to send her over the edge, and not the kind of edge she wanted or needed in her life. Things had to be interesting. Exciting. Sometimes dangerous. Diane liked that. She thrived on it. Give me a Taco Bell burrito grande and a car chase—to go.

Mel came back with a plate loaded with a variety of cheeses and crackers, which he placed on the coffee table in front of Diane. He returned with grapes and two goblets of white wine. "Pinot grigio all right?"

"Perfect." Whatever that was. But if he was drinking it, it was probably decent. What did she know about wine? The house wine at the Chase. Some kind of cabaret something-or-other that she'd only had once because its color reminded her vaguely of the cough syrup she'd had as a kid. Diane nodded, took a long sip of wine—it was good—and took up a cracker and cheese knife.

"I feel like I been rode hard and put up wet," she said between mouthfuls. God, she was hungry. She hoped he'd come up with a real dinner, not just the snacks. Mel looked at her quizzically. "Like, when you ride a horse," she explained, "really ride him, you got to walk him around, cool him off before you put him back in the stall. Put him up while he's still sweaty and he'll get all stove-up and muscle-sore and everything. That's how I feel right now. We been runnin' since I can't remember."

"Incredible," Mel said. "I can't imagine." He had a soft voice with a slight nasality to it, as though he were just coming down with a cold.

"I can't, either, and I just did it," Diane said. She shoveled in another bite. She tried a smile, and Mel tried one back.

"How exactly did you get out?"

Diane ran down the details of the escape, punctuating her sentences with bites of cheese and cracker. Telling it brought it back vividly; by the time she finished her recounting, she was exhausted all over again, but wound up, too.

"So the truck driver," Mel said, "you left him on Twenty-sixth?"

Diane nodded.

"That means he's probably already talking to the cops. We have to move quickly."

Diane stopped midbite, looking around as if she expected the door to blow open.

"I think he's probably still incapacitated," she said. "I taped him up pretty good. I felt bad for him, but it had to be done."

"But we can expect him to be talking to the cops before too much longer, right?"

"You never know. He might just decide to mind his own business."

"What do you think?"

"I really couldn't say. He didn't seem like a bad dude. Could be he's got a little pot in the truck, or speed. You know those truck drivers, they live on that stuff. He might not be in a hurry to have an encounter with the law."

"I think he's gonna call the cops."

"Yeah," Diane said. "So do I. Guess I was just hoping."

She didn't quite know how to take him.

"So if you're a New York City lawyer, tell me. Where's your shiny suit? Where's your pointy-toed shoes?" She smiled to show him she was kidding, just in case he missed it.

"I save those for court," he said. "This I do for recreation."

He smiled back, mimicking her smile it seemed to her. She wasn't sure he was happy with her attempt to break the ice.

She looked at the floor, thinking about the hotshots she'd gone up against in the courtroom in Breard County. But even though Mel was a lawyer, he seemed like a pretty nice guy. She stood and walked over to the window, looked out at the park. People walked designer dogs and pushed chi-chi strollers holding babies in designer clothing. They all seemed so . . . together, so . . . at home. Diane soaked it all in, feeling rather like a character in a virtual reality game, a collection of lit pixels on someone's video display terminal. She wished Gail would hurry up.

"Have you made plans?" Mel asked.

"No," she said. "Shoot, I didn't even know where we were going until we got here. And now I don't know where I am."

Mel smiled. "You're safe here," he said.

Diane nodded. "Thank you for that."

"Gail didn't mention that there would be anyone with her. I was a bit taken aback."

"It happened kind of suddenly," Diane said. "I mean, don't think she was planning to take me, but she couldn't have got out of there alone. Not the way we did it." She sat back down, looked at Mel earnestly. "Not to brag," she said, "but Gail was lucky to have brought me along."

"I gather," Mel said.

"You don't have to worry about me," Diane said, "though I guess I might as well get it over with and tell you I used to be a cop. Before I got framed."

He didn't even blink. "Well, I knew her new cellmate was a cop. She told me on the phone. But I appreciate your honesty. How did you come to be a police officer?"

Diane took another sip. "Stumbled into it, I guess. I was thinking about law school."

"Really? So it's not like your father or mother or uncles were into it and you followed in their footsteps."

"God, please, no. If there's one thing I don't want to do in life it's follow in either of my parents' footsteps. God bless 'em, but they're just a couple of fuckups."

Mel cleared his throat. "Let's check the news, see if you two are notorious yet."

Diane followed him to a small study and took a seat on a leather couch. Her body heat warmed it instantly. Gail emerged from the back of the apartment, wearing a terry bathrobe, her hair wrapped in a towel.

"How's your ankle?" Before Gail could answer Diane turned to Mel. "She needs a doctor. She needs stitches."

"Come," Mel said to Gail. "Sit. Let's take a look." He grimaced when he saw the wound. "She's right," he said. He went down the hall and returned with a towel. He lifted her swollen ankle onto the couch, placed it gently on the towel. "I'll make a call. Be right back. Do not answer either the door or the phone. No matter what."

"Try the shower," Gail said to Diane. "It's heavenly."

Diane stuffed another cracker into her mouth, washed it down with wine, and headed for the bath.

By the time she returned from her shower, which had been quick, but efficient, Gail had finished off the grapes and the cheese and the crackers.

And by the time Mel returned from his trip to the phone booth, Diane had put together a couple of Spanish omelets and some hash browns and the women were eating slowly, savoring the taste of a hot meal made from real food.

"I hope my stomach doesn't freak out," Gail said.

The television was tuned to NY1, the city's all-news cable channel: talking heads intercut with video footage, some live. There was talk of local political scandals, talk of the latest abduction and murder, talk of the latest fourteen-year-old mother who'd sent her newborn down the trash chute to the incinerator. Nothing about escaped convicts.

"We're cool," Diane said. "Maybe he just fired up his engine and went wherever he was headed."

"Maybe he's still giving his statement," Mel said. "That can take awhile."

Later that evening, after the doctor, a close personal friend of Mel's, had come and gone, leaving Gail's ankle properly

stitched and bandaged, and leaving Gail with an admonition to
stay off it for twenty-four hours, Mel came to Gail in her
room. She was on the bed, reading what was supposed to pass
for an intelligent magazine for women, but it seemed loaded
with beauty tips and weight-loss tactics and inane suggestions
for how to calm down and take control of your life. Nothing of
substance. Mel sat next to her, looking vaguely uncomfortable.

"What?" she said.

"I don't know how to put this delicately. I think you should
lose her."

Gail was stunned, and then for a moment thought he was
right, and then knew he wasn't.

"I can't," she said. "If it wasn't for her, I'd be in custody
right now, with an attempted escape charge."

"I understand that. But you're both out now. You need to go
your own way."

"I'm not ready to do that just yet. She doesn't have any kind
of network, Mel. Nobody to help her. She needs me, or she'll
get caught for sure."

"What, you're her mother all of the sudden? You need to
disappear, and we can help you do that, but it's going to be all
over the news, sooner or later, two white women on the run.
You have to split up."

"We won't."

"How so?"

"How not so? We disappear, that's all. We've already disappeared. And we're on the road tomorrow. Outta here. Gone."

"Not in your best interest."

"I owe her. We made it together. Not solo. Together."

"You don't owe her."

"No, you're right. I don't owe anybody anything. But she
deserves a hand. She was framed, for God's sake. Out and out
framed."

"Not your obligation."

"Totally true. But I want to help her."

"Why?"

"Because I feel like she needs it, and I feel like I can."

"You haven't changed."

"I have. Completely. But I haven't given up on what's right."

"This is right? To risk going back there? For a cop, no less?"

"Truth of the matter? I got nothing to lose."

"Truth of the matter, you've got your freedom to lose. You've been locked up eighteen years, you ready to go back for more?"

"I'm not going back."

"Lot easier to catch you if you match the profile."

"There are loads of white females out there, **lots of couples**, lots of friends, what's to distinguish us?"

"Are you in love?"

"No! Do we act like we're in love?"

"Your dedication to her is impressive."

"It's not predicated on that."

"Okay." He relaxed a little. "As long as your judgment isn't impaired."

"No more than usual."

Mel laughed, tugged at his tie to loosen it.

"You have some money. Your parents." He took an envelope from his back pocket and held it out to her. "Fifteen thousand," he said. "There's more. Invested. But I shouldn't be taking any large withdrawals from it. In case someone's watching, which they no doubt will be from this point forward."

Gail reached for it, thinking of the time her father bailed her out, how vulnerable and proud he'd been on the drive back to Connecticut. And her mother, who'd never said anything about providing, who'd only been happy to have Gail home for the weekends during those college years. An eternity ago. They were good people. She wished she could have been closer to them.

"I could contact the authorities," Mel said, "try to negotiate your return and get you out on time served."

"You're not serious."

"No. But it's my duty as your lawyer to tell you."

"Forget about being my lawyer. Be my friend."

"As your friend, I say stay free."

"Yeah."

"Which means getting away from your pal out there as soon as you can. She's dangerous, I can tell."

"How can you tell? You barely know her. Come on."

"She has an attitude."

"Don't we all. She's pissed off. You can't believe what they did to her."

"So most likely neither can a jury. Get away from her."

"It's not that simple."

Mel sighed and looked toward her.

"It never was, for you." He sank back. "Gail, I don't want to see you locked up again."

"I don't either."

"The ID man is coming tomorrow. Get your driver's license, get away from here, get a job, get a life, get a family. You deserve it. You've done your time. Go."

"I can't bail out on her."

"What do you owe her? You don't owe her anything. You did her a favor, now do yourself one. Gail, listen to me. You've got people. Friends who will help you. Who know you deserve a life. You've done more than enough time, we all know that. So go. Have a life. Can you run with that?" He ran a hand through his gray curls. "Look at her. She's going back. I can tell you right now. And if you're with her when they catch her?" He shrugged.

"I wouldn't have made it without her," Gail said quietly. "She literally pulled me up and out of there." She took in the scent of old wood and furniture polish. She had forgotten what wood smelled like.

"Gail," Mel said, "your father and mother each asked me to take care of you should you, when you, got out. You can't stay with this girl. She'll get you arrested."

"I can't just abandon her."

"It's not abandoning. It's the smartest thing for both of you. She'll realize it, once you broach the idea. She's a cop, for crissakes."

"She used to be a cop."

"Once a cop, always a cop."

"Not in this case."

"And why not?"

"She's had everything she believed in shaken up."

Mel smiled to himself. "Like someone else I know," he said quietly.

"Have you heard from Tom?"

"Changing the subject?"

"Yes and no."

"No. I haven't. No one has. But he's another one you should steer clear of."

"I was just curious."

"He's somewhere in the Midwest, according to rumor. Maybe doing what I'm telling you that you should do: get a life."

"I need a little time to adjust, you know."

"I know. I know. Believe me, Gail, I understand. But the safest thing for you right now would be to take up residence somewhere far from here, get a job, get some friends, and just go about the business of everyday living. You will adjust. The most important thing is that they don't find you and take you back. And that's all the more reason to distance yourself from her."

Gail leaned toward him.

"I can't. No. More than that. I won't. Not yet anyway." She knew he was probably right, she had plenty of doubts herself. But this was larger than her doubts. It was a matter of loyalty. She was not going to leave Diane stranded in New York City. Or anywhere else for that matter. She had to help her.

Diane walked in then, stood in the doorway waiting for someone to say something. Mel and Gail sat looking at her.

"Won't what?" she said finally.

"Mel thinks we would be smart to go our own ways."

"Maybe he's right." Diane looked at Mel long and hard, evaluating. "On the surface, I'd say he probably is."

"Is that what you want?" Gail felt the smallest pang of hope that Diane would say yes, but was relieved when Diane straightened and shook her head adamantly. No way.

"I need somebody to watch my back," she said. "And so do you."

She looked at Mel, and Gail looked at Mel. Mel looked at the ceiling, and then back to them. "I'm only trying to do what's best. For both of you."

TEN

Diane tried not to stare as Mel hustled them toward the trains, dodging people expertly, shifting his shoulders to the right or left, missing oncoming humans by mere millimeters. Gail was behind her, right behind her, close enough that she twice stepped on Diane's heel, but Diane was so astonished at the sea of beings they were swimming through that she didn't even turn to give Gail a look. This was incredible. There were more people in this one building than in the entire town of Bolton. How many were cops? She felt exposed, vulnerable in a way she never had. She kept expecting an assault from the side, a tackle, a takedown. Handcuffs.

Penn Station smelled like a circus tent, and then Diane saw a popcorn stand down the corridor. July hot, and even though the place seemed like it might be air-conditioned—it was hard to tell with so many people packed in there—she felt little trails of sweat curling down the back of her neck. She wasn't sure it was from the heat. She turned to glance at Gail and almost looked past her, still unused to their new hair colors and cuts. Plus the makeup. It just didn't seem like Gail, but that was good. Black linen slacks and a longish black cotton halter with an African print design in pale blue and gold accentuated her slender lines. Beneath the slacks, black calf-high side-zip leather boots covered and supported her bandaged ankle. She glanced again at Gail, trying to assure herself that neither of them would be recognized. And if her own face held an expression similar to Gail's, she would be happy as a pig in shit. Gail betrayed no hint of desperation: She looked like all the other commuters and travelers focused on getting to their trains on time or getting to their office on time or getting wherever it was they were going on time.

The shops lining the corridors went by in a blur, windows full of stuff: little green Statues of Liberty, I ♥ NY fingernail clippers, neckties, coffee cups, miniature yellow cabs, books, shoes, shiny black shirts with bright orange flames burning across the chest and sleeves, Mets shirts, Yankees shorts, Knicks boxers, Giants jackets. Aromas assaulted her nostrils: the scent of souvlaki, the delicate bread smell of bagels, the garlic-green-steamy-crispy tang of stir fries. She was trying to be cool, look normal, blend in, even though she was nervous as all get-out, and even though she was, her taste buds went into full bloom, and her mouth watered from the smells emanating from the various restaurants and delis. Deli. She liked that word, it was one she'd grown up without, but it was fun to say and made you sound like you were worldly, she thought, or at least an awful lot more worldly than if you'd had the misfortune to grow up in a town where the only restaurant was the Korner Koffee Kup, gathering place of geezers and gossips, go for the counter service unless you wanted a table bad enough to wait three eons before Donna would arrive with that grimace of hers, anticipating the hard labor of carrying a couple of burgers all the way from the kitchen. Diane walked briskly on, like nothing in the world was out of sync, but felt her thoughts getting away from her, her mind going into that scattered space she despised so much every time she caught herself there, just a total waste of energy and emotion, things rattling around and bouncing off the walls of her skull, bits of memory, bits of anticipation, bits of things she thought she'd never seen before but nonetheless the images were there, the broken phrases of thought were there, but all of it summed to nothing. Zero, zilch, nil, nada—nothing. She wanted to focus, but was afraid to, and knew that was why it was happening. Think about anything but the here and now, fade out, forget that she was a fugitive walking through Penn Station in New York City, just about as exposed as a body could be. Fugitive. She didn't want the look, and she didn't want the energy.

Mel was walking fast, like everyone else, and Diane had to work to keep up with him and not get cut off by the hordes. She could feel Gail close behind her.

Criminals and fugitives gave off a certain vibe, and some cops could tune into it like they were a receiver, their dial set to KRYM: crime-time radio. It didn't even have to be a look you gave off, it was just something about you that said trouble, and if you ran across a cop who was tuned in, you were made. Busted. They wouldn't even have to look twice. So Diane worked hard to think like a tourist, stuffing her trepidation way down into the back of her skull where it might not leak out into the air around her and attract heat. But the pressure was scattering her thoughts; it reminded her of the time her brother Kevin had shot a bottle rocket into a quarter watermelon she was just starting in on. Sitting on the curb taking those first delicious bites, juice dripping down her chin, and she was watching him shoot off fireworks when the Orange Crush bottle he was using as a launch pad tipped over and the rocket headed right for her, zigzagging the way they do, and before she could move the thing struck, lodged in her watermelon and blew up, sending chunks of red fruit and black seeds all over her and a good twenty feet into the air around her. That was what her brain would now do if she didn't get somewhere safe and get there soon. But she didn't know where safe was, much less how to get there.

Someone bumped into her, hard, stunning her back to Penn Station. She whirled around, but Gail grabbed her arm and whipped her back into forward march and pushed her ahead.

"Forget it," Gail said. "Just follow Mel."

Follow quietly. Diane reined in her temper. Follow quietly and look like you know what you're doing, and think about anything but what you are doing. This was no time.

They passed an old woman pushing a grocery shopping cart with dozens of plastic bags in it and all tied around the sides and hanging off the handgrips, walking that side-to-side walk, her ankles thick as her knees, head tied in a turquoise bandanna, and a bunch of *Martha Stewart Living* magazines stacked up on top of all her other belongings. Diane started chuckling, ducked her head down so no one would think that she thought it was funny, because it wasn't and she didn't, it was only her stupid cop sick sense of humor: laughter in self-defense. She stopped herself and looked up: Here came two New York City patrolmen. Walking right toward her. Hard-core dark blue, coming right smack at her and Gail and Mel. Adrenaline flooded her system, made her skin sting right down to her fingertips, and it took everything she had just to keep her breath. She put her head back down and chuckled some more, or tried to, but it came out kind of like she was choking, so she stopped and focused on Mel's back as they walked toward the cops. She wondered how many times, when she was in uniform, she'd had this effect on people. Not on regular people, but on criminals. What was it her brother had told her that time she caught him reading Edgar Cayce out in the backyard? Karma is meeting yourself. "Right," she'd said. "Maybe he should call himself Edgar Nutcayce," which got a smile from Kevin, but she was thinking to herself that maybe the guy had hit on something there. Karma is meeting yourself.

Here they came, all in dark uniforms, the harness cops, the unis, but they were talking to each other, not really looking, and then one of them, the taller one, looked at her sharply, and even though she tried not to make eye contact, it happened, and she just kept looking and hoping that he thought that she thought he was good-looking and that was why he'd caught her looking at him, but his face didn't tell her anything, he just looked with that look that she was sure she'd had many times herself, the look that you held for civilians, who didn't know shit and never ever would, the look that kept the wall up between you and anyone who wasn't a cop. She looked, and he looked, and it was like time went into slow motion. She saw his heels striking the grimy floor, saw the ripple in his trousers from the impact of his steps, his arms swinging with authority, and the dead giveaway, this thing that got undercover cops made unless they worked hard not to do it: his right arm swinging wide to arc around the .45 automatic in the holster on his hip. It became a habit, bringing your arm around so as not to hit your gun, and to most people it just looked, when you weren't in uniform, like part of a swagger. But he was in uniform, and looking hard at her, and she couldn't cut her eyes away, didn't know the right moment, how to make it look like anything but what it was: complete and wholesome fear, and she felt her knees give and took a little stagger step and just at that moment Mel turned and slipped an arm through hers and gave her a big smile and pointed over toward something that she couldn't see and said, "There they are!" She let him guide her away from the cops, into the crowd, into the sea of people, and Gail trotted a couple of quick steps to catch up, slipped into place on the other side of Diane, and the two of them took her away from the heat.

She walked between them until they guided her to a stop and the three of them stood staring up at the huge black electronic board that held a dizzying number of trains and departure times and destinations. And then they were urging her to move again and the next thing was she was standing on a long, raised concrete platform smelling the odor of massive amounts of electricity, so much electricity that it actually smelled, and staring down at the hard steel rails below.

Mel let go of her arm to pull Gail close and give her a huge, wonderful hug. Diane stared, and the strength of the bond between the two of them left her feeling like she was standing in the middle of a desert staring at an oasis in the distance and, as thirsty as she was, she knew in the rational part of her brain that the oasis was only a mirage. When the embrace ended, Gail turned toward the doorway to the huge Amtrak car, wiping tears from her eyes. Diane looked away, embarrassed for some reason that was completely escaping her at the moment, and offered her hand to Mel. He took it, and then pulled her to him and gave her a warm, gentle hug. She pressed her head against his shoulder, wondering if it was unusual that she was twenty-four years old and this was the first time in her life she'd ever touched a pinstripe suit. It was sort of scratchy, but not too scratchy. She couldn't tell how it felt to be hugged by this man she'd met just day before yesterday. She didn't know if he was only being polite and hugging her so she wouldn't feel left out, or if he somehow liked or respected her because she'd helped Gail escape.

"If it comes down to it," Mel said, his lips up close to her ear against the noise of the train engine that had started up across the platform, "if it comes down to it, you do the right thing. She's suffered enough. If you go down again, don't take her with you." He stepped back and held her shoulders, looked her hard in the eye. There was no threat. There was no plea. It was simply a statement of what he knew was the right thing to do. Diane nodded, and tried to think how to explain to him that Gail was her partner now. They were partners the way cops had partners. Life or death. That bond had been created the moment they went over the concertina wire.

She put her mouth close to Mel's ear and said, "I'm not going down."

When she took one last look, from the steps to the train, Mel was watching her board, his lips pulled into a grim line. She turned and stepped into the car, wondering that she would respect him. Had they met under different circumstances, before her ordeal, and she'd caught him doing what he'd done for Gail and her, she would have arrested him. Now, everything was twisted inside out, she didn't know left from right, or up from down. She didn't know anything.

Inside the train, Gail closed the door to the sleeper behind her and let go the handle of her green carry-on with wheels and a retractable plastic handle. Some things had been made more convenient out here in the world during the years she'd been locked up. She leaned against the door and sighed hugely. Looked around.

"Another unbearably tiny room," she said. "When do I get some space?"

"When we get to Texas," Diane answered. "It's famous for it." The walls seemed to be made of beige plastic. She tapped at one. Sure enough.

Gail furrowed her eyebrows sternly. "The tickets say Chicago. That's where we're going."

"Yeah, and when we get to Chicago, we get off and get with your friends and get new ID and then we get tickets to Texas."

"Diane."

"I'm goin' to Texas, girlfriend."

"Let's just try to get out of New York for now."

"Swell."

"The only reason for you to go to Texas is if you have some perverse desire to either get killed or get rearrested and sent back to prison. Which is it?"

Diane sat down on the small couch and raised up the shade on the large plate glass window to her right. Another train was next to them. She pulled the shade back down.

"I'm sorry about out there," she said quietly.

Gail looked puzzled.

"I almost lost it," Diane said. "Those cops. I was bugging out."

"I thought you were going to ask him to come with us." Gail laughed softly, and then saw how embarrassed Diane was and stopped. "Don't worry about it."

"I am worried about it. It was completely uncool. I gotta get myself together."

"Just believe nothing's out of the ordinary. We're travelers. Like the rest of the passengers on this train. That's all. Just act normal."

"I have a feeling that normal for you is not normal for me."

"We have some time to chill now, or will momentarily. I'll feel a lot better when we're out of this station. On the move."

"What scares me is that I know there are cops out there who are tuned in. Either one of us gives off the wrong vibe, their antennas will go up and we'll be in cuffs."

"So don't give off the wrong vibe."

"You know how to do that? I'm used to picking up on it, not sending it out."

"Yeah. Don't give off any vibe. Put yourself somewhere else, mentally. Just don't even be there." Gail was giving advice like she knew what she was talking about, but it was more a case of trying to calm Diane down. The girl was rattled.

"Lotta cops aren't even aware of it or don't believe in it or whatever, but the good ones pick up on it. They know to follow their gut."

"You?"

"That's how I got in this switch to start with."

"I'd keep listening to it."

"It's telling me go to Texas."

"Tell it to think again."

"I'm serious, Gail. I'm dead-on serious. You don't understand." Gail stood up and faced her. "I do understand. You don't understand! You ever been on the lam before?" She waited. "I didn't think so. There are some things you do and some things you don't even consider doing. What do you think is at the top of the list?"

"Criminal Investigation 101: They always go home."

"So why are you even considering going there?"

"I have to."

"Listen to what you're saying. Think. You don't have to."

"They framed me."

"And what makes you think they won't do it again? Or worse?"

Diane sat silently, doodling with the laces on her boots. Gail was right about that. The creeps would totally do her in if they could. When she finally answered, it came out as barely more than a whisper, but full of quiet determination.

"They can't hurt me if they don't catch me."

"You think I ever in a million years thought I'd get arrested and catch a seventy-two-year sentence?" Gail shook her head vehemently. "I thought I was smarter than the best they had. The authorities were nothing but a bunch of dumb-asses chomping on doughnuts. And from what it sounds like, you'd have a hell of a lot more to worry about than getting arrested."

Diane sighed. "I can't argue with you. It's just something I have to do."

"You sound like a moron."

"Hey, why don't we just drop the subject, okay?" Diane's volume edged upward, entering anger range. "You're gonna do what you think is best, and I'm gonna do what I know I have to do in order to be able to live with myself. That's what it comes down to."

"I didn't say you are one, I said you sound like one. You're too smart to do something so stupid. Come on." Gail opened the door to the tiny lavatory in the corner of the car, stared morosely. "Thought I'd seen my last stainless steel toilet," she said, as though there'd been no harsh exchange whatsoever. "At least there's no drinking fountain on top of it."

Diane propped her feet up on her suitcase, which, but for its navy color, was the same as Gail's. What did Gail know, anyway? She could make it without her. "Whatever," she said glumly.

Gail sat down across from Diane and rubbed a hand over the fabric of her seat. "I can't get used to sitting on soft furniture."

"You'll have time."

"Like you know," Gail said, but smiling, trying to ease the tension. "You weren't even in for that long."

"Three minutes is long enough," Diane said. "Getting dragged through that front gate is long enough." She raised the shade and lowered it all in one motion. "Thinking about it is long enough."

Another smile from Gail. Good. The train started forward with a mild lurch, and then rocked slowly back and forth as it lumbered through the dark.

"Finally." Gail stepped across Diane to raise the window shade. They were in fact moving. She sat back down, raised a high five to Diane, who slapped it and laughed out loud.

"So I guess the question is," Diane said, eyeing the sleeping arrangements, "who gets the bottom bunk?"

Gail pulled open the door to the dining car and scanned the room. One diner: a suit reading the *Wall Street Journal* and sipping coffee. Good.

Diane seemed to know where she wanted to sit, so Gail followed her to the last table on the right, pressed up against a corner, next to the door at the opposite end of the car. Diane slipped into a seat with her back against the wall. Gail sat across from her, next to the wide window that stopped about halfway across the table.

"Don't you want to sit where you can see out?" Gail looked at Diane.

"No." She spoke quietly. "I want to sit where I can see everything in this room, and where I can get out the door fast if anything comes down. But you go ahead, enjoy the scenery. I'll keep an eye out."

"Don't watch too hard, or someone's going to notice that you're watching. We're cool here. Lighten up."

Diane sat back, picked up a menu.

Gail eyed her. "Are you . . . ?"

Diane rested her arms on the table, leaned toward Gail. "Packing? One of us has to."

"No, one of us doesn't. It's safer if you don't."

"Wrong."

"We have to talk about this."

"Not here."

Gail thought about getting up and returning to the sleeper, but decided to hang in. Best not to create a chasm. She and Diane needed each other, at least in the short term. The most important thing was that Diane had a pretty solid idea of how the cops thought, how they would proceed, and where the pitfalls might be. And as much as Gail didn't like Diane carrying the gun, part of her felt a kind of relief, as though Diane were her protector. She felt almost chastised, but let herself look out the window anyway. The train was rolling now, headed north along the Hudson River. Look out the window. That's what an ordinary traveler might do. She couldn't get over the beauty of the wide waters, the lush greenery sloping toward the riverbanks. She had taken it all for granted before she went inside. Now, it stunned her nearly to tears.

Diane sat looking at the menu, equally impressed with the scrambled eggs, fresh asparagus, and smoked salmon in a phyllo cup and the homemade corned beef hash with two over easy and warm toast. When Gail looked at the menu, she was overwhelmed by the choices. The decision was not limited to matzo pizza or peanut butter and jelly. She doubted that she'd be able to make up her mind.

"You know what a phyllo cup is?" Diane peeked over her menu.

"Is this a joke?"

"No," Diane said. "It's a question. I've never heard of it."

"Pastry," Gail said. "Thin. Light. Crispy. Kind of like the pastry in baklava."

"And what's that?"

"I see what you're looking at. Get it. It'll be good."

"But what's the pastry like?"

"I'll tell you what it's not like. It's not like a tortilla." Trying to make peace.

"Ha-ha. Is it like pie crust?"

"Yes. The flakiest pie crust you could imagine. Falls apart. It's good."

"They served it in the chow hall?"

"Very funny. I remember. From when I was a kid."

Diane watched as Gail's hands took up the white napkin from the white plate on the white linen tablecloth. They were trembling ever so slightly. The silverware gleamed in morning sunlight streaming in through the wide window next to the table. The train had speed now, rolling along the tracks, jostling gently every so often. Diane looked again at Gail, who was staring down at the plate in front of her and clutching the napkin close to her stomach.

"Gail." Almost whispered. "Are you okay?"

Gail slowly put her napkin in her lap and looked at Diane. "Yes. I am okay. I'm fine."

"What is it?"

Gail laughed gently and shrugged.

"It's all just so . . . just so . . . civilized." She took a sip of ice water from the goblet before her. "Diane, you know how it felt in that place? You know how awful it was for you for even that little while you were there?" Diane nodded, almost cringed at the memory.

"Well, I went in there, think about this, I'm kind of in shock here—I've been in there since you were six years old."

Diane rocked back. It was incomprehensible. She couldn't imagine being there that long. Six years old. Forever ago. She didn't have many memories from six years old, but she did remember that it was the year her Uncle John had come to visit and taken her and Kevin out to Carlsbad Caverns and they'd seen all those hundreds and hundreds of bats come hurtling out of the caves just at sunset. And then he'd taken them home to his place, a small ranch out near Lubbock, which was as flat and god-awful a place as anybody could imagine, or at least that's how she remembered it. But he had three horses, and he'd let Diane and Kevin take the two gentler ones out riding in the brush, and they'd had as much fun as ever they'd had in their lives. It nearly broke Diane's heart when Uncle John packed them back up and drove them the daylong drive back to East Texas and their mother. She had fallen in love with Sylvie, the buck mare she'd ridden almost daily for two solid weeks, and the last thing she wanted was to go home to what she knew was there.

But their mother looked different when they arrived—her face wasn't so red and puffy like it sometimes got, and she smelled of spearmint instead of martinis, and she had a real smile for them, though there was something scared about it. Even Kevin gave her a hug, though Diane could tell he didn't trust what was happening. Her mother held her for a long moment, and then she hugged Uncle John and thanked him for everything and asked him in for iced tea. He accepted, but only stayed long enough to tell her she looked real good and he hoped things would get easier for her now before he climbed back in his sky-blue GMC and headed for the highway.

Later that night Kevin and Diane had been sitting out in the backyard under her favorite pine and she'd said something about their mother seeming so different.

"She's sober," Kevin said, but there was still anger pushing out from his voice. "She's been in rehab."

"What's rehab?"

"It's where you stop drinking or doing drugs, whatever it is you been doin', Pipsqueak."

"I'm not a pipsqueak." He'd been calling her that forever,

and it had turned from insult to pet name between the time she was three and now. "How long does it last?"

"Sometimes forever," he said. "You know my friend George. His daddy went in nearly four years ago and he hasn't had a drink since. Seems like it took for him."

"You think it'll take for Mom?"

"Let's hope so," Kevin said.

It seemed like it had. Their mom stayed with it, clean, even got a job at the Korner Koffee Kup and started making her bed in the mornings and telling Kevin and Diane to do the same. That was the only thing Diane didn't like about her mom being sober and all—suddenly she had to start making her bed every day. That part sucked. But she would have made her bed forever, even taken it apart and put it back together again every morning, if it had meant her mother would stay away from the alcohol.

It wound up only being six weeks, or at least that's how Kevin would recall it years later, that she had to make herself fluff up her pillow and yank the covers into place after she got up in the morning. After that, her mother didn't care again.

Diane shook off the memory; she hated unpleasant intrusions from her past. Gail was gazing out the window.

"So after all that time," Diane said, and Gail jumped and that startled Diane, and then they both started laughing. "Sorry," Diane said.

Gail shook her head okay. "What were you thinking? I know it wasn't breakfast."

"You reading my mind now?"

"For a moment you looked like you were going to cry."

"I did?"

"You did."

"I was thinking that my mother was a fuckin' drunk."

"Kind of harsh?"

"Maybe. Still, true."

"They used the term 'alcohol dependent.' Inside. The counselors."

Diane gave her a look: I never would have guessed.

"I used to help out sometimes. At the meetings."

"What were those like?"

"Nice people," Gail said. "Struggling with some pretty heavy baggage."

"Convicts. Dope fiends. Drunks. Sounds like a fun bunch."

"My girlfriends and I, in high school . . . There was a time you'd have thought we'd all grow up to be junkies. But no one did, that I know of."

Diane was still shaking her head slowly, simply not getting it, when the waiter arrived and stood ready with his pad, saving Gail from further discussion with her. There'd been enough acrimony already. Maybe it was just nerves, Gail thought. Maybe it would get easier. Or maybe she should do like Mel said and ditch this chick.

"You really still remember what phyllo tastes like?" Diane shifted gears into polite good-friend mode in front of the waiter. Gail nodded yes.

"Then I'm definitely having that."

"Make it two," Gail said. There. That wasn't so difficult.

After brunch, they went back to their sleeper.

Gail felt oddly secure there, probably because the train was moving. There was something reassuring about being in motion, isolated from the larger world—by her own choice now—and traveling. It wasn't like she was sitting in an alleged safe house and cops might blow through the door at any minute. There was fear, yes, but at the moment she could chalk most of it up to paranoia. Then again, the threat was as real as the young maniac sitting next to her in the sleeper: the cops could very well blow through the door any moment . . . provided they had boarded the train in New York. But if they'd done that, they would have already busted them. She didn't really have to worry about it until they approached a station, and Cleveland was still hours away. Until then, she could come and go if she pleased; take a stroll through the train, go to the dining car for meals. It was somewhat frightening; she realized that there had been comfort in being confined, in not having choices, in having to do as one was told. The lack of responsibility had been, in its way, liberating.

But stifling as well, and more so. It was such an odd headspace. She had wanted, for all those many years, more than anything to be free, but now that she was, freedom—with its attendant responsibilities—seemed in itself confining. She had to choose. She had to decide. And there were consequences stemming from her decisions and choices. Inside the walls, she'd had nothing left to lose. Out here, she could lose her freedom.

Diane pulled the gun from beneath her shirt and stuffed it down next to the cushion on the couch.

"That why you like loose-fitting clothes?"

Diane looked at her sharply. "No need to frighten anyone."

"You're frightening me. Get caught with that, it's another whole case, on top of the escape charge, and that's on top of what we still have to serve."

"Duh." Diane turned to face her, cocked her hip, and put a hand on it, nodded yes, ever so slightly. "Let's see, I got twenty, plus whatever they add for the escape—I'm sure that's at least five, plus another whole case. Gosh! I'll be in there for a long, long time if I get caught. You? You got twelve, plus whatever for escape, but I guarandamntee yah, you won't get nothing for the gun 'cause, just in case they do catch us, I'll give you my word right now: it's my gun, you had nothing to do with it, you tried to talk me out of it. Okay?"

"I'm comforted," Gail said, not exactly sincerely.

"Let's face it, girlfriend." Diane took the gun back out and tucked it into her suitcase and zipped it closed. "Better?"

Gail ignored her.

"They catch us," Diane said, "we're just plain fucked. So we might as well do whatever we can not to get caught."

"Not violence. They can take me back before I will do violence."

Diane's mouth dropped open, only slightly, but her astonishment was apparent. "Hey," she said, "whatever."

"We have to come to some kind of agreement."

"Look, I gave you my word. You won't have to deal with it."

"I have to deal with it if you use it on somebody."

"I don't think I'll have to. I know how it works."

"You can't say that."

"I'm not gonna ditch my pistol. Forget about it."

There was no reasoning with her. Gail stared outside the big picture window. A billboard: Welcome to Pennsylvania! America begins here. Like New York and New Jersey didn't exist. Like Pennsylvania was the be-all and end-all. Redneck heaven. They'd had Tom locked up there, in Allenwood, for several years of his bit. She wondered where he was, what he'd done—besides not get in touch with her—since his release more than two years earlier. No doubt he'd hooked up with someone who would wash his clothes and cook his meals and open the mail and jump into bed whenever the mood struck him, which was pretty frequently. Gail couldn't even picture having sex now. It had been so long, all she knew was that it would have to be perfect. It would have to be with the absolute right guy in the absolute right circumstances. She'd been without it too long to just jump in the bushes with the first guy who was willing to fuck. Maybe part of it was fear that she was no longer attractive, that she was over the hill, no spring chicken, too long in the tooth, that there wouldn't be a guy who was willing, though she laughed at herself for such a thought. There was always a guy who was willing. Able or not, that was the question. The green flatlands of Pennsylvania rolled by. *Freedom is just another word. . . .* She knew she'd have to think about it sooner or later, the question she'd been able to avoid so easily in the rush of escape, the overwhelming physical exertion, the mind-bending reality of it. Where was she going and what was she doing? Now, this instant, she was still running. But she couldn't do that forever. She had to think about the long term, about what she would do with her life, and mostly about what she could do within the constraints of existing as a fugitive. The larger choice was between only two options: live as an outlaw, underground, and just go like hell until they caught her again, or reenter society and try to pull it off as a law-abiding civilian. Establish an identity. Find meaningful work. Become part of a community. Maybe even enter a relationship. And she'd read stories about women who had children even when well into their forties, some as late as in their fifties. Perhaps she wasn't entirely too old. Maybe she could even—she stopped herself, afraid to hope. And look at Sara Jane Olson. On the lam as a model citizen for twenty-four years, and then one afternoon, driving her minivan down a suburban street in St. Paul, the cops pull her over. End of freedom. The *New York Times* headline, she still remembered it:

WAS THIS SOCCER MOM A TERRORIST?

What if she succeeded in making a new life, like Mel said, what if she had children and raised them lovingly and made it through all the turmoil of family to the day of her oldest's graduation, only to be stopped by the cops on her way to the ceremony and hauled back to prison? How much did the authorities want from her? How much would they take? Would they take everything they possibly could, every minute they could steal from her, just because they could? It might be easier, in some respects, to stay outside the law, to forego any attempt at normalcy. She wasn't even sure she wanted it, regardless of whether she was capable of it. When she thought back to her upbringing in her eminently normal family, even though she loved her parents and over the years had come to respect them for who they were (and their politics had improved once she was convicted), when she thought back to those suburban days, she wasn't at all sure she wanted to reenter that. It could be as stifling as prison had been. Perhaps even more so, in an insidious kind of way.

Diane's eyes were closed, and Gail felt her own lids giving in to gravity and exhaustion and who knew what else; she felt the blanket of sleepiness falling warm and fuzzy over her body. She could not have fully known it in prison, but now that she was out, she realized that during the entire time she'd been in there, she hadn't really rested. She'd slept, yes, her eyes had closed and she had dreamed, but she'd never actually rested. She hadn't been able to get to the place where recuperation and regeneration took place. She heard a huge sigh escape from her, and God, it felt so good, she let her eyes fall shut, and it felt so good.

The door to the sleeper slammed shut and Gail started

awake, momentarily confused, until she realized the dark-headed young woman with cropped locks was Diane. She looked scared, her back pressed against the door as she stood clutching a copy of the *New York Post*.

"You're not gonna believe this." She handed the paper to Gail.

They were on the cover, side by side. Grim black-and-white prison mug shots, numbers under their chins, beneath a thick black headline:

TWO FOR THE ROAD
Renegade Lady Ex-Cop and Female Former Revolutionary Make Daring Prison Break

Gail sat staring at the paper, thankful that the photo they'd obtained of her was almost twenty years old. Her eyes were fierce with defiant disdain, her hair wildly curly and all over the place, spilling onto her slender shoulders. She glanced at her reflection in the mirror on the sleeper door. Unrecognizable from the mug shot. If she still felt any defiance, which usually she did when she let herself feel, she was able to mask it. Her eyes were quiet now. And her hair was sculpted. If she put on a business ensemble, she could pass as a lawyer, or stockbroker, or CEO. Disgusting. But useful.

Diane hadn't fared so well, as her photo was only a few months old. But her haircut and color had done a lot. Gail didn't think just any cop on the street would recognize her, provided she didn't pull out the revolver and start waving it in someone's face. She looked pretty punk, in a fashionable way.

"Did you read it?"

"No!" Diane sputtered. "I just saw it, somebody left it in the dining car and I grabbed it."

Gail turned to the story. There was a photo of Sundown FCI, looking like a masochist's castle, and another shot of Gail with several other prisoners, taken, she recalled now, when the literacy program was still happening and the feds wanted to promote all the wonderful rehabilitative programs they offered. Something to do with the following year's funding. She looked a little calmer in that one, even almost smiling. But it, too, was ancient. Nobody was going to make either her or Diane based on what was in the paper.

"These people," Gail said, "these assholes." Diane stood waiting. "I bet it was Johnson. Had to be."

"What, for godsake, tell me."

"They quote some unnamed source who works in the prison as saying it was apparent that I had been planning the escape for some time, and they speculate that I somehow forced you to come with me."

"Right." Diane smiled. "What are they, stupid?"

"Would you work in a prison if you could get another job? Any other job?"

"It might work in our favor." Diane sat down on the small couch next to Gail, peered at the article. "I mean, if they really think that, then they'll also think that I'll be trying to get away from you, or maybe even that we already split up."

"I think the smartest thing for right now is to present ourselves as mother and daughter."

"I have too many mom issues to pull that off."

"Fake it."

"Look, let's just be friends. Not relatives. Besides, you don't look old enough to be my mother."

"Prison preserves you. Clean living, regular schedule. Keeps you looking young, even if you feel like the Methuselah tree, 4,643 years old. In California. Some days in that place I felt just like it: totally rooted and been standing there for thousands of years."

"Mom." Diane bolted up. "Not gonna work."

"Why not?"

"Because that word leaves such a bad taste in my mouth."

"You talk about her like she was a monster."

"She was. Kind of."

"She was sick, Diane."

"How do you know? You never met her."

"I've met a lot of people like her. And I'll tell you this. You would do well to forgive her and move on. I know we don't know each other really well and all, but it seems to me like you're carrying around a serious amount of anger. I know how that feels—"

"Maybe. Maybe not."

"I know how it feels to carry around a lot of anger. It'll eat you up. You need to let it go."

"And just how do I do that?"

"You have to figure that one out yourself, I'm afraid."

"Yeah, well, another time. What else does it say?"

Gail scanned the article. "*America's Most Wanted.* We're gonna be on *America's Most Wanted* this week."

"Holy shit."

"And the Internet. We're posted on the Internet. I've never even seen the goddamn Internet."

"No sweat." Diane was pacing, three steps each way, practically banging into the walls. "Only about a zillion people have access. We are so fucked."

"Don't say that. We're not. Sit down, please. We just have to use our heads. I mean already we don't look like ourselves. And believe me, our ID is solid. Mel's connections are the best. The best."

"What else?" Diane sat down next to her again. Stared at the paper.

"Looks like they couldn't get to any relatives for comment. Says you claimed innocence. Says I renounced violence."

"Brilliant." Diane rested her elbows on her knees, let her head fall forward to where Gail couldn't see her face. "Have you?"

"Yes, Diane, I have."

"You wouldn't have if you were me."

"Maybe not. I can't really say." Gail saw tears dropping onto Diane's hands, slowly, plop . . . plop, delicate and clear. She reached to rub Diane's back. She didn't know where the gesture came from, except that she wanted to ease the girl's pain.

"We are so fucked, and I want to kill those motherfuckers," Diane whispered. "In my heart, that's really what I want to do."

Gail's hand jerked away and she felt a chill on the back of her neck as murderous intention filled the small space between her and Diane. She had been around murderers. Even celled with one for a while. The ones she had known were the gentlest of souls, as though the commission of the act had opened within them a huge cavern into which sadness flowed constantly, but never quite filled. And never could. But this was different. This was premeditation in the happening, an energy coming out of an anger vicious enough to drive Diane to kill.

It was a quiet, terrifying despair.

Gail slumped back in the seat, watching as Diane pulled herself upright and smudged the tears on her face, slapped her hands against her camos, drying the tears on them, and stood up. She raised her arms and leaned against the window, staring out at the scenery rolling by. There were houses now, in bland colors, weathered. Outskirt territory.

"Looks like we're coming into Cleveland," Diane said finally. "At least, it should be. In Chicago, I'll go my way and you go yours."

"You're making a mistake. You can wait. You can think things out."

"There's nothing to think about. I have to go find them and force them to tell a judge what they did to me."

"At gunpoint? I don't think that kind of confession is acceptable in court." A chuckle or a snicker, Gail didn't know what the sound coming out of her was, except an attempt at a laugh. "At least not if the judge is aware of it."

"It may not have to be like that. I don't know yet."

"Then you shouldn't go. Not until you have a plan."

"That sounds real good, Gail—I mean Liz—but it's not like any plan is foolproof. I could go in there with the best plan in the world and it could still get totally blown away by a complete silly accident. I mean, just like I had a plan to go to law school, and I got seriously sidetracked. And I can't even think of a plan until I go back and try to piece some things together. I gotta talk to some people."

"You've heard of long distance?"

"You've heard of phone traces?"

"You've heard of pay phones?"

"I'm going. You don't have to come with me. You have no obligation to come with me."

"How do I know you won't burn me? You know my ID, you know what I look like. What happens if they get you and you decide to cut a deal?"

Diane whirled around, her face contorted with anger. "Fuck you!"

Gail stood up, got in close. "How do I know?"

Diane stood for a long moment, her breath coming hard and fast. Whoa. Slow down. What was the problem here? She was trying to do the right thing. The right thing for herself and the right thing for Gail. "You know because I'm telling you I won't," she said slowly, her voice controlled and low. "I give you my word, and my word, my friend, is good."

Gail looked at her, and knew she was telling the truth. It wasn't so much that she even really thought Diane might betray her; if she'd ever thought that seriously, they would both still be back there in that cell. What she really wanted was for Diane to calm down, slow down, think about what she was doing, and change her mind about going to Texas, at least for the time being. She wasn't even sure why she felt that way. Maybe it was because she saw so much about Diane that was like herself back when she was a twenty-something hothead, albeit Diane was focused in an entirely different direction. And because she knew Diane would wind up doing serious time, if not life, or even death maybe, God she couldn't even think about that, not for Diane, not for anyone. She knew this much: Diane was not a bad person, but she was a very confused and angry and messed up person right now, and in that state she was capable of making the ultimate mistake. She'd been a cop, for godsake.

"Diane," Gail started, but she was stopped by the sudden slowing of the train, which pulled her forward in her seat and caused Diane to sidestep in order to remain standing. They were at some kind of platform, but not yet in a station, or at least it didn't look that way. The train came to a stop. Diane looked at Gail—a glimpse of fear, but only a glimpse, and then a flash of determination.

Gail didn't like it at all.

Diane pressed her cheek against the window. Gail joined her. They couldn't see much, some grayish buildings and a long concrete platform, beyond that, myriad railroad tracks leading into tunnels in front of them, and all seeming to merge into three or four tracks that stretched back in the direction from which they'd come.

It was eerily still and motionless in the sleeper, after so many hours of humming along the tracks and the gentle swaying of the rail car. And then they heard the door to the sleeper next door opening, and men's voices, official-sounding.

"Shit," Diane whispered. She headed for the door. Gail grabbed her arm, motioned her to sit back down. "No!" Diane hissed. "What would you do if we were just passengers on this thing? You'd go out and find out what the problem is. Or maybe you wouldn't, but I sure as hell would, and that's exactly what I'm gonna do. Now let me go." She jerked her arm loose from Gail's grip and opened the door. Gail sat down quickly, opened the paper to hide the pages featuring her and Diane. She thought she was going to faint, molecules danced in the thin air of the sleeper. And then the cops were at the door. Amtrak police? Amtrak had police? They did, apparently, and the Amtrak police had a German shepherd with them.

"May we see some identification please?" Gail dug in her bag for her brand-new driver's license as the dog handler entered the sleeper. Diane stepped in the lavatory doorway to let him enter, digging her license out of her thigh pocket.

"Here you go," she said. Gail handed hers over silently, thankful that her hands didn't tremble. The cops' presence in the sleeper, the dog's wet nose quivering, seeking scent, Gail smelled the polyester in their uniforms and the leather of their gun belts, she smelled the dog, heard its panting, and there were tiny bursts of static from the radio on one of the cop's belt, and she sat quietly, trying to make herself into Jane Q. Citizen who was frightened at being this close to police but had absolutely nothing to hide. She forced herself to swallow.

Swallow hard.

She had nothing to hide.

The cop took the driver's licenses, and pulled out his radio. "Six seven-one to base, I need a ten-seventeen on two subjects, first subject last name King, first name D-e-b-o-r-a-h, middle initial E., white female, DOB 12/07/61, New Jersey DL 169566989. Second subject last name Wright, first name Niki, middle initial L., white female, DOB 3/15/79, Oklahoma DL 9146874076. Over."

"Ten-four, six-seven-one. Stand by." Gail looked at Diane, unable to understand the gibberish coming out of the radio. Diane had heard it perfectly, and knew that at the moment the dispatcher was feeding the info into a computer that would check virtually everywhere for them. NCIC: National Crime Information Center. If Mel's ID man wasn't perfect, she and Gail were in deep shit. She sat down next to Gail, watched the dog follow her handler's snapping fingers, sniffing carefully, her tail wagging.

They sat some more. Gail's nose wrinkled at the scent of cologne coming off the cop with the radio. Every time he shifted his weight, which was often, a little of the smell wafted over to her, his scented cop molecules entering her nose, invading her body. It was sickening. She sighed through her nose, trying to clear her sinuses.

"What's your dog's name?" Diane asked.

The handler stared at her in a not exactly friendly way before answering reluctantly, "Ginger." The dog turned at hearing its name; the handler snapped his way to the lavatory, Ginger following. She stopped and sat, looking up at her master. Nothing to report, sir. Diane watched them slip back out into the corridor, past the radio cop, who was staring at them, one hand on his walkie, waiting. They sat. Ginger waited outside the door. Diane couldn't help herself. As she looked at Ginger she kept hearing George Clinton's funk-laden rapping: ". . . dope dog, got to have a habit." Renfro had brought it into the station one day, and they'd had to listen to it about eight times to get the lyrics right, but they and everyone else who wandered into the kitchen, where breaks were taken, howled when they finally started hearing the words.

Gail heard more gibberish spitting out of the radio, and Diane heard, "Six-seven-one, both subjects clear."

"Ten-four." Six-seven-one shrugged to his partner, nodded curtly to Gail and Diane and exited the sleeper, pulling the door tight behind him.

As it clicked shut, Gail melted. "I do not fucking believe this," she said. "Is this America? Are we still in America? Or did they somehow transport us to Europe in the early forties? What the fuck was that?"

Diane stood up and peeked out the door, closed it, and locked it. "One of two things." She was all business. Gail saw the cop in her. "Either they had a snitch who told them there was dope on this train, or . . ."

"Or?"

"Someone who says they're your trusted friend isn't really your friend."

"Mel is solid."

"Gail. Those cops had some information. You could tell it by the way they were acting. They weren't just taking a shot in the dark. They know something. The question is whether it's about us."

"Obviously they don't, or we would be on our way to jail right now. The ID held up."

"Unless they just wanted to make sure we were here so they could follow us."

"Follow us where? What's the point of that?"

"You gonna tell me you don't have friends in low places?"

"Underground."

"Yeah. Way underground. Think the heat doesn't salivate at the thought of tailing Gail Rubin?"

"I don't think that's what's happening."

"Do you know that's not what's happening?"

"Well, we can't get off here, or they'll know something's wrong."

"No. We'll wait until we get to the station. Whenever they finally finish searching this thing."

They sat there, the air in the sleeper growing stale from lack of circulation, Diane and Gail sweating. Gail did the cross-word in the *Post*. That took ten minutes or so. Forty minutes later, the air came on and the engines fired up. The train rolled forward, slowly, toward the station. A black-and-white sign said Cleveland. Diane began gathering her things.

Gail wasn't sure why, but suddenly she thought it was the

wrong thing to do. Their tickets said Chicago, and that was where they should get off. And then she thought it was the right thing to do and got up to begin gathering her own things. Shit. Who could tell. Who knew. She didn't. This must be what it felt like to mainline methamphetamine. She couldn't think.

"We should stay," she said to Diane.

"Huh?" Diane plopped down on the couch, holding on to her suitcase handle, ready to roll. "We gotta get outta here, man."

"No. We've got to stay put until Chicago."

"You're crazy."

"If they see us get off the train, they'll know."

"If we see that they're looking, we won't get off. But if I've got a chance to get off this thing, I'm gone. I'm not gonna sit here and get arrested."

"You're panicking."

"No, I'm not. I'm calm as can be."

The train was in the tunnel now. Dim, dingy lights flashed past the window, the interval between them growing longer as the train slowed, and then they were in a huge lighted cavern, and the train was slowing, slowing, and it stopped.

ELEVEN

Gail sat, watching as Diane stood at the door, her knuckles white from the grip she had on her suitcase, the handle extended, ready to roll.

"Mistake," Gail said quietly. "Big mistake." She settled into her seat, pressing herself against the cushions as though prepared to resist arrest.

"They're gonna bust you," Diane said, her voice taut. "They're going to take you back there."

"I know what I'm doing."

"Neither one of us knows what the fuck we're doing, but I'm going on what I saw and what I feel, and I'll tell you right now, sure as I'm standing here, you stay here and they're fixin' to arrest your ass. For real."

Gail dug in her bag, pulled out a wad of bills, held them out to Diane. "You'll need money."

Diane stared at the cash, didn't move.

"Take it."

Diane reached for it, started to put it in her pants pocket, stopped suddenly.

"Come with me. I can get us out of here."

"Yeah?" Gail's voice was angry. "You got a plan?"

Diane stood mute, then knelt and zipped open her suitcase, grabbed new clothing out and began changing. Not that she knew why. She was stalling out of fear maybe, or maybe hoping that Gail would relent. Fighting panic, maybe. A moment later she was shoving the cash and her DL into the pocket of her jeans, relacing her boots, sticking her gun into the waistband of her jeans. She tossed on a light cotton button-down to cover the gun, shoved her city clothes back into the case and zipped it shut, put it in the corner of the cabin. Hesitation slipped up from behind and put her in a choke hold. Run. Don't run. She didn't know. Right at this moment, when she *had* to know, she didn't. She did not know what to do. She sat down on the couch next to Gail.

"This is gonna sound crazy," Diane said. "But I'll meet you in Chicago."

"I can't give you the contact," Gail said. "I can't do that."

"You don't have to. Just meet me at, I don't know, meet me at whatever Hertz rental car place is closest to the train station."

"Great plan."

"You gonna show or not?" Diane watched Gail gaze out the window, past her, like she wasn't there, staring at someplace Diane had never been.

"Tomorrow at five P.M. If you're not there, I'll come again the next morning at nine. If you haven't made it by then, I'll start watching the news to see where they popped you."

"Or assume," Gail said, "that I made it. That I'm in the wind."

Diane stood again, wishing Gail would change her mind, wondering if Gail was right and if she, Diane, was about to blow it big-time, walk out off the train into the loving arms of the law.

There was a moment, something hanging in the silence between them, the sensation that something was breaking, like a promise maybe, only there'd been no promises made. Diane wanted to say something that would convey to Gail her gratitude, but she didn't know where even to begin looking for the right words. Whatever she said, she thought, would come out sounding trite, sounding like some kind of excuse for bailing out on Gail. Because that had to be what Gail was thinking: Diane was bailing—and maybe making one very huge mistake in doing so.

"Whatever happens," Diane said, "good luck. It's been, you know, whatever it was." With that, she was out the door, leaving her suitcase, carrying only a black nylon backpack she swung over her shoulder as she went. Glad she hadn't found words. After what they'd been through. And whatever Diane had thought about criminals while she was still in uniform, all of that had been turned inside out by her time inside. Gail was stand-up. Gail was an inspiration. This might be goodbye forever, and she would miss her.

She dismounted the train smiling at the conductor who stood on the platform making sure no one took a tumble on the way out. Scanned the platform. Nothing. But she felt naked, standing there. And she thought she'd felt scared and exposed in Penn Station. She hadn't known the meaning of the words. She looked around again, even as her feet moved beneath her, carrying her along with the crowd, walking through air that seemed thick as water. She was underwater, walking against undertow, needing to breathe, wanting to rise to the surface and suck in air.

No cops. There was the escalator. No cops. She floated toward it, flowing with the human current. Things going well. She was walking away. Getting away. But it couldn't be, things couldn't go like this, so smoothly but realer than real: things, objects and people around her, the very air around her taking on a thickness and density that pressed at her, making it difficult, still, to breathe. She walked, surrounded by crowds, utterly alone. She needed her partner. She needed Gail.

Gail sat, the walls glowing hallucinatory beige, shimmering with something that looked like heat waves off a highway in a fierce afternoon sun. She thought she was seeing molecules of air dancing around the cabin and realized she was on the verge of fainting. Her ankle throbbed. She leaned forward, put her head between her knees, and stayed that way she didn't know how long. Until the feeling passed, and she was left sitting alone in the cabin, willing herself to stay put, trying to push down the barrage of questions that were time-lapse blooming in her brain, breaking from plain brown cocoons and fluttering around like butterflies caught in a bell jar, banging off the sheath of glass that was her skull.

She shouldn't have let Diane go. She couldn't stop her. But now the girl was on the loose, and who knew what would happen if she got popped. She might easily cut a deal. She probably would. Everybody did, these days—even the fucking Mafia guys yapped away to the heat when they got busted. Everybody punked out. And God knew the cops would rather have a revolutionary, even a former revolutionary, behind bars than they would one of their own.

Diane walked briskly along the platform, falling in with other departing passengers. She put a look on her face that belonged to someone who had to be someplace soon, urgency in place of panic. Remember Penn Station. Remember how cool Gail and Mel had been. Remember to believe that you are not a fugitive. The station swirled and blurred around her. She focused on the small things, a woman stupid enough to travel in stiletto heels, a teenager with pink hair and so many piercings that she looked like her face might start leaking any moment, on the mild echoing hum of humans in transit, footsteps falling and conversations. She spotted an exit sign and watched it grow closer. She could get there. She could get there. Just keep walking.

And then, to her right, there they were, the cops and the dog, standing near what looked like a main exit. They were looking for someone, scanning the area, eyeing the travelers. Diane knew the look, knew the stance. The dog looked from her handler to the scene before her and back again at her handler, her nose raised to sniff for fear. She was on her feet, sensing the tension, awaiting a command.

Diane veered left and headed for an archway. To TRAINS. Back the way she'd come, somehow. Functioning on intuition now, as lost as she'd ever been in her life, but moving as though she knew precisely where she was going and how to get there.

She slipped past a family and onto the escalator down.

Down and down and down, slower than time. The thing crawled, Diane walked the moving stairs, edging around suit-

cases, excusing herself with attempted politeness when someone gave her a look. She reached the platform, Train 909, the
Wanderlust Limited Daily, and Gail sitting inside, playing it
cool. Diane walked past, using raw willpower not to reboard
and drag Gail out of there, warn her what was happening, but
Gail wouldn't move, she was sure of it, and now there wasn't
time. Gail had made her choice; it was out of Diane's hands.
Fuck it. Just go. Move and keep moving. She made as if heading for the front of the train, past an occasional conductor
helping people board. She slipped her other arm into the strap
of the backpack, centered it on her back, slipped the gun
around to the front of her waistband.

Almost to the front of the train now, her eyes following the
track parallel to the one Gail's train sat upon, on the opposite
side of the platform. No train there, and ahead the blackness
of the tunnel leading back out somewhere into the world. Diane looked up to the windows of the train she was pretending
to board, to the very front where the engineers should be at the
controls. She saw a man's back, and glanced behind her down
the platform. People were busily boarding. One shot. She had
one shot.

She slipped over the edge of the platform onto the empty
tracks, landing more lightly than she'd anticipated, almost
stumbling. Her backpack caught on the edge of the platform;
she jerked her shoulders hard to wrench it free and fell hard
against gravel, leapt up and pressed her back quick and hard
against the concrete. She edged toward the darkness of the
tunnel, moving hunched over, scuttling down under cover of
the platform until there was no more platform and she was in
the gloom and cool of the tunnel. She stopped several yards in,
pressed herself against the wall and ventured a look. Her eyes
traveled the length of the platform, past last-minute boarders
rushing to make the train, past conductors picking up their yellow metal steps and placing them against the pillars in the center of the platform, to the escalator.

She shrank back; her breath stopped.

The cops. The dog.

On the escalator. One of them had his radio out and was talking into it.

She looked back once more, saw them entering the train. Gail. She turned and ran.

Stumbling at first over railroad ties, until her eyes adjusted to the dim wattage from the green and red and amber lights posted along the tunnel, and then she could go faster, gravel crunching under her feet, the beat of an army marching double time, echoing before her down the subterranean passage. She ran and ran and ran. Like she'd been doing forever, it seemed, like she'd been doing all her goddamn life.

She breathed hard as the backpack pounded her back. She pulled the gun from her waistband and ran with it in hand, alarmed suddenly that it might somehow discharge into her leg, or worse, her gut, if she left it put. She gripped her gun and ran and sweated and breathed and ran. Steady now, steady now, just keep going.

Suddenly there was a wide space in the tunnel, some kind of offshoot, and against the wall a couple of old refrigerator boxes tacked together into a shanty. Two gnarled and hairy figures huddled in the opening, and they leaned toward her, their eyes wide, eyeballs white against sooty skin. She swept past them, giving them a glimpse of her weapon in case they had thoughts of coming after her.

"No sweat," she panted, "I'm already gone," and their mouths dropped open as she passed, and one of them called after her, "Roll on, sweetheart!" She didn't look back. She picked up her pace.

Soon there was a lightening in the tunnel, and then she saw dusk. Maybe two hundred yards away. Hard to tell in here. She ran faster, sweat pouring down her forehead and into her eyes. She swiped at them with her sleeve; still they burned with salt.

Gail. Maybe they already had her. Maybe she was still sitting there on that train, unaware that she was busted. Diane ran with whatever the thing was inside her now that once had been hope. She ran and kept a picture in her head of Gail making it out of there, slipping past all of them unnoticed, like a ghost.

• • •

A commotion in the corridor, sounding about two cabins away. Gail recognized that one cop's voice, the dog handler, *Seek, Ginger, seek. Seek,* and the snapping of his thickly padded fingers. Then muffled words in deep tones crisp with authority, barked out like military orders, and a guy's voice shouting, "Fuck you, man, you can't do this!" That she heard loud and clear, and the dog growling a low threat, and then some bumping around and the sound of something dragging down the corridor.

The sounds of arrest. The sounds of a prisoner being dragged off to segregation. It roared in her ears, reverb on full, clanging in her head, dead memory, but this was real time, this was happening. She should have gone with Diane, gone when she had the chance.

She sat in her sleeper, afraid to move, afraid to breathe.

Afraid she was next.

She didn't know how long. How much time passed.

The sounds faded, disappeared. She moved and raised the shade. Pressed her cheek to the glass, trying to see what was happening. On the platform, she got a glimpse of the cops, some guy handcuffed between them. Ginger at heel, her tail bobbing purposefully, and then they were out of her limited view.

She heard a sigh escape, collapsed onto the seat. Wait. Just sit here and try to be calm and wait.

Half an eon later, she heard the rumble of the train's engines, felt the vibrations from below. Thank God. Now go. Just let's get out of here.

A knock on the cabin door brought her instantly to her feet. She turned, doing a three-sixty in the middle of the small sleeper, raised the shade, and looked helplessly at the hard, thick Plexiglas window. No one on the platform now. The walls swirled around her, and she had to catch her balance. She knew who was outside: men in uniforms. Men with guns. For the briefest instant, she wished she had one, too. Then she stopped herself. Composed herself. For some reason she smoothed her shirt.

She opened the door, fully expecting to be shoved against the wall and cuffed.

It was a porter. A black man in a trim white shirt and black trousers. Smiling. His mouth was moving, saying something, but she couldn't hear it over the "Hallelujah Chorus" blasting inside her head. She twisted her lips into a smile, bit her cheek to keep from laughing as relief washed over her, filled her with a giddiness.

"Ms. King?"

Stood a moment, then nodded. The name hadn't registered.

"Yes," she said, trying to see past the porter into the corridor without seeming to. No cops. That she could see.

"I have a fax for you." He handed over a plain brown envelope, nodded politely and strode away.

She checked the corridors again, closed and locked the door. Stood there, leaning against it, holding the envelope, looking at it. She smiled and shook her head, laughing, or attempting to, at herself. A fax. Her first fax ever in her life.

She recognized Mel's scrawl, with the loopy flourishes. It was a single page. Plain paper; no heading. No *TO*. No *FROM*. Sent from a Kinko's in New York. It said: "Your old friend called to ask about you. If you want his number, call me at your convenience. But I wouldn't. Hang loose."

Tom. She sat down, quickly began the tedious business of tearing the fax into a thousand or so small pieces. Later she would visit the public bathrooms in the passenger cars of the train, distributing the remains of Mel's message in various bathroom trash cans and toilets. Maybe she was being too cautious, but just as some people actually believed one couldn't be too thin or too rich—usually anorexics in haute couture—Gail knew she couldn't be too vigilant. She sat awhile, waiting for her heart to stop pounding.

Tom. Gosh, all she'd had to do to get his attention was escape from prison. What a guy. She knew Mel was right. She should stay as far away from him as she could. Don't even call Mel. Let Mel tell Tom he hadn't heard from her.

The train moved forward, and Gail sat, amused at the smile on her lips. Getting away. She was doing it, getting away. Her neck began aching and she focused on getting the tension out of her shoulders, out of her back, telling the muscles to relax. The train was really moving now, pulling out of the station. Goodbye, Cleveland. This was good. This was perfect. Why the fuck had Diane freaked out? Everything was fine. Or almost. Sort of. Maybe. Six hours to Chicago. She wondered if Diane would be there. She wondered if she should even show up. She felt a giddiness overcome her, but instead of throwing up her guard, she let it envelope her. She let herself fall into it. She slid down in the seat and stretched her legs out before her. She was doing it: getting away. Escaping. She couldn't remember when she'd felt this way. Like she was in charge of her life. Like she had some kind of control over her future. Like she had to use her wits to survive . . . outside a cage.

And then she recognized it: the exhilaration of risk. And she knew when she'd felt this way.

Tom. It would be interesting to know where he was, what he was up to. And she was certain he was up to something.

"Who knows?" she said softly. "Who cares?" And then she realized she was talking to herself and went back inside her head. She used to catch herself doing that sometimes in her cell when nobody else was around. Just to hear a voice that wasn't shouting out commands or screaming obscenities. Sometimes it was the voice of a friend, others times it was that of a prosecutor, cross-examining her in the matter of her life.

No doubt he had a new audience now. That was what she'd been, it occurred to her. Tom's audience. Not at first. At first he'd made sure she felt like the most important person in the world to him. But later, though the passion didn't abate, that's what role she fell into. Part of his audience. Seventh row center, to be sure. But still.

"Maybe he's grown up." Out loud again, though quietly. Talking with a friend over coffee. *Who are you kidding?* Inside her head. The voice of reason? The visitor she most and least enjoyed spending time with. The visitor who was often too busy thinking to stop by for a cup of tea.

Dusk going to dark fast. Diane crouched under a low oak atop an embankment, the tracks below twining into the station like some twisted steel nerve network. Sweat poured off her, but she'd almost got her breath back. She waited. Waited for the cops and their dog to emerge along the tracks. She waited more. Twenty minutes. Thirty.

Nothing.

Full dark now, and she heard traffic, the sounds of a freeway, down over the other side of the embankment. She stood up, looked around. She was right at the edge of things, where highways converged and twisted in cloverleaf exits and huge green signs announced the names of interstates and streets that meant nothing to her. She scanned the landscape, the littered edge of downtown, and her eyes fell on a sign that boasted *CLEANEST RESTROOMS IN AMERICA*. She could hide in the bathroom, as she had in sixth grade after four girls tried to rob her outside the pharmacy on Main Street. Right out in broad daylight after school, the four tough girls in town. Diane had fought them off, kicking and swinging, surprising the shit out of them, and then darting into the pharmacy and running past the fountain counter in the back to the ladies' room. They left her alone after that.

She started hiking, her backpack slung casually over one shoulder. She walked toward the cleanest restrooms in America right there on the edge of Cleveland, striding in the way she imagined some trust-fund college kid touring Paris in the summer might walk. And then she dropped that gait and walked her own walk, eyeing the landscape like an artist.

It was farther away than it looked. Diane asked the cashier for the key. He handed her a huge Slurpee cup with a hole cut in the bottom, the restroom key dangling from a string secured through the hole with a large knot.

"Guess it's hard to lose this, huh?"

The pimple-faced whiteboy behind the counter nodded and looked to the next customer. Diane ducked around the corner and keyed the lock.

The door auto-locked behind her. She stepped to the sink, looked into the gleaming mirror. No wonder the kid hadn't wanted to talk to her. Her short hair was curled up and kinked into place with dried sweat. Her face was smudged with dirt.

Man. Just back from hell. . . . She splashed water on her face and yanked at the paper towel dispenser. Finger-combed her hair. Looked again. Better. She took a pee—sweet relief—and straightened her clothes, slapping dust from her jeans.

Back in the EZ Mart, she pulled a twenty from the bills Gail had given her and purchased a phone card.

Outdoors again, the smell of gasoline and concrete still warm from the day. She stood for a long moment, wondering if she was making a mistake. Over across the freeway, the towers of downtown Cleveland, renovated Cleveland, the new Cleveland, glittered in the night. It wasn't a mistake. She wouldn't be here more than ten minutes. She realized then that as long as she kept moving, they'd most likely never catch her. Not unless someone snitched, and she'd make sure that didn't happen. Just keep moving. She picked up the receiver.

There was a sleepy hello and then she said, "Renfro."

"Diane?" Awake instantly. Alert. Maybe even alarmed. "Where the fuck are you?"

"Other end of the line," she said.

"Are you okay? 'Course you're okay. You okay?"

"Yeah. I'm okay. How are you?"

"I'm . . . fine." A silence then, neither of them knowing what to say.

"Got a new girlfriend?" Trying to kid.

"Half a dozen of 'em." He cleared his throat. "Diane, what are you doing? I mean, I read about it, it's been on TV. Holy shit, girl, are you out of your mind?"

"I couldn't just stay there and rot."

"But you got the papers I sent, didn't you? There are legal avenues."

"Yeah, well, I wound up on a dead-end street."

He made a sound like he was trying to laugh. "You gotta come back. You got to fight the case."

"Not without knowing they won't lock me up again." A breath. "Listen, feel free to say no, but I need some help."

"I guess you do."

"I need the trial transcript. From Churchpin's trial. Or whatever that was supposed to be."

"You're not the only one who wants it. But the damn court reporter hasn't finished transcribing it. Taking her own sweet time."

"So when's she supposed to be done?"

"Even the judge is screaming at her. Should be any day."

"I need it."

"How do I get it to you?"

"I'll call you back when I figure it out. But it'll be awhile."

"How long?"

"I don't know. But get your hands on it as soon as you can."

"They found your car."

She felt her face flush warm at the memory, the embarrassment of having to tell sorry-ass Lowe she'd blown it.

"Where?"

"Couple a hundred miles from here. Out in the woods somewhere east of Nacogdoches."

"Any suspects?"

"Nothing. Your briefcase was gone. Whoever stole the ride wiped it down real clean."

"Not a hair? Not a fiber?"

"It's at the impound lot over at the S.O. I don't know as they've gone over it all that closely. They looked for prints."

"Assholes don't even want to know who it was. *That's* what's happening there."

"And your pal Efird quit."

"Efird? Really?"

"Chief wanted him to start seeing some shrink—about the drinking, you know, and the trauma from what Linda did to him. I think he shoulda done it, but he figured it would put him in a holding pattern as far as promotions went."

"Probably true."

"Maybe. Anyway, he's outta there. Told the Chief he'd had enough bullshit to last three lifetimes and slapped his badge on the desk and walked."

"He was never my pal."

"Coulda fooled me."

"It's really kind of important to me to be taken at my word at this particular point in my life."

"I'm sorry. I guess I just don't know what to say. I miss you like all get-out, and I'm scared to death for you."

"I miss you, too." Saying it made it hurt all the more. "Do you know where Efird went?"

"Why?"

"I'm not sure yet. But I'd like to know."

"I heard he moved down by Nacogdoches somewhere. Living in a goddamn mobile home." A sigh, and then, "You should've told me."

"Told you what?"

"About you and Efird."

"I told you already, it wasn't anything."

"Except you passing out cold and spending the night at his place. You never even mentioned it." His voice was tight.

"Where the hell'd you hear that?"

"You wouldn't believe the shit that's getting said about you since you got locked up."

"I believe it's gettin' said, but that doesn't mean you should believe it happened."

"Just tell me."

"What."

"You and Efird."

"Nothing. Nada. I did pass out, but somebody doped me, not like it was from too much alcohol. And nothing happened. Nothing."

"Why didn't you tell me back then? When it happened?"

"I thought you'd get all pissed off, like you are right now."

"I wouldn't have."

"Then why are you now?"

"You should've told me."

"My mistake. I'm sorry."

"Diane. You gotta come in."

"Poor fucker. Just gave up, huh?"

"There's gotta be a way to work things out."

"I can't believe you're even saying that to me."

"I want you alive."

"Not if it means I gotta live in a cage."

"Di—"

"I gotta go. I'll call again." She hung up, scanned the area. The highway was right there. She could hitch.

No, she couldn't. She went back inside to ask directions to the bus station.

The slow grind of metal against metal brought Gail awake. The train was lumbering through a curve, the wheels scraping against the tracks. She got up from the bunk, raised the shade. Chicago.

She edged into the minuscule space in front of the sink and brushed her teeth, combed her hair. She still wasn't entirely used to her new appearance, but at least it no longer jarred her when she looked in a mirror.

When the train halted, she was ready to step out of her sleeper. Other passengers were emerging, most of them sleepy-eyed. Gail tried to look likewise as she wheeled her case in front of her, and Diane's behind her, down the narrow corridor.

And off the train. She stood on the platform, stunned that there were no cops waiting for her. Crowds pushed past. Gail stood, expecting the worst, certain she was surrounded by undercover heat, afraid to move for fear they would draw guns and—a shiver went through her; she shook her head and shrugged and forced herself to walk forward.

No one even noticed.

She followed a series of signs through a congested wing of the station, trying not to stare at all the people who were yakking into cell phones. It was weird, seeing them all walking and talking into the little handheld devices. What had they done without them? Maybe thought about things? Pondered the meaning of life? She wished she could see all the radio waves, words and words and words riding on them from phone to antenna and back to phone. The air around her must be saturated with words, all these millions of words converted into electronic pulses by some kind of technical alchemy, zapping through the ether at a speed she couldn't fathom.

And then the building opened up to reveal a huge and beautiful waiting area with an arched travertine ceiling, milk-white windows at either end of the room conforming to its curve and flooding the interior with light. Travelers sat among the rows of polished wooden benches, some dozing, some reading, some blabbing on their phones. She wanted one herself, but had heard that the authorities could pinpoint the location of a cell phone within a matter of a few seconds. She wasn't sure that was true, but considered her paranoia on the subject to be healthy.

She spotted the ladies' room and wheeled in. Entered the handicapped stall.

When she came out, she had only her own suitcase with her. Diane's she left parked in the stall, next to the toilet. She dropped Diane's shoes into the wastebasket, tossed a couple of paper towels on top just as someone entered the restroom. Gail exited quickly, looking down as she smoothed her shirt, not to smooth it, but to keep the woman entering from getting a good look at her face. Even as she was doing it, she thought it unnecessary. But necessary. As necessary as movement, and right now movement was essential.

There was a Starbucks in the waiting area. It seemed that they were everywhere, at least they had been in New York, and now here was another one. She wanted to try something, but wanted even worse to keep moving, get out of the station. She walked briskly, past the Elgin-faced clock that said 7:22 A.M., past the Starbucks, out through heavy wooden doors into the morning. Huge stone columns rose up in front of her, looking not unlike the ubiquitous pillars of justice that fronted any federal courthouse worth its name.

She didn't know where to go. She had a phone number in her head, memorized while she was at Mel's, but wasn't ready to make the call. He'd given her a calling card too, something bought at a drugstore, basically untraceable. But she wanted to wait until Diane either showed or didn't. She headed down Adams Street, walked until she saw a coffee shop, ducked in.

It was air-conditioned and smelled of bacon. She took a booth, pulled a menu from the holder. Coffee-shop standards, but once again she was overwhelmed by the choices. She settled on coffee and a bagel. She wondered where Diane was, and thought about getting a paper, but even if Diane had been popped it wouldn't have made this morning's edition.

She was almost finished with the bagel when she was stopped midbite by the sight of two Chicago cops pushing through the glass door of the restaurant. She gulped, made herself keep chewing, glanced away from them, but wasn't sure where else to look. Her heart became a Ping-Pong ball, bouncing back and forth between her lungs in a championship playoff. Move slowly now, everything's fine. They're just ordering coffee. She picked up her check and grasped her bag and wheeled it to the register.

They were six feet away from her, neither of them talking, just standing there while the counterman poured their coffee into to-go cups with a blue-and-white image of the Parthenon printed on them. Who should she pray to? Zeus, get my ass out of here but fast.

She paid and walked out, knowing that they weren't going to stop her, but not believing herself. Left on Adams, back toward the train station. These were good shoes that Mel had come up with, easy to walk in. She walked fast. But not so fast that it looked like she was running from something.

Taxi.

Taxi taxi taxi.

Get me out of here. Get me out get me out.

Five o'clock sharp, and Diane sat on a bench just inside the rental area, pretending to read a paper, waiting for Gail, and wanting really badly to wash the smell of bus out of her hair. The Hertz on South Canal Street, the closest to Union Station, had a line at the counter, busy people wondering why there weren't more staff members on duty to handle the customers. They stood waiting impatiently for service. Diane sat patiently waiting. Just waiting. Maybe for Gail. She hoped for Gail.

She tried not to look at her watch every three minutes, but by quarter to six she was certain Gail had been busted. She didn't know whether she was feeling angry or sad. Maybe a little of both. But she would stay, give Gail a little more time to show. Maybe if she just sat here long enough.

People came and went, families and businessmen mostly. A couple of teenagers came out, grumbling it wasn't fair they couldn't rent a car without a major credit card, eyeing Diane's boots with envy.

So scratch plan A, Diane thought. She sure as hell didn't have any plastic. She'd never had to rent a car. She'd had her own since she could drive, though it was a stretch to call some of her early junkers automobiles. She stared at her boots. Prison-issue black steel-toed lace-ups. Totally hip. Totally cool. She hadn't realized at the time why she wanted to wear them so badly. She'd thought it was because she found them practical, good boots for an escape, where you'd be running through who-knew-what-all kind of landscapes. But now she understood it was because she wanted to take something from them, she wanted to *steal something* from the prison. She'd shined them up nicely at Mel's. They looked almost new, but they were good and broken in. She imagined herself giving Gib Lowe a serious kick in the ass. Sneak up on him while he was bent over and— *thunk!*—expand the circumference of his sphincter.

A taxi pulled in. It was her. It was Gail. Hot damn. Diane jumped up and was at the rear door before Gail had finished paying the driver. She climbed in next to Gail.

"We coming or going, ladies?" The driver's thyroid eyes stared at them from the rearview.

"Going," Diane said. Then, to Gail, "They're down to mini-economy size." She turned back to the driver. "Is there like a Holiday Inn or something close by?" He nodded yes and reset the meter, pulled out.

Gail surprised Diane by giving her a hug and a light kiss on the cheek. "I'm so glad you're here."

"So. Am. I." Diane let her head fall back on the seat, closed her eyes.

"How was your trip?" Gail was smiling, just barely.

"I took the scenic route. Yours?"

"There was some excitement on the train."

"I thought there would be."

"So how is it I'm here?"

"You tell me."

"Some other fool got grabbed."

Diane saw the driver eyeing them in the mirror and nudged Gail.

"Yeah," Gail said, "West Virginia was wild. But I needed a week to myself. Your father, you know, I love him, but, I just needed some time. What'd you think of Swarthmore?"

Diane sighed loudly. She'd never heard of Swarthmore, but the way Gail said it made Diane certain it was a school. "I just don't know." Diane tossed her hands, let them fall onto her lap. "I can't decide."

"I wouldn't worry about it too much right now. You have lots of time. And you haven't seen Northwestern yet."

"Good school," the driver said. "My son goes there."

Ah. "Graduate or undergrad?" Diane asked.

"He's a junior."

"I'm shopping for a grad school." Diane nodded.

"All's I know, he wants to go more than four years, he picks up the ticket. A regular degree'll get him a good enough job."

"Depends what he wants to do," Diane said.

The driver hit the meter again and eased to stop in the porte cochere of the Holiday Inn.

He wished Diane luck in her quest and directed a knowing look at Gail—it never stops with kids, does it?—which she tried her best to return. She and Diane entered the hotel like two tired travelers. Diane set her backpack next to her and took a seat on one of the lobby couches. Gail plopped down next to her.

"So why couldn't we rent?" Gail asked.

"Gotta have a credit card."

"I do. Mel gave me one."

"Nice of you to let me know."

"It never came up."

"Okay. So do you want to go back? Head out now?"

Gail let herself relax into the couch. It felt so good not to be moving. Her body needed rest. Her mind needed rest.

"I'm wrung out," she said. "Let's stay here a night. I think we're okay. We're cool."

"I was hoping you'd say that. I did a four hundred meter sprint yesterday."

"I can't wait to hear."

"I feel like dirty dishwater, and it might even be a relief if someone pulled the plug and let me run on down the drain."

Gail stood. "Wait here while I get us checked in."

Gail picked up the remote and settled on one of the two double beds in the room. Found the on button. The TV came to life, on the screen a series of choices: movies on demand, free TV, hotel services . . . It was all confusing. She chose Free TV and the screen switched to CNN. A heavily made-up Asian woman was talking about the stock market. Beneath her image, headlines scrolled across the screen. *Priest in Akron OH charged with sexual abuse of thirty-seven altar boys between 1964 and 1972 . . . tornados kill three, injure twenty-nine, in Beeville TX . . . An abandoned suitcase in the ladies' room forces evacuation of Chicago Amtrak station, delaying travelers for three hours. Suitcase was empty . . .*

"Shit."

"What?" Diane joined her in front of the television.

"Your suitcase."

"What about it?"

"I left it in the ladies' room at the train station this morning. Someone reported it and they closed the station for three hours."

"Why'd you do that?"

"What, I should leave it on the train for the cops to find? I don't think so."

"No. You did the right thing. I mean I guess you could've left it on the street or something, maybe nobody would have freaked out about it."

"I was in a hurry."

"I know. I'm not on your case. It just seems like you feel bad about it. I was offering a suggestion."

"A little late."

"In case it comes up again. It could come up again."

"Let's hope not."

"Gail. Don't feel so bad. Those people sat around for three hours. You sat around for eighteen years."

"I didn't exactly sit around," Gail said. "I accomplished some things." And now she thought, it was time to stop accomplishing. She would not do anything to bring any attention to herself. Not even things of a helpful nature. She would become Susan Q. Citizen. She would so conform to the expectations of society that there might even be times when she would begin to doubt her own existence, her actual status as a sentient being on planet Earth.

Diane might still be considering a bang-bang, shoot-'em-up, rootin'-tootin' reentry into Texas, though she seemed to be coming around to reason, but regardless of what Diane did, Gail had her own vague plans. She wasn't sure where she would go, or how long she would even stay in one place.

But wherever she went, and wherever she wound up, she would tread so lightly that no footprints would ever be left behind.

TWELVE

Gail peered through the hotel door peephole. The man standing in the hall wore a suit and tie, had neatly trimmed, slicked-back black hair. A broad forehead, fierce but friendly eyes. He was holding a soft-sided brief case. Her reaction, not panic, but caution, told her she was adjusting to her new status. She called through the door. "Who is it?"

"Rick Reed." She recognized the voice from her phone call to him earlier. She looked again. It took a moment, but finally she put the image of the man in the hallway together with the memory she carried of Rick from his days in Free Now. She opened the door, locked it behind them. They stood looking at each other, and then Rick grabbed her and gave her a huge hug.

"They done you wrong, girl. They done you bad wrong."

"And would've kept right on doing it." Gail smiled, motioned him into the room. Diane pulled her attention from CNN. She'd been watching for hours now, since Gail had mentioned the suitcase. Every time the banner came crawling along the bottom of the screen, she would say, "Here it comes again. How many times they gonna run this thing?" Though she knew the answer: until something more enticing happened.

Gail introduced them, using first names only, though she was sure Mel had briefed Rick on Diane. Rick shook Diane's hand and then took a seat at the small glass-topped table in the corner of the room. There was a fold-up display advertising the restaurant, promising knockout doses of alcohol disguised in tropical-colored liquids. Kind of weird for Chicago, Diane thought, but then probably every Holiday Inn all over the world had the same specials going this month. She sat back down on her bed, where she could keep an eye on CNN, but kept her ear tuned to Gail and Rick.

"You look good," Rick said, but Gail was sure he was being kind. The years inside had taken a toll, she knew. Rick, on the other hand, really did look good. Healthy, with lively blue eyes and lips that curved up into the hint of a smile even when he wasn't smiling. Right now he wasn't smiling, he was pulling new ID out of his briefcase. Passports, even. Those weren't easy to come by. He placed them on the glass tabletop.

"Somebody made travel plans? For us?" Gail opened a passport. It was her photo, the one taken at Mel's just after her makeover. Her eyes looked slightly stunned but keenly alert, like those of something wild caught in the glare of headlights on a lonely country lane.

"Just so's to have options," Rick answered. "Get someplace you're comfortable."

Gail saw Diane turn and start to say something, think better of it, go back to the TV.

"We need fresh plastic," Gail said. "The trains, it's like there are cops everywhere."

"You should see the airports. They got that thing reads your retina for ID at O'Hare. Testing it. Imagine once that's in place. Like something out of a Tom Cruise movie." He dug in his case again. Came out with a Visa. "No preset spending limit," he said. "But Mel said to tell you to use it only when you absolutely have to. And we'll have to change it in ninety days or so." He smiled. "And he said to remind you it's all coming out of your account. Not directly, of course." He sat, looking at Gail and nodding, like he was still trying to absorb that she was actually there across the table from him.

The driver's license was from New York this time. Now she was Nina Roselyn Fisher. She picked up Diane's passport. Blair Ellen Parker. Of Baton Rouge, Louisiana. She nudged Diane, handed her the passport. Diane looked at the name, the place of birth. Tossed the passport back on the table.

"No problem," she drawled. "I'm already Blair. And don't nobody fuck with me. I'm from Baton Rouge."

"Don't be too ready to show it off, cowgirl. You two need to lay real low."

"Just joking," Diane said. "You ever been to Baton Rouge?" Rick nodded no.

"That's why you didn't get it," Diane said, and shot him a smile that mostly said they were in a situation where they had to get along, so best if they both rolled with it.

"So how's your life been?" Gail pulled Rick's attention away from Diane. "What're you up to these days?"

He sat back in his chair, loosened his tie, unbuttoned his crisp white collar.

"I went from Free Now to Read Now." He chuckled. "With a few years of lying low myself."

"I seem to recall they indicted you."

"They indicted everyone they even thought they *might* have a chance of, if not convicting, at least pressuring into a plea bargain. What'd they indict, like twenty-seven people on that case? Of which eighteen walked? Some of those juries were outraged at the evidence they were expected to convict on. It was crazy. And they never even *caught* the ones who were actually in the bank."

"You're talking about the robbery. I was talking about my case, Tom's, the guns, you know, the—"

"I wasn't in on that one. I mean, I wasn't indicted. They got you, they got Tom, they got Hal and Billy, but those two only for conspiracy, not actual possession. Chris and Michelle weren't even named."

"Chris? Michelle?"

"You didn't know? Of course not. They were on the way over when the cops fell on you. Chris"—Rick glanced at Diane—"was supposed to hook up with you guys. Put things together."

Gail tried not to show surprise. Put things together. As in bombs. She hadn't known who else was involved. Tom had just said they were to sit on things until someone showed up to take over.

"I thought you knew."

Gail shook her head.

"You heard from any of them? Hear from Tom?"

"Not directly." Gail caught herself massaging her hands, one with the other, the way she had several times when she was on the witness stand. She stopped and placed them in her lap.

"What about Chris and Michelle?"

"Not a word. From anyone."

"For almost twenty years?"

"It would have been foolish for anyone to contact me, don't you think?"

Rick looked curious, like he was waiting for more from her, but she turned to Diane.

"You mad 'cause they made you from Louisiana?"

Diane stared at her. "*Hey-ull* no," already doing her Loozianna thing, "I don't give a flyin' fuck where ah'm from, girl, I care 'bout where I'm goin'."

Gail grinned and shook her head and turned back to Rick. "Read Now, you said?"

"A literacy group. We work with underprivileged children in urban Chicago."

"I did the same thing in the joint. Had to put together my own program."

"Maybe we could use it."

"Feds own it. Probably never see the light of day."

"Maybe someday. When you get established somewhere. We could communicate."

"Maybe. Underprivileged children? Don't you mean ghetto kids?"

"Yeah, is that like one of the weirdest words ever compounded, or what? I mean, privilege implies a special right or immunity, no? So how can someone be underprivileged? If everyone—we're talking theory here, man—if everyone has the same privileges, those privileges are no longer privileges, They're just everybody's right."

Diane looked at him. He was getting worked up, jerking at

his tie, leaning toward Gail. "There's really no such thing as underprivileged," his face going red, "unless one presumes that everyone deserves the same privileges, in which case we're no longer talking about privileges. The word loses its connection to its definition. Who came up with that term anyway? Probably some rich Republican bitch looking to push her old man into the White House."

Diane was staring at him, looking like she might burst out laughing. Gail raised her hands helplessly. "I see you haven't lost any of the old fire."

"Not true." He laughed at himself. "I'm actually pretty close to burnt. What I see, day in, day out."

"I hear that," Diane said. She picked up the remote. Settled on the local news.

Rick glanced at Diane, gave a half shrug, looking at Gail seriously.

"I'm really sorry," he said.

"For what?" Gail didn't feel he owed her any kind of apology.

"For what happened to you. You got a really raw deal. And you were always such a nice person."

"Hey." Gail shook her head, smiling. "We were all kind of crazy back then. Believers. Too much belief is a dangerous thing."

Rick shook his head slowly, half laughing, but not the ha-ha funny kind of laugh.

"I can't imagine if we'd ever . . ."

"Succeeded?"

"Exactly."

"So when did you leave? When did you decide to go another direction?"

Rick looked over at Diane, and back at Gail, questioning. Diane raised her head off the pillow and said to him, "I'm not even here, sweetheart. Not even in this room."

He leaned forward, elbows on knees.

"I think it was when I realized how easily I could have been there. That day."

The bank. He wasn't going to come out and say it in front of Diane, not anything specific, but Gail knew what he was

talking about. He had been on standby to drive one of the vehicles that day at the bank. Luckily for him, the first-stringers
had showed up.

"You have a family?" Gail reached down to touch her ankle,
which was starting to itch. Healing.

"I did." Rick eased down in the chair, crossed his legs. "I
mean I still do. Two kids. I'm divorced."

"Sorry," Gail said.

"Hey, it happens. A lot. But I get the kids every weekend,
and my ex is cool about things. I just . . . I think I was looking
so hard for some kind of stability—and I have to admit, probably some kind of good cover—that I rushed into it. Her clock
was ticking, and we both know we made a mistake." He
shrugged, and then broke into a smile. "Except for the kids. Our
kids are great. Just the best." He caught himself then, straightened in his chair. It was like he couldn't get comfortable.

"It's okay, Rick." Gail smiled, a little tiredly. She had a feeling she was going to have to get used to this kind of thing,
sooner or later. People with children feeling sorry for her because she was on the other side of forty and still childless. Inside, it hadn't mattered so much. Everybody in there was
isolated, parentless, childless.

Gail pulled herself out of memory. All that was doing was
extending her time inside.

"Did she know?"

"My wife?"

"Yes."

A pause. "No."

"How long were you married?"

"Almost eight years."

"And you never told her?" Gail was stunned. "How could
you be that close and that far away at the same time?"

"I'll let you in on something. Unless you wind up with
someone from the old crew, someone who already knows who
you are and where you've been, don't ever, ever even *think*
about revealing your true identity. First, it's unfair to put anyone, especially someone who doesn't know anything about,
shall we say, the status of your freedom, in that position. And

second, you'll have about a one hundred percent better chance of getting picked up."

Gail nodded. He was right. She saw a look on Diane's face that made her uncomfortable. The first time she'd seen Diane look, was it—guilty?

"Did you feel the distance?"

He shook his head no. "I was, and am, still fundamentally myself," he said. "I have a new name, I have new numbers for the government. I pay my taxes, but I cheat when I know I can get away with it, because those fuckers deserve it, and I do what I can to help ghetto kids learn how to read. They're great kids. I love my work. But it drains you."

Diane swung her legs around to the side of the bed facing the table.

"So how come you're all in a suit and everything?"

Rick smiled at her. "Usually I'm not. Thought the occasion demanded it. You know, incognito, that kind of bullshit."

Diane nodded.

"So." Rick sighed. "I won't ask where you're going. I mean, if you want to tell me, that's fine."

"I don't know yet," Gail said, and saw Diane glance at her. "And I'm sure you don't want me carrying your business card around."

He laughed, shaking his head no, no offense, but of course not. "If you see Tom, or anyone else, give 'em my love."

"Thanks for these," Gail said. Rick stood to go, looked confused for a moment, so Gail opened her arms for a hug. His embrace was warm, and she wished she could stay there for a while. It felt safe. Or at least she could pretend it felt that way.

The map was spread out on Diane's bed, Gail's finger tracing a line southwesterly toward Oklahoma City. Outside, the city of Chicago was lighting up in the cool blue gray of dusk. The television droned in the background. Gail couldn't get used to it, but Diane insisted they stay tuned to the news.

"Looks like about a twelve-, thirteen-hour drive. If we push on through."

"You can drive that long?"

"I can, but it'd be nice if you could spell me now and then."

"I haven't driven for almost twenty years. I don't know if I remember how."

"No sweat. Half the licensed drivers in the country don't know how to drive. Anyway, it's like riding a bike. You'll be back in the saddle in no time flat."

Gail shrugged, not so sure, stared at the map.

"Holy shit." Diane grabbed the remote and upped the volume.

"It was like, they totally took me by surprise. They looked harmless. To me it was just a couple of women who needed help, and I was willing to do that. They said their car had broken down, gave up the ghost, and they needed to get to the city . . ." It was the dump truck driver—Gail couldn't remember his name—the skin around his mouth broken out in a near-perfect rectangular rash.

"Who'd've thought?" Diane said. "Allergic to duct tape. I feel bad."

Gail moved to her bed, directly in front of the tube, sat down. Diane climbed next to her, sitting cross-legged on the bed, leaning toward the TV, glued.

"Mike," Gail said.

"And he said he wouldn't tell," Diane said. "And you were ready to believe him. See? Sometimes I know what I'm doing."

Gail was silent.

". . . and then that one, the younger one, we get to the city and next thing you know I'm looking at a damn .357 or something, I know it was *big*, it was a big-ass gun . . ."

Mike got a little shaky then, his eyes darting back and forth and his eyelids fluttering back tears, but he caught himself, "I'll be damned if I'll ever stop for *anybody* again. I thought she was gonna shoot me. I really did. I'm telling you, those girls are not playing around."

The reporter hadn't finished thanking Mike when the mug shots came up, full screen, side by side, numbers under their chins, chins that were thrust up in almost identical attitudes of defiance.

"Look," Gail said, "we're on TV. We're full-fledged humans now. We exist in reality."

Diane just stared at the tube, heard the reporter's voice describe them as "the revolutionary and the renegade," heard the reporter's voice say that authorities had reason to believe the escaped convicts might still be in the New York City area, but that it was also very possible they had fled the city.

"In other words," Diane said to the TV, "you don't know dick." She sighed, and Gail thought it sounded kind of contented. It definitely wasn't a worried sigh.

A commercial came on, and Gail hit the mute button.

"So."

"So?"

"It didn't look anything like you."

"Thank God. Yours, either. But you had an attitude, huh? When they brought you in?"

"Enough for both of us," Gail said. "I think."

"I don't doubt it," Diane said. Gail took it as a compliment.

Later, when the lights were out and the TV off and they were each drifting in their thoughts, Diane flipped onto her side, facing Gail.

"Rick," she said. "He was your boyfriend?"

"Almost," Gail said.

"You trust him."

"Obviously."

"How do you know he's okay?"

"There's no *knowing*. But I trust him as much as I trust anybody."

"Me?"

Gail turned to look at her. "I'm not entirely sure I trust you. Or I'm not sure I trust you entirely."

"Why?"

"I guess trust is not the right word for what I'm trying to express. I do trust you. I just don't trust your judgment."

"Now you really do sound like a mother."

"Don't dismiss experience."

"Oh, my God."

"I'm serious. I've been around."

"Mostly you've been locked up! Like almost a fifty-fifty split, isn't it? Between free and locked up? And the free was basically your childhood. Now you're gonna tell *me* how to behave?"

"I'm just asking you to take a step back, look at the situation carefully."

"That why we're going to Oklahoma? Right next door to Texas?"

"We can hook up there. Friends from grad school. It'll be safe there."

"Know why the state of Texas doesn't slide off into the Gulf of Mexico?"

"Why."

" 'Cause Oklahoma sucks."

"That's not even funny. It's juvenile."

"True, but it's how I feel about Oklahoma. Got no use for it whatsoever. Flat, dusty, ugly as sin, and drier than a popcorn fart." She paused. "What on earth possessed you to go to school there?"

"Native American cultures."

"The white man pretty much bled all that out of them. I been to some reservations. Like going to the zoo, only the creatures in confinement are human. Sadder than shit."

"I worked on one. Right after I graduated."

Diane was silent for a moment, and then said quietly, "I've got some Indian in me."

"Really?"

"My great-great-great-grandmother on my father's side. Maybe even another great in there. Not that I know much about it. Only that she supposedly was Warm Springs Apache. It's really just a rumor, I guess. My mother told me once. I wanted to know more. But she didn't know herself."

"We could look into it. The people we'll stay with there, one of them teaches at the university. They've got access to all kinds of records and archives."

A long silence then, so long that Gail felt herself drifting toward sleep, and then through the haze she heard Diane shift, rustling her covers.

"Gail?"

"Hmm?"

She wanted to tell Gail about the phone call, about Renfro, but thought better of it. Maybe when things were more settled.

"Nothing," Diane said. "Just thanks. For taking me with you."

Gail smiled, though she knew Diane couldn't see it. But it was there in her voice when she said, "Couldn't have done it without you."

Diane lay in the dark, hearing Gail's breathing settle into the rhythms of sleep, as she had for all those nights in the cell. She thought back to Rick Reed's visit, how something about him seemed slightly artificial, the way instant mashed potatoes, though they looked fluffy and delicious, always seemed to carry a slight taste of cardboard from the box they'd come in. Probably he was just nervous about being around a cop. Or an ex-cop. But she knew how they thought, and even regular old civilians had the same attitude: once a cop, always a cop. The same way the cops thought criminals never changed. It was all mixed up in her head, and none of it making any sense.

Unable to sleep, she got up and went to the window. Twenty-fourth floor, and she was looking out at the chunky Chicago skyline, buildings lit and glittering, still plenty of cars on the street. She kept seeing Mike on TV, hearing his voice as he told America to be on the lookout. For Gail. For her. Two desperate convicts. God, there was so much bullshit in the world.

Everything in her was pulling her back to Texas, and at the same time she felt as though she were headed for doom. It was strangely liberating, making her feel almost giddy and light, like she was standing there firmly in the grasp of gravity but also floating through some weird place of weightlessness. Or maybe like the Graviton, the whirling cylinder that stuck riders to its sides with centrifugal force while the floor dropped out from under them every year at the Breard County Fair. She'd been six the first time she rode it with Kevin, and she'd made him take her back on five times in a row, even though they had to stand in line again each time.

She had to go back. That was all. She looked out at

Chicago. She could never live in a city like this. You couldn't see more than three or four stars out there tonight, what with all the ambient light. Light pollution, that's what it was. Night should be night, lit up by the moon and stars, not by neon and flood vapors.

"Diane?" Gail propped a pillow behind her, shifted to sitting up.

Diane returned to her own bed, sitting cross-legged, facing Gail.

"You know what it is?"

Gail shook her head no and waited.

"I'm not the kind of person wants to strike out from home and go to some big city to seek fame and fortune. I like Breard County. To be honest, I wasn't kidding, what I said about quitting the department and going back to school when all this happened. I was kind of fed up with being the police."

"Maybe you should."

"I didn't realize they admitted fugitives these days. How liberal."

"Diane, it's all changed now. You can't go back there. You've got to shift your frame of reference."

"You know how to do that? 'Cause I'm not at all sure I do."

"We'd have to fix you up with a different undergrad degree. It's not like you don't really have one. It just needs a new name."

"Maybe you can give me better grades." Diane laughed. "That'd have to be a three-point-eight average, though, at least."

"Diane, I'm serious. Though we wouldn't spike the grades. It's that Dylan line: 'To live outside the law, you must be honest'."

"I was only kidding."

"It seems like you're kidding on the square."

"I'm not. But whatever."

"It's something you could do. You'd have to get settled somewhere, get a job, build a life for a year or so. Then you could start applying. It's actually a really good way to get yourself into your new life."

"I'm not sure I'm through with my old life yet."

"Listen to yourself, Diane. It's a really good idea. I forget whether it was Watson or Crick, you know those two guys who came up with the model of DNA? One of them was talking about how he decided what to do with his life, and he said you should just listen to the gossip in your head, that there would be something, some subject, that would interest you to the point that it returned again and again in your internal conversations, and that was the thing you should pursue."

Diane lay back on her bed and got under the covers. "I guess I'll have to start paying better attention to myself." But she already knew the gossip in her head. Intimately. Or at least the gossip that had taken over since the DEA agent read Miranda to her. And it kept getting more and more insistent.

Gail plumped her pillow, a real pillow, soft and fresh. And a pretty decent mattress, too. She remembered family vacations, when they would pull into a Holiday Inn after a day spent cooped up in the car and her father would give her quarters to feed into the little metal box by the bed that made the mattress vibrate all over for five jiggling minutes.

"I just think it's a really good idea. You're talking law school, right?"

"I guess. That's where the gossip in my head goes. To matters criminal." At least it wasn't entirely a lie.

"I hope you'll think about it. Seriously. I think you'd be good. And knowing what you know now, you could do some good, too." Gail rolled over to face the wall, just as she always had in the cell to signal the end of the conversation, sleep time. Only in here the wall wasn't inches from her nose.

Diane stared at the light seeping in through the windows. Listen to the gossip in her head. That was the problem. The gossip in her head was all about Breard County and Sheriff Gib Lowe and District Attorney Al Swerdney. And about Rick and Juanita Churchpin. The gossip in her head, whether she wanted it to be or not, was about settling the score.

THIRTEEN

Diane pulled out to pass a line of trucks, then checked the speedometer and thought better of it. Best to stay within ten of the speed limit. But she was finding it difficult, being used to driving with relative impunity. Being used to driving with a badge in her pocket. And more than that, she was in a hurry. Trying not to show it, but still. Rolling through rural America, past houses, farms, acre after acre of corn and wheat, as far as you could see, she wanted only to get Gail to Wherever, Oklahoma, and then get herself south. To Texas. To home—and whatever was waiting there. She felt oddly confident, but underneath the layer of cool, when she let herself go there, she was scared out of her wits. So she didn't go there. She stayed on the surface, where she could think clearly, unencumbered by emotions like fear and loathing. That was where she needed to hold herself: alone and lonely. Outside the window, the flatlands of middle America rolled by, calm and level as the surface of a pond at dawn, though not nearly so reflective.

"You want to take over?" Diane arched her back, then pressed herself against the seat. Chicago had been asleep when they pulled out, well before sunrise, in their rented silver Taurus. Afternoon was waning now, and she was feeling the fatigue of having driven all day.

"I will. If you need a rest." Gail still didn't want to drive at

all if she could help it. She wasn't confident of her ability to
steer metal tonnage down the road at fifty-five miles an hour,
and besides, she was feeling uneasy. Breathless. Like she needed
to sit and look out the windows at the scenery rolling past and
collect herself, try to let the days since the escape catch up to
her. Things were out of sync. If she thought back to the first
time she considered it—truthfully—that would have been before they even took her out of the courtroom that day, right after the judge had consigned her to a term of imprisonment of
not more than seventy-two years. The thought hadn't even
taken shape in the form of words in her mind; it had been
vague and blurry, not more than a kind of awareness that no
matter what, she would not stay locked up for that long. Maybe
it was that the form of escape was so conceptual then: the actual logistics of the escape were necessarily vague. She might
escape by going over the walls, or digging a tunnel, or effecting
a disguise and walking out the front gate. Or she might escape
by hanging herself or swallowing pills. She could not very well
plan an escape from a prison she hadn't yet seen or felt, did not
know intimately. All she knew was that she would not do that
much time. She refused. But then, when she'd got there, after
six months or so, when the shock wore off and life inside became if not completely tolerable, at least doable, she forgot
about it, as much as any prisoner ever forgets about it, but at
any rate it no longer occupied a prominent place in her
thoughts. That was when she threw herself into helping the
other prisoners. So many of them had so much less than she.
She was white, educated, from a comfortable upper-middle-
class background that meant certain doors were open to her.
She remembered the moment she realized the opportunity
she'd been given. She passed by the phone, where the line of
mostly dark faces waited for their three minutes of talk time,
and heard a young woman saying, "Oh, you know, it's pretty
nice here, you know, three meals and a warm bed, you know,
and ain't nobody beatin' up on me, I can't complain . . ."

Diane moved a hand from the steering wheel; it caught
Gail's attention. They were behind a station wagon, Indiana
plates, and in the back a couple of kids pressed their noses flat

against the back window and waved happily. Diane waved back, and the kids kept waving, looking at Gail, and then Gail waved and the kids' heads disappeared from the window, and the waving hands followed.

"They should be wearing seat belts," Diane said, her voice sounding as if it were on autopilot.

"Are you sleepy? I'll drive if you really need me to."

"I'll go awhile longer." It wasn't that Diane couldn't do the whole day at the wheel. That was what patrol had been about. Eight hours at the wheel, mostly boredom, punctuated by mostly mundane calls, and occasionally some excitement. Efird had said detective work wasn't a whole lot better, but at least your back didn't ache from all that time driving around in a squad car, and you didn't have to carry forty pounds of equipment on your belt.

"It doesn't have to be Oklahoma," Gail said. "You could go anywhere."

"I know." What Diane didn't know was how she'd feel about leaving Gail behind. It wasn't as if there were friends and family to return to. She couldn't actually go home. Neither of them could. But in a way she had it better than Gail. If she could figure a way to clear her name, she *could* go back. People would respect her, maybe even more than they had before she'd gone away. But Gail. Gail had no home to go to. Her only friends were either prisoners or ex-cons or people she knew from the movement. She couldn't really risk settling among any of them.

"These people we're seeing," Diane said. "They're?" She let the question hang, not fully asked.

"Old friends," Gail said. She sighed. "I met them when I was in college here. They were from back east, part of the movement, but fell away from it after the bank robbery. A lot of people did. Most of us wanted nothing to do with that kind of violence. They went to California, grad school, then came back here, settled. I don't think they're on anyone's lists anymore."

"Don't be sure."

"I didn't say I was. But I think this is a good bet right now. We can regroup. Make some decisions."

"They didn't, you know . . . Oklahoma City?"

"God, no, Diane. How could you even think?"

"I didn't really. But, I mean, even senators sometimes change parties."

"We weren't a political party."

"What were you?"

"We were a bunch of kids who wanted to change the world."

"That why you robbed a bank?"

"I didn't. That was a core group of hardliners. Most of us had no idea it was even going down."

"But that's not what the prosecutor thought."

"Maybe. Or maybe he was looking toward a promotion."

"Kind of hard-core tactics, isn't it?"

"Yeah," Gail said. "Almost as hard-core as the guys who prosecuted you."

Diane was silent. The sky stretched blue for as far as she could see, a smattering of puffy, searingly white clouds hung high above the distant horizon. She saw the shape of a rabbit, outlined almost perfectly, its legs frozen midjump.

"Where's this coming from, anyway? You suddenly don't trust me?"

"I'm just nervous," Diane said. "I don't know these people. Any of these people who are helping us. Helping you. I'm feeling kind of like a pet or something, you know, like you couldn't find anybody to watch me so you had to bring me along."

"That's silly and you know it." Gail did not wonder aloud what it was, what she meant when she said it was more than a tagalong. But when she took stock, thought about present and recent-past circumstances and prospects for the future, Diane was her closest friend in the world. *Right now,* she reminded herself. It was a circumstantial friendship, or partnership, or whatever it was. But that didn't explain the feelings in her chest when she thought about Diane doing something foolish like going back to Texas and facing up to whoever these cretins were that she couldn't stop dwelling on.

"You know what I thought about when Oklahoma City happened?"

Diane's head jerked sharply toward her, eyes questioning, and then she went back to the road.

"I mean after the initial shock, and the horribleness of it, later on, when the analysts started doing their unending thing. When they were talking about how the bomb was made, that it was made out of common fertilizer . . ."

"How easy it is to make bombs?"

"That, too," Gail said. "But I couldn't stop wondering why we're fertilizing crops with explosives."

"Look at that," Diane said, waving a hand at a huge combine out in the middle of one vast field, a giant green mechanical monster thrashing its way down a long row, one of hundreds of rows, thousands even, stretching toward the horizon. "There's your answer. These aren't any small family farms we're drivin' past. These babies are megafarms, owned by corporations, and they'll do anything to cut costs and increase yields. Just that simple." Diane nodded in the direction of the combine. "Like something you'd expect to see on a lunar expedition."

Gail nodded.

"They got air conditioning now, and really large sound systems inside the cabs."

"Where would you live, if you could choose anywhere?"

Diane thought for a moment. "Maybe someplace tropical. Hawaii maybe. Someplace where it's hot. Or maybe Arizona. I'm not sure. You gonna stay in Oklahoma?"

"I don't know yet. I just want wherever it is to be someplace I can eventually feel safe about."

"You're joking, right?"

"Not entirely. I do hope, as the years go by, that I'll be able to relax. I've got a lot of catching up to do. All I know right now is that everything's changed. It's a different world out here than it was when I went in, and I want to live. I want to live my life, you know. It's like I've got a second shot at it, and I want it to be worthwhile. Fulfilling. I want to learn and explore, and I want to make some good, solid friends."

"You sound like an ad for some college. Or the military."

Gail was quiet for a long moment, and then she sighed. "I think about a family," she said. "Sometimes I wonder if I still have time to make a family."

"What, like you're going to marry some accountant or something and disown your past, pretend it never happened? Look for happiness chasing crumb snatchers in suburbia?"

"You're tough," Gail said. "So cynical so young." She looked out the window, as the combine became a green dot at the edge of her vision, and then empty fields filled the car window. "I don't even know if I can have children. I'm past that magic forty-year deadline, you know? The odds are increasingly stacked against me."

"You really think you want a baby?" Diane's voice was softer, willing to give somewhat to ease the question's landing.

"Yes. I want a baby. It's not something I think. It's something I feel."

"Renfro used to talk about that. I never could wrap my head around it. Family. But I wouldn't be so fast to count myself out, if I were you. They can do a lot these days."

"I think the toughest part might be finding a husband."

"Who says you need a husband?" Diane looked across the seat, had her head in that tilt that Gail had come to know, the one that spoke of the sensibility gap between them. The one that said Gail might be older and wiser but she still didn't have a clue. "Nuclear families are way in the minority now, you know. I read it in a magazine. The husband and wife and one or two kids type family. Down to about twenty percent of the population. Everybody's either divorced or gay or opting not to marry, refusing to buy in to the tradition. And the legal hassles. Not to mention the heartache."

"What happened to joy? To the satisfaction of giving yourself to a relationship—a family relationship?"

"Gail? What is with you? I mean, where's this coming from?"

"Who knows. Maybe it's some kind of adjustment anxiety. Maybe I'm feeling pressured to fit in."

"Big-time, I'd say. But there's no rush."

Gail shrugged, gave Diane half a smile. *Tick, tock, tick-tick tock.*

"Hey, I'm rooting for you. I hope it works out for you. It's just not what I'm after."

"You may find yourself rethinking as you get older."

"Maybe so. I just—Shit!" Diane took her foot off the accelerator, the reaction automatic, letting the car slow without showing any brake lights.

"What?"

"In the mirror. Highway patrol."

Gail tensed in her seat. "Okay. We're not speeding?"

"Hell, no. I may be crazy, but I'm not stupid."

"Just stay behind this truck. Keep driving."

"I kind of thought I might."

"We're not doing anything wrong. Just drive."

"He's coming on fast."

"I know. I know."

Diane followed the truck, dropping back just a bit to increase her following distance. Scanned the area. Nothing but fields and flatness. Nowhere to run, nowhere to hide. The cop was in the left lane, gaining on them, drawing closer.

"He's after someone, looks like."

"Not us. He's not after us." Diane couldn't tell if Gail was stating a fact or praying out loud. The cop car was three car lengths back, then two, into her blind spot and emerging out of it again, right next to them. Diane glanced over, then glued her eyes on the road in front of her. Like anyone would do, she hoped. She forced her hands to relax on the wheel. *Just drive. Just drive along the road like the law-abiding red-blooded American citizen you are.*

Then the squad was past them, passing the truck in front of them, and out of sight.

"Damnation," Diane whispered. She counted to ten before putting on her signal and easing into the left lane.

"What are you doing?" Gail's voice held alarm.

"To see where he's going."

"Who cares where he's going? As long as he keeps going."

"That's what I want to find out. If he's gonna keep going."

The car was well ahead of them now, vehicles in the left lane slipping quickly into the right to let it pass. Diane watched until the car was far away from them, still showing no sign of slowing, before she eased back in behind the truck.

"Okay," she said, "Okay." She looked over. Gail had closed her eyes, her head resting against the seat back, looking for all the world like she was asleep. "Sometimes it's a bitch not being the police." Diane was talking to herself. She set the cruise control and flexed her knee. Turned on the radio and hit scan until she heard Bonnie Raitt—*Let's give them something to talk about*—and settled on that. She drove, wondering how on earth Gail could sleep, wondering if Renfro'd had any luck.

The sun was low on the horizon, and Diane thought surely Gail would wake up when she pulled in to the rest stop, but Gail's eyes showed no signs of opening. Diane got out, filled the tank, paid cash, and pulled over to the parking area. Still Gail slept. Diane watched her, the flickering of her eyelids as she dreamed. She needed the bathroom, but did not want to leave Gail vulnerable, asleep in the car out here where just anyone could approach unnoticed. She waited for Gail's eye movements, beneath the pale closed lids of her eyes, to stop, signaling the end of the REM cycle, the dream sleep.

"Gail?" She touched her shoulder. Gail stirred, pulled herself out of slumber. Sat staring out the windshield and blinking, rubbing her eyes.

"Where are we?"

"Just north of Oklahoma City."

"You're kidding."

"I'm not. I gotta pee." Diane got out and headed for the ladies' room, veered into the Qwik Stop to get the key.

Gail sat, her face numb from sleep. She couldn't believe she'd slept all that way. And that deeply. She hadn't slept that way since—she couldn't remember a sleep that deep. Ever. She was having a hard time getting conscious. It was as though she was looking through the sheerest sheet of gauze; even what she knew must be the garish orange and red colors of the plastic sign on the Qwik Stop were blunted. She forced herself to get out of the car, stood, and stretched. Rubbed her hands across her face. Walked on wobbly legs toward the ladies' room.

When she got back to the car, Diane was in the driver's seat.

"You okay?" Gail stood at the window.

Diane nodded.

"Let me make a call."

Diane watched as Gail walked sleepily to the pay phone near the station entrance. Gail dialed a number, talked briefly, rubbing one eye, and then wrote down directions on a scrap of paper. Diane hoped these people, whoever they were, were as solid as Gail said they were. It seemed to her somehow too easy, that Gail had a network in place just waiting to take care of her. But maybe that's how it was. Maybe Gail's crew was trying to make up for all those years Gail had spent inside without once opening her mouth about her accomplices. It was almost like they shared the cop code, the wall of silence. The one that probably helped put Diane behind bars.

The house was north of town, exurban, at the end of a long, gently winding drive leading past pine and low oak from the two-lane county road that would take you east toward Arkansas. Gail felt a thrill surge through her as Diane eased the car to a stop in the driveway. She wondered how the years had been to her friends.

There were two stories, of cedar, with a flagstone patio beneath a deep roof overhang, creating a kind of farmhouse front porch. The large oak front door had a lion's-head brass knocker and stained glass accent windows near the top. Hand-thrown clay pots full of dark pink and white impatiens hung in braided jute hangers around the perimeter of the porch. There was a large cedar picnic table; beyond it, a couple of rockers.

Attached to the gently sloping roof of the two-car garage was a basketball goal, and past that, in the yard, a trampoline. Gail took it all in as she and Diane approached the front door, wondering that she hadn't imagined Chris and Michelle would have children. Of course they would. They'd been married the year after the robbery, or so it seemed. All Gail remembered for sure about the date was that she'd been in that awful red-painted plywood phone booth outside the control room, on a collect call to her mother, who said an invitation had come to the house with a note saying how sorry Michelle and Chris were that Gail wouldn't be able to make it. They wanted her to know that they were thinking of her. She hadn't been in prison very long yet. Then. She still had hopes of getting out in four or five years, although that early in her sentence, even that seemed an eternity.

They weren't out of the car when Michelle came out the front door, wearing a flowing brown paisley full-length skirt and a tan tank top of some fibrous material, linen or hemp, maybe. Her hair was long, over the shoulder, a mass of curls and ringlets. She came to Gail with arms open and a welcoming smile, and her greeting to Diane was no less effusive.

"Come in, come in." She swept them toward the front door, the drawl in her words surprising Gail.

She stopped suddenly and turned to look at the Taurus Diane had parked in the drive.

"Maybe we should put it in the garage," she said.

Diane nodded and returned to the car, started it up and waited while Michelle pulled up the garage door before easing the vehicle inside and killing the engine. The door issued a metallic screech as Michelle struggled to pull it closed.

"Chris promised he would put some WD-40 on there," Michelle said. "One of these days."

She led them out of the evening heat into the air-conditioned house, through a tiled entry into a spacious room that held the kitchen, dining area, and living area. "We wanted a kind of loft effect," Michelle said, looking around proudly. "Iced tea?"

"Sounds great," Diane said, looking around, admiring the comfortable southwestern furnishings. Lots of wood and cushions, Mexican blankets, a large stone fireplace. One entire wall was a bookshelf, overflowing, the others were adobe, everything very earthy. Gail recognized a ceramic storyteller on the mantle above the fireplace, a grandmotherly figure with tiny children sitting in her lap, on her shoulders, clinging to her arms, all listening with rapt attention as grandmother wove for them tales of the spirit world.

"I like your place," Diane said as she took the large glass of tea offered by Michelle.

"You should have seen it when we bought it," Michelle said, leading them to the living area, settling in a rocker. "A wreck. Totally. We've redone it bit by bit over the years."

Gail sank into the overstuffed cushions of a couch, and Diane settled next to her.

"So." Michelle twirled a ringlet around her index finger, took a sip of tea. Diane sipped, too, still taking in the decor. She felt an uneasiness creeping into the room, or maybe it had come through the front door with them. She did not feel welcome.

"Where's Chris?" Gail asked.

"He went to get some fish for dinner. We thought we'd grill. You eat fish?"

"Yes," Gail said.

"Fish have eyes," Diane said. Michelle looked at her oddly.

"I'll make an exception," Gail said. She thought of the fish sticks they served on the chow line at Sundown. Breaded clumps of tasteless white mush. She addressed Michelle. "Fish sounds lovely."

Michelle kept twirling and took another sip of tea. "I hope there's tuna."

Diane stood up, placed her tea carefully on a coaster on the table. This place was *Better Homes and Gardens,* and she was afraid she would spill something or leave a smudge on the couch, do something crass. Nothing was out of place. There wasn't even any dust that she could see. Maybe they'd cleaned up for company. She hoped so. She'd hate to think of anyone living with such constraint, though she knew there were people who did. She'd been in a house or two like that, on calls, but usually by the time the cops arrived, the veneer of order and tranquillity had been cracked, if not shattered.

"Mind if I jump on your trampoline?"

Michelle's blue eyes widened for an instant, and then her lips broke into another gracious smile and she said, "Of course. Make yourself at home."

Diane grabbed her tea and made her exit, thankful to get out of there. She didn't know what kind of history Gail had with this girl, but whatever it was, the two of them didn't seem to be clicking, and it was painful to watch. She headed out across the lawn, unlaced her boots and took off her socks, climbed onto the springy black netting of the trampoline. She went gently at first, getting the feel of it. She'd only been on one of these things a time or two in her whole life, but she remembered it as being fun.

Inside, Gail picked up a small bowl from the heavy rough-hewn oak table in front of the couch. She guessed you would call it a coffee table, though its density seemed to call for a weightier name. She could just wrap her hands around the bowl. It was pale white, with a kind of lavender wash over it, and inside was a darker lavender. The outside had been taste-fully pitted with some small sharp object prior to glazing and finishing.

"Sandra made that," Michelle volunteered, "our daughter. She called it 'A Bowl Full of Air.' Took second at the art fair."

"How old is she?"

"Freshman year at Rice. But that was from high school. Ryan, our boy, is a junior there now. He's working as a camp counselor this summer. Sandra's doing a summer thing in Paris. A regular Francophile, like her dad." She paused, sighed. "I was scared when we first moved here that our children would grow up to be cowboys. We've been blessed."

Gail nodded. "I'm happy for you." And she was. Happy that Michelle and Chris had been lucky enough to have escaped—did she dare call it the folly of youth?—seemingly unscathed.

Michelle looked earnestly at Gail, and something in her changed. "I'm so sorry for what happened to you." She put down her tea and stopped twirling her hair and leaned forward in her chair. "I didn't know what to say, before," nodding at the door, "I just want you to know. I—we, we all—everyone. We felt awful for you. I thought about you so often. It's such a *helpless* feeling . . ."

"It's okay." Gail sipped her own tea and delicately wiped a droplet from the corner of her mouth.

"Maybe it is, maybe it isn't. I mean, I look back on it and on how we were. How we were all so sure that what we were doing was right, was *needed*, how we knew everything was so critically fucked up and how we thought we had the answers, the solutions, how we thought we were the ones who would change the world, make it better. All that talk about willingness to give up your life for your beliefs." She shook her head, smiling sadly. "Some revolution, huh?"

There was the sound of a car pulling up, and a moment later they heard Chris come through the front door, the crackle of grocery bags being shifted.

"Honey?"

"In here."

"I brought a surprise." Chris set the groceries on the counter that separated the kitchen from the living area, his narrow face breaking into a smile when he saw Gail. He was taller than she remembered, in jeans and a light blue denim shirt, but maybe he hadn't been finished growing when she knew him before. It looked like he'd topped the six-foot mark.

"Long time, no see," Chris said, and moved to give her a light kiss on the cheek. "How was your stay at the Hotel Hades?" Still smiling, his tone conversational.

Gail laughed, happy that his ebullience, which he had always carried with him regardless of circumstance, was apparently still intact. Diane came in, barefoot and carrying her boots, looking over her shoulder at something.

"So," Chris said, "recognize this stranger?" And then someone else entered the room.

Gail stared. "How could I not?" But she didn't move, didn't stand to greet him or smile or throw her arms out in welcome. She felt frozen. Numb. He stood there, a smile trying to break free, held in check by apprehension. His brown hair was short, what had been a shaggy beard trimmed neatly in a goatee. He worked out, apparently, his chest and arms amply muscled beneath a textured gray Henley. She might not have recognized him, so much bulkier now than when she'd known him as a wire-thin radical with crazy hair and fire in his eyes. The fire was still there, but the flames were under careful control.

"Tom," she said. He smiled then, and moved to her. Lifted

her out of the chair and kissed her cheeks and pulled her close. Gentle. He was so gentle. He held her as if he were afraid she would disappear, leave him holding air. He held her quietly, ever so kindly, and kissed her eyes.

Gail felt him holding her, the reality of him after so many years of imagining him, and wrapped her arms around him as much to support herself as to assure herself that it was really him. She had not thought to feel this way. She had thought, after all that time, all that silence between them, that she would feel no more for him than cool curiosity about what had motivated him to disappear from her life. When her knees had strength again and she was standing on her own, she slipped her hands up his back to his shoulders and rested her head against his chest, as though listening for a heartbeat. She was not sure what this was she was feeling, but she wanted it to stay, and she wanted to stay right where she was. Holding him. Being held by him.

"I never thought we would see this day," he whispered.

Standing behind the grocery bags on the counter, Diane watched, and then looked to see Michelle with fingers to her trembling lips, on the verge of tears, and Chris, beaming happily at being instrumental in the reunion. And then Tom moved and gave her a look at Gail's face, and she realized all three of them were seeing what they had expected to see: seeing the moving reunion of two long-lost lovers, but that was not what Diane was seeing, and that was not what was happening. Diane saw on Gail's face a disbelief mixed with the desire to play the part that her friends wanted to see, and the inability to do so. Gail didn't even *know* this man, and it didn't look to Diane as if she wanted to get reacquainted. There was too much pain in it. There were too many years of silence between them. She wanted to say something, walk over and take Gail's hand and get between her and Tom and face him down. Ask him what the fuck business he had coming into Gail's life now after having been gone so long. She stood silently, half hiding behind the grocery bags, wishing that Chris would wipe that fool smile off his face and get a grip on reality. The guy might test well enough to become a professor of whatever, but as far as Diane could see, he was a moron.

"I think this calls for a celebration," Chris said. "Did Michelle show you the wine cellar?"

"Why, no," Diane drawled, affecting the tone of a Dallas socialite, adding a little squeak to the end of the no. Gail glanced at her, shot her a quick, mechanical smile that came and went in a demisecond. Diane saw concern in Tom's eyes as he looked her over, but he erased it quickly and stepped back to let Gail pass. Gail followed as Chris led everyone down the hall and through a door, down a set of steep steps into the basement.

"Chris has become somewhat of a connoisseur," Michelle said.

"Myself," Diane interjected, "I think they can all pretend it's about bouquet and aftertaste and acidity and whatever else they want, but what it really comes down to is the buzz." Gail's glance told Diane to lighten up; Diane returned the look.

Michelle laughed and put a hand on Diane's shoulder, "I think you're exactly right."

There was barely room for the five of them to fit into the cellar itself; three walls were lined with racks practically filled with bottles. Diane was impressed. Chris squeezed past her to retrieve a bottle from the middle of a wall of shelves. He spoke over her head to Michelle.

"What do you think, Babe? A Saint-Emilion? I have a great '98 Angelus here. Been waiting for the right occasion." Then to Gail, "Red's okay?" Gail nodded, feeling confined, eager to get out. "Good then." Chris turned, waited as the others filed out into the basement. He was just closing the door when he slapped his forehead. "Wait a minute. What am I thinking? I know exactly what we need." He reentered and emerged a moment later with a second bottle, displaying it to Gail.

She looked at the label: Duckhorn Vineyards. It was a cabernet sauvignon, but about all she remembered of wine were the bottles of Bully Hill Chris used to show up with at the Free Now meetings, bottles with labels like Bulldog Baco Noir and Love My Goat Red.

"Haven't times changed," she said.

"Nooooh," Chris practically moaned. "Check out the vintage."

Gail looked again. *1986.* "The year I went in."

"Exactly," Chris said. "This stuff's been bottled up for as long as you were."

"Must be worth a lot," Tom said. "Aged to perfection."

"Goes for close to three hundred a bottle," Chris said. "Of course, I never pay retail."

Diane stared at him. "Three hundred dollars? You're kiddin' me, right?"

Chris, his eyebrows raised in self-defense, lifted his chin almost imperceptibly. "No," he said. "I'm not. And when you taste it you'll see why."

"Okay, okay." Tom headed up the stairs. "Let's pop the fucking cork, man!"

Gail stared at the bottle, and then at Chris. "When did you buy this?"

He thought for a moment. "Oh, come *on,* Gail! No way. I got it a couple of years ago." He was sincere. His gesture had been spontaneous. He wanted to do something special for her.

"How could I know?" she said. "I mean you always were a little—"

"Weird? Yeah, but not weird enough to put away a bottle of wine the year you went to prison. Tell her, will you Tom?"

Tom stopped and offered a hand to Gail, nodding his head up toward the kitchen. "He's not *that* twisted."

Chris slipped past them and bounded up the stairs, and Gail did not pull her hand from Tom's as they followed him, Diane and Michelle behind them. It felt—she was afraid to think it—it felt like *before.* Before she had numbed herself to the idea of reunion. It felt like what she used to think about late at night in her cell, remembering Tom's touch and the pull between them. Those times when it was only the two of them, when the meetings were over and he would pour them each a glass of wine and light the candles and put something soft on the stereo and explore her body with kisses and tiny moans, and my-God-my-God it had been so long. She climbed the stairs, holding his strong warm hand, alive like she had not been since forever. She had to stop. Had to. Her breath caught in her throat. This was not how she wanted it to happen. She slipped her hand free, and Tom let it go easily, glancing back to smile. She took hold of the rail, gripping it tightly as she pulled herself up toward ground level.

In the kitchen, Chris made a great show of decanting the bottle, and poured glasses of bottled water while they let the cab breathe a bit. "One thing I could live without," he said, "is the water in this part of the country. It's full of either sulfur or chalk, depending on the whims of the soil lines. Ours is chalky. You'll notice it in the tub."

"You can't drink the water anywhere anymore," Tom said. "But half the time the bottled stuff is just as bad. Look at what Coke and Pepsi are doing. You've seen Dasani, right, in the bottled-water section? That's the good old Coca-Cola Company. Taking municipal tap water and running it through a filter, bottling it, and charging money."

"I had no idea," Michelle said. "They never stop, do they? Maybe they really are part of the CIA." She chuckled at herself.

"I refuse to pay money for water," Diane said. "I mean, I won't buy it in the store. Maybe it doesn't taste the best in the world, but right out of the tap is fine by me. I guess if you grow up with something, you get used to it. I don't even notice."

"Chlorine?" Tom said. "You can't smell the chlorine in tap water?"

"Not if it's coming out of a well."

"Right. Then you only have to consider agricultural runoff."

"You can test for that now," Chris said. "They've got tests for just about everything."

"Right," Tom said, "except presidential aptitude."

Gail looked from one to the other, trying to follow the conversation, but Tom's presence was quietly overwhelming her. She watched as he and Diane jockeyed for position until Diane let herself be squeezed back to where she had to reenter on Tom's left, between him and Chris. Gail could feel the heat coming off Tom's body; he stood gesturing as he spoke to Diane and letting his arm rub against Gail's, seemingly unaware of it, but at the same time letting Gail know he was acutely aware of it and wanting more. Wanting her. Alone, to himself. Wanting them together. She was not sure she could bear it, the roiling emotions inside her, making her heart pound and her thoughts swirl as though she were some helpless teenager in braces who thought herself eminently undesirable suffering through her first high school prom.

"Chris," Michelle said finally, Gail wondering if Michelle had somehow tuned into her distress, "how about that wine."

Gail watched closely as the ruby liquid curled into her glass, her mind flashing on the day she was brought through the front gate of the prison on the bus, an old school bus painted dark blue, windows sealed with tight crisscross mesh wire that cut the sky into cloudy gray diamonds and smelled like a handful of old nickels. Still cuffed and shackled, she was taken off the bus and in through the receiving gate of the prison. She could still see it, the layers of yellow paint on the huge metal door, the brick walls twenty feet high, the looks on the faces of the prisoners off to the left, fenced inside the Big Yard, feeling bad for the new arrivals, feeling good that more coming in meant more had to go out soon.

". . . our dear friend Gail," Chris was saying. She picked up her glass, held it before her. Chris glanced at her, saw she was back with them. "Who stood up for what she believed, as well as for those who believed with her. To Gail, who is in our eyes truly a heroine. May your time outside be as productive as the time you spent in custody, and may you find sufficient happiness to ease the bitter memories of your long sojourn inside the walls—no, wait, not just sufficient happiness, may you find bountiful happiness, and well, I'm full of shit here, all I can think is just thank God you're out. We love you. Thank God you're free. Long may you run."

Glasses clinked, and Gail felt tears welling. She took a slow sip of the wine, and it was not sweet at all; she wouldn't have wanted it sweet. It was smooth and dry, and that was just how it should be. She brushed away the tears just as Chris and Michelle took her in a hug, and then Tom joined, wrapping his ample arms around Gail and Chris, and all four of them swayed in each other's arms, holding their glasses of '86 vintage cab aloft, being careful not to spill it. Gail caught a glimpse of Diane, who had moved over to lean on the counter and was sniffing at her glass, and though Gail would never have believed it, she saw tears beading at the rims of Diane's eyes.

She stepped back, raised her glass again. "To my friend Diane," she said, offering her glass to Diane, "because you can thank God all you want, but if Diane hadn't been there, I wouldn't be here."

Diane held up her glass. Gail heard the chime of crystal as their glasses touched, and Diane went from one bare foot to another, rolling the wine around on her tongue, enjoying it. Finally she swallowed, nodded approval to Chris, looked square at Gail, grinning, and said, "Fuck 'em and feed 'em fish sticks."

Chris cracked up, stomping his foot and shaking his head. "My sentiments exactly." And then, earnestly, out of the blue, "What was it like, being a cop?"

Tom cleared his throat and asked Chris if there was a phone he could use. When Chris pointed to the wall phone, Tom nodded his thanks and took the receiver, excusing himself before heading down the hallway for privacy. Diane watched him go, wondering why he couldn't talk in front of his friends. "So?" Chris was addressing her.

Diane's mouth edged up at one corner in a hint of sardonic grin. "Oh," she said. "The question. People who aren't cops, even people who swear they'd never in a million years be a cop, everybody always wants to know what it's *like*. Like there's some kind of mystery to it or something weird about it. It's mostly boring. It's always different, and it's always the same. I don't know. I guess it's kind of like being in a gang, you know, you hang out wearing your colors and drive around looking for trouble."

"So how do you cope, day in and day out?" Michelle slipped a hand into her husband's. "When you confront people who hate you for what you do, or who're angry because you're writing them a ticket, or out of their minds with grief. How do you deal with that, emotionally?"

Diane felt like she was an invited speaker in a Sociology 101 class. But these were obviously very nice people, very sincere people, and they honestly wanted to know. She ventured a glance at Tom, who had returned to the group and had an arm around Gail's shoulders now, but was paying close attention to the conversation. Gail leaned her head down to sip at her wine, avoiding Diane's eyes.

"Emotionally? You have to shut it down. You can't be bawling your eyes out when you need to be getting someone who's injured out of a wreck and into an ambulance, or when you're trying to get details of a rape so you can find the motherfucker who did it, or whatever the situation is. So, truthfully?"

They nodded in unison.

"You laugh about it. You shut it down inside and make bad jokes about it."

Michelle sipped from her glass, keeping her eyes on Diane.

"It's called a cop sick sense of humor. It gets you through the day. But sometimes, when you're around people who aren't cops, don't know cops, and you laugh at an inappropriate moment . . . they don't get it. Think you're a real sicko."

"But you're saying it's actually a coping mechanism." Chris looked at her intently. She nodded.

"That explains a lot," Gail said, but she was smiling at Diane, trying to get her out of a discussion that Diane didn't seem to be enjoying.

"So tell us what you make of this," Diane said to Chris, holding her glass to the light.

He swirled his wine and took a careful swallow. "Hmm." He took on the air of a stuffy professor, flashed a quick smile, and returned to character. "I would say"—he cleared his throat—"I would describe this particular wine as brooding, the nose is classic black fruit, plum comes to mind. In the mouth I detect dark chocolate and oak, which introduce a certain juicy cherry and unsweetened chocolate. Balance and integration are excellent, as are the depth and structure."

"Damn," Diane said. "I bet you're hell grading essays."

Michelle, Gail, and Diane shared a look, Michelle somewhat guiltily but no less sincere. Tom winked at them and raised his glass to inspect.

"I'm not sure," he said. "I mean, I don't know a lot about this." He had Chris's attention. "I agree about the brooding nose, but I get cassis and chocolate. And I like the way the solid entry leads to a stout, full-bodied palate. Nice, firm tannins, and I especially appreciate the varietal lead pencil accent."

Gail and Michelle stood, trying not to laugh.

"God," Diane said, "I haven't tasted lead pencil since second grade."

"Okay, okay," Chris said, "go ahead and make fun. But you gotta admit, it's a kick-ass glass of vino." He finished his off.

"Agreed," Michelle said. "Now why don't you fire up the grill, and we'll get this fish ready to cook. Is it tuna? Did they have tuna?"

He nodded yes on his way out the door, Tom in tow.

Michelle unloaded the vegetable drawer onto the counter: three different lettuces, a cucumber, some carrots, a red bell pepper. "This should do nicely." She grabbed a tomato from the windowsill above the sink and pulled a hard maple cutting board from beneath the cabinet.

"I'll do that," Gail said. She picked up the frisée, the red leaf, and the arugula by turn. "Diane," she said seriously, "we can't eat this. There's no iceberg."

"We'll pretend," Diane said.

Michelle glanced over, happy that her friend was enjoying. She handed Diane the packages of fish and a large platter. "Let me just get this corn soaking and we'll be ready to go."

"You cook it in the husk?" Diane asked.

"Soak it for a while, put it right on the grill. It's delicious that way."

"I bet it is." Diane laid a tuna steak onto the platter. "So this is what it looks like in real life?"

"Before they can it. Yeah." Michelle rinsed her hands and stepped over to check out the fish.

"The last corn we had was raw," Diane said. "Fresh off the stalk, so to speak. In fact we were sitting right next to the stalks."

"That seems an eternity ago." Gail was happily ripping apart lettuce, tossing the pieces into a salad spinner. "I don't know, Michelle," she said, "this all seems pretty . . ."

"Yuppie?" Michelle said. "Upscale?"

Gail nodded. "Not that I say that judgmentally. It's just, I never pictured it, you know, back when we were . . ."

"I know. I never really expected to have adult furniture. But here it is. Home sweet home."

"But," Diane said, "are you happy?" She hoped it came out like a joke, but she did want to know.

Michelle grew thoughtful for a moment. "Yes," she said finally. "I'm happy. I love my kids. I love my husband. We've got it pretty good, with both of us teaching at the U. Things are . . . good."

"And you don't miss your radical days?" Diane stood, holding the platter of tuna, ready to take it out but not wanting to leave the conversation. "You don't miss the excitement? The, what, the brotherhood—"

"Camaraderie," Gail said, "I miss that. But not the rest of it."

"You mean the way the guys could sometimes be jerks? Like we were just there to, like, do laundry and go out for coffee and stuff like that?"

Diane laughed at that. "Wait a minute. I thought you guys were supposed to be cutting-edge. I thought you were supposed to be enlightened. You telling me it's not just the cops who are pigs? I mean, when it comes to gender-related issues?" She put the tray down, leaned on the counter on one arm, cocking her hip out. "Listen to this." In a loud whisper, telling on someone. Gail and Michelle turned, ready to listen. "One night, my sergeant was riding with me, they have to do that twice a year and do a report on how well you do your job, so it's my turn and he's driving, and we get this family disturbance call in some apartments over on the east side of town. So off we go. When we get there, he pulls up right in front of the apartment, it was an upstairs one, but you're not supposed to pull up in front, you're supposed to park a little ways down the block, for safety reasons. But he pulls up right in front, and we're just getting out of the car when *kaboom!* this asshole fires a fucking shotgun at us, hit the front door of the car, right on the shield and the Protect and Serve decal, and we're running for cover and *kaboom!* he fires another round. Unbelievable. So we're calling for backup, and I get down behind a car in the parking lot and the sergeant's down behind another car. No more shots and all these squads start pulling in, taking up positions around the parking lot, and in a matter of five minutes there were a *lot* of weapons aimed up there at that window. Anyway, long story short, we're out there for hours and hours. Turns out the guy was in his ex-wife's apartment and had come there to kidnap the kids, but she talked him out of it and got out with the kids before we got there, but he's in there drunk as a skunk, and then the chief and the deputy chief and the captains are all there and they've got a fucking command post set up in another apartment. At a certain point they radio for me to come to the command post, and I don't know if I'm in deep shit because the sergeant has tried to cover his ass and say I'm the one who parked in front of the place, but it turns out to be that—"

The front door slammed and Chris blew into the kitchen holding a spatula, Tom right behind him.

"There's heat," he said breathlessly. "You got two choices. Hide in the cellar. Or hit the road." He looked from Gail to Diane and back again. They stood, frozen.

"Wait," Michelle said, "how do you know—"

Chris took a Motorola radio from his shirt pocket, held it aloft. "Kevin," he said. "He's down the road." Then to Gail. "I'd tell you to run, but I don't know how many of them or where they are. Kevin saw only one car."

Gail looked at Diane and Diane looked back. They didn't know.

"Look," Chris said, "if they have a search warrant, I'll make noise, you all head out the back. I'll keep them busy to give you time." He looked at Tom. "I think that's your best bet." To Diane, it was like he had metamorphosed out by the barbecue grill. He went out as a dorky professor and came back as General Colin Powell. To Gail, he had become the person he was when she last saw him.

"Let's go," Tom said.

Chris led them down the basement steps and into the wine cellar. "There's a corkscrew down here somewhere." He smiled. "But don't open the Rothschild!" A wink and he closed the door. Virtual blackness.

"Sit down and get comfortable," Tom whispered. "From this point on, we don't move unless we hear him yelling."

"Wait a minute," Diane said. "Who put you in charge? And why the fuck are you even hiding?"

"Nobody's in charge," Tom said. "We gotta work together here, *Officer*, or our asses are gonna be back in jail before the clock strikes midnight. I've been in tight spots before, and look, here I am—in one piece. Now I suggest you lose the attitude and we all just—"

"Whatever." Diane's voice was sullen. Who the fuck did this guy think he was?

"—cooperate with one another. And in the interest of being polite, I'm on parole."

"And?"

"That's why I'm hiding. I can't associate with my former associates. I'm going to be quiet now, so that no one can hear us."

Fine with her. Cooperate. Her pistol was in the car, in the glove box. Shit. If they had to run she'd just have to hightail it to the garage while whoever-the-hell-it-was that was headed down the road toward them right this very minute did their searching. If they even got that far. She couldn't figure it: Why would there be somebody on them now? It wasn't like they could have picked up the trail on the highway. She'd been careful. Nobody, but nobody, had tailed them. She let herself fold onto the cool concrete floor until she was cross-legged, one shoulder up against the glass noses of the wine bottles in the rack behind her. She felt totally, completely, helpless. At the mercy of the whacked-out professor upstairs, even though he didn't seem so whacked anymore. It had all been an act, or maybe not. Maybe he was really two people. He was this nice guy who taught freshman English at the college, and he really was nice and a little bit goofy, until something from the past tapped him on the shoulder, and then he turned into the tough, calculating, radical he'd once been full-time, bent, above all else, on survival. Who wouldn't be, in that position? All she could do was sit and wait. Try not to get worked up. Try to stay level-headed, clear-thinking. And be ready to run.

Again. Shit. She calmed herself, breathed slow and steady, rubbed the back of her head, right under the base of her skull, telling her adrenals as she massaged the pressure point to wait just a fuckin' minute before squirting that juice into her blood-stream. She didn't need it quite yet.

Gail heard Diane settle to the concrete floor, and then felt Tom settling down next to her. He slipped an arm around her waist. She wondered if she should move away, create a distance between them. But she didn't want to. All those years, those years of staying shut down, denying the basic human need to be touched, to love and be loved. Those nights, thinking about him, knowing *why* he hadn't been in touch, but not knowing *why not*. Tom pulled her to him and pressed her head against his chest, leaned to kiss her hair.

"Not a day went by," he whispered, close in, his lips brushing her ear. So softly she wasn't sure she heard him. And when she was sure what he'd said she wanted in the worst way to believe him.

A long, annoyed sigh came out of the darkness.

"Chill," Gail said quietly.

"No problem," Diane replied. "I'm so chilled I've got goose bumps."

Gail wondered if this was what single mothers felt, when they finally got asked on a date and had to deal with a recalcitrant child. But Diane had to know that however desperate Gail might be for family, she was anything but easy. She could fall into Tom's seduction, that would be simple. But *easy* was a path completely obscure to Gail, like some trail hidden beneath wild, weedy overgrowth. She could not see it. It was not in her to look for it. If she even tried to walk down it, she'd trip and stumble. She knew full well that Tom was taking advantage of the situation to try to smooth over the pain he'd caused her. She knew, too, that he didn't see it that way. He wasn't bullshitting anybody, not in his own mind. He could lie to himself as adroitly as the finest high-minded politician.

And she could sit there in the dark and tell herself all that, but her body was taut as a nylon rope in a tug-of-war, her skin glowing with the anticipation of his touch. She was ready to bolt, and at the same time she did not want to move from the delicious position in Tom's arms. She was wrapped once again in his strength, and her thoughts took off, whirling uncontrolled, moving so fast she felt the need to latch on to one, grab it and try to hold it still until she could examine it, try to make sense of it.

There was a clomping of boots on the floor above, more than one pair, and the sound of authority in a man's deep voice. Some kind of off-balance response from Chris, and then more questions, more I-don't-know tones of response. Gail took a deep breath, let it out quietly. She eased away from Tom, just slightly, allowing the cool air of the cellar to slip between them. It was okay, doing that, feeling the familiar distance between herself and any living creatures that might be in the vicinity. That, she knew. She heard the voices upstairs, tuned in to them, listening for any hint that things were going awry. More questions, whoever it was doing the asking could've sung baritone at the Met, but she couldn't make out any words. Then she heard Michelle's voice, musical, light, but sounding very serious, and some more words from the authority. Then a shuffling, a turning, and the boots went back out the door.

"Praise the Lord," Diane half-spoke, half-sighed.

They sat in the darkness until they heard Chris at the door, and then the cellar filled with light, making them squint and cover their eyes. Tom got to his feet easily and offered Gail a hand. She let him help her up.

"I'm still a a little stiff," she said, "from all the running."

"I can't see how you wouldn't be," Tom said.

Chris waited until they were all out of the cellar before ducking in and grabbing more wine. "I don't know about you guys," he said, "but I'm opening another bottle. Or three."

Diane slipped in after him and grabbed a couple herself.

When Chris looked at her she said, "No sense you having to run up and down the stairs all night." He chuckled and pushed back the door for her.

"So," Chris said, huffing up the stairs, "U.S. marshals. Two of them. I don't know how much they know, but they didn't act like they were hot on anyone's trail. Or even particularly interested in what they were doing. Said they were following orders, didn't say from where, to check out all"—here he nodded at Gail—"your former associates. It almost looks to me as if someone's taking your escape as an opportunity to update their files."

"Not so far-fetched, given the mood of the country these days." Tom's brown eyes held relief; the crease that ran vertically between his eyebrows softened somewhat.

In the living room, he took a seat next to Gail on one of the couches, but gave her room. The room looked different to Diane, and then she realized that blinds had been lowered, curtains pulled tight.

"The car you're in," Chris said. "The plate's clean?"

"It's a rental," Gail said. "Under an alias."

"We should still change it," Chris said. "I'm sure they've got it now. Broadcasting it all over the fucking place."

She sat, listening to Chris recount the mild interrogation he and Michelle had undergone. He was controlling his voice, but not well enough that the effort at control wasn't evident, betraying his nervousness. Diane didn't blame him. She was still plenty rattled, still hadn't shaken the feeling she'd got when she realized she was in a cellar with two other fugitives and zero in the weapons department. Not smart. She stood up and went to the kitchen, poured herself a glass of wine, and stayed there, drinking too fast and listening from behind the counter. Then she slipped out the door and went to the car to retrieve her gun.

When she came back in they were all waiting for her, sitting on the couch staring at the door.

"Where'd you go?" Gail asked, her tone light but forced.

"To get something from the car," Diane said, her look telling them not to ask any more questions.

"We have to split soon," Gail said.

"No shit. I'm ready to go right now." Diane had her hip cocked out and her thumb tucked into the waistband of her jeans, her hand resting at what seemed an odd angle, until Gail realized Diane's hand was resting on an imaginary holster.

"No," Chris said. "You should wait. Just a couple of hours maybe. Give the marshals time to move on." He motioned for Diane to join them. "Have a seat," he said. "More wine?"

"I'd better not," Diane said. "If y'all don't mind I'll just go lie down for a while, try to get some rest. I've been driving all day."

She ignored the look Gail shot her and went down the hall to the guest room she'd been assigned—Chris and Michelle's son's room—and slipped the gun under the pillow on the bed. Above the headboard was a poster of some gruesome-looking heavy metal band. There were some wrestling trophies on a high shelf of the bookcase. It was strange, being in a total stranger's room as a guest. She had often enough been in total stranger's houses and rooms, but always as a cop. And it was strange, the feeling she had right now, the feeling that she was, in spite of it all, still a cop. She stood staring at the books in the bookcase, but few of the titles meant anything to her. They were the books of a teenage boy who seemed mildly interested in reading. She recognized *The Catcher in the Rye* and *The Lord of the Flies*. It wasn't like the bookcase was stuffed to overflowing. There were tokens there, perhaps books he'd been made to read for school and had surprised himself by liking. She realized she was looking at the bookshelf as though she were on a case, looking for clues. But no crime had been committed here. It was like some variant of déjà vu where she felt she'd been here before but knew she hadn't and so it had to be that she'd been somewhere else in similar circumstances, similar enough to make her feel this way. Or maybe it was just that she missed it. She missed the hunt. The search for clues. And when the moment came where the evidence added up to an arrest warrant: the catch. What a rush that was. She missed it.

Stuck down on a low shelf was a shoebox of baseball cards and Magic cards and even a couple of old shiny Pokémon cards. She picked it up, began looking through, not sure why. Beneath the cards, her fingers hit a packet. She pulled it out. It was about the size of a single Reese peanut butter packet, but done in camouflage. On the front, black block letters: Camo Condom. Beneath the lettering: *Don't let them see you coming.* She wondered if Michelle knew her son had them.

When she put the shoebox back, the book that had been standing next to it caught her eye. A hardcover, red lettering on the spine: *Deep Cover.* By Mike Levine. The ex-DEA guy. *The Big White Lie.* She wondered if whoever found her car had found the book in her briefcase and opted to tuck it away somewhere before calling the sheriff to report they'd seen a Bolton cop car parked in the middle of the woods outside Nacogdoches. Maybe the prick who stole her squad had escaped from the trauma of having stabbed three teenagers for no apparent reason by sinking his teeth into *The Big White Lie.* More probably he'd sold it at a used book store down the street from the pawnshop where he no doubt hocked her Samsonite. And then it had showed up again, the bright white cover with the thick black lettering that caught her bloodshot eyes from its spot on Efird's bookshelf—and never in a million years would she have thought Efird had even a book in his apartment, much less three shelves of them all lined up neatly—on what she'd come to think of as "the great morning after." And then Efird wouldn't even let her borrow it. Asshole. She pulled the book from the shelf and tossed it on the bed, planning to read herself to sleep, because after this evening's events, she sure wasn't going to get there from any other direction. And then she remembered the wall-to-wall shelves in the living room and went out to see what she could find there.

Michelle and Gail were setting the table. Chris and Tom had returned to the grill. Gail, about to place a fork on a napkin, stopped cold when she saw Diane, her eyes raised into a silent question. Diane shrugged it off and went to the bookcase.

"You might not go for most of those," Michelle said. "We lean to the left when it comes to literature."

Diane heard cheerleaders in her head, saw them dressed in the red and white of the Overton High School Cougars, bouncing up and down, shaking their pom-poms, . . . *lean to the left, lean to the right, stand up, sit down, fight, fight, fight* . . . and most of the town of Overton in the stands on a Friday night with nothing else to do, shouting the cheer, but not doing any of the leaning or the standing up or sitting down that was supposed to go with the words. She wished Chris was making Frito pie instead of grilled tuna. She could still taste it: they made it in those flimsy cardboard containers, the same ones that held a large order of fries, only with Frito pie it was a snack-size bag of Fritos poured in there and a ladle of steaming chili poured on top and then a sprinkling of grated cheddar. The snack bar at the Paris High School stadium made the best Frito pie in Texas, she was convinced, though the Overton team had never made it past district, so for all Diane knew maybe Abilene or El Paso had decent Frito pie as well. Even on the rare occasions when she'd gone to college games, she hadn't found a Frito pie as good as the ones they made at the Paris Wildcats games.

She realized she was staring at the bookshelves and not seeing anything. She renewed her search, though not fully sure what she was looking for. She saw something workbook sized: *The Anarchist's Cookbook*. Next to it a thick one: *Female Perversions*. Then, *A Bright Shining Lie*. But no *Big White Lie*. Maybe she could find a paperback somewhere. Or somehow her copy would come back to her. A friend of hers in school, a girl who took her nose out of books only to eat or sleep, had said once that it wasn't so much that she found books to read as it was that the books found her and presented themselves to be read. Standing there in front of that massive shelf full of books, Diane thought she might be able to do what Gail had suggested: escape back to school. Hide out in the ivory towers. Probably not a whole lot of marshals would think to look for her in the halls of academia. And wasn't that what she was thinking about doing before she fell into this mess? So she'd have to find something other than law school, because, sure, they might think to look for her there. Then again, where would they begin, and how would they find her if she had solid ID? Maybe law school was precisely where she should go.

Diane lay in her bed in the darkness, having decided reading was not the way to go tonight. She heard Chris and Michelle in the kitchen, water running and dishes clinking, and Chris saying something and Michelle laughing. Maybe they really were happy. Maybe some people were happy having families.

Long after Chris and Michelle had turned off the lights and gone to bed, after the dishwasher in the kitchen finished its cycle and stopped its sloshing and humming, Diane lay awake, waiting for the clock in this boy's room to show three A.M., when they would split and hope no marshals were waiting. She missed her old life, even if she hadn't been totally enamored of it while she was living it. It was a hell of a lot better than this. Missing Renfro. At first she thought maybe she only missed having sex with Renfro, but when she thought about it, it was much more than that. Or maybe she was only feeling that way because she knew she needed some things and he was the only one she could trust to get them. She didn't know. It was getting all confusing and, at last, she was feeling a weight to her eyelids.

She heard a cricket chirping somewhere in the room. The sound was familiar from home, and she hadn't heard it in a long time. There hadn't been any crickets in prison. Smart move on the part of the crickets. Cockroaches loved prison. Plenty of crumbs around from prisoners stashing food they weren't supposed to have in their cells.

And then the cricket, too, got quiet, and the central air kicked off and the gentle whoosh of air coming from the vent in the ceiling stopped. From down the hall she heard the sounds of Gail and Tom making love.

It sounded like Tom was doing a good job.

She felt her fingers creeping down toward her navel, and then past it, and then she closed her eyes and saw Renfro, his eyes pulling her to him while he was inside her, and that look on his face, for all the world like he loved her.

FOURTEEN

A hand on Diane's shoulder brought her bolt upright; she swept an arm under her pillow and came out holding her gun, scanning the darkness, fighting through haze to consciousness.

"Ho—!" Michelle yelled, then caught herself, finished in a frantic hiss, "—ly shit!" She stepped back, her hands raised. "Diane it's me, Michelle." In a low voice now, calming tones. "Put that thing down. Time to go."

Diane was on her feet, stepping into her jeans, grabbing her boots. Heart thumping in her chest, but no panic, sending blood where it needed to be. Efficient. She was in auto mode, moving quickly but not so hurriedly that it would backfire and cause her to stumble. She stuffed the gun in her waistband and slipped out into the hallway. Michelle followed her with her backpack. She heard Tom in the hall ahead of her, whisper cursing as he tiptoed, shoes in hand, like a drunken husband trying to sneak into his bedroom just before dawn.

"What are we being quiet for?" Diane practically yelled. "No one's here yet, right? No one's chasing us?"

"You never know," Michelle said, talking normally now.

Tom was behind the wheel and Diane slipped into the backseat, not saying anything, not asking why was Tom driving, what was going on. He turned to look at her.

"Where's Gail?"

Diane let her mouth fall open. "How the fuck am I supposed to know? She was with you." Diane sat, too, wondering how long they would sit there before one of them made a move to go get Gail. Then Michelle came out.

"She's not coming," she said, a worried look on her face, the fingers of her right hand bothering a curl near her cheek. "She won't say why."

Tom grabbed his door handle, but Diane was faster, out her door and turning over her shoulder to say, "I'll handle it." Her voice told Tom to stay out of it.

Diane heard sniffling as she approached the bedroom. Gail was curled in one corner, her knees drawn up, her arms wrapped around them. She was rocking ever so slightly, forward and back, ever so slightly. Tears trailed down her cheeks.

Diane knelt next to her, put her hands on Gail's shoulders. Gail jerked away.

"I can't," she said. "I can't keep going."

"Gail, you have to," Diane said gently. "It's not like you've got a whole lot of say in the matter. Come on." She lifted, urging Gail up. Gail pressed herself back against the wall, shaking her head adamantly no, balking like a thoroughbred being led into the starting gate.

Diane backed off. Sat down next to her. Said nothing. Rested an arm around Gail's shoulders. Gail sobbed, caught herself, fought it, felt a heat building in the center of her chest, a bomb waiting for detonation.

She didn't know what was happening to her. She could feel her face twisting up, her lungs begging for air; she was choking, she couldn't see. All the years, all those years in the cage, and now she wanted desperately to run free, but reality was holding her frozen: the realization that she would be running for the rest of her life. There would be no escape, there would be no respite, she would live in fear of getting caught, getting locked up, of having a taste of life and then having it stolen from her. And she was sorry. She was sorry more than any of them could ever know, and who were they anyway to say what justice was, how could they know what punishment was enough when they were the ones meting it out and had never tasted confinement, did not know the ravages of solitary.

And then she felt Diane's arms around her, Diane pulling her up and draping an arm over her shoulders and dragging her from the room. Like a soldier dragging a wounded comrade away from the front lines, Diane took Gail from the invisible cage and pulled her down the hallway, and to the front door, and through it to the car.

Tom came out the door and helped Diane get Gail into the vehicle. Diane belted her in and closed the door, crawled into the backseat. Michelle and Chris stood staring.

"Is she okay?" Michelle whispered. Then, to Gail, louder, "Are you okay?"

Gail stared out the windshield, nodded a barely perceptible nod.

Chris tossed the bags in the trunk and ran around to give Gail a kiss.

"Call us when you can," he said to Tom and ran back to the porch.

Before they were out of the drive, the house had been darkened and locked. Diane pictured Michelle inside, trying to make herself look sleepy for when the knock came on the door. If they would even knock. Maybe they would kick it. But she didn't think it would give with less than a battering ram. All that heavy oak. It was a beautiful door. And maybe no one would even show. Maybe the authorities had been satisfied when they questioned them earlier. Right. Maybe the pope was a Baptist.

She sat back, strapped on her seat belt, and watched Gail. This was a very fucked-up situation.

Tom drove fast, and expertly. In under a minute it seemed, he had them off the main country road, which wasn't much to start with, and on some tinier country road, sand coated with oil it looked like, and blasting through the woods at a speed that turned the tree trunks into vertical brown blurs in the headlights.

Diane pulled an ankle across her leg to put on her socks and boots. She was going to have to ask why he was along, she wouldn't be able to help it, but thought she would wait. It did make things easier. She didn't have to drive, and the addition of a white male to the party might help them escape detection. And she might need help with Gail, who had apparently dropped off to sleep. Maybe she had learned that in prison: when things get so totally fucked up that there is apparently no way out, just close your eyes and dream.

Tom was intent on the road. Diane looked over her shoulder, half expecting to see headlights. Behind the car, dust roiled up, burnt sienna clouds in the red of the taillights, flashing even redder when Tom hit the brakes, which wasn't often.

"Where you takin' us?" Diane was looking for some kind of landmark, but all there was were trees, and a road that appeared the same no matter whether you looked forward or to the rear.

"How's Dallas sound?"

"Good," Diane said. "Sounds perfect."

Gail's head popped up. "No," she said. "Arkansas, New Mexico, Colorado. We do not need to go to Texas."

"It's good," Diane said. "Dallas is fine."

Gail turned in the seat and glared at her. "We are not going to Texas."

"I thought you were asleep," Diane said. "I thought you were out of it."

"I was," Gail said. "Out of it. Not asleep. I was very out of it."

"You're okay."

"Yeah." Gail nodded. "I just bugged out. I'm sorry." She turned to look at Diane. "Thank you," she said, "for helping me out back there. I'm sorry."

"No need to apologize," Diane said. "That's what partners are for." She hoped Tom was listening.

Gail turned to him. "You shouldn't even be doing this," she said. "Your parole."

"Fuck parole," Tom said. "I just won't get caught, that's all."

"Ah," Diane said, "famous last words if ever I heard 'em."

"You never heard them from me," Tom said.

"Guess we'll see." Diane shifted in her seat, slipped the pistol in her waistband over to the side just a little. There. "How far to Dallas?"

"Once we hit I-35, about three hours." Tom looked over at Gail, reached over to rest a hand on her shoulder. "It's the safest thing for me," he said. "And for you two. I can get you there and be back home before noon. And Chris is making calls first thing this morning. There'll be fresh ID there. You can get another rental and split." He glanced over the seat at Diane. "There's nothing that says you have to stay in Texas any longer than it takes to get yourselves ready for the road."

Diane sat back and made a motion like she was zipping her lips shut. She wasn't sure whether Tom saw or not. Gail definitely didn't, or she wouldn't have rested her head back and settled in her seat the way she did.

For some time after they were on the interstate the car was quiet. Diane had trouble slowing her thoughts; it was like five different plans were competing with each other, trying to get chosen for the team. Finally she wriggled down into her seat, leaned her head back and closed her eyes. It wasn't like vigilance would help right now. And the marshals would be looking for two women, not a couple.

Diane stared up, out the car window into the dark sky. "I just wonder how they knew to come there looking for us."

"I really don't think they did," Tom said. "If they had, they would have looked harder. I think it was just like Chris said, they were using Gail's escape as an excuse to update their info on all her known associates. If they stumble onto you two in the process, so much the better."

"I'm not so sure." Diane folded her arms across her stomach, trying to calm herself. Nobody said anything. "I mean it seems really odd to me. We didn't have any problem in Chicago. We hooked up there for the ID." She turned to Tom. "You know the Chicago people? Do you know anything about that part of it?"

"All I know is that whoever you hooked up with there was cool. Nobody burned you guys. Nobody. If they had, we'd all be in custody right now."

"I wish I shared your confidence." She turned around to

look at Tom. "I mean why else would they have come there. They knew we were there."

Tom glanced back at her, looking like a vacationing dad about to lose it with the kids in the backseat.

"Diane," Gail said.

"No." Tom's voice was low, controlled. "Let's hear it."

"When did you know we would be there?"

"Late yesterday afternoon. Chris called. I didn't even know who would be there. Chris just insisted that I come for dinner."

"But you had all evening, basically, didn't you? What about that phone call? Who was that to? Who'd you call?"

"Diane!" Gail's tone was just short of a scold. "You're *interrogating* him."

Tom looked embarrassed then, glancing over at Gail before answering.

"I canceled a date," he said. "I was supposed to go dancing with someone." He glanced again at Gail. If she cared, she showed no sign.

"Diane," she said, "chill. Look, sure, it could have been Tom. But it wasn't. I know this. It could have been Rick, back in Chicago. But it wasn't. Of course it wasn't Mel. It was *nobody*, Diane. None of my people would do that."

"Then how the fuck did the marshals know to come there? Who the fuck tipped them."

"Nobody." Gail folded her arms and settled in her seat. "It was just like Tom said. Don't you think some asshole in the feds knows who Chris and Michelle were? Knows their history? Of course they do. But Chris and Michelle, as you saw, are leading very straight lives these days."

"There's no motivation for any of them to rat," Tom said. "Okay? None of us, *none* of us, would ever do anything to put Gail's freedom in jeopardy. She's done enough time. We're doing everything we can to keep her free." He wrapped an arm around Gail, pulled her close. "Double for me," he said.

A silence fell. Diane slumped into her seat. Tom aimed the car into the night, the concrete highway stretched out straight and level before them, rolling into the beam of the headlights as though it were being spun out from a reel, the painted white strips between lanes flashing by rhythmically. Diane watched them streak past, coming out of the dark and slipping beneath the front fender of the car.

"I'll drive back as far as Norman and leave the car somewhere, plateless and disabled." He patted the dashboard. "Poor baby. I'll get the bus there, back to Oklahoma City."

"You know what it was?" Diane sat up, leaned forward, speaking to Gail. "Why they called me to the command post that night? When the guy shot at me and the sergeant?"

It took Gail a moment to realize Diane was talking about the story she'd begun last night. Was it last night? Right at the moment Gail didn't particularly give a shit, but thought it best to humor Diane. "What was it?"

"They wanted coffee," Diane said. "They sent me to the 7-Eleven for a pot of coffee."

"Who shot at you?" Tom spoke gently, stretched an arm across the seat back.

"Just some drunken asshole," Diane said. "He filled my squad car door with double-aught buck."

"What for?"

" 'Cause he was drunk, I guess. Wanted to shoot the police. Didn't you ever want to shoot the cops?"

Gail didn't like the tone of Diane's question. Or the way Diane was saying *po*lice. It was like she was looking for trouble, trying to heat up another argument.

"No," Tom said. "Whatever differences I had, I never wanted to shoot the cops. Or anyone else for that matter."

"You should have seen it," said Diane, laughing softly now.

Jesus, Gail thought, talk about mood swings.

"Me running along," Diane said, "darting from one skinny-ass tree to another, a pot of 7-Eleven coffee in one hand and my .357 in the other. Hoping the guy hadn't moved from the front windows of his apartment to the back." Diane kicked her legs up onto the seat, stretching out sideways, and sighed heavily. "Women get fucked, and fucked around. That's how it's always been, and that's how it'll always be."

"I don't know," Tom said. "Change takes time, unless

you're willing to take radical action. That's the theory anyway." His turn to sigh.

"Tell me something, Tom," Diane said, "how is it you and Gail got identical sentences and began serving them on exactly the same day and yet you got paroled more than two years ago, and if we hadn't blown out of that joint Gail would still be in there, looking at—what was it, Gail?—twelve more years? That what the parole board wanted from you? How'd you swing that release, Tom? 'Cause I gotta say, looking at it from the outside, it would appear to me on the surface that if it wasn't just a case of the guy driving down easy street and the woman getting fucked, then you must've ratted. That's the only way I know something like that could have—"

"Diane!" Gail shouted, anger turning her face red. "Who the fuck do you think you're talking to? Who the fuck do you think you *are,* making accusations like that. Christ! I don't believe— You know, if you're so sure you're surrounded by traitors, why don't we just pull over and let you out? Is that what you want? You want to go out on your own? Because I don't even want to be around you if you're thinking my people are anything but solid. They're the best friends you could have—if you had a clue how to have friends in the first place—and you are really, really pissing me off with this bullshit!"

"Look," Tom said, speaking slowly, calmly. "I don't know why you're bugging out over my being here. I'm with you two. On your side. This woman sitting right here next to me is one of the most important people in my life. I love her. I always will love her. And I will do all in my power to help her. Whatever trip you're on is yours. I don't plan to interfere."

Diane rested her head back again. Fuck it. She didn't know how Gail was feeling about things, but she did know that she'd be glad when Tom was headed back to Oklahoma City. Okay, so he hadn't talked to the marshals. She believed that now. He wasn't a rat. She didn't know if his heading back right away was only on account of his parole or if it meant he'd be out of the picture permanently, but she hoped he would get gone. She hoped he would leave Gail alone. He wasn't right for her, any moron could see that. He was taking advantage of her, even though Diane was sure he thought it was love. Some men, that was all they knew of love. Love was finding a woman to keep your house and make your meals and lay down with you whenever you wanted, and otherwise to stay the fuck out of the way. She thought he was like that, Tom; that was how he struck her. Used to being taken care of. She couldn't believe Gail would fall for that. But they had a history, a heavy history. What did she know about how it was twenty years ago, what kind of choices Gail had back then. Her own mother hadn't seemed to have many. Maybe that had been why she loved to go swimming in vodka. A way of coping with the fact of being female. Even in these days, there were plenty of times Diane felt like she was banging her head against a wall, trying to make detective. And if she did, they'd all say the only reason she made it was because she was a woman. A token. Or else she'd slept her way there. And what the fuck was she even bothering with all this for anyway, because right now they had to get their asses to Dallas and get new ID and a new ride and start all over again. Once again. Again and again and again. She wondered if that's how it would be forever, if she even chose to take Gail's advice and get back in school and forget her old life and start a new life, like a life was something you could shed every year the way snakes shed their skins. She was not cut out for this. She wanted the life she had. Even as far from perfect as it had been, it was a pretty good life, she realized, now that it had been taken away from her. And if she could just get it back, she would have a lot more insight now as to what steps she should take to make it better than it had been. She'd be a hell of a lot nicer to Renfro, for one thing. Take the man seriously. She might try to tell herself it was just sex with Renfro that she was missing, but it wasn't. It was Renfro. All of him.

She let herself relax in the seat, made the tension drain from her muscles and tried to find a place to put her head that didn't twist her neck into an uncomfortable angle. She was about to doze off when headlights glared in through the rear window.

"Gail?"

"I don't know," Gail said. "It doesn't look good."

Diane eased up in the seat and peeked out the back window. High beams now, coming on fast, gliding along two feet above the road surface, all business, and then they were close enough to light the rearview with glare, and on came the high-tech red, white, and blue of the Texas Highway Patrol's new millennium Visibar.

Diane mashed the button on her seat belt and sat up, hanging over the seat back, her head and shoulders thrust between Tom and Gail. She turned from one to the other. "Would somebody please go ahead and tell me how the *fuck* this happened! Why is the heat on us? How did it happen?!" She was halfway over the seat, yelling in Tom's face, accusing him with her eyes.

Tom's voice was low and came out like a growl. "They catch us, I'm going back, too. Now sit back and put your fucking seat belt on! I don't want you getting hurt."

He made an arc to the right; the wake-up bumps running next to the fog line at the edge of the highway sent their rude rattling vibrations up through the tires as Tom eased the car down into the bar ditch and up the opposite side and into a field, driving gracefully and fast until they were fully onto the flatland, where he got a fresh grip on the steering wheel and mashed the gas pedal to the floorboard.

Diane cinched her seat belt tight and braced herself against the door. Damn, this boy knew how to drive.

Behind them, the HiPo car was just coming up out of the bar ditch, having tried to clear it at too sharp an angle and gotten sideways before making it out. They'd gained time on him.

They raced across a field of flat dirt dried almost hard as concrete, with scraggly brown Johnson grass sprouted up everywhere. Tom plowed over it like it wasn't there, heading for a stand of oaks that looked to Diane about a thousand miles away, but in reality was only a half mile or so in the distance.

"C'mon, motherfucker," Tom said through clenched teeth, glancing into the rearview. Diane looked behind them and all she could see was dust. She guessed Tom was talking to the car. The dust lit up white, and then some red and blue sliced through it. The cop was on them again, gaining.

Tom banged the steering wheel. "Fucking worthless piece of shit. Move, baby, move!"

The engine sounded like it was going to blow. They hit a bumpy patch and Gail's head banged against the front passenger window. If it hurt, she didn't say anything.

"We got one shot," Diane said loudly.

"Diane," Gail said, "swear to me right now you're not gonna use that thing."

"Like I said," Diane replied. "We got one shot. Tom, you get us into those oaks and we all three gotta bail and run in different directions. He's gonna have to choose one of us to shoot at or chase. He can't pick off three moving targets before we're into the darkness."

"So who do you think he'll choose?" Tom shouted above the noise, hunched over the wheel, driving like a bat out of hell.

"I think he'll choose the guy. Who do *you* think he'll choose?"

"What if it's a lady cop?"

Diane laughed. "You're it," she yelled. "You da man!"

Tom aimed the car between two low-hanging oaks and nearly crashed into one on the other side of them before the car skidded past it. Diane popped loose her seat belt and gripped the door handle, thinking *Here we go again* and at the same time wondering at the oddness of the thoughts her own brain tossed up at the strangest of times. The trooper chasing them, he most likely had the right to use deadly force. Tight call. She hoped he was the cautious type. As Tom braked, he cut the wheel hard and hit the accelerator, slinging the car around so the headlights aimed at the trooper before the vehicle rocked to a halt. Diane jumped from the rear seat almost before the car was stopped, bolting like a racehorse. Out of the gate and across the unforgiving dirt, hearing the scream of the trooper's vehicle as he veered around the oak stand. She felt the headlights wash over her and threw herself to the ground, landing harder than she'd expected, rolling, almost knocking the wind out of herself. The engine sound went to her left and she heard car tires scrabble against the dirt as the trooper made a sharp turn.

In darkness again, she spat grit from her mouth and pulled herself up, went into a sprint, hoping to God there were no gopher holes in the field. She ran, putting distance between herself and the noise and lights of the trooper's car, the hot, dry night air burning her throat, and in her head, trying to send him a message, *go for Tom, go for Tom, go for Tom.*

She ran, boots pounding against the ground, dust still choking her throat. She ran and felt it not in her muscles, but in her bones. The muscles were exhausted; she felt the shock and jolt of each footfall shoot up into her knees, and through her knees to her hips.

She ran until she fell, gasping, to the earth. Breathed in the scent of the sunburnt Johnson grass, a scent that smelled like home. Lay there swallowing air, gulping it, her legs quivering from exhaustion. She knew she had to get up, move on, and keep moving, but she couldn't. Not yet.

She lay there until the sound of the trooper's engine faded and she could hear the questioning song of the crickets. They'd always sounded to her as if they were calling to the darkness: *Anybody out there?* She hoped he'd gone after Tom. She hoped Tom had gotten away, but she hoped he'd gone after Tom and given Gail a chance to escape.

She lay listening to the crickets until her vision returned and she could raise her head up off the ground.

Before her, miles away still, but definitely there, the lights of Dallas rose up, casting a glow into the night sky, a bubble of light with just the faintest tinges of yellow and pink to it, rising high into the sky, obliterating the stars.

She put her head back down on the dirt and licked her lips, trying to come up with some moisture. Her tongue felt swollen, as if a dentist had gone in to numb her mouth and hit a wrong nerve. She sat up, reached around to tuck her gun back into place.

"Okay, Diane," she said, "get up off your ass and walk." She sat there, unable to move.

And then she heard a beating against the air, an insistent *thwop-thwop-thwop* that sent her mind spinning and threw her legs into gear. She ran for the oaks, hoping to get there before

the searchlight from the helicopter could find her. It was gaining on her, slicing through the darkness, widening into a giant
circle that skimmed across the ground, chasing her even if it
didn't know it. She ran.

Glanced over her shoulder: the thing was closing in, maybe
fifty feet short of her as she pushed herself past what she'd
thought was her limit, pushed herself forward through pain
and to the other side of it, her body running so fast her own
mind could barely keep up; the light, the light, the giant blades
of the copter beating the air so goddamn efficiently, and it was
loud now, getting so close, too close. She looked up, saw it
black and ominous, hanging in the sky like a giant bug with its
bulbous glassy eyes, and the light, traveling over the land, lick-
ing the dirt and grass and weeds, she glanced up again and
stumbled, falling hard to the ground but bounding back up,
moving on all fours as she regained her balance and pulled herself upright, still moving, then into a run again, getting her gait
back, and the light closing in and she couldn't look anymore.
She could only run, push herself, run and run some more, just
move, all out, giving it everything she had, and then she stumbled, hit the ground hard, air gone from her lungs, her body
spasmed, unable to suck in the air she desperately needed,
from somewhere she saw the light, coming at her, slithering
across the ground, ready to bathe her in heat and glare. She let
her head fall to the ground, smelled dry dirt and burnt weeds,
she was breathing again, gulping air, and her eyes closed and
she waited for the light.

She didn't know if she heard it first or realized the light
hadn't found her. The steady maddening whop of the helicopter blades went away from her, still close, the noise was, but
moving away. She opened her eyes and was in the shadows still.

The copter had veered off to the right and was headed on a
diagonal across the field.

She sat up. She pulled herself to her feet, staggering like a
sullen drunk. She fought gravity and took steps, fell into a run,
or something close to it. She did not stop. She ran.

Dallas glowed in the night before her, glass and mirrors,

mirrors and smoke. The helicopter noise grew fainter, not much, but fainter, as it arced around in the air above the field.

The land fell away before her, and she scrambled down the bank of a dried-out river, splashed across a pathetic few inches of water at the center of the wide, flat riverbed. And then up the other side, clawing at red dirt, and there in front of her, not thirty feet away, were three perfect circles, almost white, side by side, three concrete culverts, tunnels beckoning her, offering refuge from the helicopter searchlight, leading who knew where, but somewhere under the sidewalks of Dallas for sure. Drainage culverts for the street grates that filled when the rains came in spring, the thunderous storms that dumped thousands of gallons of rainwater onto the streets in the space of less than an hour.

She edged back up to follow the copter, saw its beam zigzagging across the field, and in its light: Gail. Gail running as Diane had, running desperately, running when she did not physically have it in her to run anymore, running on willpower alone.

"Get away," Diane whispered to herself. "Please, God, let her get away." Something caught in her throat, a cry. She had to force herself to stay where she was, motionless, when everything in her wanted to go to Gail and pull her to the safety of darkness.

And then the light cut sharply right, leaving Gail staggering in the darkness, and Diane saw what the copter had found. There was Tom, screaming something at the sky, gesturing like a psycho, screaming and waving his arms. Diane couldn't hear what he was saying, she could barely see his mouth moving, but he was screaming at them, she could tell. And finally was able to make out what he was doing with his arms and hands, all that crazy waving. He was giving them the bird.

Diane let her body tumble and slide back down the embankment, ran crouching across it and slipped into the closest culvert, ran in full speed, not even having to duck, so large was the circumference of the drainpipe. Maybe twenty feet inside she came to a halt. The sounds of her breathing echoed in the tunnel, the choking, wheezing gasps that raked her windpipe with pain.

Before her lay perfect darkness. She held her hand out in front of her face, close enough that she could smell the dirt on her palms. She couldn't see it. She could feel sweat pouring down her face, pouring out of her skin everywhere. She turned and looked back toward the entrance. A circle of blue-black night glowed in the distance. She could go no farther, at least not until daylight, and even then it was doubtful she could proceed in the tunnel, not without some kind of light.

She slumped against the hard curve of the concrete, slid down to a crouch, her feet at the edge of the thin trickle of water dribbling down the center of the tunnel. She leaned forward, resting her arms on her knees, her head on her arms. She'd been running forever. All her life.

She leaned her head back against concrete, raised her arms, draping them over her head, and stayed that way until her breath came back. Then she rested back on her knees again. Her tailbone was going numb from the concrete. She smelled a dampness, a small swampy odor from the slow draining water that she knew was probably milky green.

It didn't matter how uncomfortable it was, it was comfortable enough.

She couldn't move. She could not will her body to do more than try to maintain stasis: keep the blood flowing and air going in and out of her swollen lungs. She couldn't think, couldn't find any words in her head. She was simply there, a being in a world of hard white stone and near absolute darkness.

She did not know how much or how little time passed. Time was irrelevant, a concept for mathematicians and scientists. Who cared.

And then she heard footsteps, quiet and moving fast, footsteps coming into the tunnel.

She stirred. The footsteps stopped.

The chocking sound of hard breathing held in, forced to near silence. But not big or heavy, not male. It couldn't be.

A pebble, or something like it, some kind of small stone,

bounced against the concrete and rolled into the water, its noise made louder by echo.

And then a whisper.

"Diane?"

Diane cleared her throat, but said nothing. It was Gail.

"Diane, it's me. It's okay." Letting herself breathe full on now, blowing air out hard, the way she used to on the track after sprinting the last two hundred meters of a miles-long run. Diane recognized it.

"It's okay," Gail said again. "I followed you in. I saw you come in here. I lost them. We're okay."

Diane sat silently, waiting to be sure no troopers would come crashing in behind Gail, ready to run into the darkness if she heard the rattle of equipment on a Sam Browne, the spit of static from a radio. Keyed up, so far into alert that fatigue melted from her now, pouring off like the sweat that had only a few minutes earlier stopped dripping from her body.

"Diane. Please."

Diane stood up, and heard Gail's breathing stop. And then, an almost matter-of-fact tone, an almost laughing voice, words that didn't know what attitude to take, whether the situation was tragic or hilarious. "You're about to really piss me off."

"Come on in," Diane said. "My tomb is your tomb."

She heard Gail's giddy whispered laugh, and her footsteps drawing closer. And then Gail's arms were around her, feeling as sweaty and caked with grit as her own, and their heads were on each other's shoulders and they were rocking back and forth, ever so gently, holding each other, giving and getting strength, rocking and rocking.

"Tom," Gail said finally. "The light. The helicopter. They were about to get me. He took them away from me. He drew them off."

"I saw," Diane said.

"He said run, and I just ran. I ran and ran and then I saw you coming up the bank of the river, but I couldn't make it that far. I hid under some bushes until they went away. I think they must have got him or they would have kept looking. He

told them something. Some story. He must've. He got them
away from us."

Diane felt something warm against her cheek, and droplets
on her shoulder, and she held Gail closer and let her cry it out.

Room 329 at the Harvey Hotel smelled almost exactly like
room whatever-it-was they'd taken in Chicago, at the Holiday
Inn. That one no doubt being combed by marshals now, or
maybe they'd already finished. Gail took a deep breath: aroma
of industrial strength carpet shampoo and some kind of Ajax
knockoff, polyester bed clothes and artificially cooled air. The
air-conditioning unit hummed from its spot beneath the window, strategically placed not to block the view.

Her clothes were stiff from having been washed in the bath-
tub and air-dried over the shower curtain rod. Their suitcases
were no doubt in an evidence locker somewhere, or else being
picked over by U.S. marshals looking for clues. They wouldn't
find anything but clothing in them.

Gail stood to the right of the air conditioner, avoiding the
icy blast blowing up from the vents on top, staring out the
plate glass window that overlooked seemingly nonstop traffic
in both directions on Interstate 75. As far as the eye could see:
hotels, strip malls, gas stations. Everything looked new, like it
had been erected within the last month or so. The only telling
sign of wear was in the surface of the parking lots, blacktop
bleached gray-black by the relentless Texas sun. Consumer
heaven. Depressing. She watched cars pull into parking lots,
drivers get out, some shepherding small bouncing children toward the large Toys "R" Us across the highway. Gail had
thought it was the prison diet that put weight on so many of
the women, though many of them came in large, but right now
she wasn't seeing many skinny people headed into the McDonald's and Burger King (practically next door to each other), or
the Sizzler next to them. She watched those coming out the
doors, some of them waddling to their cars, talking on their
cell phones. The country had gotten crowded while she was
locked away. More cars, more stores, more fast food joints,
more people. And the people, it seemed, had gotten heavier.

Like the country itself was getting bloated and slow, even though everything was moving faster. She turned from the window. Diane was gazing at the tube, hitting the remote, switching channels through a cacophony of screaming announcer ads until she hit the image of a prison, a prisoner in khakis being led toward the front gate and a smoother, soothing announcer this time, doing that not-quite-talking-not-quite-whispering thing . . . *then at ten, it's Street Time. Welcome to life on the outside* . . .

Gail turned back to the window, heard the announcer talking about the rest of the evening's lineup. Welcome to life on the outside. Yeah. Life on the outside.

The ID man, who looked like an insurance salesman, had come and gone, leaving them with new DLs under new names with their new likenesses. The passports would take awhile. He'd set up quickly and waited patiently while she and Diane dug into the boxes of L'Oreal he brought. Gail went blond, Diane opted for red, though a subtle, natural shade of red. Gail hadn't recognized what he was offering when he held out two disposable cell phones. Not even three by four inches, barely a half inch thick. Sixty minutes call time, prepaid. Use up the time and toss them. Or get buggy about the possibility of a trace and throw them out. It's disposable! Toss it and buy another one! Gail asked about being tracked, and Mr. ID said no way could they trace these phones to anyone. They might be able to home in on the phone, but there was no way to tell who it belonged to, and there were so many of them out there already, on the networks and operational, that the feds didn't have time to try to decipher which bad guys were using which phones. By the time they figured it out, the phone was taking up its minuscule piece of real estate in a landfill somewhere and its former owner was in possession of a new one, with a new number.

She felt a heaviness descend on her, a pressing down, as though the planet had slowed its rotational speed, upping its gravitational pull. She wondered where Tom was, though she knew. He was in jail. The question was which jail, and under what terms. She wondered if a bail would be set so he could be free until his revocation hearing. Because after that he would definitely not be free. He was going back inside to finish his sentence, a parole violator. He had done it for her. He had taken them off her. Sacrificed his freedom so she could get away. He would do another two years behind bars. She couldn't absorb it; couldn't fathom it, that kind of love. That level of devotion. But she could feel it, washing over her, lifting her up, engendering within her a determination to stay free, stay outside the walls.

She looked out the window again, at the sun hanging low above the huge domed rooftop of a shopping mall behind the smaller strip mall stores off the expressway access road. Maybe she could walk there, though it didn't look like anybody walked in this town. So far, she hadn't seen a single pedestrian.

"Let's go pick up a rental," she said to Diane.

Diane hit the mute button and looked at her.

"You got any clue how hot it is out there? It's July in Texas, man, heat of the afternoon. We could go later."

"Let's get it over with. I feel too vulnerable here without a car."

They took the motel shuttle to DFW airport, a half-hour ride past sun-bleached strip malls, apartment complexes lining parts of the highway, huge canvas banners tied to some of them advertising the deal of the month, or a free this or that if you signed a two-year lease. And then more fields, briefly, and then neighborhoods, set back off the highway, but not far enough, and more strip malls, and huge warehouse-type stores, massive low-slung structures, home improvement stores, cowboy boot stores, furniture stores, electronics stores. Gail sat, staring out the window, amazed at the sheer number of stores. What could they be selling that she had managed to survive without for nearly twenty years? She'd survived with food and books, basically. And paper and pen. It had kept her mind reasonably sharp, she thought. Sharp enough to realize that what she was seeing outside the window was Obscenity, American-style.

She and Diane were the only two on the shuttle, seated way at the back, where the driver couldn't hear them. Not that he seemed to want to. He had a CB radio and was speaking rapid-fire into it, Arabic maybe, or Urdu. Oblivious to everything but traffic and his radio.

Gail turned to Diane.

"Is it like this where you grew up? Where you worked?"

"Yes and no." Diane looked out herself, as if to make sure of her comparison. "Where I grew up is a really tiny town, a really poor town. None of this kind of stuff. There was a grocery, a pharmacy, the church, the church thrift shop, the post office, the gas station. I think that was about it. Where I worked? Yeah, it was a lot like this. Not so many highways, not nearly big like the Dallas–Fort Worth metroplex—"

"Whatever that is."

"—but, yeah, there's, like, a Cineplex and a Home Depot, a Wal-Mart, all that kind of stuff."

"Depressing as hell."

"At least you can go to the movies. I had to go thirty miles to the movies when I was a kid. Until they ran cable into Overton."

"I'm thinking about heading west," Gail said, watching Diane for a reaction. Diane went stone still, her face a mask of calm.

"Where?"

"I'm not sure. New Mexico to start with. If that doesn't work out, maybe Arizona. Maybe just keep trying places until I find one I like enough to stay or else go till I hit the Pacific."

"You know I want to," Diane said.

Gail's eyes caught Diane's. "For real?"

"It'd be the smart thing to do."

Gail's head went just sideways, barely perceptible.

"And fun," Diane added quickly. "Not just smart. I mean, look, we lived in an eight-by-ten room for months together. Surely we could get along in the larger world."

"I'm not talking about anything long-term, Diane." Gail raised her eyes and smiled. "But I think it would be good for both of us, to be able to count on each other for a while, until we get some kind of, I don't know, some kind of *stability* going. Or something."

"I've got your back, for sure."

"Yeah. Right now, that's cool. So I'm asking, I mean, we kind of had to just head to the closest place where we could get some new ID, you know; it's not like we could go back to Chicago. But I'm talking about now, we've got to decide, you know, where we're going and what we're doing."

"You want to get out of Texas." Diane's voice went glum.

"That's not even a question," Gail said. "We *have* to get out of Texas. *You,* especially, have to get out of Texas."

Diane sat for a long time, staring across the blue interior of the shuttle and out the windows on the opposite side.

Gail saw tears welling in Diane's eyes, slipped an arm around her.

"Diane, you have no choice."

Diane nodded, her head down. Gail felt Diane's shoulders go slack beneath her arm. She squeezed, hugging her friend, brushed her red hair playfully.

"You look good as a redhead."

"Thanks." Diane glanced at the shuttle driver, saw him occupied and wiped at her eyes. "All right," she said.

"You're coming?"

"I need to think about it. You weren't planning on checking out tonight, were you?"

"I don't exactly have a plan. I don't know about you, but things seem okay. I mean, we've lost them—for the moment, anyway. But after night before last, I think we could stand to spend another night here. Rest up. Though I can think of places I'd rather be."

No one gave them a second glance at the airport. They got the car and were on the road back to the motel in time to beat the evening rush hour, which, according to the radio, would begin sometime just before four that afternoon.

They weren't back in the room ten minutes when Gail decided to go to the mall across the highway.

"We need clothes," she said. "And I want to get some running shoes."

"You don't seriously want to run." Diane was in her motel

position, lying on her stomach on the bed, a pillow propped under her chin, the remote in one hand.

Gail shook her head no. "I just want to have the right shoes, should the occasion arise. It seems to happen when I least expect it."

"It can't happen again. It won't. I can feel it."

"Like I said, when you least expect it."

"You taking the car?"

"I was planning to walk. I'd like to move at human speed for a change."

Diane chuckled. "It's too hot out there. I'm staying put." She could have taken the heat; she liked the heat. But she didn't want to take a chance on drawing any attention to herself and Gail. Who knew? They were a couple of hundred miles from Bolton, but somebody, anybody, could be up here visiting a cousin or something, and they could go to the mall, and they could spot Diane. Not that she'd be easily recognizable, but you just never knew. And she realized then, that this was how it would be as long as she stayed in Texas, or anywhere close to it.

"Anything in particular you want?" Gail stood staring at the TV. Diane had the sound muted, was watching the news of their escape crawl across the bottom of the screen. The police video had made for some exciting viewing. The helicopter spotlight on Tom, standing there in the middle of the field, waving his arms like a maniac. They had blurred out his hand. Can't shoot the bird on the tube.

"Just a pair Levi's I guess," Diane said. "For now. You pick the shirt. I'm a ten."

"Want me to get you a pair of shoes?"

"Can I trust your judgment?"

"Better than you can trust your own, sweetheart. What size?"

"Eight and a half. Something with air in the heel."

"No problem."

Diane lay back on the bed, a look of absolute and utter boredom on her face.

Gail took her room key, only it wasn't a key, not like the real keys attached to green plastic rectangles printed with the room number and the motel name and address on them that she remembered from traveling with her parents. This looked more like a credit card, only it was smooth and of flexible plastic, with no indication of what room it would open, only an arrow instructing which end to insert into the door entry.

Diane saw her staring at it and said, "What?"

"I don't know. I just have these moments. Like déjà vu in reverse or something, like I've been transported into the future only it's not the future, it's the present. It's just strange. How much everything's changed."

"It's called a keycard, babe. Keyless entry's the thing. Like on the rental, the electronic entry. All that shit's supposed to deter thieves, but you already know my boring theories about locks and burglars."

"The experts must disagree with you."

"The experts are the ones came up with the theories. They know newfangled locks won't deter real thieves. They'll only challenge them to rise to new levels of competence. It's all just a support system for the illusions of safety they sell to Joe Citizen, who sees every evening on the news how danger lurks everywhere. But it sells. Oh, how it sells."

"Thanks for reassuring me." Gail slipped the card into her bag, along with her new cell phone. "I feel so high-tech."

"You ain't seen nothing,'" Diane said. "Enjoy your shopping."

Diane had been right about the heat, and by the time Gail reached the mall she was soaked. The blast of cool air that came out the door went to lukewarm as it hit the blast of heat coming in from the street with Gail. She stepped in through the second set of doors, felt the cool on her skin, slipping around her neck and under her arms, as though seeking moisture.

The place was huge. A seemingly endless succession of stores selling whatever you could possibly need or desire, and as Gail made her way down the wide tiled corridor, she saw a great many things that nobody in her right mind could possibly need or desire. There was an inverse ratio between the ugliness and uselessness of an object and its price, though Gail tried not to be too subjectively critical. If a painting done on black velvet of dogs playing poker brought a swell of artistic sensibility to someone, who was she to say it was dreck. She strolled along, looking for a shoe store, feeling like she'd gone through some weird consumer looking-glass. The Muzak was depressing, the hum of the huge air-conditioning, or whatever it was that was filling the space with a low, barely audible rumble, made her fear the place might fall victim to faulty engineering and collapse, and the smells wafting out from the food court, with its collection of garish plastic signs above reeking steam tables looked after by bored, pimply high school dropouts were enough to make her appreciate the food she'd gotten on the prison kosher line. A single phrase floated through her head, rolling past again and again, being sung by a church choir in Boise . . . "o'er the land of the free, and the home of the brave," and a huge crescendo, and people cheering, and then it would happen again. And again. She tried to mentally turn down the volume, since she couldn't get rid of it. No luck. Another song. She needed another song, but all that would come was "Plop, plop, fizz fizz, oh, what a relief it is." She kept trying, walking and looking for the shoe store, a shoe store, or any store where she might find a pair of running shoes, and then, suddenly, there it was, the Nike Store. The ubiquitous swoosh, the swoosh that was on *everything,* the swoosh she expected to see superimposed on the moon one of these fine nights. It went against her beliefs to buy a pair of shoes with that swoosh on it, that swoosh that stood for cheap labor, overseas sweatshops, and cool, cool, hot, ever-so-cool shoes. But right at that moment, she felt that if she didn't get some fucking shoes and a fucking pair of running shorts and a fucking tank top she might just lose it and go over and gorge herself at the food court on pretzels that were cholesterol free but loaded with so many calories that you could live off one for a week, top that off with yogurt that wasn't even really yogurt—they said it stood for the Country's Best Yogurt—but one look at the ingredient list and you knew it really stood for This Can't Be Yogurt, and don't forget KFC and the urban legends stating that the name has been changed to protect the corporation from lawsuits for claiming they were selling chicken when the things they were selling in the shape of chicken thighs and chicken wings and chicken breasts belonged to creatures who'd been genetically engineered to the point where they were no longer legally chickens. Could they take the crow out of roosters, too?

Finally. Finally the song had stopped. Gail stood staring in the window of the Nike Store. *The* Nike Store. They would shorten it to The Store one day. And then it would just be the symbol out front. The swoosh. No words. No need for words in a world that could only interface graphically. Rather like a return to the seventeenth century, only they looked at stained glass windows in massive Gothic cathedrals, windows that told the story of God's love, and of God's cruelty. No need for vocabulary, not for the unwashed masses. Just look at the pictures, look at the symbols. You'll know what's for sale inside, and that's all you need to do to be happy: recognize the trademark and buy buy buy.

Gail entered. Fuck it. She needed shoes, and as much as that she needed out of this place, but fast. A clerk came over. She showed him a shoe and said size eight in blue and eight and a half in peach. He left. She went to the shirts and found mediums. She went to the shorts and found mediums. Light blue for her. Peach, in a slightly different style, for Diane. But it all looked a lot alike. Everything had logos. Everything. They should pay people to wear their stuff, since they were advertising with it. She returned to the shoe display and sat down. The clerk came back. She tried on the light blue shoe. It fit. She nodded and said thank you I'll take both pairs. He put the shoes in their boxes and carried them to the register, where she paid cash and took her packages and exited the store.

She made it in and out of Filene's in record time, emerging with jeans and a couple of nondescript summer tops for her and Diane.

She looked up the corridor. She looked down the corridor. She wanted to scream.

She remembered passing a Spencer Gifts, a black light glowing from inside the store and posters in the windows. Some things *could* withstand the test of time, apparently. She saw the sign and headed that way, toward the exit where she'd entered.

It was like opening an oven door, the blast of searing air Gail felt exiting the mall. She held on to her breath; the heat was trying to suck it out of her lungs. Cars glittered in the parking lot, nearly blinding her. She cast her eyes away and headed across the vast expanse of the parking lot, toward the sound of traffic rushing down the interstate, toward the traffic light where she'd walked the narrow sidewalk along the underpass.

She would pick up a paper in the lobby. There were free *USA Today*s available there. She would read the paper and wait for the afternoon to cool and then she'd go out for a run. A leisurely run, try to burn some of the excess lactic acid out of her muscles and get rid of the soreness it created. But it would be crazy to run right now, in this wilting heat. Unless the cops were chasing you. She laughed at herself.

The young man behind the front desk in the lobby nodded cordially, but she could tell he didn't really see her and thought that was terrific. It put her at ease as she entered the elevator. There was bottled water in the courtesy bar in the room. A big bottle of cold water would be just the thing.

She slipped her key card into the lock, heard a click, and saw the red light go green.

She let the door ease closed behind her, heard the slow quiet whoosh of its hydraulic hinges.

The TV was off. The room was silent. Maybe Diane had decided to go for a walk, or down to the restaurant.

She walked in past the entry, looked at the beds. Looked at the chair. Looked at the desk.

That was when she saw the note.

FIFTEEN

Fuck it all.

She might be a fool, or she might be saving her life. Too early to tell. No way to tell. But move it on over, John Wayne, she was either going to walk away from it a free woman (if there was such a thing) or die trying. And right at that moment, right at that particular moment as she drove down the highway, the act of driving effortless, second nature, she didn't care if it cost her life. Her life was expendable just at that moment. Her life—as it existed after what Sheriff Gib Lowe and District Attorney Al Swerdney had done to it—was not worth saving. She'd be happy to move on, thank you very much.

Outside was flat and near desolate, acres and acres of wheat or weeds, depending on the farmer, and the sky stretching pale blue from the horizon to deep space, big as tomorrow.

Renfro was waiting for her call, and she was sure there would be something in the transcripts he'd gotten from the court reporter late one night, narrowly escaping from her apartment, as he put it, with his virginity. There had to be something in there, some little slipup made by Lowe while he was on the stand. There had to be something there. You couldn't lie the way Gib Lowe did and not cross yourself up at some point during your testimony. There'd be something in those pages that could lead her to the truth about the murders and her own setup. And after what Renfro had told her about Efird, she wanted to see Eef as well. First she had to find his place, because she would have to catch him by surprise. No way to tell how he'd react to seeing her. He might actually be stand-up, or at least pissed off enough at the department not to want to turn her in. She'd known he possessed an outlaw sensibility since the time he told her—when she asked him about what he thought it took to be a good detective—that the best cops are the ones who'd've made the best criminals.

And whether he was up to the task or not didn't matter. She was doing this. She had to, or her life was over. She couldn't begin again until this was taken care of. It didn't matter how far she ran or what she did with what would become no more than the remnants of her life. The burden of unfinished business would be a weight on her, pressing her down for the rest of her days, making it difficult to breathe, like some kind of asthma of the soul.

The handle of her gun rested next to her right kidney, or close anyway. It felt comfortable there, even though it was digging into her skin just a little. It was strange coming back here like this. An outcast. A fugitive. A disgraced peace officer. She remembered in her interview, that first one, after she'd aced the written exam, and the physical agility course and the shooting range, when a lieutenant sat behind a desk and asked her how she thought she'd feel if she had to take a human life in the course of her duties as a police officer. If she felt she *could* take a human life in the course of her duties as a police officer. She had given it some thought, even before the interview, but she took her time answering because she wanted to be sure before she said the words, so much so that the lieutenant seemed to be running out of patience. But when finally she said she was sure she could, she was sure. She wasn't just saying words to get a job. And now, well . . . would it be in the course of her duties as a police officer if she walked in and blasted Gib Lowe and then took the elevator to the DA's office and shot Al Swerdney? Even if she was no longer a cop, she knew they were crooked, knew they were incapable of performing their jobs honestly, and—she could not deny it—she wanted in the worst way to shoot the motherfuckers. She could say that to herself and know that it was the truth, but that she was actually, seriously, really considering murder scared the shit out of her. Was she, really? She felt a knot in her throat and tried to swallow it down, but found that she couldn't swallow. She sat there, choking on the realization that she was capable. That, if there was no other way, she might well do it. That she was in contemplation of cold-blooded murder. Not an irrational, rage-fueled, spur-of-the-moment action that resulted in death. She was thinking, seriously, that Gib Lowe and Al Swerdney might need to die, and that nobody was willing to do the job but her. There was nothing she could do to put them down there on death row in place of Rick Churchpin. Renfro had said once that she belonged on the endangered species list for being a cop who didn't believe in the death penalty, even after she explained that it seemed to her that locking somebody in a cage for the rest of his life was a far harsher punishment than frying him or giving him the big fix. The death penalty meant escape from incarceration.

But now? Knowing the rage of unjust imprisonment, knowing what it was like to have your life ripped out of you? Knowing that it had been accomplished by two men of good standing in the community, two knights in shining armor, two good guys, two pillars of the First Baptist Church of Bolton, two devious, plotting, greedy, ambitious, lying, vicious motherfuckers who didn't give a shit who got knocked in the mud and left for dead as long as *they* accomplished their goals. Knowing that, Diane thought, driving down the highway through the afternoon heat, beneath the endless sky, across the territory she had once been sworn to protect with her very life, knowing that—yes, she could. She could extract justice the old-fashioned way, the way justice and injustice had been done for years and years and years in Texas and parts west. She could walk up to Gib Lowe and look him right in the eye and just plain shoot the sorry-assed bastard dead. And then take the elevator to the DA's office and blow good ole gangbustin', gospel-preachin' Al Swerdney right over the back of his padded leather office chair. Be done with the both of them.

She might even get away. And if she didn't, so what. She knew how to do time, and it wouldn't take long to put her on death row her own self, and if she didn't fight it, she could be out of the world in less than two years, easy. And if she did fight, well, it might be that finally, somebody would listen. Somebody would hear. It sure as hell wasn't as if she had anything left to lose. They'd taken her word, her honor, her job, her boyfriend, and they'd smeared her name with dirt. They'd taken everything from her. And they were killers, only they didn't have the guts to do it themselves. They used the state's machinery for their dirty work.

She felt the rage building inside her, she sat perfectly still and steered the car down the razor-straight highway and felt it inside her, burning her up and turning her cold at once. Yeah, she thought. Gail was right. I should've never lifted this piece from that hunter's cabin. Should've left it right there where I found it. She reached back and touched the handle of the gun, just to make sure it was real and there. It was. She felt an energy rising from within, coming out of the rage, surging from deep in her gut, a tingling that spread up her spine and into her brain and branched outward through her limbs. It was the same kind of sensation—though very different, too—that she got when she found a warehouse door unlocked in the middle of the night and knew the odds were good that there were burglars inside and it was her place to catch them. It was danger. The awareness of danger. The thing that was throwing her was that it wasn't hitting her from outside. It was coming right up out of her gut, flowing through her, filling her. And then it took her through the rage, past the rage, into the miasmic middle of it and out the other side. And she was filled with a calm she had never felt before. Utter. Complete. Calm. She knew then. That she could kill them.

Gail sat on the bed, staring at the note.

Hey. Sorry I can't say a lot on paper. I've got to do what I told you I have to do, got to straighten it all out, whatever that means. I'll take my phone if you need or want

to reach me, but I won't drag you into this. Thank you for
all your help, and for being the truest friend I've had. I
wish you all the best and I will never forget you. Love, D

P.S. I'll turn the car in as soon as I'm done with it.

This was so fucked. She was insane. Diane was insane, and
Gail had to accept it. And stay as far away from it as she
could. But first, she had to get the hell out of this motel
room. Get where Diane couldn't find her, or tell someone else
how to.

The truest friend Diane ever had? That was pretty fucking
lonely. Or maybe not. Gail tried to think how she herself
would fit in, how she would relate to someone, anyone, who
hadn't done time. That was the thing. It changed you forever.
The physical confinement *expanded* you; it opened internal
horizons, made visible to you what was there all along but hidden to the naïve eye. And nobody who hadn't been there could
understand, not sufficiently. She understood what Diane said
in her note. They were friends forever in a way that neither
could ever be with someone who hadn't been locked up.

And now Diane had bailed out. Gone out on her own before
she was ready, headed no doubt for more than she could handle. Gail slumped on the bed, feeling the way she imagined a
mother must feel when she discovers that her teenage daughter
has eloped.

She was trying hard not to care, trying to get to that place
she had taken herself so many times during those years inside.
The place of nothingness: of no feeling, of not even really existing. Trying to be a *hardened convict.* She laughed.

What was the girl's problem? Gail didn't have to ask. Diane's *problem* was the same one Gail had gone to prison for, all
those years ago: she was suffering under the misguided notion
that life should be fair, or at least that humankind should be
fair. Nature was not fair, nature just *was,* in all its grime and
glory. But humankind had consciousness, had memory, had
will. Humans should be fair. The justice system should work.

Diane wanted her day in court, and Gail knew what that was like, the kind of rage that being denied could engender.

Back to life, back to reality. Gail went into her bag and came out with the tiny blue plastic cell phone with the small kangaroo logo above the keypad. She put the earbud—which sounded more like something a dermatologist would remove from your ear than something you should insert into it—into her ear. The mouthpiece was a perforated black plastic bubble on the cord that attached the earbud to the tiny disposable phone. This was too weird. Might as well be sci-fi. All this plastic shit everywhere. Please, recycle *me*, too. A decade or so away from *Soylent Green,* are we? Gail punched in Diane's number, one of the several she had memorized, and hit the call button. She hadn't noticed before, but centered above the red call and green end button, was a lone button in the same ominous red color as the end button: 911. God forbid you should have to remember to hit three buttons instead of one. But maybe its purpose wasn't so much functional as psychological: it was a real live panic button, there to remind you that things could go terribly, horribly wrong just when you least expected it. You would need help. You would need help so badly you wouldn't even be able to remember three simple numbers. All you'd be able to do was push the panic button. Don't forget the panic button. It's there to remind you to be scared. She shook her head sadly, realizing that while she had been locked away for all those years in a place that was loathed and dreaded by law-abiding citizens and criminals alike, corporate-government America (who could tell the difference anymore?) had created in the land of the free a culture of fear, a culture that permitted them to prey upon citizens at will. And the populace could only whisper *Protect us, we don't care what it costs, just keep us safe from all the monsters hiding under our beds.* Nineteen eighty-four was here; it had merely arrived a couple of decades late.

She dialed the number of Diane's cell.

She heard a ringing, and then a click, and then a computer generated voice said *Please leave a message.* She pressed end. Great. Wonderful.

Nothing to do but wait. Wait and hope Diane would, for whatever reason, decide to get in touch. Maybe to apologize for taking the car. Right. She lay across her bed. She had a few moments anyway, before she needed to split. She needed to think, decide where to go next. She'd need new plastic, and probably, to be safe, new ID. Not that she thought Diane would burn her to the heat if Diane wound up jailed—a very likely scenario—but better not to have to worry about it. She'd hang in Dallas awhile, wait to see if Diane got in touch, and also call Mel's ID man and let him know she needed to be reprocessed. She was planning calmly and getting more and more angry at Diane. She grabbed the USA Today. Take a moment. Calm down. Read the paper. Maybe do the crossword.

A set of photos stopped her cold. There on page two, those same miserable mug shots from the Post, but beneath them, photos evidently taken by the security camera behind the check-in desk at the Holiday Inn in Chicago. Her chic black hairstyle, Diane's punky blonde look. The shots were that grainy black-and-white garbage, fuzzy as bunny tails. Evidently the Holiday Inn hadn't upgraded its technology in a while. Thank God for small favors. Below the security photo, in color, the image of a balding reddish-blond guy in uniform, a badge shining above his left shirt pocket: Sheriff Gib Lowe. The sheriff, according to the article, believed Diane, and therefore Gail by association, should be considered armed, dangerous, and more. They were an affront to the peaceful nature of women everywhere. Reminded him of when his hunting dog, Buster, came down with rabies, and much as he loved Buster, the disease had progressed past the point where Buster could be saved. The high sheriff had to put a nine-millimeter through Buster's skull, for the good of the community at large. And for Buster, too. The sheriff couldn't stand to watch a good dog suffer like Buster was suffering. And though, when it came to Gail and Diane, he had no evidence—scientific, forensic, or even anecdotal—to back up his numerous presumptions, he felt certain that the duo was headed for Texas. If they weren't already within the state's borders, they would be soon. Get the kids and pets inside and lock your doors. Gail didn't so much read the article as stare at it, picking up bits and pieces of the sheriff's comments, swallowing them like they were spoonfuls of Pepto-Bismol, the pink liquid her mother insisted on giving her when she had a stomachache, and which inevitably made her puke. She wondered if he'd be taken seriously. It didn't seem likely, seeing as his comments were totally speculative, but why were they even talking to him and what did his dog Buster have to do with her and Diane? Gail realized that Diane had not been exaggerating when she said the sheriff was whacked. The man was obviously a fucking lunatic. And if . . . no, not *if* . . . *When* Diane showed up in Bolton . . . Gail didn't want to think about it.

She would wait until dark to check out. No sense running around in broad daylight, even if she didn't look like the old her in the photo. She hadn't really considered leaving the country, wanting some time to adjust to her freedom and get some kind of background established before making any decisions about where to settle permanently.

She packed her bag and left it, unzipped, on Diane's bed, and then lay back on her own bed to take a rest. When dusk came, just before nightfall, she would go out for a run, contemplate Nike the Goddess of Victory, and advertise for Nike the corporation, one of the several that treated the women and children of assorted Asian nations like shit. She would run until she couldn't think anymore and pretend that the exercise had helped clear her head.

Nobody had her back. That sucked. Gail would handle herself alone, or she would find the help she needed. Gail had friends out here. That was the difference. Gail came from a world where it was accepted that you might wind up doing some time for the cause, and it was quietly acknowledged that when you finished your bid and were released from prison, you would come out to a circle of friends who would help you any way they could. Diane envied that, was able, now, to understand it.

But except for Renfro, and even he was a big maybe, Diane had no one. She didn't know even where her brother was, and her mother was probably still in a stupor, worse than useless—

needy. Show up there and Diane would wind up doing laundry, dusting, and making runs to the liquor store. And anyway, the marshals no doubt had that address. The rest of her friends were all cops, all out of the question.

So fuck it. She had one shot: to get to Renfro and Efird and figure out what the hell happened and then take it to someone, she didn't yet know who, but find someone who would listen and do something about it.

And if that didn't work she'd consider going to plan 2, which involved firearms.

So it was good Gail wasn't here, because she wouldn't want to bring Gail into any kind of shit storm like that. But she missed Gail now, in a way she hadn't anticipated. Out here alone. Flying solo. Headed home. Funny how flat everything looked. She'd never noticed before.

"No-no-no-no-no. Not home," she said, talking to herself out loud. "Definitely not headed home. It's enemy territory, and don't forget it for one fuckin' minute." She passed a field with a smattering of cows trudging along the fence line, eyeing the parched weeds on the other side of the barbed wire as they headed for the barn.

She wondered if they were seeing green, there on the other side of the fence, where there was none. There was no green anywhere, just various shades of brown and beige and an evening sun getting its last licks in, as though urging the fields to spontaneous combustion.

About an hour east of Dallas, the terrain began to change. It was still flat as all get-out, but there was some green showing now, mostly in the form of evergreen trees. She was driving into the piney woods of east Texas, and the weather was changing, too, a line of thunderheads coming up out of the south. It was starting to look kind of spooky out there, with the slender pine tree tips spiking into the darkening gray sky.

She caught herself pushing eighty twice in ten minutes or so, and after the second time set the cruise control in order not to get too far past sixty-five. She gave herself twelve, over seventy-seven m.p.h., knowing that no self-respecting highway patrol would write anyone for less than fifteen over the limit.

She put the radio on, hit the scan button, and left it operational, picking up sounds in three-second clips before the radio automatically sought the next station. It ran through its course four or five times before she heard Emmylou Harris: She hit the button to freeze on the station. Emmylou Harris could always get her attention. . . .

At a gas station near Gum Springs, she stopped and put fuel in the car, though the Taurus didn't actually need much yet. The station was actually a gas station, not a minimart, not a convenience store. Just a filling station, built of stone and mortar with a plate glass window and an overhang to protect from inclement weather. There was a small brass bell on the door to announce the arrival of customers, and beneath the ancient cash register an assortment of dusty packaged candy. Diane looked around, spotted what she'd really stopped for hanging on the wall behind the register: phone cards. They were plastic, credit card–sized American flags, with "Freedom of Choice" in script, centered, and in the lower left corner was the black-and-white image of a little boy in overalls, a phone receiver held to his ear, his smiling face letting you know that nothing in the world was more fun than talking on the phone.

Diane handed over one of Gail's hundred-dollar bills, wishing she had something smaller so as not to be remembered should someone come asking after her, but the clerk, a wrinkled-up, blue-haired woman obviously suffering from osteoporosis, took the bill and made change without a second glance.

"Have a nice day, dear," she said, her voice as dry and thin as a newspaper clipping from the era of FDR, and returned to her chair beneath the phone cards to light a cigarette and take up her knitting. Diane said thanks, you too, and pushed open the door, enjoying the sound of the bell, scared half out of her wits about the call she was about to make. But it was simple. He'd come through, or he wouldn't. Nothing she could do about it.

He answered on the first ring. She gave him the phone number printed on the pay phone and pressed a hand on the receiver hook, disconnecting the call, but making it look like she was only leaning on the phone, still engaged in conversation. Even while she was doing it, she wondered if it were necessary; there was nobody around but the smoking granny inside the gas station.

The storm looked to have blown over without dropping any rain whatsoever. It was still hot and dry, the sun still hanging high, the ground still parched and thirsty.

When the phone rang, Diane took her hand from the hook. He was out of breath.

"You're here?"

"Close," she said.

"What now?"

"You've got it?"

"I got it."

"Is this cool with you? You're up for it?"

"Yeah, yeah. No problem." He sounded to Diane like he was seriously sweating it. His nervousness came through the receiver.

"You don't have to. I'll understand."

"No!" He calmed himself. "No. I want to. I read it. Read it all last night, and you're right. I think."

"About what? Which part am I right about?"

"About they framed him."

"And me?"

"I believe you. Okay?" His breathing was slowing; he was calming. He took a deep one, blew it out slowly. "Sorry. I ran all the way over here. I believe you, okay? I never really didn't believe you. It's just that I kind of kept trying to fit the two sides of the story into my head, thinking they could eventually make sense. It took me awhile to understand that they couldn't. Never would."

"It's not a game."

"No shit, Sherlock."

"You're not just doing this in hopes of getting laid?"

He laughed, as she'd hoped he would, laughed long and loud and then cut himself off abruptly. "I've missed your body bad, bay-bay, but it'd take more than sex to get me into this kind of switch. I'm doing it in hopes that you won't have to go back, or that you won't get . . . that they won't—"

"Can you meet me now?"

"Now's good. I'm on days."

"South of town, the old Couillard farm?"

"Okay."

"Forty minutes or so. And listen."

"What."

"This isn't . . . you're not . . ."

"What?" The flat tone warned her not to insult him with the question.

"I don't know," she said. "I just don't want to see you get, you know, mixed up in trouble."

"I already am," he said. "Get it through your head. I love you." She was silent.

"To answer your unasked question," he said, "it's not a trap." He hung up.

She walked away from the phone booth in a daze, spotted her car there next to the gas pump, walked to it, or tried to. What was it her mother had said that time, after rehab? One day at a time, her mother had said, just put one foot in front of the other.

Fuck it. It wasn't like Renfro was expecting her to marry him or anything. He was helping her out. He knew she'd been fucked over in the worst possible way, and he was helping her. That was all. No, that wasn't all. He loved her. He had said it, and she had heard it.

He was so good at getting confessions, good at relating to offenders. He could sit there and talk to you, and you'd want to tell him the awfulest things you'd ever done. Diane had been with him when he'd gotten a rapist to confess on the side of the road, after pulling over a van that matched the description given by a bruised and traumatized teenage girl at the hospital. Diane backed him up, and stood watching while he made friends with a rapist, convinced him to come clean, convinced him that the only way to survive was to admit the wrongdoing and hope to start over again. Was that what he was doing now? Would he try to convince her, as he handed over the transcript, that she had to start over? Would he tell her he loved her and then slap the cuffs on her wrists?

She couldn't think. She had to think. She had to be there with her wits fully functional or she wouldn't survive.

She drove carefully, on a two-lane blacktop now, and no traffic to speak of. At one point a dark green Chevy came up behind her, leaving about three car lengths between its front bumper and her rear one. She could see two males in the vehicle. She slowed, not suddenly but gradually, like someone who's not paying attention to their driving and lets their speed fluctuate. The car didn't pass her. It slowed down as well. But in the rearview she could see the guys inside it were smoking and talking and maybe they weren't paying much attention to their own driving. She slowed some more, to a full ten under the speed limit. Still nothing. That's when she put her signal on and pulled onto the narrow gravel road shoulder. The car shot past her, not even a flash of brake lights. She sat there until it disappeared over the horizon before pulling back onto the road.

There wasn't another vehicle in sight when she made the left onto the farm-to-market road that ran past the old Couillard place.

Renfro was waiting there. She saw his car parked back next to the barn where old Mr. Couillard used to milk his cows before the middlemen put him out of business. There was a large painted plywood sign posted on sturdy four-by-four posts, red lettering on white background: FOR SALE, 77.34 ACRES, ZONED INDUSTRIAL. WILL BUILD TO SUIT. Mr. Couillard had gone to live down in Corpus Christi with a daughter's family right after the milk bandits, the middlemen intent on sucking every penny of profit from the farmers, forced him to stop doing what he'd done for close to forty years and the developers moved in for the kill.

She drove past without slowing, heading down the road until she'd clocked five miles on the odometer before swooping around in an easy U-turn and heading back to the farm.

She wheeled off the main road and down the gravel path that led back past the deserted farmhouse to the barn and pulled to a stop next to Renfro's ride. He looked at her like she was someone he thought he might have met but wasn't entirely sure he had. He stared as he opened his car door, a nervous smile on his face. Diane killed her engine and got out, walked around her car to where he leaned up against his driver's-side door. He seemed to recognize her then and opened his arms. She fell against him, and he wrapped her to him tight, his face pressed against her neck. She heard him whispering thank God, thank God, and she could've drowned in the scent of him, wrapped in his quiet strength, letting herself feel for the first time since they'd taken her to jail what a good and decent man he was and just how much she'd really missed him.

"You did a good job," he said. "Passing you on the street, I might not have recognized you." He mussed her hair. "Kinda short, though."

"It's been sort of a process," she said. "If I have to change my appearance once more . . . I guess it's either a wig or a Mohawk."

"Let's hope you don't have to," he said.

Gail stopped at the front desk to inquire about a runner's map. The clerk, a trim young man with impeccable grooming, pulled one from beneath the counter and placed it in front of her.

"How far are you looking to run?"

"I think a mile will do for this evening," Gail said, thinking that the real answer was *until they stop chasing me.*

SIXTEEN

Diane closed the transcript carefully, placing it on the seat between her and Renfro. It contained Sheriff Lowe's testimony, and that of the forensic odontologist called by the state. The other volumes were in a bag in the backseat. Probably two thousand pages of trial transcript. Nothing but the truth, in ink, on paper. The sun was sunk just below the horizon, the sky going lavender. She looked sullenly at Renfro. He raised his eyebrows in a question.

"I don't get it," she said. "I thought you said this proved they framed Churchpin?"

He shifted around to lean against the passenger door.

"I didn't say it proved anything," he said. "I told you I think you're right that they framed him. And I do. You read that testimony? The odontologist?"

"Whatever the hell that is."

"The bite marks on one of the female victims matched Churchpin's teeth?"

"Yeah, I know who you're talking about."

"I went on-line, plugged him in. He's a legit dentist, and he's what they call 'board eligible' at the ABFO, the association that hands out certificates for the specialty, but he's still gathering points to take the exam. They have to get a certain number of points before they can be tested to become legit. One way to get points is to testify in court cases."

"Shouldn't they have to get certified *before* they're allowed to testify in cases?"

"Seems bassackward to me, too. But that's not what bugged me out. Guess where the guy went to high school?"

Diane shrugged.

"Round Rock." Renfro leaned toward her, so close she thought he might be about to kiss her. "Class of '76," he whispered. "Guess who else went there and graduated that same year?"

Diane waited.

"Gib Lowe. They were on the track team together."

"Lowe was on the track team?" Diane was so shocked her voice squeaked.

"Shot put. His buddy did the discus."

Diane deflated back into her seat. "What does that prove? It doesn't prove anything."

"I know that." Renfro shifted again, getting worked up. "But don't you think it's a little cozy, the DA calling one of the sheriff's old high school buddies to testify in this extremely important case where he desperately needs a conviction? And the guy's not even certified? Don't you think they should've got someone with the finished credentials?"

"Of course. But it's not enough. Not even close."

"It's better than nothing."

"Look, Renfro, I appreciate this. I really, really appreciate this. But a jury already bought this guy's testimony—"

"And so did the DA, from the looks of it. Green cash money, no doubt."

"Scumbag." She took Renfro's hand. "When did you do all this? When did you have time?"

"I made time," he said. "I thought about you every day."

"Thank you." She pulled his hand to her lips and kissed his fingertips. "That's sweet." She let go of his hand, and he let it fall onto the transcript like he was helpless to control it. "I missed you, too."

"Efird hasn't been much help," he said. "I've tried to talk to him about Churchpin, but all he wanted to talk about was you." He let his arm fall across the seat back, touched her shoulder gently. "Like he was obsessed or something." He leaned in, looked at her closely.

"There was nothing," Diane said. "Ever. Nothing."

He nodded. "I almost wrote you about it. But, I don't know, the thought of other people reading our letters. I thought about putting it in with the legal mail, but it seemed too risky."

"You'd have got fired. Chief wouldn't approve of you corresponding with a convict."

"I didn't know what to say, anyway. I didn't want to chase you away, any more than I already had."

"It wasn't like I could run anywhere."

"Apparently you can."

"I had no choice."

"I can't believe you pulled it off. It's pretty amazing, Offic—" He cut himself off.

"So you said Efird won't talk to you?" She tried to smooth over it, the realization between the two of them that things had changed so much. That Diane might well have to go, disappear from Texas and any chance they had of a future together. Unless Renfro was willing to leave his own life behind and go with her, and what were the odds of that?

"How the hell'd you—"

"I'll never tell," Diane said, her tone joking. "Where's Efird stay these days?"

"I'll have to show you. It's kind of off the beaten path."

"You can't come with me. He freaks out, your career is down the tubes. You've heard of harboring a fugitive?"

"He freaks out, you could get hurt."

Diane slipped her shirt back and twisted in the seat to show him her gun.

"I'll be fine," she said, half laughing. "I'm a felon now. Other people are supposed to be scared of me." She wanted to be joking, but the words she said dug at the back of her throat on the way out. Felon. Convict. Monster. Something other than a human being, something to be feared and despised.

"I'm backin' you up on this." Renfro's eyes were determined. "Unless you got somebody else going with you. Where'd your partner go? Y'all split up?"

"She's where she is, and—nothin' personal—but that's nobody's business but mine and hers. I couldn't ask her to expose herself to this. This is my problem."

"You're not going out there alone."

"Oh, yes, I am. I am *not* going to put you in this mess. Anymore than you are already. No way, no how. Anyway, he's not going to hurt me. Now draw me the map. Please."

Renfro sighed, picked up the transcript and began sketching a map on the back cover. "You'll call me, right? I'll put my cell phone number here for you, too."

"No," she said.

His head jerked up sharply. "Just call me. Let me know you're all right when you finish up."

"Don't write it down. Tell me. I'll memorize it."

He stared at her.

"*If* something should happen," she said, "I don't want anyone finding your number on me. You don't have a sledgehammer with you, do you?"

Renfro shook his head no, still drawing the map. "Why?"

"Insurance," she said.

"Bullshit," he said. "But the Home Depot's open late tonight."

"When'd you get a cell phone?" Diane watched him write a road name in neat block letters. She liked that about him, his fastidious handwriting.

"About a month after you left," he said. "You know, all these women calling to ask me out and all." He looked up and smiled at her, winked. She reached to touch his cheek.

"I'll just bet they did."

"I turned them all down," he said. "Told them their appeals for dates lacked conviction." He pulled her over next to him, put an arm around her. "So tell me," he whispered, "you have any hot little affairs there inside the walls?" He traced a finger along her collarbone, headed south toward her heart.

"Think I'd tell you if I did?"

"I'd hope so."

"I didn't."

"Nobody hassled you?"

"Not about sex."

"So it's been awhile."

She nodded, feeling his fingers at work on the button of her blouse, feeling a warmth from his touch that was spiraling right down her center, filling her with desire.

"I can't believe you're here," he whispered, leaning to kiss her. "I thought it was gonna take me years to get you out of there." He pulled her to him, whispering again. "I missed you bad, girl."

He held her then, they sat wrapped up close to each other, watching as shadows filled the car and the first stars appeared. After a while, he lifted her face to his, a smile playing at this lips.

"You know," he said, "you won't catch Efird home before the bars close. Wanna go play in the barn?"

The mattress was comfortable. The room was dark. The air-conditioning unit hummed, offering a kind of white noise that drowned out the sound of cars passing on the freeway outside. Gail lay there, her eyes closed, trying to talk herself to sleep.

Trying in vain.

The room at the Marriott North, conveniently located on the LBJ Freeway, was so similar to the room at the Harvey, the one she'd left just after nine that evening, that Gail was beginning to think she could travel the world and get the sense that she was merely going in circles and coming back to the same hotel room, no matter where in the world she went. It reminded her of the very last movie she'd seen in the prison auditorium, before all the politicians jumped on the tough-on-crime bandwagon and the authorities stopped showing movies on Friday evenings. What was it—*Groundhog Day*, yes, where the guy kept waking up day after day to discover it was still Groundhog Day. It was like that: no matter how far she traveled, she kept waking up in the same room.

She'd faded out early, and now the alarm clock on the nightstand glowed 11:24, a dot indicating that it was P.M.

The night had barely started, and here she was waking up.

She wanted more sleep. It seemed out of the question. Still, she didn't move, didn't get up. Even if she couldn't sleep, she would give her body rest. Lie there motionless, focused on relaxing, try to conserve her energy, and hope for some form of rejuvenation.

If she wanted to make it out here, if she really and truly believed that she should be free, then there were decisions to be made. She needed to think it out, move carefully, not let herself be swayed by passion. Objectivity was imperative. That was one major difference between the Gail who got caught and locked up and the Gail who was out now, back in the world. To a large degree, it was up to her whether she went back or not. Sure, blind luck could function on either side: some cop might stumble across her and snap to the situation. Or might not. Luck was part of it. But she had to do all in her power to avoid that situation. Which meant not going after Diane. Which meant leaving Diane to her own fate. Which meant abandoning her friend.

All those years, no decisions to make. No chance to make a decision even if you wanted to. It was all sorted out for you. You were there, in prison, no chance of going anywhere. You ate what they fed you, when they fed you. You went where they told you and did what they told you to do. Even knowing they were morons, they were slaves, they were too scared to strike out in the world on their own. The best they could manage was to suck on the government teat, and like pigs in a litter, they fought for the nipple among themselves. And *they* told *you* what you could do and when you could do it. But they couldn't get inside your mind. They couldn't take away your freedom of thought. That was the problem now, the major adjustment Gail knew she had to make. When there was little or no chance of taking action, thought could run free and talk was bargain basement cheap. Now she had to follow up. When she felt something strongly, when she *believed*, she had to take action on the belief or else abandon it, admit that she no longer possessed it as belief, only as idle speculation.

Diane was her friend. Diane had got her out of prison. If Diane hadn't been there to pull her up into the tree and drag

her through the woods and bandage her wound and do the
dirty work of survival, Gail would be still in her cell, her hands
cupped and trying to hold on as she watched her life drain
through her fingers like water.

And if she went after Diane now, she would be risking her
freedom.

She looked again at the clock. Mr. ID had said he'd be there
early. He'd do a passport. She could go anywhere then. Europe. Asia. Or some island somewhere, someplace raw and remote, where there wasn't all this plastic, where things didn't
beep and buzz all the time, where the air smelled green.

Early would be good. The earlier the better. If she went af-
ter Diane and got picked up, it would be a form of betrayal.
Betrayal of Mel, of Chris and Michelle, of Rick Reed, and of
Tom. Especially Tom. She wondered where they had him.
Putting herself at risk unnecessarily would be a breach of faith.

She could go. She was free to go. No one would blame her.
Least of all Diane.

Diane eased slowly down the lane. There was Efird's trailer, an
old, corroded turquoise-and-white Champion dropped in a
small clearing at the end of the curving dirt drive. He'd made
sure he got way the hell out in the country, that was for certain.
There wasn't anything around for miles that Diane had seen.
The rusting remains of a barbecue grill sat several feet away
from what passed for steps leading into the mobile home:
wood planks on cinder blocks, all spray-painted silver. A string
of plastic jalapeño pepper lights sagged from an outlet next to
the front door over to an arthritic-looking apple tree ten feet
distant, shedding a pinkish red glow onto the beaten patch of
bare earth that functioned as a patio. Beneath the tree, an impressive pile of glass beer bottles in green, brown, and clear.
And another pile of larger bottles next to that. Almost exclu-
sively Wild Turkey, looked like. The boy was doin' some
drinkin'.

And apparently he was home early tonight. A yellow glow
came through the windows. Diane wasn't out of the car when
the trailer door opened and Efird stepped out, pistol in hand.

"Who the hell's there?" His tone was half threatening, half joking, as if he were aware of his macho act and poking fun at it.

"It's the used-to-be-*po*lice," Diane said, forcing a laugh, making sure her voice held no threat. He froze on the rickety cinder block steps, one hand still on the doorknob, trying to connect the voice to his memory. Diane shut the car door and walked toward him, hands held out to her sides where he could see them, and as she entered the reddish glow from the patio lights, she saw Efird's mouth drop open, his eyes bulge with disbelief.

"Holy shit!" It was something between and a shout and a whisper, something between happy-to-see-you and what-the-fuck-are-you-doing-here, something she couldn't quite pin down as either happily surprised or scared half to death. "Holy shit!" He stepped down nimbly, stuffing the gun down the front of his pants, opening his arms as he swaggered over. "Hellfire and damnation, girl, is that you? What the *fuck*, Wellman? You tryin' to get your ass *arrested?*"

"Been there, done that," Diane said, returning Efird's hug.

"Come on, come on," he drawled, "Come the hell on inside. Shit."

"Efird, wait." Diane stepped back, stuck her hands in her back pockets. "I don't want to be any trouble. You know. If you tell me to go, I'll go right now, and it'll be like I was never here. I don't want to make trouble for you."

"Hell," he said. "*Hail.*" He made a show of looking around, checking the sky above them, peering into the woods. "You see anybody? I sure don't see anybody. I don't even have a fuckin' phone out here. Hell with 'em. You come on inside."

Inside was a wreck, or close to it.

"Pardon the mess," Efird said. "I haven't really unpacked everything yet. This is temporary. My uncle uses it for hunting. Rest of the year it's vacant." Diane nodded, staring at the boxes stacked about the living room, the stacks of books piled on the couch, the dirty clothes tossed under a small end table.

They sat at a padded booth in the kitchenette. Efird took from the dish rack a couple of Texas Rangers tumblers, the eight-ounce size with the crossed bats and baseball design that

Diane had seen offered free with a fill-up at Exxon stations. Efird put them on the white Formica tabletop and grabbed a bottle of Wild Turkey from its spot next to the salt and pepper shakers, began pouring. Diane waved at him to stop, saying that's enough a couple of times before he listened and began filling his own glass.

"Want some ice?" He capped the bottle. Diane shook her head yes. Efird leaned out of his seat and reached to open the refrigerator, grabbed an ice cube tray and cracked loose some cubes. Offered it to Diane. She pried a couple out and dropped them in her glass. And then a couple more, hoping they'd melt fast.

Efird tapped her glass, took a mouthful of whiskey and swallowed it whole, sending a shudder the length of his body. Diane took a sip, felt the burn down the back of her throat.

Efird set down his glass and leaned on his elbows. Looked at her. Drank again and looked some more.

"You believe what they said about me?" Diane swirled the ice cubes around in her glass.

"Not for a goddamned minute. When I told Jimmy Ray Smith, he about shit his pants. I think he was planning to ask you out for dinner. Next thing we know, you're in jail and we're sittin' there scratching our heads."

"Me, too. Fuckers show up with a search warrant, and come up with cocaine. I swear to you it wasn't mine. But it was my word against the fuckin' DEA and the jury believed the DEA. You know. They marched out their chemists and their agents and put on a dog and pony show and the jury went for it."

"Dog fuck the pony or'd the pony fuck the dog?"

"The only one who got fucked was yours truly."

Efird downed another mouthful and shook his head slowly. Diane couldn't tell if he was trying to smile or trying not to cry.

"I woulda been there," he said. "At the trial, if that pussy of a chief hadn't sent down orders that nobody could go. We couldn't have any contact with you whatsoever."

"Lightweight," Diane said. "Always was kind of a punk."

"Shit, girl." Efird sighed, drank again. "But I gotta tell you." He leaned in conspiratorially, dropped his voice to a whisper.

"I think it's cool as shit you broke out of fucking federal prison. Hot damn! How many motherfuckers can say they accomplished that in their lifetimes?"

Diane smiled, met his eyes.

"So where's the other woman, that radical chick?" Efird was positively gleeful.

"I think she headed to Sri Lanka, or someplace like that. Said she was going to some commune over there." Diane laughed quietly, nodding. "Told me I could come with her, but I don't know, it just seemed like something I'd never be able to get into. She was pretty cool, though." Diane looked down at her drink then, just in case her face might be offering some clue that she was telling lies. Efird might be tipsy, but she knew he could latch onto a lie like it was gospel and he was a Baptist preacher. She took another sip of whiskey, shook her head. "Lotta folks in there were all right. Kinda surprised me."

"I bet," he said, eyeing her. But she didn't see any suspicion on his face. "So what're you gonna do?" he asked. "What are you even doing in this part of the world?"

"Trying to straighten things out. I'm sure Lowe was behind it, wanting to get me out of his hair before I dug up something he didn't want known about Rick Churchpin. If I could just get in to talk to Churchpin . . ."

Efird snorted. " 'Fraid he's not doing much talking these days."

"He never did. Not since his mama got killed. And not much before that."

"No. I got word yesterday. Dude killed himself. Got hold of something sharp enough to slit his wrists."

Diane sat staring at Efird, watching his lips form words. She knew she should be feeling something, some kind of sadness, sorrow, or anger. *Something.* But she was numb. Her pulse steady and smooth, her heart doing its job in her chest. Efird's lips were still moving. She pulled her attention to his words.

" . . . far as I'm concerned the world's a better place without Rick Churchpin in it."

"What'd he ever do to you? I thought you liked him at one point in your life."

"I did. He was a good kid. Would've made a fine cop. But he went and blew it. Let me down in a big way."

"You think he killed himself? Or do you think somebody helped him?"

"Nobody had any reason to kill his sorry ass, except the parents of those three kids. Nah. He did himself."

Diane sat, her face blank, wondering if her chances of exposing the truth in the Churchpin case, and thus her own, had died along with him.

"They had it on the news this evening," Efird said. "You didn't see?"

"No." She sat, not knowing what to say. "Why'd you leave?" Her words came out low, almost in a whisper.

Efird looked up, the whites of his eyes gone pink from bloodshot, his eyebrows pulled low in concentration. But however bad it might have got for him, the drinking, Diane saw that he was still taking care of himself. He was shaving. He was brushing his teeth and washing his hair.

"The department? I'd just had enough, finally." He rested his chin on one hand, the drink getting into his head now. "I had enough horseshit, and I had enough money saved to get by till I decide what to do next. Me and Jimmy Ray's thinkin' about becoming PIs. Figure we could do real good that way, make money and not have to put up with a bunch of bullshit from a bunch of whiny-ass brass who don't know their asses from the eighteenth hole. Plus be partners. For real."

"Sounds good," Diane said. "I hope it happens for you."

"Maybe you could be our first customer, or what is it they're called . . . client. Our first client."

"Unless you get your shingle out, like, tomorrow, it may be too late for me. I gotta get something together fast, Efird. They catch me, I'm back in prison for a long fucking time." She stood up, stretched, ambled toward the couch. He got right up and followed after her. The boxes prevented her getting close to the couch unless she actually wanted to climb up over them.

"It's the kitchen or the back bedroom," Efird said. "Everyplace else in this wreck is full of all the worthless shit I've managed to accumulate. No place to sit."

Diane turned, rattled her drink between them.

"You got someplace to stay tonight?"

"Yeah," she said. "I got a friend expecting me."

"Bet I can't guess."

"Betcha can't, either. I'll tell you this and save us both a minute: it ain't Will Renfro."

"Oh, I get it." Efird laughed, turned, and headed back to the kitchen booth, practically having to duck not to hit his head on the low roof of the trailer. "Him you'll protect. But me? I'm expendable."

"I told you outside. I offered to go."

Efird waved an acknowledgment, and Diane followed him back to the booth.

"He's still a cop."

"And I, thank God, am not." Efird stood a minute, thumbs tucked in his belt, hip cocked out. "He know you're in the neighborhood?" He folded himself into the booth.

Diane shook her head no, absently tapping a finger against the tabletop. "And I don't want him to."

"Good enough," Efird said.

"I had planned to ask you to go visit Churchpin, which there's no way I could ask Renfro to do. Try to find out what was in that letter he wrote to his mother."

Efird swallowed some whiskey. Sighed loudly. "I don't have a clue about the letter, but I can tell you Churchpin was moving a lot of dope," he said quietly. "Some folks—myself included—suspect it might have been coming to him from somebody in the Sheriff's Office."

Diane felt a charge shoot through her body, firing from her brain, and wondered if hounds felt that same thing when they picked up a scent.

"Linda hinted at it." Efird said, his voice catching on her name. He cleared his throat and sniffed, his eyes grew hard. "Before she went and blew her fool head off."

"Efird, you shouldn't talk about her like—"

"It's what happened," he said. "I'm tellin' it the way it went down."

In the silence, Diane heard an owl hoot somewhere off in the woods.

"Pretty," she said.

"Yeah." Efird shifted in his seat, picked up the saltshaker and tried to balance it on its edge. "Couple of my snitches thought Churchpin's connection might have been Lowe himself. Gettin' it out of the evidence locker. Moving it through Churchpin."

"Why didn't you—"

"Hell," Efird said, his voice rising up into falsetto, "Look what the fuck happened to you! You think I'm gonna accuse the sheriff of Breard County of dealing dope and my only evidence is the word of a sorry-ass speed freak on probation for whoopin' his girlfriend's butt? I got more productive things to do with my life." He stood up again, leaned against the kitchen counter and finished off his whiskey, draining the glass. "Though I'm not quite sure yet exactly what they are." He laughed at himself and placed his empty glass, slowly and carefully, on the counter.

Diane didn't know why, but she found the way he put the glass down, so slowly, so gently, vaguely threatening; she felt her insides tighten up as though they feared taking a blow to the gut. She leaned back to cover her anxiety, stretched an arm across the back of the bench seat, exposing her front to attack. The illusion of being at ease.

"So that's really why you left."

"What, 'cause of some kind of guilty knowledge?" He looked like he wanted to spit. "Nah. I told you why I left. Too much bullshit. Too much paperwork. Too many asslickin', pussy motherfuckers getting promoted." He sat back down and refilled his glass, taking what was left of the ice cubes from the tray on the table and dropping them in. "Sure you don't want to go to Sri Lanka? I'd go with you in a heartbeat. They wear fuckin' grass skirts there or what? It's tropical, right?"

Diane smiled at him. "Efird, I can't do *anything* until I clear my name and get this conviction overturned."

"I know that," he said seriously. "I'm just not at all sure you can. I'd think about gettin' the hell out of here, if I was you."

A silence fell, and Diane heard June bugs banging against the screen door, drawn to the light, their hard, dry, brown shells striking the metal mesh, making dull pinging sounds in the night.

She looked over at the screen door and shrugged. "I don't know."

"I wish I could give you more," he said. "That's all I got."

Diane took a sip of her whiskey and set the glass back in the ring of water it had made on the tabletop. "No idea who killed his mama?"

He shook his head no. "I seem to recall the sheriff took over that investigation."

"And I seem to recall you saying there was no way you would let him take the case away from you."

"Can't fight city hall."

"Sweet, Efird. That's really sweet."

"Hey. No need to come at me from that direction. I had my reasons."

"You're right." Diane backed down, softened her tone. "I'm just a little frustrated, if you can imagine."

He nodded.

"And of course the case is still open. Churchpin's mom?"

"Far as I know."

Diane stood up, stepped over to the sink, set her glass on the counter.

"So." She looked once again at the boxes and books on the couch and living room floor. "Guess there's not much sense unpacking everything if you're gonna move again soon." Diane tapped the screen to chase the June bugs away before opening the door.

Efird stepped over and pulled her to him, offering a hug. "Hell of deal you pulled off." He stepped back, shaking his head and smiling. "Someplace I can get in touch? If I come up with something?"

Diane shook her head. "I'm staying pretty mobile. But I'll

stop back before I head out, or whatever. I don't really know what I'm doing right now."

"You get it touch if you need something. *Anything*. I'll help you all I can, girl. You know that."

She nodded, walked to the car.

She strapped on her seat belt, saw Efird's silhouette in the door, his arms pressed against the doorframe as though he were trying to widen it. He slapped at something on his neck and stepped back inside the trailer, pulling the screen door shut after him, giving her a sharp, tiny salute goodbye.

SEVENTEEN

When the knock came, Gail was at the door instantly. She'd been up, dressed and waiting since before the sun rose, her thoughts vacillating between ideals of loyalty and desire for safety. She had gone to sleep hoping to be startled from sleep by a call from Diane, and had awakened to a blurry sense of happiness at not finding herself in her cell, followed by a crushing sense of disquietude when she remembered Diane's foolishness.

She barely spoke to Mr. ID, who arrived, as last time, in the guise of a businessman. She took the envelope he presented with a grateful smile, confirming that Mel had taken care of payment, and quickly closed the door.

That was it. Her bag was packed, her breakfast was done, her cell phone was fully charged. She opened the envelope and checked out the passports. Diane's was there, too, though Gail's had the newer photograph, the one Diane was not aware of. They looked impeccable. She hoped. But however good the briefs might look, there was only one true test of their integrity: the customs booth.

Gail picked up the remote and pressed the proper buttons to check out of the hotel. She left the keycards on the dresser and calmly wheeled her new suitcase out the door.

An airport van was parked at the edge of the port cochere. As Gail approached, the driver got out and took her bag.

"DFW," she said. "Air France."

On the way to the airport, she took out her cell phone and tried once again to reach Diane, but once again an anonymous voice said *Please leave a message.* This time she didn't hang up.

"D," she said, "I've got something I need to get to you right away. Please call me back so we can make arrangements. I'll need to hear from you within the next three hours or so. Please get in touch. I hope you're okay."

She could put the passport in a locker at the airport and hide the key in the ladies' room. Or if Diane could give her an address, she could mail it. She still couldn't quite believe Diane had run off. She appreciated Diane's desire not to expose her to whatever danger Diane had headed for, but she couldn't help feeling abandoned. Diane should have talked to her first. Let her, Gail, make up her own mind about whether to be involved or not. The world had thrown them together in that tiny little cage in upstate New York, a situation built on a foundation of absurd chance, a roll of the dice. Had Johnson put Diane in a different cell, Gail would not be headed for the airport with a fake passport in her bag. She would most likely still be in prison, awaiting charges for attempted escape. Or she might even be dead. She hadn't been able to tell Diane, but it was Diane's almost unwavering fuck-it-all attitude that gave Gail the courage to make the break. She saw so much of her own youthful self in Diane that she never stopped wondering how Diane wound up being a cop. How someone so fundamentally rebellious would fall into a job enforcing rules and regulations. But Diane's determination to seek justice had inspired Gail to realize that justice had been done in her own case, and done some more and more and more, until it wasn't justice anymore; it was cruelty and petty politics that was demanding she serve more years, and that realization was what led her to try the escape. Probably years too late, but it was better than finishing her sentence. It was, now that she thought about it, the only honorable thing to do.

She thought back to the time she'd run away from home, in second grade, when she and Carole Johnson from down the block had made peanut butter and jelly sandwiches and gone to live in the doghouse that the Petersons had left out near their trash cans in the paved smooth alleyway after their dog had been run over the previous spring. By late evening, as the summer stars were beginning to shimmer, most of the neighborhood was out looking for them, and soon enough Mr. Johnson's head appeared, almost completely upside down, in the doorway of the doghouse, making it difficult to tell whether he was frowning or smiling.

She had a feeling now that she knew what her mother had felt like that day, only she didn't have the same options that her mother had. Gail didn't want to leave Diane behind, but Diane hadn't left much choice. Gail had no intention of sitting in that hotel waiting for Diane—or the heat—to show up.

Out the van window, Gail watched the underbelly of a single slender cloud on the horizon going pink with the coming of day. Already the airport was busy. She counted eight planes in the sky, circling into position for landing or arcing around after takeoff. She marveled again at how crowded America had gotten while she'd been locked away. She wondered if the same thing had happened to Europe.

Diane opened her eyes and felt her lungs compress at the sight of her surroundings. The motel room was not much more than a jail cell minus the bars. Some kind of toxic carpet laid over bare concrete—without any padding, from the feel of it as her bare feet carried her toward the bathroom. The window unit was working hard against the morning sun. Diane thought she could smell the glue used to stick together the pieces of the brown Formica furniture, but decided maybe it was just the odor of whatever chemicals they used to clean the room. Depressing as hell. The place was one of those low-slung two-story cinder block jobs set close enough to the highway that passing trucks rattled the windows. But more than toxic chemicals, the room smelled like the beer-stained sweat of a thousand traveling salesmen, guys hanging on to the bottom rung of the white collar ladder while their kids grew up without them. Diane had met more than one of them on domestic disturbance calls. Some of them got so used to being on the road that they didn't know how to act when they got home.

She took a plastic cup from the stack of inverted, individually wrapped plastic cups on the flimsy baby-shit brown plastic tray that held a matching flimsy plastic ice bucket, no lid, no foam padding, like the ones at the Holiday Inn. She removed the sealed plastic wrapper from around the plastic cup and turned on the plastic bathroom tap to let the cold run, to flush out the water that had sat in the plastic pipes all night, probably absorbing PVC. Maybe Michelle and Chris had been right about bottled water.

But why was she even thinking about them?

Because they'd helped her. That's why. They'd helped Gail and her. They'd risked their own freedom to help Gail and her get away. They were solid. They were good people. Like Mel. Like Rick Reed. So many of her thoughts and beliefs were getting all turned upside down and shaken and mixed up, as though they'd been dumped into a blender, mixed thoroughly on high speed and poured back into her skull: purée of confusion.

She drank a glass of water, then another, and a third, and then went to dig her phone out of her bag. She felt bad about taking the car, and worse about leaving without telling Gail what she was doing. But at least Gail hadn't had to choose whether to come along. And that was what made Diane think that she'd done the right thing to slip away as she had. It took a burden off Gail, and Gail damn sure didn't need any extra burdens. So the least Diane could do would be to call Gail and let her know everything was okay and reassure her that the car would be returned. And that she wasn't out doing a bunch of crazy shit that was sure to get her busted. And that if she did somehow get busted, Gail had nothing to worry about. She might have been a cop, but she would never rat out Gail. In fact, she would deny that Gail had even escaped with her, claim total ignorance on that score.

Gail sat at one of the black upholstered bench seats near a set of Departure Information screens, scanning the *Dallas Morn-*

ing News for mug shots or headlines. No sign of them, but then the small headline **"Huntsville Prisoner Takes Own Life"** caught her eye. Rick Churchpin. That was the one. The case Diane was obsessed with. Fuck. Where in hell was Diane and was she involved? That was all. It was too strange. Maybe Diane had something to do with it. Maybe Diane had asked questions where she shouldn't have, and someone she contacted had warned whoever and they had seen to it that Churchpin woke up dead. Gail sat motionless, trying to think, trying to quiet the buzzing in her brain. What did she care, anyway? What did it matter to her, Rick Churchpin's suicide, if it even was a suicide? She didn't know the details of his case, only what she'd read in Diane's presentence report that night in the records room at the prison, and the bits and pieces she'd picked up from Diane over the course of their months together. She did know that this little bit of news gave her a very bad feeling about where Diane was and what she was doing. Gail felt bad, in a disconnected way, for Churchpin, and knowing what she did about prison, considered homicide a very real possibility. Just, why? Why had Diane split, and never mind anyway. Never mind. Get on the plane and get the hell out of here. She was reaching for her bag when her phone began ringing. Or beeping, whatever that noise was it was making to indicate she had a call. She dug it out, pressing the green button while fitting the earbud to her ear. She said hello and waited. Said hello again.

Nothing.

"Okay, I'm going to hang up now," she said, her voice coming out singsong as she attempted to cover her fear.

"Hey, homey. Don't cut me off."

A rush of anger and relief.

"Where are you?" Diane sounded like nothing had happened, like she was calling to see if Gail wanted to catch a movie.

"Airport."

"Okay, listen, I'm really sorry about everything, I'll get the car back I promise—"

"Fuck the car. Where are *you?*"

"Doing what I need to. Like I said in the note."

"The paper says that guy killed himself in his cell."

"I know."

"This is crazy."

"Tell me about it."

"You could be in danger."

Diane laughed.

"Are you nuts?" Gail lowered her voice, realizing that she'd been speaking too loudly. Passersby were glaring at her with irritation.

"Not at all," Diane said. "It just struck me as funny, I mean, kind of stating the obvious. And it's not like you're just out for a stroll in the park."

"Right."

"I hooked up with my old friend. A couple of them in fact. I'm not alone here."

"That's comforting Di—" Gail caught herself. "Why haven't you called?"

"I thought minimal exposure was the idea."

"Fine, but you could've returned my call."

"I'm calling you back right now. God, you sound like my mother might have sounded, I mean, if she'd been a good mother."

"I'll take that as a compliment. Look, we've been through too much to go and blow it now. Get the hell out of there."

There was a silence, and then a long slow sigh.

"The guy's dead. From what I understood, you needed him. Forget about it. All of it. I was about to get on a flight. I could wait for you here."

"Where're you thinking of?"

"Europe."

"Kind of general."

"We'll get specific when you get here. Come. Now."

"Arf-arf!"

"I'm serious."

"Give me thirty-six hours. If I don't have something solid by then, I'll meet you. We'll fly off into the sunrise together."

"You're being flip. You don't get it."

"I do get it. I totally get it. You don't get it. I got people down here who care about me. Who are willing to help me. Good solid stand-up guys. Like your pals in Oklahoma City. You know what I'm saying?"

"I know what you're risking."

"I'm not gonna do anything foolish. I've got a shot here to get things straightened out, okay? To undo the damage and get back what I had. I have to try."

Now it was Gail who was silent, struck by the level-headed determination in Diane's words, the evenness of her tone, the lack of invective in her message.

"I'll keep you posted," Diane said. "And if it even remotely looks like things are falling apart, I'll bail. I promise."

"I need to know how to reach you. Where you are."

"You've got my cell."

"If something happens. To you. Or whatever."

"Okay," Diane said. "You know that guy who used to write to me, when we were roommates?"

"Yes." Gail didn't reach for a pen. She cleared her mind to put the number in her memory.

"It's his cell. If you can't reach me and you start buggin' out, you can try him. But you won't have to. I've got this under control. Couple of days? Bueno?"

"Call me," Gail said. "I can't hang here forever." She disconnected, tucking the phone back into her bag, pretending to go back to reading her paper, but repeating Renfro's number to herself until she was sure she had burned it into long-term memory.

And then she dialed it.

EIGHTEEN

It was a half-moon night, not as much light as Diane would have liked, but enough that she could see without headlights as she eased down the drive toward Efird's trailer. She pulled her car around back, intending to park behind the trailer, and only then noticed an old trail leading into the woods at the edge of the clearing. She squeezed the vehicle in between the trunks of two oaks, drove slowly down the lane until she found a brushy spot where she could manage to turn the car around. It was too dark to see well under the tree canopy. She hit her headlights and the beams cut into the woods, across to the edge of the clearing.

Her breath left her. There was a body. Beneath that pine over there. Slowly, she reached behind her for her pistol, rested it on her lap as she stared, trying to focus, giving her eyes time to adjust to the sudden brightness of the headlights. She looked, and the body, sprawled on the ground, took shape. Its eyes were open in terror, its mouth twisted in pain. It was Lake Bolton all over again.

She closed her eyes, shook her head, opened her eyes and looked again.

Still. It was.

She killed the engine, pocketed the keys, came out slowly with her gun at ready.

The headlights from her car threw her shadow, long and twisted skinny, on the ground before her. She approached the body, bracing herself for blood, the sight and smell of it, the things it did to you. Around her, beyond the beams of the headlights, the woods loomed dark. She got closer, almost in a crouch now, instinct curling her body into a coil spring and making it a smaller target.

And then she was on it, and laughing. She kicked at it.

A piece of wood broke off. It was a rotting chunk of tree, one stunted broken limb pressed to the ground like a mangled arm. Diane tucked her gun away and stood there, waiting for her blood to stop rushing, feeling her heart beat against her breastbone, willing it to slow.

She looked again. Tree trunk. Stripped of its bark by the elements, the wood bleached to the color of skin. An old woodpecker hole and a couple of knots formed a face above the broken limb that she'd taken to be an arm, a face that looked like the one on the framed poster she'd seen in Chris and Michelle's bathroom, the one of that guy screaming.

She went back to her car and sat staring at the tree. Remembering the bodies that night. Whoever killed them was still walking free, but the DA could be sure of another term of office come the elections in November.

A fly came in through the passenger window, buzzing angrily, banging itself against the windshield. Diane picked up the transcript from the seat beside her, folded it in half, waited. When she tried to look at the world from the perspective of One World, One Love, or being totally nonjudgmental, or having sacred respect for all living things, or believing in the possibility of reincarnation, which she didn't do very often, it was flies that did her in. She despised flies. Always had, always would.

The thing lit on the dash and she smacked it, hard, decisively, with the transcript. The buzzing stopped. She opened the car door and leaned to pick up a twig. She wiped the remains off the back of the transcript onto the ground, leaving a splot of fly blood about the size of a corn kernel on the paper. Sheriff Lowe's testimony, deadly once again.

Then she heard another buzz, smaller, lighter, fading in and out, coming close, then veering away, even and steady, getting whiny when it got close enough to bite.

Forget about this. Where there was one mosquito, there were legions of them. She rolled up the windows and cranked the engine. She took a last look at the tree, tried to wipe the images of the dead teens from her mind, backed out to the trail, and drove back toward Efird's trailer. She killed the lights again as she got close to the edge of the woods, parking well back under the cover of trees.

Outside the car, she stood listening to the rustle of leaves in a soft night breeze. She heard something small scuttle through the underbrush some yards away. A chipmunk maybe, or were they all asleep by now? It wasn't yet ten. She had no idea when Efird would return. Most likely he was out drinking; she probably had at least a solid two hours before he'd arrive. She went around and pulled the sledgehammer out of the trunk. She should have been scared, or at least nervous, but she felt nothing more than she might if she were taking a stolen bicycle report. Just get the job done and get out of there. Even if she wasn't exactly sure what the job was. But she wanted a look around Efird's place, needed to see what he was up to, what he was hiding. Everybody hid something, and he had been close enough to Churchpin at one point in his life that there might be something there. That night at the crime scene, she had been flattered when he told her he was leaving things up to her. But in retrospect, looking back from a distance, it had been an odd thing to do. And funny how the sheriff had showed up to steal the case so soon after Efird left. Probably it was nothing. Probably she'd find some pornography, maybe some less than street-legal weapons. Standard stuff for a boy cop's digs.

Outside the trailer, she knocked. Nothing. She tried the knob. Locked. She raised the sledgehammer, extending her arms, and took a small step back to get into proper position.

She pulled back the hammer. Aiming for the doorknob, she swung it into the target, moving easily, letting the weight of the hammerhead do the work. There was a *ping!* and the door popped open, Diane jumping to catch it before it banged against the outer wall of the trailer. Keyless entry. Not a lick of visible damage.

She stepped inside, pulling the screen door shut after her. Set the sledgehammer against the wall by the door. Dark as dungeon, or almost. Moonlight seeped in through the small windows above the kitchen sink and the living room couch. The whiskey glasses from last night were still on the kitchen counter. It looked like Efird had finished off the bottle of Turkey after Diane left. There was a fresh one on the table, right where the other one had been, next to the salt and pepper shakers that looked just like the ones at Harbingers Barbecue. Probably came from there.

The living room was still in shambles. She stepped over a box, toward the couch. Headlights coming down the drive. Fuck.

She stayed low, crawled over the box, closed the trailer door, and crouched on the kitchen floor. She heard the car pulling up out front. Headed for the bedroom and was on her hands and knees, next to the bed, when she remembered the sledgehammer. She heard a car door shut as she scrambled back to the front door, grabbed the hammer, and scurried back into the bedroom.

Under the bed, she blew out a few quick breaths to slow her breathing down. Shit. What was she going to do, wait until Efird went to bed and then sneak out? A great way to get shot. She wasn't even sure why she was hiding. She could have just sat down at the kitchen table and waited until he turned on the lights to greet him. Another good way to get shot.

The front door opened, and then the screen door. She should have locked the front door.

"Eeef?" Footsteps into the kitchen now. "Efird?" She couldn't place the voice, though she thought she'd heard it before. The kitchen light went on; footsteps came toward the bedroom. She saw blue jeans and cowboy boots, barely visible in the seepage of moonlight through the bedroom window. She held her breath.

"All right then."

She pegged it when he spoke softly to himself instead of calling out for his friend. Jimmy Ray. What was his last name, Efird's soon-to-be-partner in the business of private investigation?

"I wish the fuck you'd get a phone," Jimmy Ray said, turning to head back toward the kitchen.

Diane exhaled, ever so slowly. Silently. She hoped Jimmy Ray wasn't planning to hang out and wait for his pal.

But she heard him lock the screen door in place, walk toward the living room.

And then the sounds of a box being opened. Things being taken out, books and papers, from the sound of it. He was emptying it. A shuffling of papers, a low, mumbled curse. Another box being opened.

Whoa. Jimmy Ray hadn't come here looking for Efird. Jimmy Ray was searching the place. Diane rested a cheek against the orange shag wall-to-wall. She was going to need her strength, no good wasting it being all tensed up under here.

Jimmy Ray finished the living room and moved into the kitchen. He was starting to get frustrated, she could tell. Hadn't found what he was looking for—whatever it might be—and was running out of patience. He was slamming things around, getting careless, getting noisy.

She eased out from under the bed, pulling the sledgehammer with her. Positioned herself next to the bedroom door. The rear door of the trailer was six feet away. Okay. If he heard her, she'd head for the car. If he didn't, she'd stick around outside somewhere.

She heard him slam a cabinet shut. And then he was coming down the hall. She pulled her gun, ready for him as his footsteps came closer. And then stopped, suddenly. A sliding door opened; his boots left the carpeting and clomped across linoleum.

He was in the bathroom. She heard him unzip, and a sigh as he peed.

God knew *that* was loud enough. Diane was out the door, sledgehammer in one hand, stuffing her gun into her waistband, waiting for the flush, waiting, there it was. She latched the door and crawled quickly under the trailer.

She positioned herself behind a pile of cinder blocks and two-by-fours stacked up next to the rear wheel of the trailer. The thing wasn't that high off the ground; she'didn't have a whole lot of headroom. She heard the thump of Jimmy Ray's boots as he came out of the bathroom and went back to the kitchen. And then the sounds of more searching, floating out through the screen door into the quiet country air.

A cricket started up, chirping from somewhere down at the other end of the trailer, it sounded like. Diane sat back gingerly against the lumber, making sure it was stacked sturdily enough to hold her before letting her full weight rest against it.

A while later Jimmy Ray clomped across the floor above her head. Getting to the bedroom now. She wished he'd hurry up and find whatever he was looking for. She'd catch him when he came out the front door. Find out just what it was he'd come after.

And then what? Say thanks a lot, I've got to run now, I'm a fugitive? She would have to handcuff him and leave him here, and he didn't strike her as the type who would let her do that without a struggle. He would either overpower her or force her to shoot him while he tried. And that was out of the question.

She sat, listening to Jimmy Ray get hotter and hotter, throwing things around now, yelling, kicking the walls. Yeah. Let him leave. Whatever was up between him and Efird, when she told Efird who tossed the place, she'd be in a good position to find out.

Finally, things got quiet again. The cricket stopped its chirping. She heard Jimmy Ray pacing the length of the trailer, back and forth, slowing down, taking another tour.

He was coming out the front door when headlights came down the drive. She heard Jimmy Ray close the trailer door and saw his boots move down the front steps.

The car parked, the headlights stayed on. Efird came out the door and knocked it closed with his hip.

"What the hell you doin' here?" Efird sounded seriously hostile. Diane backed up against the lumber, twisting around to where she could get a view.

"I'm tired of the bullshit, Efird. Churchpin's dead, in case you hadn't heard. Why don't you just go get the thing and let's burn it right here in this sorry excuse for a barbecue grill and agree to be done with it." Diane could see now that

Jimmy Ray had on a shoulder rig, sporting what looked like a nine-millimeter.

Efird walked over to face Jimmy Ray. Up close.

"I shoulda threw your ass in jail, is what I should've done." Efird said.

"Hah! Good one, Eef." Jimmy Ray tossed his head, flicking his ponytail. "Like you had nothing to do with it." He squinted against the glare of the car headlights and stepped around to face Efird from a different angle. Efird stepped likewise, so that they stayed face to face, sideways to the light. Now Diane saw that Efird had a pistol stuck down the back of his pants, smaller than Jimmy Ray's, maybe a .380.

"Look, there's no reason we can't the two of us head on off down to Austin like we planned." Efird spoke calmly, in a friendlier tone now, and cocked his hip out to the side in that way he had, tucking his hands in the back of his jeans, his palms out. Where he could get at his pistol quick and easy. But Jimmy Ray couldn't see that. "I mean why you're gettin' all antsy now is beyond me."

"It's not right. I'm tired of worrying you might go and get all self-righteous." Jimmy Ray's eyes went cold as he looked Efird up and down. "You owe me better than that." He moved fast, his hand going to his pistol, yanking it from the holster under his left arm, but Efird was faster, pulling his gun, whipping it out from his back and squeezing off four rounds dead into the center of Jimmy Ray's chest. Jimmy Ray stood there for a moment, looking at Efird, the coldness in his eyes going warm, his mouth contorting in an attempt to speak. He dropped his gun; his hands went to his chest, feeling for blood that had not yet begun flowing from the holes there. He fell to his knees, but before he hit the ground Efird was behind him, had him under the arms and was dragging him toward his Jag.

Diane caught her gasp before it escaped from her throat. A chill hit her right in the back of her neck and shot down her spine, raising the gooseflesh across her back. She fought not to move. Her mind was screaming *do something do something do something* until she managed to stop it with a single command: Don't fucking move.

When she went to put her head down on her arms, she realized she was holding her own weapon. She set it carefully on the ground next to her and made herself breathe. Slowly. Quietly.

She stayed low like that, listened as Efird opened the trunk of the Jag and dumped his best friend's body in there. He walked back over and picked up Jimmy Ray's pistol, looked at it for a long moment, turning it over in his hands, inspecting. Diane lost her view of him when he entered the trailer.

A moment later he came back out, still carrying Jimmy Ray's gun. He stopped to turn off the headlights of his car, then got into the Jag and drove away.

Diane sat there. And sat there some more. She sat there trying to absorb what she'd seen, trying to take it in, assimilate it. She sat there not wanting to waste any time, but needing to make sure Efird wasn't coming back.

When she convinced herself he was gone, she crawled out from under the trailer and dusted herself off, or tried to. She looked like she'd just run an obstacle course; even in the dark she could see that dirt was smudged against her chest and all down the front of her jeans. It wasn't coming off.

She walked over to where Jimmy Ray had fallen. Efird had caught him and got him into the car so fast there was barely any blood, a couple of small puddles next to the start of two grooves in the dirt where Jimmy Ray's boot heels had dragged across the ground as Efird pulled him toward the Jag.

As she climbed the steps up to the trailer door, Diane heard Gail's voice in her head: *Get the hell out of there.* Yeah. But whatever was in the trailer, Efird and Jimmy Ray both thought was worth killing for, and she had to see if she could find it.

NINETEEN

Jimmy Ray had made a bigger mess of the place, if that was possible. Boxes ripped open, books and papers thrown across the living room. Dishes out of the cabinets, scattered across the counter and in the kitchen sink. A package of spaghetti broken in half and strewn across the kitchen floor.

Diane pushed a pile of papers aside and sat on the couch in the dark. Not sure what she was feeling at first. And then she recognized it: empty. Like all those times, growing up, when she would go outside in the heat and sit under the pine tree in the backyard, escaping the reality of what was going on inside the house where she was supposed to be growing up.

Efird would say, rightly, that it was self-defense. So why'd he take away the body?

She got up, turned on the light, and stared around the living room. She didn't know what she was looking for. She picked up the papers she'd pushed aside on the couch. Old case reports, some of the suspects names familiar: burglars, dope dealers, car thieves. A paper folded in quarters caught her eye. She reached and unfolded it.

It was the sketch of the man who stole her squad, computer-generated from the description she'd given. All shaggy-headed, hair hanging over his eyes, thick beard. There wasn't a whole lot of face visible beneath all that. Efird's copy was one of the many unofficial versions that had floated around the department for weeks after the theft. Someone had typed across the bottom of the sketch: *SWM seeks young, attractive, reasonably smart female patrol officer for fun and frolic in the woods in the wee hours of morning. Must have own transportation.*

She tossed it on the kitchen table on her way to the sink for a glass of water, wondering where Efird had got it and why he'd hung on to it. Raw spaghetti crunched beneath her feet. For awhile she had suspected him of being the one who'd typed the mock singles ad onto one of the originals and left copies all over the station. If not for the fact that he'd been away then, supposedly on an extended vacation to help him get over what had happened with his girlfriend—but actually on loan to the Nacogdoches PD, working undercover—she'd have sworn it was him who'd pulled the prank. When she turned on the tap, the smell of rotten eggs wafted up from the sink. Sulfur water in the well. Diane drank anyway. She hadn't realized how thirsty she was.

She put the glass down and walked outside, across the sparse grass behind the trailer toward where her car was hidden in the woods. She pulled around and parked near the front door, the nose of the car facing south, toward the road. Ready to get out fast. At the door, she reached to plug in the chili pepper lights. If Efird didn't recognize the car she was in, she wanted him at least to know somebody was there in his place. The last thing she wanted to do now was surprise him.

Back inside the trailer, she took out her cell phone and turned it on to dial Gail's number. She would tell her to wait. She would go with Gail and put the Atlantic Ocean between her and all this nastiness. The phone took the digits as she pressed them in, but when she hit send, nothing happened. She tried again. Same thing. No signal.

She went to the bedroom, also a shambles, bedclothes strewn on the floor, clothes yanked out of the closet and dumped. Dresser drawers hanging open, their contents tossed. She reached into the top one and pushed aside some socks and underwear. Nothing. The one below held T-shirts, and beneath one of the Ts she found a .25 automatic. Probably a throw-down. There was another pistol in the bottom drawer, a Glock 9 × 19. She checked the clip, locked it back in place, cranked a round into the chamber, and pressed the safety. That gun she stuck into her waistband, in front, where anyone could see it. Her own pistol she left stuck in back, hidden beneath her shirt. She bent to loosen the laces on her right boot, stuffed the .25 down in there and retied the lace.

She returned to the couch and sat down. Her back ached from all that time hunched down under the trailer. She cleared the rest of the couch, tossing things to the floor, and stretched out to rest, lying on her side so the weaponry didn't dig into the flesh. But she didn't want to get to comfortable, and sleep was out of the question, though it was after midnight.

The sound of a car coming down the drive woke her. She bolted up, checking for her pistols as she headed out front.

Efird parked the Jag next to her ride and got out smiling, ambled toward the door.

"Been here long?"

"Somebody's been in your place." Diane turned to lead the way inside.

"What the hell?" He stood staring. She had to admire the way he managed to look shocked.

Diane leaned to peek out the door. "Jimmy Ray's not with you? Isn't that his ride?"

"He let himself get picked up at the club," Efird explained. "Went home with some blonde."

"Oh." Up close now, she could smell the fear in Efird's sweat. "Damn, Efird, you look like you just finished a three-mile run. You're soaked."

He cracked a smile and winked at her. "Jimmy Ray's not the only one gettin' laid tonight. I managed a little quickie myself." He sniffed at his armpit. "Do I smell bad?"

She stepped closer and sniffed at him. "No. You're fine."

"Who the hell did this?" He swept an arm around, looking again at his trailer. When he walked into the kitchen, the spaghetti crunched under his boots. He grabbed a couple of glasses from the mess on the kitchen counter and slid into the booth, reaching for the whiskey. He stopped when he saw the sketch. Looked at Diane and then picked it up and tossed it over on the cabinet, next to the sink.

"None for me, thanks," Diane said, sitting down across from him. "I've got some driving to do tonight."

He poured himself a double and took a swallow, sighing with relief.

"That my pistol you're totin'?"

She nodded yes. "It was out on the bed. Guess you have to figure whoever did this wasn't looking to steal your valuables."

"Can I have my gun back?"

Diane slipped the Glock out and handed it to him. "There's one in the chamber. I wasn't sure if whoever did this might not be coming back. Still not."

"Well, now. I'm loaded for bear." Efird put the pistol on the table beside him. "What brought you over? You find something out?"

"Only that it's time to split. Get the hell out of here. Far away. Don't come back."

"Could you be more specific?"

"No." She placed her hands in her lap, let one slide around closer to where her gun was. "I know you killed Jimmy Ray."

Efird's head jerked back, almost as if he'd been hit with a left jab. "What did you just say?" He was half whispering in disbelief.

"I was here when he pulled his pistol on you. I saw you shoot him."

He shrank just a little, but quickly took a breath and came back to himself.

"I guess you did," he said quietly.

"What did he want? What was it he was looking for?"

"I don't think you want to know."

"I can keep you out of jail," Diane said. "I can tell them I saw what happened."

"Not without getting locked up yourself."

"Not if I can prove I was framed."

"That's gonna be hard. On account of the guy who framed you is seriously dead right now."

His words hit like a blow to the solar plexus, knocking the air from her lungs, almost paralyzing her. She stood up quickly, and Efird jumped, shifted sideways in his seat, one hand moving to cover the Glock on the table. Diane glared at him, raised her arms into a stretch, nice and slow, calm, not a hint of threat in her movements. He relaxed, shaking his head.

"Damn, girl," he said, "why don't you go on and startle a man?"

"Sorry," she said. "I just don't quite know how to take that little bit of news." She moved toward the living room, stood staring at the mess Efird's buddy had made. "Jimmy Ray, huh?" She turned to look at Efird.

He sat in the booth, nodding the way she'd seen him do when he had just cleared a case and was readying himself to go out and make an arrest. The gotcha nod. Justice come home to roost.

When she turned again to the living room, her back to Efird once more, she saw it. Face down on the floor, sprawled there, its bright white jacket askew. *The Big White Lie.* She glanced at Efird and stepped over a box to get to it. Picked it up, and yes, it was hers. The one she'd had in her briefcase that night. There was her ex libris inside the cover. She closed the book and put the jacket back in place, tucking the flaps in neatly as she walked back to Efird and sat down across from him, resting the book on the table between them.

"Jimmy Ray give this to you?"

Efird shook his head no and took a long swallow of whiskey, peering at her over the rim of his glass.

"You got any other stuff belongs to me? My briefcase? My good pen?"

Diane sat, motionless, looking into Efird's eyes, and it was as though a cloud of energy came rolling across the table toward her, a salient mass of particles, flowing out of him, and when it hit her, she had to push against it to avoid getting knocked backward. It flowed around her, above her and below her, surrounded her, filling her with absolute, chilling dread. And then it was past her and gone. She felt as if she'd been hit—hard—in the stomach. There was no air left inside her. She was helpless to breathe.

In that moment, she knew beyond doubt that she was sitting across the table from the man, or one of them anyway, who had done the Lake Bolton murders.

"But he put the dope in my apartment, right? I got that part right?" She hoped she wasn't sounding unbelievably stupid. She'd just needed to say something, anything, fast. Keep talking, keep Efird talking, while she figured a way out of this. If there was one.

"I said he did, didn't I?" Maybe she wasn't reading it right, but Efird's tone sounded anything but hostile.

"How do you know?"

"Trust me. He put the coke in your crib, and he sent one of his snitches to the feds. DEA had no idea they were part of a setup."

Jimmy Ray. And Efird. She felt a slow anger building inside her, starting somewhere between her heart and her stomach, spreading from there, until it had filled her brain like a swarm of hornets. Her breath was labored and images from the arrest, *her* arrest, flashed in her head, leaving her feeling sick and dizzy.

"That motherfucker." Her words came out slow and quiet. Keep the blame on Jimmy Ray. Keep the focus away from Efird and totally on Jimmy Ray. Don't let Efird think—what? Don't let Efird think she was sore at him? Right. And then something about the level of rage she was feeling pushed her over to the other side of the emotional spectrum. She was calm. Completely calm.

A scuffling noise outside brought Efird to his feet. He hit the light switch, throwing the room into darkness. Dim red light from the pepper lights on the patio seeped in through the kitchen window. Diane saw Efird crouch toward the front door, peek out. He turned and crept past her and down the hallway to the rear door, the one by the back bedroom.

Diane turned to watch him. Maybe she could make it. Out the front door and into her car. She peeked out the window, gauged the distance. Edged toward the end of the booth seat, eyeing Efird, who was staring intently out the back door. Diane moved to stand, and Efird turned suddenly, glanced at her, then bolted out the door, shouting. "Get out of here, motherfucker! Go on. Git! Now!"

Diane sat back down slowly, resumed her position at the table. No way she'd get to the car before Efird could get a bead on her. No way.

Efird returned, took a drink, and slid down in the booth, stretched his arms out on the seat back. "Fuckin' coons," he said. "Goin' after the garbage. Again. I swear I'm gonna kill that trash-eatin' little fucker." Diane saw a small bloodstain on the side of his blue denim shirt, right near the seam, but didn't acknowledge it. He sighed quietly, the sigh of someone who is about to undertake a task they most certainly do not want anything to do with.

"You know what he wanted? Jimmy Ray? When he came here today?"

"I figure it had to do with Churchpin."

Efird nodded. Stood. Turned and opened the freezer door. He lifted a box of frozen pizza and took from beneath it a large Ziploc baggie. Tossed it on the table in front of Diane. She opened it and removed the paper that was inside.

The letter. From Churchpin to his mother.

"You don't have to read it, I'll tell you what it says." Efird sat down again, leaned on his arms, halfway across the table. "It says that after Linda left him, he talked her into hooking up with me. Probably told her he'd beat the hell out of her if she didn't. He was my snitch, you know. One of 'em, anyway. Best of the bunch. It says that he's sure Linda didn't commit suicide, that he thinks I shot her when I found out she'd been running her head to him about my business."

"Let me guess."

"Methamphetamine," Efird said, letting the word roll slowly off his tongue. "Crystal meth. Speed. Go-fast. My mama didn't raise no fool. I did that undercover work down there in Nacogdoches? Jimmy Ray clued me in right away, and it didn't take long for me to understand how much money there was to be made in drugs, and how I could use Rick Churchpin to distribute for me. I mean, it's not like it was my own genius of a business idea. Been done plenty of times before."

He gave her a wink and said, "Wonder why I'm telling you all this?"

She nodded.

"Because you're an outlaw. You're a fugitive. You can't tell anybody, and even if you do, nobody's gonna believe you. You're felon, a fuckin' drug dealer."

"Did you kill those kids out there at the lake?"

Efird bit on his lips, let out a sigh, and stared at her. A memory flashed across his face, a sadness that glistened in his eyes and was gone almost instantly.

"I'm sorry I had to make a fool out of you. Taking your car and all."

Diane stood up and reached for the sketch on the cabinet. "It's not that good a sketch. I can see why nobody picked up on it." Diane sat, looking from the sketch to Efird and back again. She placed it on the table, making a circle with her hands, cropping the eyes and nose from the rest of the sketch. There was a similarity, but it was vague at best.

"But couldn't it be me?"

She shrugged. "I didn't get that good a look, but I guess I don't have to tell you that."

He laughed, ran a hand through his close-cropped hair. "I clean up real good, don't you think?"

Diane made a sound that was supposed to be a laugh. She felt dizzy, trapped in the Gravitron, whirling and whirling, stuck to the walls by centrifugal force. Trapped.

Efird sat there, smiling rather smugly. Diane sat, waiting for the dizziness to pass, feeling totally and utterly stupid. Big mistake, telling him she'd seen him kill Jimmy Ray. Yeah, big mistake, but it had done the trick, loosened Efird's tongue. And now there was no way he would voluntarily let her walk out of here breathing.

"Why'd you dope me?"

"I wanted to know how serious you were about taking down Gib Lowe and Al Swerdney. I needed you to be honest."

"Hardly seems like that would matter if they had nothing to do with setting up Churchpin, or me."

"It mattered that you were stirring shit up. I knew if you dug long enough and deep enough, you'd be able to prove Churchpin didn't do the murders. Hell, you might even have figured out I was the one in the sketch."

"Well, I didn't."

"Neither did that dumb-ass sheriff. God must've been handing out bucketfuls of stupidity the day that boy was born. But I want you to know, I didn't go out there that night planning to stab those kids. Fuckin' Jimmy Ray." He stood up again, began pacing the kitchen, three steps across, three back, his boot heels striking the pale blue linoleum with authority, until the sound of crackling pasta made him sit back down. "You know," he said, "Rick Churchpin brought his punishment on himself. Got all wired up one night and ran his head to those kids while he was selling them meth, told them Jimmy Ray and me were his connections. Then *they* decide to blackmail us. Stupid little punks looking for a lifetime supply of crystal. You don't fuckin' blackmail the cops."

Diane sat, listening to his words, and knowing he was telling the truth, but it was such a small truth, a sordid and meager truth, a pathetic truth. Three teenagers, gone violently to the other side of existence. Churchpin dead, and the only person who gave a shit about his dying also dead. Linda, Efird's girlfriend, dead. Maybe Efird cared. Maybe that's why he was living on Wild Turkey. Or maybe he'd killed her. Diane had never given credence to those rumors, but after what she'd just seen?

"But I swear to you," Efird said, "I had no idea Jimmy Ray was gonna twist off like that. I mean he was pretty wired up himself that night, but man . . ." Diane thought she saw him shudder.

"Juanita?"

"No. Not me. That was Jimmy Ray all by himself."

"And Rick? His suicide?"

"Jimmy Ray's got friends in low places."

"How'd you wind up with the letter?"

"Later that night, after we closed down the bar, we were both pretty drunk, but he was drunker. Silly bastard had it sittin' out on the seat of his car."

"Efird. If Churchpin didn't kill those kids, why in God's name did he confess to Lowe?"

"Who the hell knows if he did? Lowe's a fucked up bastard and maybe he just did what he had to so as to make his case. Or maybe Churchpin figured he was better off in jail than out here on the streets. He barely got away from Jimmy Ray that night at the lake."

"He was there."

"Yeah. That stuff about his tire tracks matching was not manufactured evidence. I don't think he wanted to face Jimmy Ray out on the streets."

"Or you."

Efird shrugged. "Or maybe he figured in his own twisted mind that he really was responsible for the murders, and in a way he was. Maybe he thought he deserved to stay in jail."

"I guess he wasn't counting on the death penalty." Diane sighed. "Efird, that is as just about as fine a set of rationalizations as I've ever heard."

"Darlin', it makes as much sense as all the rest of the shit I saw while I was wearing a badge."

"All this over some powder."

"It's not about the dope, darlin'. It's about the money. Dope's just another form of currency. Unless of course you're strung out." He sat, staring at the letter on the table between them. "Myself, I haven't touched the stuff since that night."

"Efird," Diane said, "I don't know how you think you're gonna be able to live with this."

"Break out the Bible, honey, let's get it on." He shook his head slowly, smiling sadly. "You been taking lessons from Al Swerdney? I don't need forgiveness, girl. Not from you. Not from anybody."

"You're fucked up, you know it? You're a waste."

"Probably true. Nothing I can do about it."

"Don't you think they're gonna look pretty close at you when Jimmy Ray goes missing?"

"They'll look. But they won't find anything. And Jimmy Ray had enough enemies to go around for everybody. Hell, he's been working dope for damn near eleven years. There's plenty of folks seriously pissed off at his little white ass. I won't even make the top ten—"

A knock at the front door brought him up short. He stuffed the Glock in his waistband, motioned Diane up, and put her in front of him as he went to the door.

He nudged Diane, and she opened the door, staring in astonishment at Gail. Everything in Diane was tuned to the man standing behind her. And then she felt Efird's arm move and the barrel of the Glock was pressed against her temple.

"Howdy," Efird said to Gail. Low and dead serious. "Who the fuck are you? And come on in." He stepped back from the door, pulling Diane with him.

Gail edged into the trailer, trying to keep some distance between her and the madman holding Diane at gunpoint. She nodded at him, walked slowly forward.

"I just came to get her," Gail said. "We're leaving the country."

"And just how the hell you gonna do that? Walk?" Efird's voice was threaded with anxiety, a tremor ill-concealed.

"I parked out by the road," Gail said. "All you have to do is let us leave, and it will be as though we were never here."

"We'll see," Efird said. "First we got to talk." He reached an arm around Diane's neck, pulled her back close against him. His grip told her he wasn't planning to let anyone go anywhere.

She felt his lips against her ear. "You're packin'. What you holding back there?" He was up close against her, the pistol in her waistband pressed between her back and his belly.

"My pistol," she said quietly. Efird let go of her neck, and she felt him lift the gun. He stuck it in his waistband and reached around her neck again. She stayed loose, offering no threat. "Let us go. We'll disappear. It's like you said. Even if I talk, nobody's gonna believe me."

He backed into the living room, his eyes on Gail as she approached slowly.

"Keep coming," he said to her. "Come on and have a seat."

Efird released Diane and motioned them both to sit on the couch. Stepping over, Gail tripped on a box and Efird raised his weapon, aiming at her head.

"Efird, no!" Diane shouted, grabbing Gail and pulling her close. The two of them sat down slowly.

Efird pushed a box to the floor and sat down in a chair across from them.

"Okay," he said calmly. "Now we just got to figure out what's the best course of action to take here."

Diane and Gail nodded carefully. Gail took Diane's hand, squeezed it quietly, invisibly, and Diane knew that she should simply sit there and try to keep Efird talking, keep him engaged, keep his attention.

"I have tickets already," Gail was telling him. "We're going to France. I can show you the tickets. And our passports. I have our passports."

Efird looked like he was considering, but he didn't take his gun off them.

"You know," Gail said, "I don't know you. I don't care about you. And I don't care what you did. All I care about is getting my friend here and getting as far away from the U.S. marshal's office as I can. I mean, come on. We're fucking wanted."

"Efird," Diane said, "let us go. I promise you'll never hear from me again. Whatever you got goin' on, that's for you to deal with. The man who framed me is dead. It's over for me. I don't aim to have anything else to do with seeking justice, or any of that bullshit. Just let us get the hell out of here. It'd be best for you."

He was listening. They could see that he was paying attention, considering the options.

And then his face changed, a cloud passed over his eyes, and his features hardened.

"If I let you go," he said, "I'll be living the rest of my days wondering if you're coming back, or if you've already come back and some judge has issued a warrant for my arrest." He leaned back in the chair. "How do I know you won't get over there to wherever the fuck you're going and then just drop a dime on me? Call the DA and give him the lowdown." He leaned forward again, his wrist flopping casually back and forth as he aimed his gun at Diane, at Gail, back at Diane, and back and forth slowly, almost casually. "No," he said.

Diane leaned forward and crossed her arms over her knees.

"I have a friend outside," Gail said. "In the car. I told him if I wasn't back in five minutes he should call the police."

Efird stared at Gail, soaking in the information. Then he laughed, loud, almost braying with hilarity.

"You expect me to believe that?"

"It doesn't matter whether you believe it or not. It's real."

"Efird," Diane said, "think about it." She rested her head on her arms and let her hands drop down toward the floor, like she was begging, like she was too exhausted to argue with words. Her right hand dangling now so close to where she had the .25 tucked into her boot. She knew she would have to come out fast and empty the thing into him.

And then, suddenly, Efird wasn't looking at them, he was looking at the screen door as it opened and Renfro bolted in, gun drawn, scanning the room. He threw down on Efird, not a word, just the look in his eyes that said *I'm gonna kill you, motherfucker, prepare to die,* and then Efird swung his gun around and pulled the trigger and the blunted roar of his gun going off filled the trailer as Renfro dived for the floor and Efird stood, aiming again, this time on his target, crouched and dead on, and Diane pulled the pistol from her boot and stood, moving toward Efird, a blur, and she stuck the .25 at him, point and shoot—*bam! bam! bam!*—straight into his chest, and Efird turned to look at her with this question in his eyes like where did you come from, and Diane approaching, *bam! bam!* And throwing the empty gun to the floor and grabbing the Glock from Efird as he crumpled downward and collapsed next to the chair, looking like a contortionist the way his arms and long legs folded beneath him, five neat bullet holes in his chest, a perfect cluster of shots, opening the way for Efird's lifeblood to drain from his body.

Renfro pulled himself up from the floor and stumbled toward Diane.

He put an arm across her shoulders and pulled her over to lean against him. "Thank God," he said. And then Gail too, was at her side, and Diane felt Gail's arm slip around her waist, and the three of them stood staring down at Efird's body.

"I think," Renfro said finally, "we should vacate the premises."

"Yes," Gail said. She wasn't there. This wasn't happening. She would listen to Renfro and do what he suggested. She had to get to the airport.

Diane didn't even try to think. She heard what Renfro said and took Gail by the arm and walked Gail to the car. Their rental. The one they had been going to escape in. The one she had snuck away from Gail in. Diane got in and sat behind the wheel, was sitting and sitting. It seemed like forever. And then forever was interrupted by the flashing red, white, and blue of a squad car turning off the highway, tear-assing down the driveway, churning up dust in its wake. Running Code 2: lights only. Silent.

Diane sat, staring.

"Fuck," Gail said. She felt herself shrinking, like her entire being was getting smaller by the second, withering, drying up, turning to dust. She was evaporating into fear and the realization that she was going back.

"Gail!" Diane opened her door and reached to pop open the trunk in one movement. "Out this side, and down low," she said. "Around back and get in the trunk. Fast." Gail scrambled out the driver door and around the car, throwing herself into the trunk and pulling it closed after her. She heard a thump and felt it lock closed. Diane on the outside.

Diane eased back to the driver's side of the car and hung an arm over the top of the door, rested one boot on the car floor next to the seat. She watched the car approach and hoped whoever was in it hadn't been able to see the trunk go up. She could not put a sentence together in her head. Gail. Prison. Efird. Escape. There were words in her head, free-floating, fluttering like butterflies.

The car skidded to a stop. The passenger door opened.

Sheriff Gib Lowe stood surveying the scene. His deputy

emerged from the driver side just as Renfro came out of Efird's trailer and nimbly skipped down the steps.

"Sheriff," Renfro said, "just the man I was hoping to see."

Sheriff Lowe tucked his thumbs into his Sam Browne and rocked back just a bit before reaching to shake Renfro's outstretched hand. Renfro nodded in Diane's direction.

"I guess I don't need to introduce you two," he said. Smiling. Everything hunky-dorey.

The sheriff eyed Diane, and she thought he might pass out right then and there.

"Young lady," he said, "I believe you're wanted at the moment."

"Sheriff," Renfro said. "She didn't do it. It was a frame, like she said from the start. In fact for a while there we thought you might have been in on it."

"Churchpin," the sheriff said, still looking at Diane. She nodded yes, slowly.

Renfro pointed at the mobile home. "You got yourself a body in there," he said to Lowe. Then he nodded, in Diane's direction. "And over there you got yourself a police officer needs to be reinstated."

"That won't be necessary," Diane said. Renfro looked at her, disappointment on his face. She shook her head no, firmly.

Sheriff Lowe eyed them suspiciously. "Who's inside?" he said.

"Detective Efird," Renfro said. "And I don't exactly know what he did with the body, but a little while ago he shot Jimmy Ray Smith, a state narcotics agent."

Sheriff Lowe stood. Listening.

"I heard him confess," Renfro said. "Boy sat right inside there next to that kitchen window and told Officer Wellman he was the one, along with Jimmy Ray Smith, who did the Lake Bolton murders. And plenty of other stuff."

Diane listened as Renfro laid everything out for the sheriff. Renfro had heard everything Efird said. What Efird had thought was a raccoon digging in the trash had been Renfro sneaking up next to the window. He'd been out there all along. Diane tried to listen, but all she could concentrate on was that Gail was still in the trunk, and they needed to get the hell out of there. She saw the expression on Gib Lowe's face go from disbelief to anger and then to something that looked like sympathy as Renfro talked on.

She walked over and got behind the wheel in the car, hoping to urge Renfro to hurry up. He glanced over at her and said a few more words to the sheriff, who nodded solemnly. Then Renfro was walking toward the car, and yes, they were getting out of there. They were to meet the sheriff at his office within the hour. There were statements to give. There was a process, a protocol, that had to be gone through. Diane was not free yet.

Diane started the car and had put it in gear when the sheriff hailed them.

"Hold up just a minute." He huffed toward the car. Came around to Diane's side and leaned one beefy hand on her door.

"I'm sorry about what happened to you," he said. "Really sorry."

"Thank you." Diane made the words sound as sincere as she could, though she thought it would be a while before she knew if she meant it. She didn't know about Gib Lowe anymore, whether he was criminal or just criminally inept.

"And by the way," he said, flashing a quick, businesslike smile, "you ought to go on ahead and get out of here so you can empty out that trunk. It's likely to be gettin' a bit stuffy in there." He rapped a knuckle against the roof of the car and turned to walk back to his latest crime scene.

Diane pulled away slowly, not wanting to churn up a lot of dust. A little ways up the driveway, she said to Renfro, "I don't believe it. Do you think he knows? I mean, knows what's—who's—back there?"

Renfro nodded. "If he does, he's pretending not to. Believe me, if he thought for one minute it was cocaine, he'd've asked you to open it up."

"He really thought I was a wrong cop?"

"Seems that way. I know he wouldn't listen to word one out of my mouth when I went to see him about you. He was convinced those charges were righteous."

"How could he have been? Anybody who knows me—"

"He didn't know you."

"Still doesn't."

"He trusted you enough to let us drive away. You gonna show?" Renfro shifted in his seat. "Or split?"

Diane didn't answer. When they got to the highway, Renfro directed her left.

"There's a roadside park on up this away."

"I know," Diane said. "I'm a trained observer. Remember?"

He smiled at her, "Yeah," he said. "I remember." He reached over and took her hand, gave it a squeeze.

Diane squeezed back, and then withdrew her hand and banged it on the steering wheel, hitting harder than she'd intended, hurting herself. "Damn him," she said.

"I know," Renfro said. He took her hand back, rubbing it gently where she'd whacked it against the wheel. "I know."

TWENTY

Gail was drenched in sweat, her eyes glassy, when they opened the trunk. Renfro helped her out. She stood gulping in fresh air. He helped her over to a picnic table. She sat, looking around.

No squad cars. No flashing lights. Nothing but a straight and level highway stretching in either direction, disappearing into darkness.

"That's it?" she said. "We got away?"

"Come on," Diane said. "We'll get you to the bus station. And if you promise to be nice we'll let you ride up front instead of putting you back in the trunk." She cracked a grin, her eyes teasing.

Gail stood up slowly, looking at Diane. The girl was home. It was apparent in her demeanor. Gail wondered at Diane's seeming calm after what had happened at Efird's.

"Are you okay?" she asked.

"Yeah," Diane said. "Fine. You?"

"Fine," Gail said. "Yeah. I'm fine."

"I mean," Diane said, "considering. I'm fine considering what happened. But I'm okay. I'll be okay."

"Yeah," Gail said. She wished Diane hadn't come back here. She wished Diane had just stuck with her and the two of them had left the country. But then who was she? Who was she to say what Diane should do or shouldn't do? She wondered nonetheless that Diane would want to return to such small-ness. Then she saw how Renfro was looking at Diane, with af-fection and caring and love in his eyes, and she understood why Diane wasn't flying off to Paris with her. And who knew? Who knew what would happen? She vowed silently to stay in touch with Diane. At least send postcards now and then, see how Diane was doing. She would have to choose a pseudonym.

Renfro took the driver side. "We'll put you on the bus in Longview," he said. "I'll make sure the Sheriff doesn't get all press happy until you call us that you're boarding a flight. That sound okay?"

Gail nodded. "My ticket's exchangeable," she said.

"Ol' Gib Lowe," Renfro said, "he'll for sure be wanting to get in front of those photographers. Gotta think about reelection."

"Yeah," Diane said. "Leave it to the sheriff to see that justice is done." But she didn't know what it was anymore. Justice. It could not function beyond the conceptual level; it could not exist in reality. There were too many broken places where things could get skewed. Look at Efird. Look at Gail.

Diane turned around suddenly. "I'm gonna do it," she said.

Gail brightened, thinking that she might after all wind up with Diane as her protégé, not that she was necessarily in a po-sition to officially mentor anyone. But they had been through so much together, and Gail, somewhere along the way, without consciously realizing it, had begun assuming that they would be together for at least a while after their escape, until they had found new lives, maybe even new lives that were intertwined in friendship. She realized that she had been hoping seriously that Diane would come to Europe with her, discover new places, learn how large the world was.

"Law school," Diane said. "I'm going."

"All right then," Renfro said. "About time."

"Of course, I have some things to straighten up first."

Gail reached and put her hand on Diane's, which was draped across the seat back.

"Call Mel," she said, "he's hooked up all over. He can tell

you who to get from around here. Who you can trust to defend you."

"I will," Diane said. "If you'll give me his phone number."

"Actually he's listed." Gail laughed. "Lerner, Gernert, Enderlin, and Chenoweth. One of the top firms in the city."

Diane shook her head, smiling at her friend.

"You should talk to him about law school, too," Gail added. "He could probably help you out there as well."

"But would he, that's the question."

"You kidding? The chance to convert a cop to an attorney? He'll jump on it."

"And just how am I supposed to pay a top-dollar New York City lawyer for his time?"

"Don't worry," Gail said. "I'm sure he feels like he owes you."

Diane looked at her friend, staring up at the stars. She hadn't seen that look on Gail's face since the day Gail had taken the mower blade from Landscape. The look that said sometimes you had to jump out there and take a risk, or else you'd stay just where you were, forever locked in prison.

Gail wasn't going back. Diane knew that much. And she, Diane, wasn't going back, either. Not to the police department. She was going home. Home to a new life.

They drove in silence for a while. When Diane turned to check on Gail, she saw that Gail still had her head back, staring out the car window. Diane leaned back, took a peek. The sky was brilliant with stars, millions of them. On either side of the highway, forest and field. Green, in the day, and beautiful.

Dark in the night and mysterious.

Don't miss
Kim Wozencraft's new novel

THE DEVIL'S
BACKBONE

Coming from
St. Martin's Press in Fall 2006

DB 09/05